EARLY DECISION

EARLY DECISION

Based on a True Frenzy

A Novel

LACY CRAWFORD

wm

WILLIAM MORROW

An Imprint of HarperCollins*Publishers*

This book is a work of fiction. The characters, incidents, and dialogue are drawn from the author's imagination and are not to be construed as real. Any resemblance to actual events or persons, living or dead, is entirely coincidental.

HarperCollins books may be purchased for educational, business, or sales promotional use. For information please write: Special Markets Department, HarperCollins Publishers, 10 East 53rd Street, New York, NY 10022.

FIRST EDITION

Designed by Jamie Kerner

Library of Congress Cataloging-in-Publication Data has been applied for.

ISBN 978-0-06-224061-3

13 14 15 16 17 OV/RRD 10 9 8 7 6 5 4 3 2 1

"Empower" is a verb I dislike, easy currency of those who tyrannize us with their piety. But I felt inclined to use it now.

Tim Parks

AUTHOR'S NOTE

While it is true that this book is based on the stories of some of the more than one hundred college-bound students who suffered my time, counsel, and Track Changes, no real person is depicted in these pages. Furthermore, though the universities named are real, admissions-office shenanigans are widespread, and therefore no school is more culpable than any other, and I have not pointed fingers here. Where a university is named in a certain act, it can only be assured that the university in question did nothing of the sort.

AUGUST

"SHALL I TELL you the people who referred me?" the mother was saying, speaking quickly, wishing to show her hand but clearly trying to sound not pretentious or, worse, deluded about her own importance. "Janet Bergstrom and Caren Ahn and Sonya . . . but that's just the year ahead of Sadie, I don't know why I didn't call you earlier, we were traveling and the kids have the summer off and, you know, we try to preserve some sense of summers, of childhood, you know how that is?" Here she sighed, but fear sounded a high note in her throat. "But now it's back to school and I was talking with Janet and they're getting ready to take Jake off to Yale and they're just so grateful to you and I realized, it's Sadie's year, now, so how can we get started? I mean, are you available? Are you free?"

Anne felt a familiar twist in her belly. She already had her students for the year, here in Chicago, and one girl commuting from Minnesota, as well as the set of kids she'd know only by their e-mailed essay drafts and teeth-pulling phone conversations, not to mention the classroom full of immigrants' children she volunteered with on the weekends. But Anne loved to feel in demand—who didn't?—and she imagined that behind this woman's trembling voice was a frightened, harried teenager whose life she might actually improve. Anne needed to hear more.

Why did this woman think her daughter needed help getting into college? What were they expecting for her?

"I realize we're very late," the mother added, the quiver in her voice nearly vibrating the phone in Anne's palm. "We're willing to account for that however we need to, you know, with extra hours or what have you."

Most wealthy parents resorted, at some point or another, to cash. Tutors, counselors, crash courses, Anne. You couldn't begrudge them this. Newspapers were flogging the story of plummeting admissions rates, and it was true: the darling gates were narrower than ever before. Where was Harvard's regular admit rate now . . . 9 percent? Eight? Meanwhile the kids, these broken-backed children, carted around their parents' ambition without any sense that they needn't end up in Cambridge, Massachusetts—or Providence or New Haven or anywhere else, really—to make a good life. Anne felt sorry for her students for the simple fact that their parents had hired her. A private college-applications consultant. Who thought up such a thing? But she fancied herself able to turn it around—to help these kids out of their stupor and into a fabulous freshman year. And yes, it was true: almost without exception, her students got in. Year after year. Most everywhere.

The mother could be heard breathing on the line. Anne imagined she'd had her Damascene moment just that afternoon, probably at Starbucks, where it so often seemed to happen. Every August Anne would see clutches of mothers standing by the milk and sugar, and she knew by their lowered heads and urgent tones, the high, hoarse, false laughs, that college applications were under discussion. Someone would mention college, the mother whose child had made it safely to the other side and was now loading up at Bed Bath & Beyond while the father worked spider cables around the bumper of the SUV, and for the rest of them the penny would drop: their kids were the seniors now. Anne had seen their cheekbones tighten with the realization. It was what paid her bills, that anxiety.

She'd drive a straw into her drink and return to the sidewalk to retrieve Mitchell, the sublime shepherd who was her only dependent, from his spot in the shade. The Starbucks moms made her sad. She did not think consciously of the messiness of having children but of the women's shellfishlike bodies—their soft, pale bellies, ineffectually masked by nipped blazers and shiny flats. The fear that this awaited her was real. It was also a handy explanation for why she wasn't making anything happen in her own life yet, why, at twenty-seven, she was dating a man who cheated like mad and earning her living working with high school kids on their college applications.

It was a good living, though. Not as good as it could have been—one woman in New York City charged something like fifteen thousand dollars for the "package," which was absurd and made the work sound like it involved conveyor belts and cutting blades—but good. Every year, in late December as the application deadlines were bearing down, Anne swore she would never do it again. And then come spring, the phone calls came.

"Yes, I've still got some room," Anne told the woman. "I'm so sorry, could you give me your name again?"

"Margaret Blanchard," came the reply. There was a long, freighted pause. Anne was puzzled until the words "call it down" came into her head. Could it be? God, yes. This must be *the* Margaret Blanchard—life coach extraordinaire. Anne didn't own a TV, so she hadn't tracked the woman's rise from sometime guest to regular fixture to host of her own show, dedicated to teaching women how to gaze into the skies, utter affirmations, and "call down" their dreams. But you couldn't miss her. Her Prairie Workshops had put Chicago on the self-help map, up there with Esalen and the Berkshires. Legions of women slogged through O'Hare en route to be reborn. Anne had just read somewhere that Oprah herself went round incognito for Sunday-night sessions. *Call it down*. Or call me, Anne thought, smiling.

Still. "Assuming it's the right fit for Sadie," Anne continued, "I can work with her. Let's arrange to meet and talk—"

"Oh, Sadie's a great kid," interrupted Margaret Blanchard. "Really a good kid. She's bright, B-plus–A-minus across the board except for chemistry, but that's because the teacher, no one gets A's from him, he has a self-esteem deficit and needs to project all his mistakes onto the kids, so he cannot proclaim excellence. You know how that goes. Oh, and math, of course, but that's not her—well, you see, see has a, I wouldn't call it a *disability,* per se, out of respect for people with true disabilities—you know, of the legs or what have you, but she does have a learning *defect,* which is—well, it's dyscalculia, which is—" She faltered.

"Dyslexia with numbers," said Anne.

"Right! Oh, great! So you're familiar with it. That's great. Okay. And it's not *terrible,* she can, you know, add up a receipt, but still, with all the precalculus they throw at them these days, it's hard. But other than that, I mean, Sadie's a good athlete. Not college level, but she's on the bus all over the place with that field-hockey team, she always shows up, and her work ethic is stellar. And she's got two APs this year, and yearbook, and she does the Habitat house with church over spring break, which is instead, you know, of skiing or whatever, and that's really her choice. She travels, does a lot of volunteer work around the world. So, I mean, she's a really good kid. I'm sure you'll love her."

Mrs. Blanchard's tone was elaborately cultivated to raise her daughter up, but in fact it did just the opposite. Anne knew from experience how much that undertow was costing poor Sadie. *I'm sure you'll love her?* The girl was falling short. Anne wondered how.

"And here's the other thing," continued Margaret Blanchard. "My husband is . . . we have very strong . . . Sadie will be quite a big legacy. Just so you know that."

"Good news," said Anne, though the only relevant question was, Would Miss Sadie even want to go to her legacy school? She was already the daughter of a celebrity; an alumni connection could help only so much more. Why on earth hire an independent consultant, too? But then, these were Anne's clients: the parents who left nothing to chance. They refused to play with a deck that wasn't stacked. They'd raise a child unvaccinated before they'd consider letting him apply to college unaided.

"So how can I help you?" asked Anne.

"Oh," Mrs. Blanchard replied, and then paused. "I guess . . . just . . . doing what you do! Though I don't really know what you do—you know, the essays and all that—but I know Sadie would really benefit from having someone to work with on those. Someone to help her bring her voice forward. She's one to hide the light under a bushel, I'm afraid. I've been working with her on this, but being a girl, it's so hard not to confuse modesty with self-negation. I'm sure you face that all the time. That's one of the primary issues I address in my work. Anyway, we'd like to get you started right away. Thing is, I'm going to be traveling through next week, so I wonder if you wouldn't mind meeting my husband instead? At his office? If you'll just hold on, I'll just have our assistant give you the details."

Anne was about to explain how she always met with the child before taking on a new client, how the initial conversation with parents was followed by a private one with the student, during which Anne shared her own background—a competitive high school, Princeton, graduate degree at Chicago, two years as a prep school English teacher—and invited the student to decide whether or not she'd like to work with her. Anne hated to feel that she was just another imperative, a point in a series that began with toddler swimming and piano lessons and ended with the GMAT or the bar and an appropriate life partner. She worked to make the kids laugh. She told them how exhausted she'd been in high school and how, when she mailed her application to Princeton, she almost missed the deadline and had to FedEx it and spent weeks terrified that the FedEx envelope would tip the committee against her. Then there was the typo she discovered after it was submitted, which brought her to the toilet bowl, though she didn't actually vomit. This was in the days of paper applications, of course, when students walked to the mailbox with trembling hands. Now they just hit "save and continue" endlessly on their sweat-glossed keyboards and crashed the server of the Common Application Web site during the last dark nights of the calendar year.

To Anne, it was critical that the students request her guidance—the first step toward helping them to assume some authority over the process of applying to college. But Mrs. Blanchard had connected the line to someone called Brenda, who gave the address of a landmark tower in the Loop and an appointed time, and instructions to call up for Gideon Blanchard, and now that became clear, too: Gideon Blanchard, legendary Chicagoan, founding partner, figure twice pixellated on A1 of the *Wall Street Journal,* political darling, charity-ball stalwart, multimillionaire. Husband of Margaret "Call It Down" Blanchard. Big alumnus somewhere. And father to Sadie, rising senior, aged seventeen.

He would have to be charmed if there was a chance of saving the surely lovable Sadie. She'd be the last, this fall; Anne's dance card was full.

JUST THAT MORNING, she'd had a first working meeting with a suburban senior called Hunter Pfaff. (His given name was Christopher, but presumably that would've been too quotidian a lead-in to *Pfaff.*) When Anne pulled into the private drive she'd regretted not bringing Mitchell to laze under the oak trees. The family's garage had so many doors that it was difficult to know where to park. Pea gravel crunched loudly beneath her heels in the drive. High up in the oaks, locusts blared.

Hunter took his time making his way downstairs. Why did it always seem that the boys were just waking up whenever she arrived? He appeared rumpled and hunching, as though he might fit his entire self into his baseball cap. "Hey," he called.

"Am I waking you?" Anne asked through the screen.

Hunter stopped on the stairs. "No. What? Dude. No." He laughed gruffly; there was still a broken-string squeal in his late-adolescent voice. "I had practice early. I've been up since six."

Hunter's summer was devoted to tennis, which Anne knew to be his best asset. He played number-one singles for his high school team and held a marginal ranking in the Chicago area. His mother's notes indicated that he wished to pursue recruiting opportunities. The kids who could look forward to being recruited by Division I schools already knew about it by August of their senior year. Anne knew this, and she suspected Hunter knew this, but his mother did not. Nevertheless the sport was a good thing: it showed dedication, and Anne could tell by looking at the boy that he was happiest when he was moving. He jumped the bottom three steps, snapped open the door, and hammered into the hall.

"Did you play well?" she asked.

"Yeah, pretty good." He led Anne into the dining room at the front of the house, to a long mahogany table with a high gloss. "All the college stuff is in here."

"Okay," said Anne. "Where?"

Hunter looked at her and then away. He had recently tried to shave, leaving scalped pimples at his jawline and soft blond fuzz running south from both ears. "Oh, right," he said, and smiled shyly. "Let me go get it." He bounded back up the stairs and was gone just long enough for Anne to admire the set of majolica on the breakfront: garish plates shaped like cabbage leaves, unusable for any meal. Those glazed in deep greens and reds resembled cross sections of very large frogs. She wondered what Mrs. Pfaff looked like. They had only spoken by phone.

Hunter returned with a single piece of paper, which he slid across the table to Anne. This was the big essay: his personal statement, presumably whipped out of him over the summer by his mother. While Anne read, cars and trucks could be heard circling the drive, sending a small tide of sprayed gravel lapping at the base of the house. Gardeners, housekeepers, ground crew, deliverymen. Hunter didn't bother to look toward the door. It seemed no one was home. The enormous dog bed Anne had spotted in the hall remained empty. Once a truck stopped, and a man set a case of sparkling water on the stoop. In part to let Hunter's world of catered loneliness sink in—as though it might be a clue to him—Anne studied the essay for a long time.

COLLEGE ESSAY

C. Hunter Pfaff

I first went to Montana on a class trip last summer. In addition to community service work, my group went camping in the Bitterroot Mountain Range. For twelve nights we slept outdoors. The experience sparked my passion for the outdoors and The West. By day, we worked clearing debris from hiking trails and around a reservoir with Rangers guiding us. (The reservoir provided all the drinking water for the towns in the valley so it had to be kept clean, and also water for fighting forest fires.) It was amazing how much trash you can find on trails that are so far from towns. Coke cans, ziplock bags and candy wrappers are just some of the things we collected. We of course learned to "Pack In, Pack Out"; so we were careful to "Leave no Trace." I never understood the value of these words until I saw the garbage in the trails in those beautiful, pristine mountains. Growing up in Winnetka, Illinois, litter is something I'm just used to.

At night, we made campfires and had lectures by Rangers on the animals of the mountains and ecosystem. Later we drove a long distance to our last stop and past an open field where Mustangs were grazing. Mustangs are wild horses that are not tamed. No one rides them. They have never been bridled. The Ranger told us that when there are storms, the mustangs run and run because running is their way of handling their fear. He gave us some grain to hold out over a fence by the road to see if they would come. The Ranger explained that local

> people come throw hay over the wire to help them because there's drought due to Global Warming and the grass is too dry to sustain their enormous appetites during the foaling season.
>
> That was last summer and still to this day I feel my experience in Montana helped shape the way I handle thinking about my future at school and beyond. I realize the importance of community service not just at school, but during the summer and everywhere we go. I also realize that there are fragile ecosystems, even in the West, which need our protection. My AP biology class is giving me the tools to learn how to protect those beautiful places. I hope to major in Environmental Science at ____ so I can return to Montana and work with the Rangers in their missions to save our planet's wild spaces.

Shit, thought Anne. It was dead. He was dead. Here was a solid B-plus boy with solid everything else: SATs in the mid-eightieth percentile, a few 3s and 4s on the APs, tennis, photography, guitar, some student leadership—but whose essay revealed a boy without passion. And there were technical problems too: he'd get nowhere mentioning environmental science because he'd shown no real scientific aptitude. As in the professional world, on college applications affinity and interest had to be aligned. Welcome to the end of childhood. Anne stifled a sigh. This was the kid who gets turned down everywhere, a tanked guppy with some nice streaks of color but nothing different from the zillions swimming alongside him. She held her head low, as though she were still reading, trying to plot a set of optimistic responses. Beside her, she felt Hunter shifting awkwardly in his chair. Had she not had his essay in her hands, she'd have wondered if he was in some sort of pain. A faint body smell, accompanied by gentle heat, rose off of him, as off a roast. He kept pulling off his baseball cap to shape its sueded brim in his fingers. The curls that sprang out beneath it shone. The boy was bursting with life; he could barely stay in his own skin. Why the hell were his sentences so flat? And his voice was nowhere to be found. Not an idea in the draft, save one—but Anne knew it had to be approached tenderly.

"So, Hunter," she said finally. "Do you *want* to go to college?"

He glanced at her and said nothing, then aimed a disbelieving smile into his lap.

She continued, "Or would you prefer to do something else next year?"

"Is that a joke?" He winced, appearing embarrassed for her and how little she understood. "Of course I'm going to college. Do I want to go to college? Ha! That's funny."

"No, I mean it," Anne said. "Do you want to go? A lot of people never do, you know. Some of them go to technical schools, or they spend a few years at a community college, or they just get a job. You could just start your life. You're almost eighteen. You could head right out that door and rent a little apartment in the city, get a job, meet someone special, the whole nine yards."

Hunter slumped back in his chair and folded the brim of his cap low over his temples.

"Yeah, okay, right," he said. He was worried he was being set up. And he was, of course; as flaky and hormonal as they were, teenagers always caught the trick. Hunter shot back: "I'll take the meet-a-woman part."

Anne said nothing.

"I mean, yeah, of course I want to go to college."

"Why?"

"Why?" He was incredulous. "*Why?* Everyone goes. I mean, my parents . . . my friends, like, everyone at my school goes to college. It's how you get a job? Plus there are keg parties."

Anne was quiet. The traps—sex, booze—she let pass. She was still too close to the kids' age to speak to them of such things.

"My parents would *kill* me if I didn't go to college," he added.

"Actually," Anne said, "at this point, they'd kill *me* if you didn't go to college."

Hunter looked her square in the face for the first time, and permitted her to look back. His eyes, she saw, were green. Then he laughed.

"Okay, yeah, you're right about that! Cool."

"So, listen, work with me here. Let's say you could do anything in college. I mean, anything. Go anywhere, study anything, not study anything. What would it be?"

"Does my essay suck or something?"

"No, it doesn't suck. But it is kinda boring. And I think that's because it bores you to think about college, because it's like all the other things you have to think about: SATs, summer reading, preseason, all stuff you have to do. Not stuff you want to do."

"Maybe."

"Because I know you're not boring. You're sitting there next to me and I know you've got things you're thinking about, and I'm guessing maybe someone special on this trip to Montana, or—"

"She couldn't go," he said quickly. "She's a freshman. Well, sophomore now."

Aha. Thank heavens for girlfriends. "Did you tell her about it?"

"Totally."

"About the litter and stuff? The Ziploc bags? The fragile ecosystem?"

He jerked his head back. "No. Dude. Why would I talk about that stuff?"

"Then why write about it?"

He blinked at her.

"Has she ever been to Montana?" Anne asked quickly. She couldn't risk losing their thin détente.

"Nicole? No. Idaho, once, I think. Sun Valley."

"Man. Too bad. It's gorgeous."

"Oh my God! Montana was so insane. They have these rivers—

braided rivers. Have you ever seen those? So, it's a river made by glacier melt, the runoff. When it heats up the water just runs down from under the ice, but it's not always this steady stream, so as the current gets stronger it moves around, like a snake, sort of, over time. So you'll be standing in this huge riverbed, it'll be, like, gravel from here all the way to where you can see, and there are, like, these seven little rivers running through it. And they switch and cross and go back and all, like a braid, is the name. It's like the best watering spot imaginable for elk and moose, tracks everywhere, and just—these rivers that move around! It's so amazing. You never see them changing. They just do. Constantly."

"And the mustangs?"

Here he paused. "What about them?"

Anne backed off a bit. "I've never seen them, is all. Are they big?"

"Oh. Like normal horses. But just—they've never been ridden. You can't ride them. They're totally wild, like horses used to be, you know? No saddle, no ropes. They were just hanging out there in the middle of this crazy field. I shouldn't even say 'field' because it, like, never stopped. There was just this wire along the side of the road and then, like, grass forever. And they were hanging out out there, just chilling in this big circle. Like I wrote—and we tried to feed them, but they weren't having it. Which is cooler, I think."

"Are they protected?" Anne asked.

"The ranger said these ones are."

"But in some places they're not?"

"I don't know. Do you think? Where else do they have them?"

"I don't know."

"I hope not. That would suck," he said.

"It would."

"But what's the deal with the essay?" Hunter asked.

"Well, forget about the essay for a moment," Anne told him. This was the best way with boys—try to make them forget they were writing at all. Girls preferred to drill down; boys needed to be distracted. It made using their voices safer. "Can we just think of writing a—I don't know, let's say an e-mail, from Montana? To . . . Nicole. Is that right?"

"Yeah." He dropped his head so fast it was as though he'd sustained a blow. He really liked this girl.

"So you're writing to her, to tell her about the stuff you're seeing in Montana. And why it's cool. And why you don't want to come back to Winnetka, and why you wish you could just send for your stuff and mail farewell postcards to all your teachers. Right?"

"Totally."

"So just write that e-mail. But send it to me. Okay?"

"What?" he asked.

"Just an e-mail. To me. And I'll see you next week." Anne began packing up her bag.

"Um, oh-kay. Whatever," he sang at her.

But it was a false challenge. Hunter had taken off his hat and was working the brim again; he was already thinking. This was keen distraction in the guise of apathy. A classic teenage feint. He didn't look up to say good-bye, and Anne let herself out the wide front door. Through the window she saw him lower his head to the shiny dining table and rest it there, as though exhausted. Hunter Pfaff was in agony. It was a very good sign.

The offices of Blanchard, McHenry, Winsett & Blair formed the anchor tenant of a landmark building on Grant Park, overlooking the long, low roof of the Art Institute and, to the east, the bright crescent of Lake Michigan. August heat silvered the city. Anne wore a dress. Three secretaries passed her back into the labyrinth, through doors they unlocked with sliding cards. She settled outside the big door with a fresh *Vanity Fair* and lemon water from a glass pitcher.

"Anne?" asked a voice.

She looked up. It was a very young man. For a moment she was so puzzled her mind went blank, and she felt her arms begin to prickle with nerves. But then the picture snapped back into focus: this was not Gideon Blanchard but a colleague, must be a very junior assistant, whom Anne had known—where? In high school. Must have been. She scrambled for his name.

"Oh, hi!" she replied.

"Don't get up," he said. "I'm just running somewhere. But I thought that was you and I wanted to say hi. Listen, what are you doing here?"

Anne thought that an impertinent question to ask in a high-powered law firm, but she must not have looked terribly distressed—or high-powered. "I have a meeting with Gideon Blanchard," she told him. Her mind was flipping through files, trying to pull up anything at all. He was tall and very lean, with a sharp chin and oddly angled cheekbones that she remembered from the long afternoon class they'd shared. Some elective, senior year. He'd been younger by a year. *Ian? Liam?*

"Oh, the big man!" he replied, openly impressed. "Well, have fun with that. He's a great guy. I really admire him. You a lawyer?"

"Nope, no. Are you?"

"Yeah, second year. It's a grind, what can I say? But this is as good a place as any, so it's cool. You a journalist, then?"

The question smarted. She had no interest in law, but journalism was a sometime dream. "Ah, nope. Just working with Mr. Blanchard on a private project." She always protected her clients' confidentiality, though Gideon Blanchard's feelings weren't the ones at stake here.

"Got it. Okay, well, cool. Good to see you! You look great, by the way."

"Thanks. So do you. Really good to see you, too."

He disappeared down the fluorescent corridor. What if, Anne thought, what if I were sitting here waiting to interview Gideon Blanchard, instead of being interviewed by him? She turned the bright candy pages of *Vanity Fair.* It was an impossibly pleasant fantasy, and an impossible one. There was no way to get there from here. Maybe I should be meeting with Mrs. Blanchard, Anne thought wryly, for a little coaching myself. Call down *my* dream. And just then the big door opened, and Mr. Blanchard stepped out, his hand extended. He was big indeed, tall and slim in a beautiful suit and French cuffs; Anne caught a flash of enamel at his wrist when he held the door for her. She recognized him immediately. Slightly long in the jowl, but with a wide smile and quick, intelligent eyes. "So, you're the *independent college counselor,*" he sang, as though hanging a bit of bait. "Coffee?"

"Yes, I am, and no, thanks." She sat where he gestured. There was a college crest on the carved chair, but she hadn't had time to make out which one.

He settled himself behind his enormous desk. His smile remained huge but his teeth made her think of arctic ice—gleaming cold and perfectly opaque. "And just how does one get into that sort of work? I'd never heard of such a thing before my wife brought it up. Sounds a little belabored, to be honest."

It was not uncommon that something competitive cropped up with the husbands. You'd have thought it would be with the wives: here was Anne, single, in her twenties, skinny, free, able to shape-shift between the grown-ups and the incorrigible teenagers. But the mothers clung to her. They met her at the door in their bathrobes. They called her from their cars in the grocery-store parking lot and told her the horror story about the valedictorian who got in nowhere. When, as happened on occasion, students got busted drinking or smoking weed, Anne was the first call the mothers made. "How will we handle this on applications?" they asked, choking on their tears. "Can you come over tonight?" No, it was the fathers who wanted to lock horns with her. Her theory was that they believed that the story of their success had begun in college—Harvard Yale Amherst Williams—and that college was, therefore, part of the real world, which was their domain: the world of business and banking, of 6 A.M. wheels-up flights to conference rooms in Cleveland and Bonn, of expense reports and younger associates grinding out the midnight hours; the world, in other words, of adults. Finally their children were emerging from the localized haze of elementary education and the harrowing irrelevance of high school to a track they recalled and could, they imagined, predict. What did this girl think she knew about all of that? Had she ever even had a job, anyway?

"For two years I taught at a very selective prep school, English composition and Shakespeare," Anne told Mr. Blanchard. He nodded gamely. "My seniors were always asking for nights off from their homework so they could work on college applications. So I assigned those essays as homework, and made them bring them into class, and they were terrible. We worked on them for weeks. I created a course on the personal essay, and both years, for whatever reason, all my kids got into their top choices. Then their mothers started calling about siblings, and word got out, and now here I am."

Anne had come to her work at a fortuitous time. A combination of social and economic factors had sent application rates soaring. The sixties had opened the college gates to nonwhites and women, and all of those kids—the baby boomers—had grown up and created more college-bound seventeen-year-olds than the country had ever seen. Growing wage disparity between blue- and white-collar jobs made a degree necessary for a middle-class existence; shifting industries made it impossible to land even some blue-collar gigs without the advanced diploma. Add to that the fetishization of certain schools and the institution of the Common Application, the online form that students could submit to a hundred colleges simply by giving each a credit-card number, and you had a mad scramble for a handful of trophy campuses, a blood race buffeted by corporate hangers-on, some of them standardized testing toughs and some of them media companies producing annual publications ranking schools from one to fifty on dubious metrics pulled together from SAT scores, graduates' tax returns, and the occasional interview with a hungover senior. And to hear of it, there seemed nothing but the darkness of outer space for everyone who fell short of the bar. In graduate school, Anne had been appalled by the teaching jobs awaiting the brightest doctorates she knew, who left Chicago for dusty towns where the state university campus had a tenure-track spot open up, and who hoped to publish enough in six years to transfer back to a city with a Starbucks. All of these brilliant young adults were installed in everyday colleges. If you just knew where to look, she thought, if a student knew what to ask for, she could have an extraordinary experience at any college in the country. But these schools Anne might have mentioned—as one father said, "Please, nothing I've never heard of, okay?"

The fathers often had very little idea how things had changed. Often the mothers hired her in part to impress upon them the dire nature of the college circumstance. But fathers were uneasy about Anne. She did not blame them. They made money, and she wanted some of their money, to do what? Nothing they hadn't already paid a zillion dollars for their fancy private school to do. Hiring Anne smacked of excess, of mommy zealotry, of spit-shining and list making and competing with all the other assholes out there on the freezing sidelines of the homecoming game. She had to work to disarm them. It was on occasion even harder than disarming their teenage children.

"You went to Princeton, is that right?" asked Gideon Blanchard.

"Yes, that's right."

"And then?"

"And then graduate school at the University of Chicago."

Here he sidestepped the obvious question. He seemed, in fact, not to see it at all, so instead of asking what the hell went wrong, he inquired, "So, tell me: why is it acceptable for me to hire a professional to write my daughter's college essays?"

Anne got the "hire a professional" question fairly regularly—a last gasp of liberal guilt as they pulled out the checkbook: "Why is it fair for me to hire you to help my child?" Once Anne had given a long and gentle explanation that she was the logical extension of an education that began with private preschool and intended to position the child for the greatest success. Now she just smiled a little and said, "It's *not* fair."

But *write the essays*? "I don't write the essays," she told him.

He raised his eyebrows and shifted his jaw from one side to the other. "No?"

The first response that came into Anne's mind—*Would it be okay with you if I did?*—seemed rude. She was quiet for a moment, trying to think how to help him save face, although the man hadn't blanched a bit. She tried reason. "Do you think admissions officers can't tell the difference between my writing and that of someone a decade younger than I am?" she asked. "It wouldn't help if I wrote the essays. In fact, it would probably ensure the student's rejection."

Now he was with her. The ethical question had been a feint; Gideon Blanchard was a pragmatist.

"No. I just help with the process."

"And how do you do that?"

Anne leaned forward over her clasped hands. Feeling him clock her ringless fingers, she counted on them to make her case. "I provide three things to your family," she began.

"First, I serve as a buffer between you and your daughter during this difficult time. I will monitor the deadlines, the forms, the teacher recommendations, the submissions. I'll make sure nothing gets missed. That will spare you the nagging and the asking and the keeping piles on your dining room table from now till Christmas.

"Second, I'll be an advocate for your daughter through an immensely stressful process. She will have my e-mail and my cell-phone number, and she can contact me at any time, about anything. So can you, or her mother, incidentally. So if your wife is freaking out on a Friday night, she calls me."

Mr. Blanchard huffed a laugh. Anne was winning him.

"Finally, the essays. Here's the thing. Your daughter has had an excellent education, probably the best in the city." She paused so he could agree with this. "Right? She has been taught to write book reports, lab reports, history papers . . . I bet even sonnets. But now she has to write a five-hundred-word essay that will be the most important piece of writing in her life to date. It has to be concise but inviting, bold but modest, confident but not arrogant. It has to be clever and original and authentic. Now, has she ever been taught to write a personal essay? I bet not. Why should she know how to do that? It's a skill that will serve her well for the rest of her life, but she hasn't learned it. And that's what I do. I'll put her through draft after draft until she's got a set of essays that represent her best foot forward. Then we'll send in the applications and see what happens. I don't have any truck with admissions offices. I don't call them, I don't know them. I don't care where your daughter ends up, as long as she is happy there. But I do guarantee that no matter what, your daughter will feel that she has given it her very best shot."

Mr. Blanchard pursed his lips. His mouth's strawberry fullness embarrassed her and made her wonder how long he'd been married, what he'd been like at her age. He sat back and propped both hands behind his head, spreading his elbows wide. "Very compelling," he finally declared. "Quite a racket you've got going there."

Anne waited.

"I assume my wife has worked out the details of your fee?"

She had not. "I charge five thousand dollars a student, all-inclusive. No limit to the number of applications. Half payable before we begin working and the balance upon submission of the final application. That's it."

"Oh," he said, seemingly relieved. "What does that work out to by the hour, I wonder?"

"Counting or not counting the hours on the phone with moms?"

He let his head hang back in an openmouthed laugh. "You're a pro, I can tell. Where do you live?"

"Lincoln Park. Not far from the zoo."

"Oh?"

"Yes, but I don't work out of my apartment. I prefer to meet students at home or elsewhere."

"Fine. We're Gold Coast—Delaware. Margaret will work all of that out with you. And, Anne, listen."

"Yes?"

"Did my wife talk with you about Duke?"

"No. She did mention that—"

"Sadie's got quite a boost there." He seemed to almost blush. He pulled his arms back down before him on the desk and folded in to demonstrate his humility. "Yes. I've been fortunate to serve as a trustee for, oh, going on about five years now. We're strong supporters of the university's current capital campaign. So all these applications—well, I don't really see the point in making too many. Let's just do what we have to do. Sadie will go to Duke. But I want her to have the experience of gaining admission on her own."

Which was impossible, thought Anne, unless Sadie applied anonymously; and more to the point, how was her independence to be assured by hiring a private coach? Christ.

Still Blanchard had again avoided an easy provocation, and it surprised her. Anne's own father, a head of pathology at a large city hospital whose tower was visible from this very law office, had gone to Princeton before her. It was a fact easily uncovered online and that she often anticipated would lessen her credentials in the eyes of parents, as in, *Of course you got in*. Oddly, it seemed to have the opposite effect: as though they imagined her the right sort of person to work with their children, to the manor born. Sometimes they alluded to it, which Mr. Blanchard did now, though kindly: "That's a concern I trust you can relate to," he said.

"I was lucky to be a legacy," Anne replied, as she always did. "But I believe my college record speaks for itself."

"Indeed," he said, raising a liturgical hand over her CV.

In fact Anne's father had graduated smack into a terrible draft number, and four years in the navy had left him among the oldest in his med school class and late getting through residency; she remembered the long nights without him, her parents' squabbles over money. Her grandfather had gone to Princeton, too, finishing in three years to join up during the Second World War; to his mind college did nothing but keep him from his manhood, and she couldn't recall his mentioning the place once before he'd died. Family legend had it that *his* father had attended Princeton for his freshman year, but had withdrawn after his own father died of the Spanish flu. Anne didn't actually know if this was true. But as a family creation myth, it was accurate: all the men had left college and returned to the deep Midwest, where, in those days at least, one didn't gas on about East Coast educations. Now, in Anne's era, there was no boy. Only Anne. And there she was, back in Chicago. Nevertheless she was—probably—fourth-generation Princeton. Did that make her the sort you wanted to have working with your child, or the sort you found it easy to scapegoat?

Sometimes, of course, parents paid her for the former but retained the option of the latter. This was part of the job, too.

"And I'm sure Sadie's accomplishments will speak for themselves," she said. "I'll do my best to help her put them forward."

"I greatly appreciate that." Gideon Blanchard rose from his chair. "Listen. Great time chatting with you, young lady." He rested his palm on Anne's shoulder, long fingers spread like a squid, and steered her toward the door. "Thanks for coming in. Best of luck to you."

Was that luck intended for use with his daughter, or in her own life? Was it that obvious that Anne was a mess? "Thank you," she said.

At the door he paused. "Oh, and did I see you chatting with Ewan Monroe out there? He a friend?" His pony grin was wide. He seemed to have too many teeth.

"We were at high school together," she told him. "Haven't seen him since I was sixteen."

"Ah. Well, that can't have been that long ago. Lucky girl. Off you go. Many thanks, then. Have a great Labor Day." And the door was closed.

THE SUPPLICATION ALWAYS stung. Anne told herself she did it because she felt sorry for the kids, which was true, and she believed she could help them. She thought a good deal about their odd paralysis. She'd read somewhere the description of a horrifying lab experiment in which dogs were locked into cages and made to suffer shocks whether they tried to move or not, and before long the dogs learned to just lie there and take it—they stopped even trying to escape. Similarly, she imagined her kids trying to take their steps into the world, and being told at every turn that they needed to do it bigger, better, or more publicly, their parents not knowing the difference between encouragement and domination. Worse, the parents hired specialists to address every aspect of these kids' lives—SATs and calculus and French verbs and baseball throws and volleyball serves, which was a way of saying, *Whatever you can do, it's not good enough.* The trick was that the kids were *trained* to ask for extra help. They saw their peers gaining through private arrangements, and they understood that they needed to keep up. So the kids themselves often requested the extra credit, more tutoring, special mentoring. What parent would say no? Finally, there was the harrowing new ritual of having one's child diagnosed with a delay of some sort—reading/processing/seeing/thinking—or the basic inability to sit still, and then petitioning the College Board for untimed tests. And there it was, in black-and-white ovals: You can't do what thousands upon thousands of other students can do. Can't show up in a gymnasium on a miserable Saturday morning, take your test, and go home. Can't suffer the nausea and the exhaustion and the overwhelming boredom, fret over the last fifteen questions, mix up your lines and have to go back and erase your bubbles. Leave trashed and with a lead-shined fist. All of these most basic indignities of secondary education had been supplanted by the graver insult of relieving students of the notion of independent challenge in the first place. By the time the children got to her, they sat warily in their chairs with hunched shoulders and waited to be told what to do. College was just the next thing—that was all. It was Anne's goal to shake them awake and alert them to the fact that real life was just around the corner. That they had four years to transition from being told what to do to choosing what to do, and that the world after college was unforgiving of indecision. When she finally did manage to get through to her kids, then it was as though a person who had been absent decided to show up—a voice appeared on the page in their essays, and a new energy drove their search. They started keeping their own deadlines and doing their own dreaming. And almost without fail, this new sense of self-possession, coupled with some insight and reasonable scholarly ambition, was rewarded by the admissions committees. In five years and seventy students, all but two of Anne's kids had matriculated at their top-choice schools. Anne was passed down from year to year by parents who refused to breathe her name until their own children had finished the process. They flew their kids in from all over the country to see her, and they flew Anne everywhere to be with them—Manhattan, Marin, Snowmass, Siena. She was sure she could help. In fact, she sometimes believed she was the only person left who could.

Unless, of course, she was just the next turn of the screw, the most elaborate device yet for robbing kids of their autonomy, and this is what worried her as she returned home from the offices of Blanchard, McHenry, Winsett & Blair. She always felt a little bit dirty after a parents' meeting, and Mr. Blanchard had been one of the worst. Plus it grated that Ewan Monroe from Modern Novel was up and coming, squirreling through those corridors as a second-year associate, while she was treading water with high school seniors. The difference in their occupations seemed a measure not of aptitude but of virtue, and also somehow of heart.

But this isn't forever, she told herself. "Not forever," she said aloud as she circled her block, looking for parking. In her father's own words, her work was an "excellent stopgap" for a young woman waiting for her life to start. Though if she were honest, it was more precisely a stopgap for a young woman waiting for her *boyfriend's* life to start. While Martin was out in Los Angeles breaking into television and scouting places for them to live, which was where he'd been since the New Year, when his latest show at Steppenwolf closed and he took a sabbatical to try for the next big thing. An agent had seen him in *Stonewater Rapture* and taken him for a drink; turned out they'd almost overlapped at Yale, and he thought Martin had the look. God, did he; his height, his breadth, his wide, clean shoulders; the deep brown curls he wore pulled back in a ponytail, gladiator-style. But what could they do? It didn't make sense for Anne to go west with him; he was crashing on floors and living by his wits. She needed to keep something cooking in Chicago until he got his foot in the door.

Remembering Martin cheered her. Just the image of him in her mind countered that beaked boy, Ewan, and his happily plodding life. She imagined their future life in L.A., a bungalow behind a jasmine hedge, eventually a child asleep upstairs. For now, Anne's home was in the lone apartment building on the block, her flat sandwiched, appropriately enough, between a gorgeous married couple on the ground floor and a batty singleton called April upstairs. On bad days, she thought Fortune was offering her the choice in starkly proximate terms. On good days, she felt perfectly poised over the happily grounded life awaiting her.

But April. My God, was she getting bad. April *Penze* was her name. Irritating in every way. A perennial paralegal hunting for a husband, *esquire,* or anyone really who would keep her in Candies wedges and highlights. She played singles volleyball on Monday nights and singles foosball on Thursdays and in the summer took singles booze cruises along Lake Michigan, Bud Light and watery G&Ts departing from Navy Pier on the half hour. Even her name was bothersome: Was that *pence* or *penzey*? *Pen-zay?* Or just plain *pens*? The word on the buzzer was like a piece of grit in Anne's days. Anne understood that her irritation was born of her terror of ending up like April: midthirties, with tinseled hair and tapping nails, like a freezing alley cat, alone. Being conscious of the origin of her aversion only heightened Anne's ire. She clung to the fact that Martin once referred to April as "that trashy chick upstairs."

April and Anne had coexisted, however, until a recent episode that had revealed that Anne's distaste was more than reciprocated—which was fascinating as well as troubling—and which had escalated matters considerably. Anne had just been returning from her morning run with

Mitchell and had paused to read the headlines of her *New York Times.* She insisted on receiving the paper in hard copy for two reasons: for the ability to do the crossword in pen; and for the pleasure of the moment when she and Mitch came in puffing from the lakefront air and stood in the vestibule, the first thin sun coming through the streaked glass, while Anne slid the paper out of its plastic sleeve and saw the day's headlines revealed. As silly as it seemed, it did actually feel like the world in her hands: the paper's dire tone was like an invitation to an important event. With all that was so distant—Martin on the West Coast, her friends grasping brass rings all over the country, her parents sitting in their lonely chairs out in the suburbs, her life seemingly perched just beyond where she could reach—the immediacy of the paper in her sweaty hands made for a moment of belonging every morning.

And often, just at that moment, April Penze would burst through the vestibule door on her way to work. She never said hello or good morning in reply to Anne; just gave her an odd look and bashed out onto the street, letting the door slam on a haze of department-store perfume. It went without saying that April didn't stoop to gather up one of the many papers on the floor. She didn't read the *Tribune* or *Crain's* or (of course) the *Times.* Maybe this was the source of her frustration; maybe she resented the daily pile of papers between her and the door. Maybe Anne simply took the brunt of that.

But one morning late that spring, on one of the first truly warm days, when May 1 had passed and all Anne's students had checked in to confirm they'd mailed deposits to their top choices, she had come in from an especially good run and was heading up the stairs to the second floor as April was flying down from the third, and where they passed, on the first landing, Mitchell shinned by April's wobbly heels, and although Mitchell was gentle as a lamb, April narrowed her eyes at Anne and said, "Keep that dog away from me."

"What?" asked Anne. In years of sharing those stairs, this was the first time April had spoken to her.

"Keep the damn dog away from me."

"He's going up to our house," Anne replied, flustered. Her heart resumed its pounding. "We live here. He's on his leash. He's just going up the stairs."

"Yeah, no shit," April hissed. Then she passed, and said again, "Just keep him the hell away from me. Filthy mutt."

The door slammed behind April. Anne felt heat rising along the sides of her neck and up into her scalp. Insults gathered on her tongue. But it was too late. Mitchell sat by their door, glossy and calm, waiting to be let in to his water and breakfast. It did not occur to Anne that April might be afraid. She could not find a shred of sympathy. April was just a flat-out bitch. As aggressive as Mitchell was mild. Rabid.

After that, they had managed to avoid each other for most of the summer. But Anne fed off of the trails of crap perfume she left in the halls, and pored over misdirected mail for clues to April's depravity. Travel brochures for Acapulco. Carpet-cleaning coupons. Something from "North Shore Cupid," who advertised to "Businessmen and Professional Ladies" and boasted of "thirty-two bull's-eyes and counting!"

But then, midway through August, Anne's paper had begun to go missing. It would be there in the pile when she left for her run at six, but it was gone by six forty-five. Monday through Friday, only, and only the *Times*. All the other papers remained. Anne imagined April taking but not reading it; one morning she even went so far as to check the trash bin on the corner, expecting to find the furled *Times* there atop the heap. No luck. Every morning, it just vanished.

So this was war. Anne let it escalate. She stepped neatly over her paper every morning, and as she ran the summer lakefront, white sun on still water, she worked over and over the problem of April. She always meant to think carefully about the conversation she'd had with Martin the night before, if in fact he had called—often he complained that it got too late Chicago time before he was able to take a break—but his words, as confounding as they were, were too passive to take the stage from April. What's more, to best April, Anne had to have Martin in her life, even though Martin had commitment problems, to put it mildly. If she'd been wise, she'd have sorted out Martin. But to hear her thoughts, to feel the churning in her belly as she pounded out five miles along the waterfront, you'd have thought it was not Martin but this strange, sad woman April she'd been thinking she'd marry for—what was it?—five years now.

THE MORNING BROUGHT three e-mails, two of which sported little red exclamation points. Anne clicked on the first, from WinnetkaOrion, and noted to ask Hunter if he'd ever studied astronomy.

> Hey Anne,
> I thought about the assignment you said, but I can't write an email to someone else and send it to you. Sorry, but it feels bogus and weird. Plus I had a long talk with Nicole about all the stuff we talked about, and she thinks I should write about Montana more and less about the community service stuff, and I wanted to know what did you think of that?
> Thanks,
> Hunter

Hunter was pushing back. Excellent. Clearly there was something he felt worth protecting. She tapped back:

> Dear Hunter,
> Nicole's idea is excellent. I look forward to reading. Please, if you can, send through to me before we next meet. Don't sweat spelling/punctuation. I'm not your English teacher.
> Best,
> Anne

She skipped over the second message, from MarionCPfaff, because the third was from Martin:

Annie,
Sorry I didn't call last night. Peter's got me lined up with a manager, which is crazy. Like a social secretary, a butler and a babysitter all rolled up into one. Have two auditions today so heading out for coffee and cigs. Will try later.
How're your kiddoes shaping up? Tell them you'll be taking Columbus Day weekend off. I don't want the pitter-patter of little elites to distract us.
xM

PS Remind me to tell you about crazy burlesque show!

Martin had nailed a certain genre of missive capable of unsettling Anne in every line. Concise and harrowing, possibly catastrophic. He was the Stephen King of romantic correspondents. Nothing was safe: not the news of the new manager, who kept him from calling her; not the cigarettes, which disgusted her; not even the sweet innuendo of his impending visit—potentially confirmed here, though who knew for sure—which was followed by an insult to her students, and thereby to her. That lone *x,* too formulaic for affection. And a postscript to leave her, kindly, with visions of naked women in her head, as they clearly were in his.

Martin's notes glided in under her radar, roughing up her heart but, on their surface, appearing ordinary and even sweet. She was left thinking that *she* was the one making things complicated. This dovetailed nicely with a larger sense in society around her, among dating singles at least, that women were generally the ones who made things complicated. So then she felt guilty and a little bit ashamed, and decided, again, that she'd stop thinking about it altogether. She clicked on Mrs. Pfaff's e-mail instead.

Dear Anne,
I hope it's okay that I'm e-mailing you. I should probably call you to talk about Hunter's college list, which we received from his

school's college counselor yesterday. Just to give you a sense, his green light schools are Denison and the U of I. And I hate to say that she's listed Amherst as a red light. Obviously this can't be a good place to start. I'd send it to you but I don't want Gerry to see it as is and I don't know how to work the scanner. I can type the schools in an e-mail to you if need be. Please let's discuss as soon as you have some time. Would you be available this afternoon maybe? I'll have my cell on at the gym and home by 4:30.

Thank you so much.

Sincerely,

Marion Pfaff

Ah, the schools. Their names were spoken like jewels: emerald and ruby, Middlebury and Brown. Each child brought home a list divided into three groups, from the least likely to offer admission to the most. Some parents considered it an opening bid. Others collapsed. College counselors had past years' statistics to guide them, and hunches, and at the very best prep schools they had years of experience placing kids exactly where they thought those kids belonged. By the time Anne was working, the top colleges were in such hot demand that the list was sent home largely as a corrective. Mothers wept and fathers raged. Schools they'd never heard of, schools whose presence atop a résumé would condemn it on their desk, schools attended in their minds only by some high school classmate, dimly remembered, who'd failed a class or two, OD'd.

For the rare child of a trustee or a major prospect, the list was a smoke screen: ten applications would be made on the pretense of this being a meritocratic process. But the first-choice school would have opened a file on the child once his PSATs were posted. The result was already assured.

For Anne, much of the work lay in managing these lists. How to carve, from the great shared dream of college destiny, a range to fairly suit each child? And how then to help bring round the parents, in their bafflement and their shame? More accurately, how to awaken these families from a fantasy that held colleges up bright and shining and implacably steady in character, to reveal each as just what it was—a living, breathing institution—struggling to serve young minds weaned on ambition and fear and heading into a job market that matched conscription to greed and made interns of all the rest?

Take Middlebury: one thought immediately of all the blond kids with a green streak, the vegans, the skiers. Take the Ivies: the Euro kids wanted Brown. Jews, Yale or Penn. WASPs wanted Princeton. Cold athletes Dartmouth. Hot athletes, Stanford. Cornell was big and seemed possible but Ithaca was a high price to pay. Columbia for the city kids. Everyone wanted Harvard, if only to say they got in.

Then the cult schools. Tufts, Georgetown, Duke. Big states that shined like Ivies: UNC, UVA, Cal. The cluster of California schools, Claremont McKenna, Pomona, Scripps. USC for the screenwriters and baby producers. Reed for the ceramicists with sky-high SATs. In the Midwest, Chicago and Northwestern—polar opposites, both polar—and Oberlin and Kenyon (mild poets and musicians). Denison rising fast. Wash U: sharp, but in St. Louis. The Boston cluster, BC BU Northeastern Wheaton Emerson. MIT, not so much—if you were the MIT type, you knew it, and you probably didn't care about other colleges except for maybe Caltech, RPI, Rice. Mid-Atlantic: Villanova, Wake Forest, Washington and Lee, and the middle D.C. schools, GWU and American. Johns Hopkins for the premeds and writers who couldn't reach Yale. Davidson, which was not Dickinson, though both deserved discovery. Vanderbilt for the skinny girls with dreams of the South. Tristate: NYU if cash was no issue or you intended to train at Juilliard. The Hudson River, art-and-English schools: Sarah Lawrence Barnard Bard Vassar Skidmore. B-plus Manhattanites turfed upstate: Hamilton, Colgate. Way upstate: St. Lawrence. The places where preppy kids went when they got turned down by their top choices: Trinity, Connecticut College, Richmond, Sewanee. Big drinkers in mining country: Lehigh and Bucknell. The Maine schools, BatesBowdoin-Colby, said in one breath, for Bostonian stars and lesser Grotonians. Williams and Amherst, twinned, tiny, elite. Funky-smart kids into free sex: Wesleyan. Funky-brilliant kids terrified of sex: Swarthmore. Outliers: Emory, Rollins, Elon, Marlboro, Carleton, Puget Sound. Colorado College for mountains and a block schedule. St. Andrews, Edinburgh, for those needing to get away. Rounding out the lights, like stars scattered beyond the constellations, every state school other than the big three, though Anne was forever wishing she could make the parents understand what was on offer there.

Anne checked a clock. It was just eight-thirty. She'd been raised never to call someone's house before or after nine. She got up to pour herself the first Diet Coke of the day. She drank copious, even vile amounts of the stuff, served up over ice with one third of an organic lemon in a glass she kept topping up all day long. The lemon would turn dusky with caramel coloring and her mouth sour with sweetener, causing her to need fresh ice and newly bubbling soda, and so on. Though Google hadn't turned up a reliable study regarding toxicity, Anne knew by the way her hands would be shaking by noon, and the fact that she had to pee every twenty minutes, that something wasn't good for her. She imagined her kidneys crimping at the edges like little calzones. It was why she switched to something more wholesome at supper time, a good red wine, which in turn she only permitted herself if she promised to run the next morning. That was the liquid portion of things. For food, she subsisted on cereal, popcorn, and miniature frozen Snickers bars, the little Fun Size ones. This was a gift of one's twenties: to live on almost no money and clearly no nutrients and still be thin and fairly healthy, with shiny hair and good fingernails. Anne was aware that it was a bit of a budget boondoggle but not that it would one day begin to disappear.

Her Diet Coke fizzed just to the top of the glass, no higher—a perfect pour. She sipped before it began to settle and grabbed two Snickers bars from their bag in the freezer, which was lodged right next to poor

Old Nassau. Old Nassau was, had been, an elaborate ornamental goldfish Anne and her roommates had bought the summer after college, in almost conscious recognition that now they ought to begin to take care of something. The fish had lived for two impossibly long years in his big round vase with a fake plant and a little bubbling rock. When the roommates had scattered—one to law school, one to an investment bank, one for a Ph.D. in microbiology and immunology, for God's sake—Anne had inherited Old Nassau. But her first year in graduate school he'd taken a terrible turn, growing first pale and then ragged, his fins falling away from him in strings. It was clear he wouldn't make it through Christmas. She didn't want to just flush him. And indeed an Internet search revealed that flushing was a slow and terribly cruel way to kill a fish. Much better, the site said, to freeze them—gradually reduce their metabolic rate until they just drift to sleep. So she'd poured Old Nassau into a sandwich bag and set him on the shelf in the freezer, next to the Snickers, and then she'd gone home for the holidays and forgotten. A week later he was solid. Encased in ice, his fins suspended gloriously, like a crystal paperweight. She didn't have the heart to toss him. The defrosting would ruin his perfect little world.

Soda and candy in hand, she moved to the couch with a book. Downstairs the building's front door wheezed open and slammed shut behind Stuart, the hot husband from 1B, who'd be leaving in his business suit. Six-thirty in L.A.; Martin would be up pacing, reciting his lines, or doing sit-ups in a sweaty haze on the floor. Whose floor? she wondered. She hadn't thought to ask. In fact, now that she thought about it, it seemed she was not welcome to ask. He hadn't thought it made sense for her to go visit yet; he'd come east when he could. Presumably Columbus Day. Besides, as he reminded her, she knew the city. She'd been to L.A. before, to work with the Harvard-Westlake girl; so what that she'd just holed up in the girl's PCH waterfront home? Anne remembered the sun off the ocean like lightning on the ceiling. Whitewashed walls, and a mute Latina who served delicious salads every afternoon at one. The student would be heading into her junior year at Stanford now. They'd worked on a glass coffee table shaped like a kidney. If one of them leaned too hard, the whole thing threatened to tip up and guillotine their knees. For three days Anne balanced her elbows carefully and sipped iced tea, and then she'd been returned to LAX by stretch sedan.

The loneliness of that grand ocean room was enough. Anne got up and dialed Mrs. Pfaff.

"So, tell me," she said softly.

"Oh, Anne," said Mrs. Pfaff, and she began quietly to cry. "It's just—I'm sorry. I was so shocked. I mean, let me read this list to you. I have it right here—hold on a sec—" Anne heard shuffling sounds and imagined frantic hands. A dog shook its collar, *tink-tink-tink,* from a tufted bed. A coffee cup was lifted and set down, and a gulp. Anne briefly entertained the beginning of a thought about women alone in their rooms in the bright mornings, fretting over men and boys, but the receiver came alive again. "Okay," said Mrs. Pfaff, squaring herself to the task. "You there?"

"I'm here."

"Here we go. Red-light schools: Amherst Princeton Penn Cornell. Yellow light: Middlebury Tufts Bates Hamilton Davidson. But Middlebury's *orange,* if you can believe it. Whatever that means. Green light: Denison Champaign-Urbana St. Lawrence Elon. I mean, *Elon*? What is *Elon*?"

"Up-and-coming, small, North Carolina."

"Well, yeah. No. I mean, Gerry went to Cornell, and don't tell him I told you this, but it always smarted because he wanted to go to Yale. And now this. I don't think she's factoring in Hunter's tennis. And what about peer counselor? There are only twelve of them, you know, six boys and six girls. It's a big, big honor! So I just, I don't know what to think!"

What Anne thought is that Hunter's school college counselor was spot-on, but her loyalty mustn't seem shaky. "What's the counselor's name?" she asked.

"Tiffany Schmitz."

Anne knew just the one. She was a pro. "All right, don't panic," Anne said. "Tiffany's job is to manage expectations. She needs parents to feel that their children succeeded, not failed, right? So she's going to go out of her way to be careful with her recommendations. She's not making the decisions here, remember."

Though, of course, to some extent, she was; Tiffany Schmitz had just signaled to the Pfaffs that she would not be pounding the table for Hunter at Amherst, Princeton, Penn, or Cornell. It would cost her too much with the admissions officers, and there would be other, much stronger candidates in Hunter's class.

"Yeah, I guess that makes sense," sniffed Mrs. Pfaff. "But, Anne, what can we do?"

"Well, we're going to be smart and thoughtful and realistic. Tell me, first, where does Hunter most want to go?"

"Oh. Well, we're just positive Amherst is the best fit for him. I mean, a small school, lots of faculty attention. Hunter really thrives with mentors. He's got a cousin there, she's going to be a junior, and she just loves it. She tells us all the time that he would be perfect there."

"Has he seen it?"

"No, we couldn't quite make it there last summer. It's so remote! But he really liked Middlebury when we saw that; we had a wedding in Woodstock, so, anyway, it's similar—in the mountains, you know, the rural thing, trees. He keeps talking about Montana but that's just a nonstarter."

"And the rest of the list? Has he seen any of those?"

"Let's see, Cornell, yes, with his dad, and Princeton, and Yale, but that's off the list. I'm forgetting the others, but yes, I think he has. No to U of I and this Edon."

"Elon."

"Uh-huh. Oh, and he liked Davidson well enough. Gerry took him to look. Said it was kind of southern, but the tennis might be a good fit."

It was almost always the case, Anne reflected, that the kids knew where they belonged. If left to their own devices, they rarely set their hearts on impossible schools. "Okay," she replied. "I think it would be good to think about which schools Hunter's seen and really liked—we should put those at the top of our list. We'll just rewrite it according to his interests, and worry about the red-light–green-light stuff later. It's good of Tiffany to be so tough; it'll help us think clearly about all of this. Has Hunter been in touch with the tennis coaches?"

"Yes. I called all of them except for—what was it?—Tufts. Didn't try there. But I mostly left messages."

"Has Hunter been in touch with them?"

"Oh, you mean, has *he* actually . . . No. Oh God—do you think I screwed up? Do they want to hear from the kids themselves?"

"It's fine, we'll follow up. Leave it with me. Just, if you could, leave me a list of which coaches you've contacted. And, listen. Amherst is—well, look. When I was applying to colleges, what was it—ten years ago—Amherst accepted just under forty percent of their applicants. They're down below the twenties now, around fifteen. It's very, very tough there. Fewer than one in five, and it's a tiny place to begin with. So let's not put all our eggs in one basket unless we have to."

"Gerry won't hear of anything else. Maybe Princeton. Not even Cornell, in truth. It's only on the list because he's a legacy."

"Has your husband kept in touch with the university at all?"

"Not really."

So Hunter was not really a legacy either. Anne was shaking her head. The poor kid really was doomed.

"So what do I tell Gerry?" asked Mrs. Pfaff. "About this list?"

"I say you tell him, 'Look at how tough it's gotten to get into schools! How silly! I'm so glad we raised a solid young man who will thrive at any of the excellent schools on his list!' "

"Are you kidding?"

"No, I'm not. And then you say, 'But of course we're going to give it our best shot, and he's a great kid, and they're going to see that in his applications.' "

"He is a great kid, isn't he? I'm so glad you think so. I really, really do."

"He's a good one. I'm really happy to be working with him. So, listen. Leave the lists with me. I'm seeing him next week."

"You're a lifesaver, Anne, really."

"Not at all. Call again whenever you need to. It's going to be fine."

But Mrs. Pfaff was crying again, so Anne gave a gentle good-bye and hung up the phone.

IN HER EXPERIENCE so far, the lone exception to the sleeping-boy rule was William Kantor, who appeared at his door in button-downs and loafers, though occasionally in brightly colored saddle shoes, with his files in his arms and a glass of ice water for them each. He had two older half sisters, long since fledged. His father was a top plastic surgeon—responsible, no doubt, for the taut grins of several of Anne's clients—and his mother ran her husband's practice, the job she'd been hired to do when the first family was still young. Since coming home from Exeter, which William hated ("If I wanted to freeze my ass off and eat shit food, I'd walk to school and forget my lunch"), he'd been left mostly to his own devices in a twentieth-floor condo on North Lake Shore Drive. Anne followed him into his study, where his computer hummed. Usually a floor-length mirror reflected the condo's wide-open view of the lake, but today it was covered with a sheet.

"Sitting shiva?" she asked.

"No," replied William. "I just find I'm self-conscious with the mirror these days. I don't like seeing myself working. I do this thing with my tongue."

"You do? I've never noticed it."

"That's because I don't work when you're around. You work. I just watch you tear up my essays."

"Maybe we should change that."

"Happily."

But the truth was, William's essays weren't getting any better. They were in a rut. Anne was stumped to understand what it was. William was writing about the question of global warming, with a specific eye as to whether it was a scientifically legitimate phenomenon. It was his view that it was not. "There's gotta be a conservative quota at these places, right?" he'd said.

"Depends on the place," Anne told him. His personal statement read like a high school op-ed piece, highly critical of environmental movements and, in particular, the Francis Parker School's efforts to recycle in the cafeteria and encourage carpooling. He didn't sound curious or even skeptical; with his Lake Shore Drive address, he sounded like a brat.

But he wasn't. On Friday afternoons, he made his family challah on the marble countertop. Anne sat and watched him roll ropes of dough while they talked. He spent weekends volunteering at the Jewish care center in Streeterville, where he knew the names of the residents he saw every week. And in the evenings, she knew, he went alone to the theater as often as he could. She'd come close to telling him about Martin, whom he would probably recognize from Steppenwolf shows, but that was a dangerous detail to reveal.

The conservative stuff was direct from his father; sometimes William's phrases were so pat that it was as though the boy were being ventriloquized. "Did you know there are more trees in the U.S. now than there were two hundred years ago?" he challenged her. "Did you know that so-called global warming stands to improve the lot of many so-called endangered species?"

William had been tipped to go to Penn. He was an excellent student and would probably get in, assuming Anne could convince him to lighten up on the ExxonMobil stuff. But he'd told her at their first meeting that he was most interested in Vassar and its terrific theater program.

"That's a women's college," said his father, when Anne later called to discuss William's list.

"Mm-hmm," said his mother. The parents were on separate extensions, at the office. William was not invited to join the conversation.

"Vassar went coed the same year as Princeton and Yale," Anne told them. "And all of them before Harvard."

"Are you sure?" asked his father.

It was amazing: any coed college that had been all male at its founding was now considered coed. But any coed college that originally had been all female would forever be a "women's college."

"I'm pretty sure, yeah," she said.

"Well, I just don't know," Dr. Kantor replied slowly. "I don't see what's so wrong with Penn. Fine theater department there, I'd think. Or hell, he can stick around here—the U of C is fantastic and right in our backyard."

"Oh, sweetie," said Mrs. Kantor, "we don't want him in Hyde Park."

"Well, he can live here and commute. Anyway, even Northwestern, as far as I'm concerned. But Vassar? What's next, Wellesley?"

"Wellesley's still all women, so you're safe there," Anne heard herself say. Occasionally she forgot to be kind. "What would be most helpful," she continued, "is if you and William could sit down together with his college counselor and determine a clear list. Ten, maybe twelve schools at most. He's got an excellent portfolio, as you know, so we don't have to make a complex exercise of this. Just decide what you feel good about, and let us know so we can get started."

"Will do, Anne," said Mrs. Kantor. "Honey," she directed to her husband, "we can talk about the Vassar thing later. No harm in just letting him apply."

But it seemed Dr. Kantor disagreed with his wife on that one, because today William looked at Anne and said in disgust, "So Vassar's off the list."

"Why?" asked Anne, as though she didn't know.

"Dad thinks it's a girls' school. Also it was really WASPy when he was a kid, so he thinks it's going to be anti-Semitic or something. Like Francis Parker is fucking yeshiva. Whatever."

"Language," Anne warned gently.

"Sorry, Hebrew school," said William coldly.

"Got it, thanks. Listen, I'm sorry. You can't even apply?"

"Not really."

"Have you looked at the application?"

"Are you kidding? I know it by heart."

"I don't even think I know it this year. Could you do me a favor?"

"What?"

"Would you just imagine what you would write if you were going to apply there?"

"Oh, I already know. I basically have it written in my head. I mean, I'm already, like, gunning to land a summer stagehand job at Powerhouse. Do you know that summer theater program? Amazing. *Everyone* passes through. I have the whole thing already down."

"Yeah? The global-warming piece?"

"Geothermal macrofluctuations. And no. It's about a play."

"Could I see your thoughts?"

"They're just scribbles."

"That's fine with me. Could I see? Or maybe you could read some to me?"

"What's the point? Do you think my father's going to go for me spending my summers in Poughkeepsie?" He pronounced the town "pug-keeps-ee," which saddened Anne even more than his father's hard line. So proud, this boy, and with no one to talk to.

"Let's not worry about your dad for a moment. A good idea is a good idea, and I'd like to hear it. Okay?"

"Maybe. I guess so. But how about later on, once we're done with a few of these other ones, since it's not exactly pressing. Cool?"

"Of course," said Anne.

"And you can't critique it," he added. "It's not for real."

"Deal."

William glanced at his mirror, remembered the bunting, and settled again in his chair. "Okay, so, what's next? Cornell?" he asked, and sighed.

ON THE LAST day of August, Anne cranked up her window-unit a/c, drew the shades, and left Mitchell collapsed on the bathroom tile to walk the muggy sidewalks of Lincoln Park to Sadie Blanchard's five-floor Gold Coast home. She'd been instructed to go to the service entrance. The bell could not be heard from outside. Anne waited awkwardly, sweating, wondering if anyone knew she was there. She flipped through her notebook again to brush up on Sadie's transcript, which Brenda in Gideon Blanchard's office had faxed through. Solid B-pluses, one C, one D that was sort of scrubbed out when the course was dropped. Asterisks abounded. It was a long way down from Duke to the next school to which Sadie could gain admission on her own. In Anne's experience, students like Sadie—genetic shoo-ins—fell into two categories: those who had no idea how lucky they were and flaunted their privilege, as though to big themselves up into the shoes they could not fill; and those who knew exactly their luck and did everything in their power to avoid being blamed for their good fortune. Kids of the former type started wearing college sweatshirts from their future alma mater in the sixth grade. Those who were more modest, on the other hand, refused to speak of the college in question. They'd be hopeless with math or science and have a tin ear for languages, fail to conjugate even English verbs correctly, but when it came to social encounters their fear of envy made them as nimble as bats in the dark. They hated to be seen.

To Anne's relief, Sadie was among the latter. She appeared at the door in shorts, a T-shirt, and flip-flops. Her tiny tan knees were goosebumped. She clutched her arms across her chest; it was cool as a meat locker inside the house.

She flashed a quick and apologetic smile. "Mum told me all about you," she said. "I'm Sadie. This"—she picked up a yipping white dog—"is Tassel. She's kind of weird around strangers."

Sadie led Anne through the back hall and into the kitchen, where a middle-aged Latina, her hair pulled into a thick ponytail, watched over a simmering stove.

"*Hola,* Inez," Sadie called.

"Hola, mi amor," the woman replied, then smiled silently at Anne and lowered her head in a kind of bow. She presided here. "Tea?"

"Nope, we're good," Sadie called. "Had an iced chai after practice. Where's Charles? I want the living room."

"Oh, he still in there, Miss Sadie. Since he come home. I tell him only to dinner, but you send him now."

"Jesus," muttered Sadie. She turned to Anne and gestured for her to follow, past a runway of sleek granite stacked at intervals with club directories, cookbooks, and piles of mail. Publicity photos of Margaret Blanchard spanned the length of the counter. There was one of Mr. Blanchard with George Bush, and another of him with the other George Bush. No kids anywhere. Anne skipped a step to catch up with Sadie, who was pushing through a three-story front hall into a grand parlor. "My little brother is in the weirdest phase right now," said Sadie.

What he was in was an elaborate fort constructed between the high sofa and the coffee table. Marble bookends pinned blankets to the chintz; books stacked to either side of the table made a small doorway, through which a boy with a bowl haircut peered.

"Charles, Jeeezus," Sadie said as they entered.

"What?" he snapped. "I'm a refugee."

Sadie sighed. "From what?"

"Jungle warfare."

"Nobody says 'warfare' anymore."

"These guys do," said Charles.

"Oh, sure," said Sadie. "Because government insurgents talk a whole lot."

Anne knelt to the floor in front of the boy's fort. "Hi," she said, as softly as she could.

He raised an imaginary rifle.

"Okay, sorry." She stood. "Um, Sadie, which insurgents are these we're fighting?"

"Probably Tamils. Charles?"

"Yep," said the boy. "Tigers. *Rawrrr.*"

Sadie removed the bookends, gathered up the edges of the blanket, and let the fort collapse on top of her brother. The boy outlined by the blanket was smaller than Anne had expected. "We went to Sri Lanka last year," Sadie explained. "Spring break. Totally amazing. The kids there needed everything—water, food, nets. We had to get lots of shots to go and, like, take malaria pills and everything. And our own water! It was totally crazy. My parents were like, 'No kids have ever done this on vacation before!' Anyway, Charles is totally, like, unable to let go."

"How old is he?" Anne asked.

"Five," answered Charles. He rose, the blanket falling to his shoulders like a cape, and walked dragging it from the room.

"Gosh," said Anne. "Where are you going this year?"

"Probably Haiti. Unless something big happens somewhere else. You know, earthquake, flood. Conflict is usually too much for us, but that's what made Sri Lanka so special."

"Ever been to, I don't know, Disney World? Or Grandma's house?"

"My grandmother's dead."

"I'm sorry."

"And no, on Disney World. No thanks. We're not into that stuff." Sadie took a seat on the chintz. "It's all commercial manipulation, and it's for little kids, anyway. We raise our spirits by raising up others."

Anne pushed aside the fort remnants and pulled up a wingback chair. The dog trotted into the room and stood on its hind paws to be lifted onto the couch.

Sadie settled the dog in her lap, and continued: "You see, my parents both have these really big jobs, and they work, like, all the time. But they make up for it by taking us on the most amazing trips. They'll even take us out of school if there's a truly special opportunity. Like that earthquake in Iran? Well, we couldn't go to Iran, but we were in Turkey working with relief efforts. It was incredibly cool." Sadie sucked on her lower lip for a moment, thinking, and then said, "Here, come with me."

Evidence of the Blanchards' Miserable Children of the World Tour hung in the back hall, in a series of framed photographs of the family in various ravaged locales: Indian slums (children born into brothels), South African slums (HIV orphans), Appalachian slums (general misery). Sadie led Anne past with a brief toss of her head. "Charles used to be too little to join us," she said, "so he'd stay here with Inez. But now he comes, too."

They arrived in an office lined with legal tomes. The boat-size desk was covered in plaques and paperweights inscribed with Gideon Blanchard's name. A crystal gavel caught the backyard sun. Sadie fetched an essay draft off the printer's tray and led Anne back down the galleried hall. The little dog followed. "Really," she added, "we are the luckiest kids ever. Isn't that right, Tassie?"

This made twice that week that Anne had been given an essay to read for the first time in the company of the student. She tried to avoid this: it put too much pressure on her first response, and made her feel she was joining an empaneled set of judges in each child's life. Her kids had had enough evaluation; they needed conversation. They needed to be listened to. A student such as Sadie perhaps most of all, because her support at Duke meant that her essay didn't really matter to anyone except Anne and, maybe, Sadie herself.

Sadie's eyes were bright. "I just finished it last night."

COLLEGE ESSAY

By Sadie Marie Blanchard

Every holiday and school vacation, my family gives back to the world by performing acts of community service. We travel or we stay at home in Chicago and work in different neighborhoods. We always have a new project on the horizon. As a result, I am extremely dedicated and passionate about volunteering. I have never met anyone more committed to generosity than we are. I like to think of my committment to community service as a five-pointed star. This metaphor enables me to explain the five ways community service is important to my life and how I serve it, and demonstrates how all five are equally important in balancing out the whole.

The first point in the star is my mother, who's committment to everything is amazing and a real example for me. My mother is a Life Coach to a wide body of people, which means she works more than any other mom I know. As a child, I used to feel sad that my mom wasn't there after school, but as I became older I realized that it was better that my mom was pursuing her own dreams. I learned this through community service. When my mom and dad take me on trips to serve overseas, or when I volunteer with my mom on a project in Chicago, I see that her dedication extends to people outside of her office. She is willing to take time from her weekends and vacations to give back to the less fortunate than ourselves. I am so proud when I see my mom doing this and I am so grateful that she has raised me with this example: my mom just gives so much and that's why she expects us to give too.

Which brings us to the second point in the star. My father. Dad is a lawyer who spends his life defending the law and upholding the constitution. It is a natural extention of his work that he also volunteers almost as much as mom. He is willing to defend the needy whether they can pay expensive legal fees or not!

The third point in my star is my brother, Charles. Now that Charles comes with us on our service trips, I have a way to boost my morale when I'm feeling down. For example, recently we were doing flood clean-up in Iowa during a long weekend. I was exhausted from studying, which I did in the car, and

> the mosquitoes were terrible, and there was not so much food so we could only eat what we'd brought with us. I wanted to give up and just go sit in the car and wait until nighttime but then I looked at some of the victims of the flood, they were children, and I imagined that it was Charles who couldn't go into his home because it was covered in filth and mud and I found the strength to keep going. My brother helps me stay connected to my work.
>
> My star's fourth point is Church. My family doesn't often get to go to Church on holidays, because usually we travel, but when I was little we went every Sunday. We don't talk about Jesus at school or at home much, and sometimes it is difficult to decide what I believe about God and my faith. When I am doing community service, I know that I am doing good. That's not why I do it, but it helps me to feel better about some of the things I don't know.
>
> The fifth and final point of my star is the future. When I look ahead to college and my life, I want to always be giving back to the world because I have been given so much. I'm not sure yet what I want to major in, but I believe that when I feel my heart is touched by working to serve, I'm in the right place and that my path will open to me.

Anne finished reading and looked up. Sadie was huddled over the dog, her hair falling like a screen over them both. Anne studied her feet, the brightly striped flip-flops, the perfect moons of red polish. The essay read young—younger than Sadie spoke; naive, spoiled, and surprisingly candid: there was a nice girl in there, bless her. Anne wanted her to have several acceptances in the spring, even though they'd be nonstarters beside Duke. The essay would have to improve dramatically.

From beneath her hair, Sadie said, "My mother thinks I should take out the stuff about her and Dad."

"Why?"

"She thinks it shows I think I'm special because my parents both work, when really the norm in the world is that. And it's only because we go to private school that I think moms are there to pick up their kids and stuff."

Man, there they were, at the most tender spot. With the boys, it took weeks of scraping at their dull sentences to find a beating heart. The girls drove straight to the center. "I think it's hard to have two parents with really big careers," Anne told her. Her own mother had started graduate school when Anne was small, and she remembered clearly the years of being told to look for their car in the pickup line because it was unclear which of a number of ever-changing college girls would be there to fetch her. For a moment she felt cold fall air and remembered one precise afternoon, and the white turtleneck she was wearing, and not having a jacket. Why would she not have had a jacket? Maybe her memory had added that bit, to explain the chill.

"Really?" said Sadie. "I think it's just normal."

"Well, 'normal' doesn't mean not hard, does it?"

Sadie shrugged.

"What do you think of your mom's suggestion?"

"I don't know. I can't think of what I would put in for those two points, though, if I took them out."

"I think we might be able to let the star metaphor go, eventually, as the essay evolves," Anne said.

"Really? But I thought that was good? As structure?"

"It does give a firm structure, it's true. But you might find down the line that you don't need it. Anyway, let's not worry about that now."

"I really like it, though."

"Okay," Anne stalled. God, who were the English teachers who taught these extended metaphors? Every year they replicated.

"You know," Anne continued, "when I was a little girl, my mom went back to school. To become a social worker." Anne's students had been raised in the age of oversharing. Confession was like a key in a lock with them, particularly the girls.

"Really?" asked Sadie. "Who'd she work with?"

"Well, she has an interest in families with small children. Single moms. People who are struggling."

"How old were you?"

"When she started school? Four."

"So not really little."

"Um, I think that's kinda little."

Sadie was puzzled. Her fingers worked the dog's ruff.

"You must be proud of her," she said.

"Absolutely. Of course."

"I can kind of understand that. My mom's job is to help people, too."

"Doesn't mean it's not a drag when you feel you're the one who needs help. Does it?"

"I guess it's, like, I don't know. When it's really bad, the kids we see, I just, you know, I think about this"—she waved her hand vaguely toward the room's double-high windows, the late city light falling behind the silk—"and I just wonder, like, why them and not me?"

Which was exactly what her parents intended, thought Anne coldly; trying to prove to their children how good they had it. Or trying to prove to themselves how good *they* were, and how deserving of fortune. A tidy transfer of guilt from parent to child.

"Of course," said Anne quietly.

"Anyway, I just think it's great that my parents give us all these opportunities to remember how privileged we are. But can you hold on a sec? I want to make sure Inez isn't putting meat in the dinner. I'm totally into the vegetarian thing right now and she keeps forgetting. Be right back."

Sadie upended Tassel onto the cushion and trotted out. Instantly Charles appeared and scooped up the dog, which looked aggrieved. He paused on his way out. "Meat is dead animals," he informed Anne. "Like, dogs."

"I know it," Anne replied. Cradling Tassel, Charles left.

"Inez is great but totally flaky," said Sadie, taking up her place. "Where's Tassie?"

"Charles," said Anne.

"Oh. Poor thing."

"I know," Anne agreed.

"He drags her into all his little forts."

"Bummer."

"Anyway," said Sadie, "do you think my essay is good for Duke? I'm applying there early decision. You know, it's kind of a big deal, because my dad is head of the board. So, like, it's all his friends who will read it. And he really wants it to be good."

"I'm pretty sure the board of trustees won't be reading applications," Anne reassured her.

"Okay, but Dad's, like, in tight with the head of admissions," Sadie told her, clutching her hands together. She gave Anne a wide grin. "They went to Choate together, isn't that wild? And I know he's just really proud of me, and he'll want to send the essay to lots of people when I get in."

"Then we'd better get started," said Anne.

SEPTEMBER

Saturday mornings, Anne volunteered at an enormous public high school on the city's far north side. Autumn marked three years since she'd been recruited by the Princeton alumna who oversaw the program, and who might have recognized in Anne the desire to serve true need. Anne had jumped at the chance. "ACT prep, basic literacy skills, that sort of thing," the woman explained. She was several years older, small and plump, with a bobbed haircut that Anne guessed had gone unchanged since she was a toddler. Anne considered her brusqueness to be compensatory, and imagined it was necessary in the classroom. She didn't seem to be married.

Anne had replied, "I don't have any training for the ACT, and I haven't ever actually done teacher prep. I'm probably best with essays."

"Oh, honey," said the woman, "these kids don't go to colleges that ask for essays."

Ever since, Anne had been, by mutual agreement, openly submissive to Michelle.

Which is why it was surprising, and a bit flattering, that Michelle had called over the Labor Day holiday to discuss a student. The telephone had set Anne's heart jumping: her apartment was silent, save for the whirring air conditioner and the occasional clink of Mitchell's tags. Martin had deemed it too costly to travel to Chicago for the long weekend, and she had begged off moldering with her parents in the dog-day burbs using the excuse of her students, even though they were all taking the weekend off.

"I think we have a ringer this year," Michelle said. "Am I disturbing you?"

"No," Anne replied. "Tell me."

"I don't know, but I think she can reach really high. She's easily the strongest student in the grade and has been since she arrived as a sophomore. Guatemalan. Pretty sure her family's illegal—I think only Mom is here. Dad may be back there, or maybe no dad. She's very shy. Doesn't get into trouble, so no one ever really asks. She's below the radar, is the thing, and I just think we're going to have to figure out how to thread this needle for her."

"Does she have the ACTs yet?"

"Yes, took them this spring. No prep at all. Composite 34."

"Wow."

"Yeah, I know, right? But the family thing's going to be a hurdle. Just getting the ACT fee waiver was hell. And talking the school into pulling together all the documentation—well, I'll deal with all of that, but we're going to have to find a way to get the FAFSA forms done, and I don't know how the family will feel about any of this. Especially if I'm right about her status."

"What does financial aid look like for her?" asked Anne. She'd only encountered the FAFSA forms twice, both times in cases of incendiary divorces. Her students were the full-tuition-paying sort, the pack mules of university budgeting.

"There won't be any contribution at all on her part, I don't think. Can't be. It would be too much for the family—they'd say no right off the bat. She'll have to work her tail off wherever she goes, in the dining hall or something, but we need scholarships, really big ones."

"I guess we need to research those?"

"Actually, at this point, I think we need to go to the top. We need a trustee. Someone who'll advocate and speed things up. I was thinking Princeton, naturally, but Cristina's got this thing for Duke."

Anne's breath caught in her throat. "Why?"

"I think because of the basketball team, oddly enough. She's got a brother, and uncles, or cousins or something, and they're all way into college hoops. So they're huge Duke fans, and I think she thinks that's the way she'll convince them she can go."

"Doubt the Tigers have the same effect."

"No. Anyway, I just wanted to give you the heads-up. She'll be there on Saturday. Cristina Castello. Have a look and see what you see. And then let's confer on this. I don't know anyone. I was thinking I could throw it open, post to the list serves—"

"Let me think about it," Anne interrupted. "I might know someone."

"Really? Seriously?"

"Might. Maybe. Let me look into it."

"Oh, Anne, that would be amazing. I knew I should call you, with all your rich-folks connections. Okay. So let me know."

By Saturday morning, however, Anne was feeling she'd been reckless mentioning her possible lead. Gideon Blanchard was hardly a friend, and, the more she reflected on it, the more it seemed wrong to ask him to advocate on behalf of a student who would be applying for his daughter's class. Maybe if Sadie were a year above or behind, but the same admissions cycle? Not that the girls would be direct competitors in the process itself. Still something seemed unfair to Sadie, though Anne couldn't put her finger on what. Sadie had so much. And she'd probably leap at the chance to help another girl. This weekend she was serving as a volunteer camp counselor at a Head Start program in south Detroit. From her e-mails it seemed that neither of her parents had been able to join her. Her father was in trial. Her mother was leading a workshop on positive empowerment at Canyon Ranch.

The battered high school building where Anne did her own good deeds was surrounded by hurricane fencing topped with razor wire. Its two-story gate was unlocked at eight by a security guard who then returned to his van in the parking lot and spent his time until noon sipping from a set of coffees on his dash. It had been explained to Anne that Cicero North straddled a gangland boundary: half of the building was in one territory, and half in the other. Three magnetometers guarded the low steps. When the school's big metal doors slammed, the entire building shook.

Still, just after 8 A.M. students came trudging in for the Excel program, a voluntary Saturday school meant to guide them to tertiary education in the absence of a true college counselor, since the school had eliminated that office for budgetary reasons some years back. Twenty or so routinely showed up. Their diligence was offset by their reticence, a learned shyness that led them to sit quietly even when they did not understand. They never failed to turn in their work, but if they hadn't understood the assignment, their pages would be blank. For some, particularly the girls, Anne suspected the hesitation was cultural, but for others it was the result of years of being ignored. They were accustomed to not understanding. They did not feel they deserved to know. Even more than the gaps in their knowledge, it was this passivity that drove Anne crazy: a more virulent form of the lassitude that infected her rich students, whose feelings of entitlement at least caused them to get their backs up on occasion. Her Cicero North kids sat in their plastic chairs quiet as cows. Their slaughter was nearing completion. They'd graduate with few options, or none, and their entrée into the world was through a gate topped with razor wire.

She started the year as she always did: by asking them to say good morning in their native languages. One year they'd gotten to thirty. She might have tracked geopolitical upheaval by the languages that cropped up in her ammonia-scrubbed classroom: English, French, Spanish, Tagalog, Vietnamese, Arabic (Egyptian), Arabic (Syrian), Arabic (Pakistani), Bosnian, Russian, Urdu, Punjabi, Hindi, Mandarin, Korean, Xhosa, Angolan Portuguese. One of two girls wearing abayas, both sitting in the far back corner, had four languages with English a recent fifth, but her voice was so soft Anne had to walk back to her desk to hear her speak. The girl sat huddled beneath her draping. Anne realized that her fantasy of lifting it off and squaring the girl's shoulders was inappropriate, though it was not unkind.

Following their Pentecostal greeting Anne unrolled the morning's *Times* for her usual opening exercise. She handed it to the closest student. "Pick any article and start reading," she asked him.

"Big one or little one?" he asked her.

"You choose. The bigger headlines are the more important stories, but they might not be the most interesting. See what looks good."

The boy hung his head low to the paper. He droned: "Senate Republicans met yesterday to consider changes to the passage of—"

"Okay, good," Anne cut him off. "So who are they?"

"They work with the president," said another boy.

"Do they?" Anne asked.

"One of two houses in Congress," said a third boy.

"Who is?"

"Republicans."

"Well, yes, you're right, but that's unfortunate and it's not by design," Anne said. "In truth, what are the two houses of Congress?"

"The Senate and the . . ." began a girl. Then silence. As in all classrooms throughout time, the second hand on the clock gave an excruciating *tick-tick-tick*.

"The House of Representatives," finished Anne. "Good. Now, what is meant by 'Republicans'?"

She scanned the Spanish speakers to see if anyone seemed confident. One moon-faced girl wore a slight smile. Her cheeks were grazed with stubbly pimples, but her wide features were graceful, and there was something sophisticated in her loose ponytail. "How about you?" Anne asked, nodding at the girl.

"G-O-P," she answered cleanly. "Grand Old Party. One of the two dominant political parties. They're the elephants, I'm not sure why. Red states. Party of Bush. They control the House—that's the other part of Congress."

Bingo, thought Anne. This was their girl. An autodidact. And she watched the news.

"Cristina, is that right?" Anne asked.

Cristina withered at the sound of her name. She nodded.

"No, it's good. You're right, on all counts."

It took half an hour to get through the six paragraphs on the front page, at which point the exercise had run its course. It overwhelmed Anne, every week, the number of definitions and references she'd have to teach to give context to a single news story. How helpful was it to talk about elephants and donkeys? Should she say, *Immigration reform will die, and here's why*? Discuss the impact of No Child Left Behind? Clearly not. Inappropriate, probably unethical. But what would be helpful, truly? In three years she'd seen a handful of kids go on to city colleges and a few state campuses. Thereafter she lost touch with them and could only imagine their lives.

But a student like Cristina reassured Anne that she might do more in that classroom than shore up her own self-respect. For ninety minutes they drilled math questions for the ACT. These kids were the only ones in their class of twelve hundred to sit the exam. Math was easier than history or politics, certainly easier than language. In her mind, Anne was working out what to say to Gideon Blanchard about this girl Cristina. She paced with an open practice-test booklet in her hand and tried to make things as simple as she could. She chalked names and numbers on the board as she dictated: "Peter and William each have twenty dollars. Elizabeth and Margo each have multiples of twenty dollars. Elizabeth has four times the amount William has. Margo has twice the amount Peter has. How much more money do the girls have than the boys?"

She looked up and waited for the students to scribble their figures. Some of the boys set to it. Cristina narrowed her eyes, worked it out, and then resumed her slight smile. The polyglot in the abaya stared straight ahead and did no work. For a moment Anne was irritated; this question was easy, and she needed them all to get it so they'd have shared purchase on the material. It would build their confidence, and hers.

"How much more money do the boys have than the girls?" Anne repeated slowly, as she remembered her own teachers doing. "How much more?"

A few voices answered, "Eighty."

Still the girl stared. "Abir?" Anne asked. "Do you have a question?"

Abir's mouth turned down. She was embarrassed to have been called out. You'll need to get used to this, Anne thought; in college, in life, *somewhere,* you'll need to be able to speak up. "Go ahead," she urged.

Finally Abir said, "Who is the girls and who is the boys?"

To: Anne@mynextfouryears.com
From: S_Blanchard@LatinSchoolofChicago.edu

Dear Anne,
Here's my revised draft. I tried to make the changes we talked about, giving examples instead of just telling, showing the reader what the experience is like and so on. I really like the idea of independence vs direction and I tried to talk about that. I took out the stuff about God and church because IMO it's probably weird to talk about that in a college essay LOL! Also I cut the star part but now I'm really not sure how to organize things. I hope it's okay that I talked about my Mom and Dad working alot, I know that's probably not good but we can change it later, LOL! Thanks xxx
Sadie

Every holiday and school vacation, my family gives back to the world by performing acts of community service. We travel or we stay at home in Chicago and work in different neighborhoods. We always have a new project on the horizon. As a result, I am extremely dedicated and passionate about volunteering. Since I was little, I have volunteered in places as far apart as Kansas, India, Sri Lanka, and Turkey.

I learned my passion from my mother, who's committment to everything is amazing and a real example for me. My mother is a Life Coach for a wide body of people, which means she works more than any other mom I know. When my mom and dad take me on trips to serve overseas, or when I volunteer with my mom on a project in Chicago, I see that her dedication extends to people outside of her office. She is willing to take time from her weekends and vacations to give back to the less fortunate than ourselves.

My Dad is a lawyer who spends his life defending the law and upholding the constitution. It is a natural extention of his work that he also volunteers almost as much as mom. He is willing to defend the needy whether they can pay expensive legal fees or not!

As a child, I used to feel sad that my mom wasn't there after school, but as I became older I realized that it was better that my mom was pursuing her own dreams. It was hard not having them at my field hockey games or Parents' Nights for the choir concert. But a lot of my friend's parents are with them all the time, and their always giving advice about what my friends should do, who they should hang out with, etc. I can't imagine what it would be like to have my mother looking over my homework every day. In fact, when I was little and struggling with things, especially math, I had to learn by myself because there was no one home to help me. At first this made me angry, but I realize now that I learned so much more by having to google everything myself.

When my parents take my brother and I to a site of extreme need, they are showing us ways that we can be good citizens of the world and give back to people in need. They never tell us what to do (except of course if we need to be shown how to help on a special site, for example in a flood where the boards are in special places or in a conflict zone where you can't leave the path because of landmines.) I realize that my mom and dad are leading by example and not by direction. They give us alot of freedom, every day to make our choices; for example to do my homework or not or to exercise or not; and they trust us to make the best choices for ourselves. By giving us that freedom, they are letting us grow into our own selves.

All this freedom means that I have alot of choice. I don't know yet what profession I would like to have as an adult. When I look ahead to college and my life, I want to always be giving back to the world because I have been given so much. I'm not sure yet what I want to major in, but I believe that when I feel my heart is touched by working to serve, I'm in the right place and that my path will open to me.

To: Anne@mynextfouryears.com
From: WilyKantor@att.net

Anne,
I've had a few more ideas for the last paragraph of my main essay. (I saw some of this absurd ANWR debate on C-SPAN.) I copied/pasted it below. I have that other thing you asked for, but it's only in my notebook so I guess I'll have to type it up or you can just read it here sometime. Thanks.
William

I think it is easy for people to feel sentimental about animals, trees, and the natural world, and forget that human beings are the biggest part of the natural world, and that our needs must come first. Who would deny the children of Alaska health care and education in order to increase numbers of caribou? Only someone who was able to get carried away on a holiday and not visit the actual people living there to learn of their actual needs. I use this as just one example of how federal law can run roughshod over the needs of the states and local communities. As my generation steps up to make decisions concerning the use of natural resources, I consider it critical that our voices advocate responsible use of all the tools available to us to enhance our communities. Therefore I intend to major in either economics or politics as preparation for law school, where I believe I will lay the best groundwork for a career in responsible public policy.

To: Anne@mynextfouryears.com
From: WinnetkaOrion@yahoo.com

Hi Anne
Here's that Montana thing, see you Wednesday.
Thanks,
Hunter

Did you ever lay back and see so many stars overhead that they blurred together like snow? Well I have. And it was amazing to think that I spent every night of my life until that day in Montana looking up and not knowing what was really there. Light from the nearby city of Chicago makes it impossible to see the stars, except for the Big Dipper and a few others, and mostly the sky is sort of pink. I had no idea what the sky was *supposed* to look like. You can't even see the constellations where I live. Now when I see horoscopes it makes me mad because I think, How are you supposed to know what all of these are if you can't even make out the stars? Why would you care, anyway?

Did you ever stand in a braided river? Or watch a moose try to get a piece of sawgrass off it's antler? Or a beaver go back and forth making it's damn? Or spot mountain lion tracks and wonder how far away it was? Well, I have. These are the things I did during the day, when at night we had the incredible stars, in Montana, in the Bitterroot Range. I admit that mostly I was wishing my girlfriend (Nicole) was there, too because I tried to describe the stars but you can't tell someone about something like that, you just have to see it. And I guess maybe it's better sometimes if you don't try to describe things, because the words aren't the same as what you see in your mind, and then you read what you wrote and it's totally this sad little version of the pictures you want to remember, and sometimes the words can kind of blur the pictures. I guess it's true that I thought for a moment that

I would keep all of the Montana stuff to myself, like a secret. But I tried to share it, because otherwise you just think about it alone. I think it's better to try.

Anyway, probably the coolest thing about my school trip to Montana (which was totally cooler than I thought it would be since the English teachers went on it with us, but they were super mellow and not at all like normal) are the wild horses, or mustangs. They were completely wild. They had never had to take the bit (that metal part that horses have stuffed in their mouths all day) and when we went horseback riding along the trails and saw them in the fields way out, I swear it's like the horse I was on felt that he wanted to live that way, like he was jealous, and I wanted to get down and take all the tact off of him and just let him free. I guess I think it's like seeing the stars in Montana. You don't know about how it's supposed to be until you get out of your own prison, and my prison is Winnetka, Illinois, and like the horse I wish I could run free.

Actually, now that I think about it, there was this one time when I was a kid when my dad and I went outside in a blizzard, and the sky was pink like I said but you could see the snow, it looked grey, falling as it came down and it was all swirling around, and when I was watching the stars in Montana it was like that, just so much you thought you'd close your eyes and it would go away, but you did and it didn't.

The September grass in the Pfaffs' backyard was thick and soft, edged with slate where the flower beds bloomed. In a distant corner a sprinkler *chick-chicked*. Overhead the enormous oak trees were still green; only the smaller maples, nouveau specimens, were tinged with yellow. Hunter kicked out his enormous sneakers and leaned back on his elbows, his ever-present cap low on his brow, and pretended not to notice the printout of his essay in Anne's hands. Beside him was a half-gallon Styrofoam tankard with a length of ribbed tubing for a straw. "Thirsty from practice," he explained. He chewed and sucked at the straw constantly, aggressively, trailing threads of spit when he looked up to respond. It was quite disgusting, actually; there was Anne, hoping to find an essay in his several paragraphs of lovely imagery and real feeling, and the kid was slobbering away like a dog. To her initial reactions—he feels trapped and angry; he's clearly in love, probably for the first time; he's nostalgic for his childhood and missing his father—she added: he'd rather repel me than risk my affection. Also: he needs some manners.

"Hunter, it's sure as hell not a college essay, but there's some great stuff in here," she opened.

"You told me not to worry about the essay part."

"I did. Which may be one reason why you were able to write so clearly about what matters to you from this summer."

"Why, because you think I'm not trying?"

"Because I think you're not trying to please anybody else."

He closed his fish mouth over the straw.

"Hunter, are you still thirsty, or could you set that down for a sec?"

"Why, it bothering you?"

"Yes. It's gross. I'm seeing your spit."

He laughed. "Nice."

If she ever had children, Anne would remember never to talk to them about manners. Just tell them how they looked, and let them choose. She noticed that Hunter's huge sneakers were not actually black, but white sneakers that had been scribbled over in black ink.

"Nice shoes, too, man," she added.

"I hate new shoes," he explained. "It's so obvious your mom did the back-to-school thing."

"You're an athlete. You need new shoes for the season."

"You sound like Mom."

Anne gazed at the back of the house: broad screened porch opening onto the flagstone patio; twin wings of rooms fronted with French doors; gabled windows across the second and third floors. White clapboard, blue shutters. There were actual butterflies frisking the tall buddleias on either side of the porch. Lovely. What was this boy so angry about?

"Is she home?" Anne asked him.

"No. No idea where she's at. Maybe shopping."

"Dad?"

"He's at work."

That put one suspicion to rest: no divorce in the works. "So it's just you."

"Just me."

So, no older siblings lurking either. She knew Hunter was his mother's only child, but there might have been halves from his father's side lying about over the summer, riling things up.

Hunter continued, "And Nicole would be over, but you're here."

"Ah," she sighed dramatically. "Sorry to hold you up. In that case, let me tell you a few things that really interested me in your piece."

"Fine."

"First, how profound it can be to feel insignificant in the face of Nature—to feel both irrelevant and deeply accompanied. Make sense?"

"Sort of," he said. Anne appreciated that Hunter's first experience of the sublime appeared essentially contemporaneous with what most likely was his first experience of sexual intercourse. Nicole the Sophomore Now was performing a valuable service to Hunter's college applications, though Anne cringed to think of someone so young performing such acts at all.

"Second," she continued, "the desire to share one's feelings but the difficulty of putting them into words. Wanting to keep things private but thinking they'd be even more special if you could share them. Yes?"

"Yeah." He was brightening a bit.

"Third, feeling like the world has been hidden from you, like you've not been able to see things as they really are. Yes?"

"Oh, totally."

"Fourth, wanting to just be free to go see that world."

"Exactly."

"Fifth, feeling guilty about that. Remembering being a kid, and your dad, maybe, and wondering why it was all okay then if it feels so crappy now."

"Eh. Maybe." He bowed over the cup again and sucked.

"So, look. These things—the stars you can't see from this backyard right here; the horses you wanted to set free to roam—these are very real things. I know you saw them this summer. But they're also metaphors. Do you see that?"

"Things that refer to other things, you mean."

"Yes, or to other feelings. This is what's so interesting about this writing. You've got metaphors in there without even trying."

"Cool," said Hunter.

"Very cool. But I want to use them to understand what's most important to you. Does anything of what I've said strike a chord with you?"

"Maybe the horses part. I think the stars bit is kind of lame, now. And I shouldn't have left that stuff about the blizzard. I could care less."

On the contrary, thought Anne. She had to find a way to meet Mr. Pfaff so she could understand.

"Okay, let's take the mustangs, then," she said. "Could you sit up? It's kind of hard when you're lying down."

"I'm awake," he muttered.

"Hunter!"

He rustled up, gathered in his legs, and slapped his knees. He seemed to fold uneasily, tightly and at wrong angles, like a broken ladder. "Sorry. I'm up. What was it you asked?"

"Hunter," she repeated. "Look. I've been to college. I don't need to apply again. But I understand you may want to apply early decision to Amherst, is that right?"

"Looks like it," he replied.

"Which means, if you get in, that you'll go there. You'll pull your application to every other school. Is that what you want?"

"Looks like it," he repeated.

She laughed, though his point was serious. "Hunter, I can't do this for you. Whether it's Amherst or somewhere else, you need to choose. We need a *great* essay. And you've got some good stuff to work with here. I'm trying to help you, but I'm not going to write it for you."

"Okay," he said.

Anne waited. The sprinkler had finished. She wanted to scan the yard for a gardener or other silent staff, but Hunter needed her attention.

"The mustangs," she prompted. "I'm wondering what it is that you wish you could run free of. What's the bit in your mouth, if that makes sense?"

"I don't know," he told her. "School. My parents. Everything."

Anne gestured toward the expanse of house. "I don't know, this doesn't look all that bad," she said.

He dug his fingers into the lawn, tightened his hands, and tore up two handfuls of grass. He let them fall.

"So you just don't like school? Having to work?"

"No, it's not that. I don't mind, like—I get my stuff done."

"I know you do. And I see there's other things. Tennis. You worked on photography for a time, didn't you? And guitar?"

"I don't really do those anymore," he said.

"Why not?"

Hunter shrugged. He had commenced violently shredding grass between his fingernails. "Look," he said angrily. "It's not like I can write a college essay about horses. So this is stupid."

"Of course you can write a college essay about horses. But you're going to be smart about it. You're going to let the admissions people know that you know exactly what you're doing. It'll be a hell of a lot more interesting than all those essays about what people want to major in or what community service they just did or what their grandmother said right before she croaked."

This earned a slight smile. She was still in the game.

Hunter brushed off his palms and took the sheet of paper from Anne. "I just think there's a way you can do things, you know, for yourself, or you can feel like you have to do them for other people."

"Yep," Anne said, excited. "So the saddle is other people's ambitions, maybe? Does that seem right?"

"Right," he said. He was studying his words. "It's in this part, about wanting it to be, you know, a secret. It's like, if you say anything, you risk it not being real to yourself anymore."

"Amazing how hard it is to protect our own desires, isn't it?" asked Anne.

Hunter thought for a moment. She watched his chest rise and fall, the brim of his cap low over his chest.

He looked up at her. "Do you deal with that?" he asked. "Like, are your parents psyched you do this? With us?"

Anne flinched. Teenagers had unfailing aim.

"I think they're proud that I'm earning a living," she told him. Then she added, unthinking, like the lonely fool she was: "But I think, actually, they'd like me to be married."

He heard the truth. "Would you like that?"

"Soon," she lied. *Yesterday.*

"Wow. But makes sense. Like, aren't you, like, thirty?"

"Twenty-seven. But thanks."

Hunter guffawed into a closed fist. "Sorry. So do you have a boyfriend?"

"No comment," said Anne. "Back to your mustangs. I think there's a great essay in there about discovering your own wishes versus delivering on the hopes of others. It has something to do with school, and something to do with parents, and a lot to do with college, which is where you have to start switching from the one to the other. Choosing your own major, making your own schedule, getting wasted or not getting wasted. You know? So it's important. And timely."

"Yeah," he said. "Okay. I see that."

"So that's the essay to write for next week. Just see what you can do. Don't be afraid to keep those mustangs in there—they're gorgeous, we want to see them. But also say what's true. What they make you think and feel."

"Okey-doke."

"Cool," said Anne. She stood and smoothed down her skirt. She felt Hunter watching her body, and felt naked from her knees down. She crossed her arms over her bag.

"See you," he said, and lay back in the grass. Then he called, "Go round to the driveway. Doors might be locked."

From somewhere came the sound of shears in a hedge. Anne scanned briefly but saw only Hunter, prone in the emerald lawn. For a moment she wanted to stalk back and slap him across the face. Then in front of her a small browned man emerged from a shadow, clippers in hand, and moved hunched, almost furtively, toward the far privet. Sweat drenched his shirt. Princes and princesses in their towers, all of them, Anne thought. Did money ever do anything other than make children lonely?

Here is what was going to happen: Anne was going to wake up one morning in full possession of the authority she needed to go out and start her life. To acquire the position she really wanted—whatever that was—and succeed. Like Gregor Samsa in reverse, she'd reach her two feet to the floor and head into the world a whole person.

She did not know how to explain why it hadn't happened yet. She had been careful and diligent. She'd earned terrific grades. There had been classes in college about which she was passionate, and books she underlined so hard she tore the page. She was desperate to understand how stories worked, and poems and plays; *how* did they make one feel? She vivisected Virginia Woolf, line by line, and the book's heart kept beating. Her professors loved her, but none of them shared with her the knowledge she needed: How did such work lead to a life full of days? What, exactly, did one *do*? Her peers, meanwhile, seemed to discover their futures easily and completely, on any given day, as though they'd reached into their pockets and found a key on a ring—appearing at breakfast senior year in suits for corporate recruiting events, or already prepping for the LSAT or MCAT. Anne sat flummoxed in a carrel full of novels and realized, come June, she had no way to make a living.

So she interned. As a student teacher, as a radio reporter, once for the blocked writer-wife of a famous film director. In the afternoons and evenings she tutored grade schoolers so she could pay rent on the bedroom she shared in an apartment that was, per the lease, to house three young, college-educated women, and which in fact sheltered four women, a stray tomcat, a guy they found on Craigslist, and the guy's pet rat.

None of the internships took. But tutoring: now, *that* she could do. In fact, she was damn fine at homework. School had been her glory; why not go back? There was always the option of doing a Ph.D. It was perfect. A long project, several years in which to dig herself deep into a subject; not an internship, but an apprenticeship. Anne wanted to go the distance. She wanted to fall in love.

She chose English literature. Several universities offered her fellowships. At home, at her parents' house in the suburbs, she unfolded her thick acceptance letters on the kitchen counter. Her mother smoothed the pages with her palm, dish towel balled in the other hand, and let tears shine in her eyes. Her father paused to survey the notes. He skimmed their opening paragraphs, then set a hand hard on his only child's shoulder and said, "I'd pick *that one*." He'd never admit his choice was based on his wish to keep her close by; they made the best offer, he said, had the best job placement and faculty. So the University of Chicago it was.

There she walked the new halls like a trainee surgeon in a hospital, given access to the brightest rooms and the sharpest tools. She signed up for Cold War and the Creation of the American Backyard and an entire seminar on the year 1851 in England. She loaded up her canvas tote at the Seminary Bookstore and dragged it home. Year one turned to year two turned to year three. Martin was proud. Mitchell loved all the free time she had to walk with him. And there she was, at play in the fields of the word, except that the amber reading rooms revealed themselves to be a sort of Neverland, where nothing ever happened, and nothing ever would. What baffled Anne was that so much passion should come to nothing; and that her former college classmates who were, say, derivatives traders, did the same thing she did with words, *only with numbers,* and thanks to capital investment and a market as bizarre as a Rube Goldberg machine, they were making millions. Literally, millions. For three years Anne stood in line once a semester to pick up her fellowship check, some thousands, a rich offering for the humanities. She appreciated that the Marxist students were always first when the office opened at nine. The very same ones who argued, in their seminar on *Moby-Dick,* that the whale signified a commodity and that the book was an allegory of the industrial revolution. To which point the queer theorists took great exception: the whale was a phallus, an argument the feminists agreed with but for violently different reasons. The postcolonial theorists claimed the cetacean was an animation of statehood, and the theory-of-aesthetics folks considered anality relevant to the discussion. The disability studies student—who herself was rumored to have chronic fatigue—stopped conversation with her assertion that the enormous whale signified the longed-for bodily wholeness, a comment she made while leaving class early, as she often did.

Anne wrote her final paper on the whale *qua whale.* Her professor was thrilled. No one had ever taken this approach before, he said: written about the whale as a whale! Except Melville, Anne thought, in despair. What happened to her college English classes, the brilliant lectures, the shared love of these books? What rabbit hole separated the B.A. from the Ph.D.? Searching for civility, Anne paid a visit to her graduate adviser. The professor nodded her dark curls and smiled. To her, Anne's malaise was a good sign.

"This means you're letting go of your primary subjectivity," she said. "And thus opening yourself to new patterns of signification."

On the desk was a single photograph of a baby girl in a silver frame. Anne tried again. "She's beautiful. What's her name?"

"She's only eighteen months old!" replied the professor.

Frustration brought tears to Anne's eyes. "Oh."

"How aggressive is it to name a child before the child can choose?"

"Sorry."

"Well, this is why you're here, right?" The professor leaned in and extended a small ceramic plate. "Breath drop? They're French. No? To think deeply about all these received narratives that bind us so. Don't forget the power of that. It will free you."

"I thought I was here to become a professor," Anne said. "To teach."

"Ah, right, the undergrads." Anne's adviser sighed. She frowned. "Dear, this is a major research institution. They're just here for tax purposes."

Occasionally Anne tried to explain just what it was that she did, as a literary-critic-in-training. At home one Sunday night, her father put down his fork and said, "These are people just wasting their days on this earth." This from a man who spent his days peering at smeared cells on slides, looking for signs of doom. Her father's comment should have freed her: it was for him that she had begun the Ph.D. program. Instead it seemed he'd rendered a verdict: her years in graduate school were wasted ones.

Anne's father was not interested in effort. He was haunted by genius. He looked for it everywhere, as though he'd lost a part of himself. Anne had desperately wished to supply the missing magic, and heaven knows he'd given her opportunities. Once, when she was maybe seven, she'd been summoned to the breakfast table, where her father folded down his newspaper and said, "Sweetie, can you add up all the numbers between one and ninety-nine?"

Anne dashed off for paper and pencil. He stopped her. "No," he said. "In your head."

And so she began to add: one plus two plus three plus . . .

His apologetic smile broke her heart. "No, you can't," he said.

"Just hang on," she pleaded.

He shook his head firmly. There was a great mathematician, he told her, who figured out how to do the sum as a boy about her age. The boy genius noticed that one plus ninety-nine equals one hundred, and two plus ninety-eight, and three plus ninety-seven . . . and from there it was simple multiplication.

"You didn't see that," he told her. "But it's okay."

Then he resumed his reading.

Or the time, when she was even smaller—four? five?—her father had just read of the tests the Soviets used to identify Olympic-caliber athletes as toddlers so they could secrete them away in Siberian training centers. He held Anne's school ruler, bright yellow and twelve inches long, by one end, pointing down. He positioned Anne's hand just beneath it, opened her grip, and instructed her: "Catch the ruler when I let go."

It clattered to the floor.

"Nope," he said, and then laughed congenially, as though at a cocktail-party joke.

Nowhere was her father's pining more acute than in the battlefields of chess. Night after night they played. In her little pajamas Anne would face him across the board. He'd castle, he'd back a rook with his queen, he'd chase down her king with a bishop and a pawn, he'd trap her over and over. She understood that he would not let her win, and she thought she agreed with this: why lie to a child? If you can beat her, you should do so. That is how things work.

"One day you'll beat me," he told her. "Someday."

But the finality of checkmate terrified her. It felt like mortality itself, with the added bolt of sadism in the predator pawns, the leering bishop in her father's quick fingers. Her dad had books on chess openings, many translated from the Russian. He talked of Bobby Fischer. Anne scanned the board and was as careful as she could be, trying to anticipate everything that could come next. By the third grade she could no longer limit her vigilance to the chessboard. In the night, defeated, she worried about school. She worried about life. She worried about everything. In this way, basic social anxiety was converted to mild paranoia. By October of that year, she was throwing up during the three-mile drive to school, leaning, buckled in, out over the curb. Her mother told her to look through the windshield between the trees. Find the horizon, she said. She asked, "How can you get motion sickness in three miles?"

The way college admissions had evolved reminded Anne of her father: as though the schools were hunting for some ghost genius, some Bobby Fischer, a fascination with singularity that in her mind was inextricably tied to thick-spined books in translation and Cyrillic characters like evil spells and the word "Soviet," and possibly the threat of nuclear war. Her students didn't have experience with fallout shelters, but they also hadn't known the days when it was enough to be a good kid. That old Siberia-scoping eye was turned on them now, but in the name of American innovation and the competitive enterprise of a new century. It was the same old crap: the ruler hits the kitchen floor, and a child learns to throw up. Every morning.

Anne actually admired the kids who pushed back. Their smart-alecky teenage gall, the willingness to, say, quit crew or drop that fifth AP or just sleep one extra goddamned half hour: she hadn't had that kind of spleen. Instead she did as she was told and tucked away her excellent grades and then emerged into the world beyond college like a mole shot out, blinded, at the edge of an unanticipated crevasse. Her friends read the currents and hopped on in: school-work-love-life. While she teetered there, paralyzed.

To fail was to fall. To plummet. Probably to die.

And because she understood this, she understood the anxiety of the parents she served, and because she understood their anxiety, she sympathized with their kids. And this made her good at her job.

There was also in her heart the darkest, smallest, cruelest fear of all, a burrowed, vicious thing with a fierce bite: the certainty that she had no contribution to make. That she had nothing to offer the world. So perhaps, Anne concluded—trying here to be brave—the best thing she could do was turn her sights to the next generation, the ones coming up just behind her, the ones with their feet newly in the door.

Alexis Grant, though she had spent every one of her seventeen years in Minnesota, had recently gained conversational Somali, the mother tongue of a small group of refugees whose children she tutored on Tuesday and Thursday afternoons. Her gift for languages had emerged early, when she demonstrated familiarity with the Latin mass her mother dragged the family to. At twenty-two months she'd sat in her car seat and called out bits of the psalms. Recalling it for Anne, her mother shuddered: the car seat had been facing forward! They just didn't know then. The danger!

Anne looked across the table at Alexis's father, who was shaking his head gravely. Alexis wore the same smile she'd had since she'd arrived at the café, fresh from her tour of Northwestern, ponytailed and clutching a tiny notebook with a pen through its spiral coils. A little sister sat quietly, diligently shaping her paper napkin into a pulpy ring.

Their mom went on.

By the fifth grade Alexis had French and Spanish. The gift lent itself to music, too, as such facilities often do, you know; she had to choose between the cello and the French horn when it came time to sit for the high school orchestra, because even Alexis couldn't play both at once! (Her friendship with Michael Schleinstock was born of her choosing the cello, leaving them both first seat in their respective instruments; this information Anne had alone, having read it in the peer recommendation Mr. Schleinstock had written for Alexis, part of the Williams application since time immemorial.) And there was math, of course. High school had scrambled to think of something to teach Alexis once she finished calc two honors. She found an advanced logic course at U Minn with a sympathetic professor who agreed to argue on her sixteen-year-old behalf to the registrar. Michael had kept up in calculus, but he couldn't follow her to logic. Wednesday evenings, after class, she called him to describe the lecture. He answered with pen and paper to hand. She seemed to slip through complex analyses like a hot knife, leaving them laid open for even an idiot to see. Once he told her this.

"Sharpness is only a function of thinness, isn't that something?" Alexis had said.

Michael had thoughtfully written that Alexis was thin. Indeed she was narrow as a bird, with pointed elbows that flaked in the wintertime, which in Minnesota was most of the time. Alexis had explained this part in one of the essay drafts her parents had forwarded along in preparation for their visit. She was careful to keep her sleeves pulled down, even in the overheated common room of the residential facility where she volunteered. The Somali children, she noticed, suffered even worse, their dark skin blue with winter scales. So Alexis brought a tube of organic shea butter in her bag and later learned it ended up eaten on toast. The resourcefulness of this thrilled her, she wrote. Not that they were hungry; that they were willing. To recognize food where she had been taught to see a cosmetic! It was like seeing nature in a highway median, a hill of trees instead of a berm. Everything about her volunteering position was illuminating. To learn Somali, which was not represented in her high school's language library, she'd had to send away to Great Britain for actual discs. They arrived wrapped in craft paper with a feathery customs form in triplicate. It might have been posted straight from Victorian England. She imagined Darwin. She felt touched by Empire. These people knew how to take care of things. Alexis thought her young charges had much to teach her about how to live.

Alexis Grant had given college as much thought as she'd given everything else, which is to say quite a lot. Night after night, she read through course syllabi on the Internet and fell in love. Professors had Web sites! And links to their work! She wished she could cobble together a school composed of the faculty she most coveted. She had written a dozen college essays already, because the prompts, if you thought about them for a moment, were really quite good; Princeton had this fun one about the most important discovery in all of human history (fire was the gimme, of course; and from there the atom; Euclidean geometry; perhaps language. She considered writing about Lascaux or Chauvet, whose images haunted her, but settled for justice, believing it not an instinct but an adaptive, if evolutionary, behavior). And Alexis's parents had read her many drafts. Many, many drafts, as they explained to Anne. Hence their concern. She had too many ideas; she was all over the map. And there were grammatical problems, some fragments, areas where Alexis went too fast. Plus it was unclear whether the colleges were looking for her to give full rein to her imagination. Mrs. Grant's Wellesley roommate lived in Chicago, and had a daughter who went to school with a boy whose older sister had worked with Anne three years before. (Ellie Wishman, Georgetown early.) They'd heard such good things; was she free?

"I do have some availability," Anne replied. Before her was a faxed document listing Alexis's grades, coursework, APs, and extracurriculars, all neatly recorded in a nonadolescent hand. "But I'm not sure your daughter needs any help from me."

Alexis blushed. The little sister's brows shot up, but her gaze stayed low.

Mr. Grant chuckled. "Oho, she's like all of us, needs a little boost here and there." All four mugs of herbal tea drained, Mr. Grant started passing round a ChapStick.

"Truly," Anne told him, "I'm not sure what I can do, beyond reading over drafts for basic corrections—which I'm sure you can do just as easily. And for free."

"We're comfortable with your fee," he said.

"That's not my point."

"We understand. But Alexis is coming out of a high school with a lousy track record with the Ivies. It's a big public, they all go to U Minn, the top students go on these state fellowships. Or to Carleton, if they're really tops. I think one boy went to Cornell, like, four years ago. I doubt the college counselor even knows her name. We had to sign her up for APs on our own."

"They don't offer AP courses?"

"They call them honors. But Alexis has taken six of the exams. All 5s."

"Again, I'm not sure what—"

"Could we just run essays by you? We can fax, e-mail, even just read them to you. You've seen those few we mailed . . ."

"I'll be happy to read and respond, of course. But we'll arrange something by the hour, because, yes, I have seen those few, and really, you don't need much help here."

Alexis spoke for the first time. "I have *a lot* of essays," she said apologetically.

"A lot," chirped the sister.

"Well, we know you won't be the same way, don't we, Marlo?" said the father.

Marlo did not look up.

"My sister's an athlete," Alexis explained.

"Soccer!" added her mother.

"All-state already," completed the dad.

"Well, congratulations to all of you," Anne said. "I don't mind lots of essays—that's what I do."

"And of course we're thinking Harvard early action," said Mr. Grant. Alexis smiled and rolled back her eyes as though in ecstasy.

Many of the most competitive colleges preferred the early decision application, which bound a candidate to the school if accepted—it boosted their matriculation rates and took some of the guesswork out of the larger spring pool of decisions. But Harvard, almost alone at the top, had a swashbuckling play called "early action," which required an early application but did not bind the student to the school if admitted. It was like a suitor offering a girl a diamond ring on the first date but letting her know to take her time playing the field. It was an astonishing feat of confidence. Or of ego, depending on how you felt about Harvard.

"I think that's a fine idea," Anne confirmed.

"Alexis looks marvelous in crimson," said the mother. For Williams's sake, in his recommendation, Michael had made just this point about purple.

"If you think she has a chance," added the father.

"Harvard's Harvard," Anne told them. "But I think Alexis seems like the sort of student who would do very well there."

"Or would it be better for graduate school?" Mr. Grant asked. "I know there isn't that much attention paid to undergraduates, and it's a little bigger than Princeton and Yale—"

"You know," said Anne, "why don't we just see how we go for the next few weeks, and we can talk about that down the line, okay?"

"Yes, sweetie," said Mrs. Grant. "Alexis may not even want to go to graduate school."

"Of *course* she'll go to graduate school," deadpanned Marlo.

"Alexis?" prompted Anne.

"I don't know! There are so many things I want to study, I don't think I could ever choose!"

"Well, then, let's get you on your way," said Anne, bundling her things. "Harvard it is, then, November first."

"We'll call you as soon as we get back to the north country," said Mr. Grant. "Thank you!"

"Yes," said Alexis. "Thank you so much! Thank you so, so much!"

The four Grants grinned: smooth-cheeked, perfect tile teeth. Only Marlo wore a touch of irony in her eyes. It was rare, but occasionally Anne worked with students who could write their own tickets. First Cristina, and now Alexis, with her border-collie brain, running down ideas like wayward lambs. Sometimes Anne wished, a bit sadistically, that she could show their files to the other mothers—the Pfaffs, the Blanchards—to demonstrate just what it looked like when a student was exceptional. A necessary corrective. Would disillusionment help them to admire their own children for who they really were?

How odd it was, she thought, that the kids who didn't really need college were the same ones who would make the best use of those four years. Bring on Cambridge: Alexis would be in a field of clover. She was what those schools were made for.

In his capacity as the incoming chairman of the board of trustees of Duke University, Gideon Blanchard thought it a *splendid,* and *worthy,* and *timely* project to help shepherd Cristina Castello through the financial aid and admissions processes.

In his capacity as Sadie's father, he thought it even cleverer: "How wonderful it will be for Cristina to have Sadie as a classmate," he said into the phone. "Assuming it works out for the girl, of course." Anne was drawing fierce cubes and spheres on a corner of her date book. Why should Gideon Blanchard make her nervous? He continued: "She'll begin with a peer who understands where she comes from and what she's facing. The learning curve will be quite steep, I imagine. You know, in terms of social interaction."

The more odious his words, the more firmly Anne remembered that he was the esteemed civil litigator. Why must she always make everything so hard? It was her mother's refrain. "Things always seem so fraught for you," she'd say. "I'm sure Sadie's public service has made her deeply empathic," Anne said now, in soothing tones, taking a torch to her own ambivalence. "She'll be an excellent contact for Cristina."

"Empathic," repeated Mr. Blanchard. "I like it. That's nice, Anne. You have a way, you know. Sadie's been reporting that her essays are coming along brilliantly."

"She's been working very hard."

"You know, I just can't get over it," he said, musing. "What better indication is there of the promise represented by our nation's remarkable system of higher education than the promotion of a young woman from an undocumented family in gangland Chicago?"

"I'm not one hundred percent sure of her immigration status," Anne began.

"Oh, of course. But let's just assume undocumented could mean visas, passports . . . hey, between you and me, a mortgage deed. Whatever it is, she hasn't got it. And now, thanks to us, she'll have a shot. It's really such a nice opportunity. This is what it's all about, Anne. It really is. Sadie will be just thrilled at the prospect, I know it."

And to her credit, Sadie did in fact seem genuinely flushed with anticipation when she opened the door to find Anne, Cristina, and Michelle waiting on the stoop. Michelle might have chaperoned Cristina alone but asked Anne, as matchmaker, to come along. For her part, Anne suspected that Michelle's demeanor might put off Gideon Blanchard. A diplomat she was not. "Do I have to dress up for the robber baron?" she'd asked Anne. "Does he want me in a maid's uniform?"

Anne regretted the ill-fitting blue pantsuit Michelle had wedged herself into—she looked like she was selling insurance, when, as the educator, she was the one who should be commanding respect. Beads of sweat stood out at her hairline and on her upper lip. Cristina was shrouded in an enormous, borrowed shirtdress. For the first time, Anne felt her ragamuffin crew from Cicero North did in fact have something to be ashamed of.

But Sadie had just a moment to feast her eyes on the poor Latina girl; Mr. Blanchard loomed in the hall. "Miss Castello," he sang, his broad shoulders darkening the stoop, trilling the *l*. Obviously he spoke no Spanish.

"Nice to meet you, sir," said Cristina softly.

"Sir!" repeated Sadie, delighted.

"Pleasure," he replied, reaching for Cristina. There was a quick handshake for each of them, accompanied by a fleeting but unmistakable expression across his eyes: an exaggerated roll of pleasure for Cristina; a slight flinching for Michelle; and, for Anne, a strobe of interest as his gaze swept down to her feet and back up again. She was ashamed to feel the tiniest bit excited about this. Cristina, meanwhile, sloped gently away from Blanchard's palm as he propelled her into the living room, where previously Charles had built his jungle refuge, and where now a pitcher of iced tea awaited on a silver trivet. Crystal highballs were distributed. Michelle considered it her job to make introductions, since Cristina was her discovery. She scooted herself up into a wing chair with both hands on the arms, like a child, and began.

"Mr. Blanchard, my name is Michelle DeLong, and I am the coordinator of the Excel program at the—"

Tipping the pitcher gracefully over Cristina's glass, he cut her off. "Miss Castello," he said, "I thought it would be a good idea to have you come round to meet my daughter, Sadie, since you girls are in the same situation applying to college this year. Then you and I can go have a little chat so I can hear more about your aspirations."

Michelle started anew. "We're just so incredibly grateful for your willingness to advocate on behalf of—"

"I understand you are a young lady of extraordinary potential," he continued, addressing Cristina more firmly now.

"Indeed," sputtered Michelle.

He wasn't wrong to relieve Cristina of the preamble; Michelle's gratitude was undermining in Cristina's presence. But also he wasn't kind. Anne wondered if this was a lesson of some sort. Gideon Blanchard, after all, was so admired.

Meanwhile Cristina's face brightened in successive directions; she was unsure where to place her loyalty.

"Thirty-four on the ACT!" exclaimed Sadie. "That's so awesome!"

Mr. Blanchard shot his daughter a dark look, but Cristina eased: she settled on Sadie as her safest confidante. Right again, thought Anne. Mr. Blanchard caught the sincere smile Cristina sent Sadie's way and gave an almost imperceptible nod.

"Thanks," Cristina said shyly.

Visibly flustered, Michelle declined iced tea.

"I only took the SATs," Sadie said. "I have to take them again in October. Sucks."

Gideon Blanchard winced. Anne suspected it was the term and not the score. "Well, we all have different gifts, don't we?" he said, replacing the pitcher and settling into a high-backed wooden chair. He leaned forward, tightening their circle, as if to draw them out of the deep upholstery. With shaking hand, Cristina set her iced tea down on the floor beside her. Sadie shot out and fetched the glass back to the coaster on the table.

"No bother," said Mr. Blanchard magnanimously. "So, Cristina, tell us a little something about your hopes for Duke University."

Cristina looked around the room, clearly unprepared. Sadie was poised on the edge of her cushion. Mr. Blanchard had crossed one leg loosely over the other knee, as if to invite some informality, though only a fool would accept it, and Cristina knew this. Michelle was spreading into the wingback, red with frustration. She spun her small gold watch round and round her wrist, *chink-chink-chink,* like a timer for Cristina's answer, fretful in the quiet. With a scowl and a quick cock of her chin, Sadie silenced the fidgeting. She was her father's daughter.

Anne was reeling. She ticked off her wrong turns: agreeing to bring Michelle; prior to that, agreeing to bring Cristina; prior to that, agreeing to call Mr. Blanchard in the first place; maybe even agreeing to work with Sadie. God, how could she have caused this? And now that they were all here, what could she say to release them?

Cristina shrugged delicately. Her hands were folded tightly, but she maintained her calm expression. Her lips were pressed together. She seemed not frightened, but thoughtful; it was a neat trick, and frankly, it knocked Anne out. Where had she learned that, and so young?

"Maybe Cristina would be more comfortable interviewing after we've had a chance to chat a bit," Anne said. "I love hearing her talk about the Blue Devils, but of course we want to give fair shrift to all the other fine institutions out there, right?"

Mr. Blanchard nodded expansively. "Indeed we do! Though not too much, right?" He paused for a laugh, which no one offered. "All right. Sadie, maybe you could start us off by telling us a little bit about why *you* want to go there."

"Um, because you did," she said.

He was stern. "I'm sure that's not all, Sadie Marie." He waited with raised eyebrow.

"Right, Daddy," she picked up. "Of course there are lots of kids who go to college and have no parents who were there before. And it's probably so fun for them to be the first, and to, you know, discover it for themselves!"

Cristina was grinning. You had to hand it to Sadie: she really tried.

She'd wear her naïveté like a diamond brooch before she'd edge the other girl. Anne risked a smile in Michelle's direction, but Michelle refused it.

"It's a spectacular university," Anne said, into the silence.

"I'm taking Spanish Four this year," Sadie offered.

"That's great," mumbled Michelle.

"Is it a difficult class?" asked Cristina politely.

"The teacher is supposed to be really sweet," Sadie answered. "Oh, and you get to go to Barcelona over spring break!"

Cristina's face lengthened as she tried to work that out. "Barcelona . . ." she began.

But Sadie had crumpled. "I'm sorry," she said. "That was probably really—oh my gosh. Anyway. It's like a way to enrich the language part of it. It's a special thing for that level class, but I probably won't go anyway because I always do community service over spring break. You know, I go to poor communities—" She broke off again, and now it seemed she might cry. Meanwhile Cristina sat placidly, listening, urging her on.

Anne wanted to whisk the two girls out the door and out into the street, where they could be teenagers and work this thing out.

Sadie worked to steady herself. She closed her clear blue eyes for a moment, then opened them again, right on Cristina, across the way. "You would probably kick butt in Spanish Four," she said simply.

Michelle was one lip curl away from an open sneer. "You think?"

Mr. Blanchard frowned in her direction. "Seems Cristina—as we say—kicks butt in all her classes, doesn't it?"

Sadie was restored. "Must be fun to be such a great student," she said. She was jubilant. Anne had the sense that she'd rehearsed this moment for years, waiting for the one soul she was specifically chosen to save. "Hey, maybe we can travel back and forth to Durham together!"

"I'd like that," replied Cristina. "I've never been."

Their rapport softened even Michelle's dark brow.

Just then Inez swept into the room, apron-clad, with a fresh pitcher of tea. Anne felt relief, like an intermission. Tassel scuffed along behind.

"Excuse me, Mr. Blanchard, Miss Sadie," Inez called. "I have the more tea here, and if anything you want from the kitchen . . ."

The dog, seeing strangers, began to growl. Cristina pulled up sharply.

"Sade, get the dog down!" started Mr. Blanchard, swatting at it, but he had misunderstood Cristina's concern. From her vantage point, Anne saw as clearly as Sadie that Cristina's smile had grown even wider, and she was on her feet in a second, leaning toward Inez, who in that moment focused on the girl and nearly dropped the pitcher in her rush to embrace her. *"¡Dios mío, querida mía!"* Inez squealed. *"Ay, ay. No sabía que era tú!"*

Mint sprigs swirled. The dog barked. Cristina backed out of the hug, remembering herself, and sat back down. *"Hola, Tía Inez,"* she said, letting them all in.

"She's your *aunt*?" asked Sadie.

"No," replied Inez, beaming at her.

"Not really," said Cristina. "She's just really close to my mom. Growing up . . . I didn't know . . ."

"No!" Inez said, shaking her head. "Oh, oh! Mr. Blanchard, he say to me, this girl she is so smart, and I think of my Cristina! But now I see you! *¡Dios mío!*"

"Oh my God," said Sadie.

"Wow," echoed Michelle.

Mr. Blanchard stood and took the tea from Inez's hands. Freed, they returned to Cristina; she patted the girl's shoulders, helpless with pleasure. "Well, how cool," he said kindly. "You couldn't have a better reference than our dear Inez. Maybe that's our cue to go to my study and talk a bit more."

"Yes, yes, you go!" said Inez, beaming around the room. "Tell him all the things!"

"Should we . . . ?" Anne started to rise.

"I'll have Inez bring the morning's papers, Inez, if you would, please," answered Mr. Blanchard smoothly. "And Sadie will be happy to—"

But Sadie was on her feet, looking gray. She held the dog in her arms. Her dress suddenly appeared three sizes too big; her tiny waist was invisible inside its boxy hems. "I've got to do . . . a thing. A school thing," she stuttered, and gave a quick wave as she left the room. They heard the sound of her feet pounding up the stairs.

Mr. Blanchard was guiding Cristina to the hall that led to his office. Anne recalled the photographs on the walls and hoped Cristina would be too distracted to notice them, but she was torn: Sadie was clearly distraught, and far more fragile than Cristina. Michelle had found the floor with her wide little pumps and appeared ready to go somewhere, though it was unclear where. She certainly would never dream of leaving the house without her charge.

Inez stood among them, wringing her hands. "I bring the papers," she told them warmly. "Oh, these girls!"

"They are both wonderful," said Anne. Her words sounded hollow. She had let both girls down, as she'd known in her gut she would. It was a horrible, horrible mistake, and now she was trapped in this living room, with one girl in the hot seat down the hall and another suffering upstairs. She wanted to hurl the glass pitcher across the room. Michelle stared at her.

"So you, you make her come talk Mr. Blanchard?" Inez asked her. Anne felt raised up by the housekeeper's pleasure; previously she had been just another soul in and out of Inez's kitchen, trailing a child. Now she was adored.

"I did," Anne said.

"Oh, thank you, thank you, Miss Anne! You make the best decision. Cristina, she go to Duke. So with Sadie! Ah, *Dios,* wait I tell her mama . . ."

"Well, Cristina and Sadie both have a lot of choices to make this fall," Anne said stupidly. Michelle frowned. "But both girls have a really great life ahead of them." Just shut up, Anne thought. She was frantic.

"I go get papers. Mr. Blanchard, he talk! You, sit."

Anne felt the heat of Michelle's hatred coming at her in waves. "You know what?" she said. "There's no need for me to sit here, is there?"

"Certainly not on my behalf," replied Michelle.

"So you'll wait for Cristina, then?"

"I will."

"I'll show myself out," Anne told Inez. "Please tell Sadie I'll call her soon."

"Yes, Miss Anne! Thank you!"

Inez swished out. Anne took a moment to return Michelle's glare. "Look, you asked me to help," she said. "I happened to have met a trustee. That's all."

"Of course," Michelle replied. "And as long as it works out for Cristina, then this is all fine. But, Anne . . ." She lowered her voice and gestured toward the bottom of the staircase where Sadie had fled. "I don't know how you sleep at night. Really, I don't."

"She'll be fine," Anne told her.

"Of course she will," Michelle said flatly. "She was always going to be. That's my point."

Anne felt defeated, and she felt it was unfair. "I do what I can," she said quietly.

Michelle sighed. She looked hopelessly shapeless in the chair, big daubs of blue suiting with uncomfortable bulges, and her plump ankles bare. Anne let herself be cruel. At least I can handle myself outside of the classroom, she thought. At least Gideon Blanchard listens to me. "I do the best I can," she added aloud.

"Yes, I suppose you do," replied Michelle.

April Penze chose to mark the arrival of autumn with a new pair of shearling-lined clog boots that smelled like a wet dog and were as furry as they were tall. She clomped into the condo-board meeting, graciously hosted by the perfect Baldwins in 1B, with a wad of leaves affixed to one sole. Already seated beside Liesl Baldwin, Anne knew her early arrival and proximate placement to be an endorsement from the couple that would drive April mad.

To see April watching Stuart Baldwin—how she gawped at him, looking up and down his handsome suit, his full head of blond hair—was to understand her every ambition. Liesl was too confident and too kind to interfere. Stuart smiled broadly and wandered around offering coffee, a dog in a room full of cats. In the far corner, two actual dogs, yellow Labs, lay side by side, not bothering to open their eyes at the knocks on the door. They had never been surprised. Anne wondered if Apartment 1B had ever been surprised by anything, or if it all just turned out fabulously, all the time. Liesl, of course, was expecting. She sat cross-legged with a glow in her cheeks like lamplight through glass. Outside it was already dark at 7 P.M.

It was impossible, on a night like this, not to think of school—not to feel school in the air, almost hear again the class bell ringing and remember the frosty mornings of new socks and stiff notebooks. Anne wondered if that feeling would ever fade, or if everyone in the room—all of them older than she, some of them decades older—felt it, every September. But what else of school remained, beside that quickening nostalgia? She scanned the room. The Baldwins: he'd gone to Dartmouth, Anne knew, because he occasionally wore his green duds to the gym; she'd gone somewhere less august, but Anne couldn't remember where. The Wozniacks, the childless couple who shared Anne's landing: who had any clue? He sold real estate, she worked in marketing. Anne suspected somewhere local and large; Saturdays she heard college football games coming through the wall. Then there was Barbara, the condo-board president, an unmarried accountant with an unexplainable rock-star boyfriend who hammered up the three flights in cowboy boots long after Mitchell's last walk of the night: clearly she'd gone somewhere, but there was no trace. Nor for the rock star. Nor for the two bachelors from the other entry, though they had Big Ten airs about them, and certainly not for the kind old lady who kept to herself beneath them. And April Penze—well, Anne didn't care to think that she'd gone to college at all. She appeared not to have any ambition, scholarly or moral.

What was it that college was intended to bestow, at any rate? Princeton loomed over Anne like a half-remembered dream, full of richness but frightening, too. She thought of all the lost opportunities, classes she dozed through or failed to dare, the years of casting about more for boys than for ideas; though perhaps, she had concluded, this was the best use of the time: four years when you are not yet ready to be an adult, when you are free to think, learn to work, and try out personas without getting into too much trouble. Like a giant playpen for late adolescents. Maybe as a service to society, campuses kept them mostly contained and mostly off the roads. But this was too pejorative. College could be a person's quickening. And if you had come from a certain background, it could change your life entirely. As it would, she figured, for Cristina Castello.

Gideon Blanchard had followed up with a quick phone call: Cristina, he explained, was exceptional; he'd already been in touch with Duke's director of admissions, whom, as it turns out, he happened to know from way back; they were going to do everything they could to ensure her paperwork was received in short order. He'd asked Anne to lunch, to discuss further Cristina's application, was Italian okay? Without waiting for her answer, he left it to her to schedule the day with his assistant. Behind his words Anne heard the panjandrums celebrating. She imagined Cristina as the lone survivor of catastrophe, swum to the side of some gleaming ship. Now all the ropes were lowered, men scrambling to bring her aboard. The hard part was done. She'd been doing it since birth.

And someday, if she was lucky, she'd be sitting in some stupid condo-board meeting, listening but not listening to the minutes proceeding—something about a special assessment for the roof and keeping the alley bins flush with the wall—and college would be behind her, and she'd have the luxury of not having to think about it at all. A luxury for

Cristina, of course, but for Anne the problem was still what to build in its place. How to live the life that all that education seemed to predict for her?

"Thank you," April Penze was saying. As ever, her voice was shrill, but she was reaching for formality, so Anne tuned in. "I'd like to talk about the dog problem," April said carefully. Her words sounded rehearsed. She was sitting awkwardly on a folding chair, legs crossed, one huge Wookiee boot bouncing slightly.

"What dog problem?" asked Stuart Baldwin.

April waved her hand dismissively in the direction of the two Labs, as if to clear their golden names. "It's the stairs—I don't think they, I mean, I don't think for the carpets, that dogs should be going *all the way up* the stairs."

"How are they supposed to get into their apartments?" Anne asked coldly.

April narrowed her eyes, revealing twin streaks of frosted violet shadow. "Well, the fire escape. Outside."

Barbara the Chair held up her hand. "Hold on. April, has there been a problem I'm not aware of?"

Anne was shaking her head. The Baldwins looked at each other and then over at their snoring Labs. Nobody else in the building owned a dog.

"It's just that I think, with winter coming, it's not right to have dogs on the carpets. Wet feet, the snow, all the dirt. I think they should use the back stairs."

"And only come in and out through the alley," Anne added.

"Well, yes."

"That's ridiculous," Anne snapped.

Liesl Baldwin shifted a bit around her belly. "Are you sure that's necessary?" she asked gently.

"Sweetheart, the back steps can be slippery," said Stuart quietly.

" 'S okay," she told her husband. "You can just take them in the ice, love."

Everyone paused for this exchange, which was enough to make Anne want to cry.

Stuart thought for a moment. "Well, I guess we're okay with that," he said.

"I'm not!" Anne protested.

"It's a not unreasonable request, I guess," said Barbara carefully. "Of course there's nothing in the condo docs about having to take pets through the back . . ."

"I pay a monthly fee to have a dog," Anne pointed out. "Carpet cleaning will be included, I imagine. And by the way, my dog's feet don't generally have leaves stuck to them." Anne nodded in April's direction. April continued to bob her leg up and down, waving the muddy clump like a flag, totally unaware.

This earned a smile from Stuart Baldwin.

"Anne, are you comfortable walking Mitchell in and out by the back stairs?" Barbara asked her.

The smile from Stuart gave her almost enough generosity to say yes—it could be done, of course, it was just a hassle of locked gates and narrow wooden stairs and passing the trash bins each way, but the point wasn't logistics, the point was April actually creating the opportunity to take something else away from Anne—in addition to her newspaper!—every single day. And to do so publicly.

"Sorry," Anne replied. "I'm happy to do that when he's muddy, which I already do. But on nice days, I'm going to use the door, the way I have for three years. If the carpets end up covered in paw prints, you'll know it's me, and I'll be happy to revisit the situation."

April set her boot down and squared herself. "Not good enough," she said.

"What's going on here?" asked Liesl.

"I have no idea," Anne answered. It was the truth. When had she become a target of April's bizarre ire?

There was no way to bring up the missing newspaper now without seeming to be entangled in something that no one would want to engage. April was casting her violet-rimmed eyeballs around the room. Finally she said, "Look, I didn't want to say this, because it's a little difficult for me to talk about . . ."

The room was silent.

"But when I was a little girl, I got attacked by a dog that looked exactly like her dog."

"A German shepherd, huh?" asked Anne.

"It looked exactly like your dog."

"Attacked?"

"Yes. It was terrible."

"Gosh, how scary," said Barbara. "Did it break the skin and everything?"

April seemed perplexed. "It ripped my coat. It was a big, puffy coat. I remember it all. So I just, I have a hard time going by that dog. I don't mind these two"—she pointed to the slumbering labs—"but there's just this thing about her dog."

"His name is Mitchell. My name is Anne."

"I know," April said defiantly.

"Wow, did you sue?" Anne provoked.

"No, I think—" April broke off. She was not a quick liar. "I think they moved away. The people with the dog."

"Well, that's good," said Anne.

"It was."

"Okay, well, listen," said Barbara. "Why don't we just ask Anne if she's willing to take Mitchell out the back, assuming that's convenient, is that okay? We know Mitchell's a sweet dog, so it's just a neighborly courtesy. Yes?"

"Wait, so do we have to do the same?" asked Stuart Baldwin.

"No!" chirped April.

"Guess not," said Barbara slowly. "But I have to say, that seems—"

"Totally unfair," finished Anne. "Dog discrimination."

"I was attacked!" protested April.

"Can we move on?" asked Mr. Wozniack. "Dinner?"

"Yes, let's," said Liesl. She reached a hand out and patted Anne's arm.

Again Anne wanted to cry: frustration at April, of course, who was a crazy raving bitch, but more at herself for getting into such tangles in the first place. This marked two days in as many weeks she'd been embarrassed to find herself caught out somehow, through no fault of her own.

Fat lot of good Princeton did in moments like this. The meeting was breaking up; the Baldwins were asking her to stay for dinner. "I've made lamb," Liesl said. Anne declined, and retreated upstairs to fume and eat alone her customary supper of popcorn and red wine. She poured the usual quarter cup of kernels into her Whirly Popper, a device that made perfect popcorn every time, no burned bits, by virtue of a hand crank that turned a little wire arm across the bottom of the pot. She worked it continuously with one hand and drank with the other. Her mother hated it. Unclear why. True, her mom made popcorn the old-fashioned way, shaken with good olive oil in a well-seasoned saucepan, and perhaps it was a feeling she had that her daughter was cheap. But Anne suspected her mother's greater concern was that her daughter was investing in things that furthered the half-assedness of her life, snacks instead of meals, gadgets instead of crockery; that she'd have greeted the appearance of, say, a Dutch oven, entirely differently. But the Whirly popcorn maker was a purchase Anne was enormously proud of, that and her black Rabbit corkscrew, whose silent, hidden mechanism was unquestionably sophisticated. The two of these together on her counter every evening formed an impressive tableau. Though the corkscrew did put her in mind of another adult purchase, this one a complicated sex toy, also, and unfortunately, termed a rabbit—because who wanted to fuck a rabbit?—which she'd bought online after Martin had mentioned he'd love to introduce "some tools" into their lovemaking. The thing was bright pink and had a horrible Hello Kitty–ish face whose bunny ears vibrated while other bits swirled. It was altogether too much, and she'd been terribly ashamed when she'd pulled it out and switched it on and seen the look on Martin's face, as though she'd brought out her hair dryer, or a waffle iron: what the hell is that for? He'd actually laughed at her. "I didn't tell you to buy a freaking auger," he said.

One week later he'd given her the thing he found exciting: a tiny pair of loosely weighted balls, yoked by a string, that she was supposed to put inside herself and walk around with, like some sort of pornographic Captain Queeg. He said they were intended to incite secret orgasms. "That's sooo hot," he groaned. "You'll have to tell me when you're coming." In truth they felt terrible, like misplaced marbles, but Anne considered herself obligated to issue a few moans, and since then he'd been sold on the idea. "Will you be wearing them when you come pick me up?" he'd asked just the other day, now that he was finally flying out to see her. Martin adored thinking he knew about her secret life.

In truth her secret life wasn't sexy at all. It was downright secretarial. Night after night, both the pink rabbit and the little balls stayed buried in a drawer while Anne sipped wine and trawled the Internet for job opportunities. She was addicted to career porn. She clicked through doctoral programs, vocational degrees, credentialing bodies and institutes and corporate recruiting pages. She read what McKinsey had to offer her, and how a career at Goldman Sachs could take her anywhere. Or how about med school? The postbac programs didn't seem that challenging. You had two years to complete all those science requirements, and they all but promised to get you in when you were done. Or vet school? Surely Mitchell served some sort of prerequisite? She was especially excited when she stumbled upon sites containing snippets of the great exams—LSAT, MCAT, GMAT; even the GRE subject tests could be good fun (she'd killed on English Literature). She'd do a few questions and find them easy and think, Life is possible. Then she'd hit a question she couldn't answer and look up, and there would be her faded love seat and the heirloom mirror her mother had installed over the dormant fireplace that showed Anne's teeth blue from wine. At this point, some nights, she cried. She had to admit the difference between something that piqued her interest and a sustaining passion. She had to admit that her friends had somehow found it in themselves to square their feet and start climbing ladders, and now they were really getting places—J.D.s, Ph.D.s, editorial roles that didn't require reviewing lip gloss. There were people looking out for them. Two of her friends, if they worked past nine, had long black town cars to bring them home. They always worked past nine and they bitched about it all, but still—a car and a driver, waiting for them? And what did Anne have? A tarty neighbor and a fire escape.

Sometimes her future seemed a climbing wall smooth as glass. Not one single handhold she could find, nowhere to dig in her toe. Once, in graduate school, a shrink had called it "dysthymia." In other words, he'd said, *You're just sad.* But it didn't feel like sadness. Sadness was to be admired: it usually followed a loss, which meant you'd had something to love. This was angrier than sadness, and terribly frightening. Anne felt like a falling thing almost at the bottom of a well. She was in trouble now, but very soon it was going to get much, much worse. She needed a rope. And it seemed a proper job with a proper name would be just the thing to pull herself up on. She'd wanted to talk about this more with the psychologist, but her student health insurance didn't cover more than three mental health visits, and he'd made the diagnosis on day three.

Tonight again found Anne filling out multiple-choice ovals online, but this time not for fun. She had a questionnaire to complete as part of her application for new health insurance, now that she had left school and joined the real world. "These things are important," her father had said. But he, the physician, didn't know. Freelance and over twenty-five? You'd better not get sick. Or dysthymic. Or run over by a car. Or have any sense of privacy:

Do you now have, or have you ever had, multiple sexual partners?

Anne stared at the question. Did they mean at the same time? At the same time in one night or at the same time over, say, a semester? Why did they select this one for her? Did they know about the pink rabbit? Or the pink rabbit *and* the wine Rabbit? My God.

The answer to their question was, Not really: there was Martin now, there had been her high school beau, and there had been—well, she'd gone to college, so a few. But *not really* was not an option. She chose *no*.

Are you now seeking, or have you ever sought, treatment for any diseases of the skin? (E.g., acne, eczema, psoriasis . . .)

Once Anne had seen a dermatologist, yes. In high school. She ticked *yes* and filled in *acne*.

Immediately the test asked, *Are you currently suffering from this condition?*

Anne closed out of the thing and called Mitchell for his walk. Her apartment felt tiny and miserable. She dutifully led the dog down the back stairs, where the blustery night was a relief. The leaves were beginning to let go, and the air had a touch of Halloween to it. It was enough to startle her a bit when her cell phone piped up, halfway down the street.

The text was from Sadie.

> NOT APPLYING TO DUKE ANYMORE. JUST THOUGHT U SHOULD KNOW.

Anne stood for a moment in the phone's blue glow. Christ. It was past eleven. The girl would be awake, sitting in her third-floor—or was it the fourth?—bedroom, or playroom, or television room, brooding and plotting to trash her life. I've got nothing for you tonight, kid, Anne thought. Mitchell was sitting quietly, sniffing the wind. Anne shivered. I'm just an almost-thirty girl who takes the back stairs.

OCTOBER

"Well, fuck her," Martin said squarely.

Anne turned the bolt and followed him down the stairs.

"She can take a fucking Xanax to deal with Mitch if she needs to. But I'd be wondering why she doesn't want you in the halls. What's she doing, running around naked?"

The streets were dark and cold. Anne hopped a step to take Martin's arm. Finally he was here. It was October, and early applications were due November 1, which meant the college frenzy had reached its highest pitch, like wasps before a frost. Anne's phone had been ringing all day. Kids were texting. Mothers were e-mailing in case their voice mails got lost. Fathers were e-mailing in case the mothers forgot to call. Lincoln Park this time of year was nothing but high school kids and hot-dog stands, but Martin at her side restored the city to a metropolis, a place of grit and glamour. His suitcases spilled across her floor like her very own wishes. It was a mess. She wanted to collapse in the same way—say, *Take me to California, take me to a life without miserable high school kids and their panicked parents, take me to something I can look forward to.* But she bit her tongue. Martin had held on to his River North apartment, but even in his absence the place was filthy, and he'd finally agreed that the cactus in the window was beyond watering. From the sidewalk you could look up and spot it browning on the sill.

"That's a grim thought," Anne told him, not wishing to imagine April nude.

"Just do whatever you want," he said. "She can have fun trying to evict you if that's her thing."

Oh, to borrow his certitude! It was in his very gait—how his shoulders plowed ahead while his hips swung ever so slightly beneath his torso, his long legs picking a horse's stride. Anne forgot how much ground he covered. She loved the clicking sound of her heels, trying to keep up.

"Jeesus, it's cold," he moaned. "Why do you live here?"

They both knew damn well why, and what she was waiting for. But Anne kept the peace. He'd just arrived. His old friend Tara had the lead in the new production at the Goodman, just opened, and Martin would be something of a celebrity in the house. It was enough.

And inside the theater, Anne found her reward: exclaiming patrons everywhere, the excitement of a new show, folks shuffling and embracing and apologizing, Martin's large hand at the small of her back. It seemed every third person recognized him. She saw that he had perfected the half-focused gaze and uncommitted smile of the center of attention—was this some Hollywood affectation? A small wave of energy preceded them down the rows, as though people sensed they should turn to look. Then Anne saw, with a few rows to spare, that William Kantor was sitting toward the front of the house, alone on the aisle, and she tugged on Martin's sleeve, but he was too slow; and what would she have suggested, that they retreat and hide? It was ridiculous. He was only a kid.

William sat with a playbill in his lap, reading the *Economist*. But of course he looked up as Martin approached, and by God, in his face it was like Christmas morning, or Hanukkah evening, or whatever; he scrambled to stand. "Anne!" he said, spotting her. "Hi!"

"Hi, William," she replied. "How are you doing?"

He looked at Martin, and back at her. "Are you? Is this?"

"William, this is my boyfriend, Martin," she said.

"Will," he corrected. "You're Martin Waverly. Wow."

"Will?" Anne asked.

He darkened his eyes at her. He had his *Economis*t in a death grip, and his other hand, which had just greeted Martin, was held against his solar plexus as though in prayer. "I saw you in *Closer,*" he told Martin.

"Cool, man, thanks."

"Your parents here?" Anne asked him.

He shook his head. "They're at services."

"Ah." Martin nodded. "Good for them."

William took this as a sign. "I think you're amazing," he gushed. Anne realized, observing his apple cheeks, that she'd never seen him admit pleasure about anything.

Martin pretended to miss the compliment, but none was ever enough. The kid was an easy mark. "Hey, so listen," he said, "why don't you join us for a drink after the show?"

"Oh, yeah! Wow! That'd be cool. Yeah. Thanks."

"Cool," Martin confirmed, and shook the boy's hand again.

They funneled past him, to Martin's reserved seats. Anne knuckled his arm. "What the hell was that?"

"What was what?" he hissed back.

"Asking my kid to drinks. Seriously?"

"What's the problem?"

"He's my student!"

"So we'll buy him a Coke."

Martin was nodding to the people on his other side as they arrived at their seats. "That's not my point," Anne continued. "I don't want my students in this part of my life, you know?"

"What part of your life?"

"My love life."

"Tara will be there, too," he reminded her. The houselights were flashing. "Not like it's a date."

"God forbid."

"Shhh," Martin said, leaning an arm around her shoulders. "Watch the show."

Three hours later Anne could not have recalled a thing about the play except how Tara looked, stalking and sulking onstage, and how Martin watched her, and how she, Anne, measured gradations of closeness between their two bodies from Act One to Act Two to Act Three. Tara wasn't a surprise—they'd met before, she was long married—but that evening, William's bright eyes cast a new spot on Martin. Anne studied him and felt, inside her, an understanding small and hard as stone. It made her want to vomit. She refused it, and it was immediately restored. Martin, sensing her withdrawal, grew cordial.

"You should listen to your teacher, here," he told William, after the show. "She's a good little writer."

"Are you?" asked Tara. It wasn't curiosity alone, but her face betrayed neither sarcasm nor envy, which made the question that much harder to answer. Anne knew Tara's husband was home with their small daughter. Meanwhile they had smuggled a teenager into a hotel bar—he'd slipstreamed Martin, coming through the doors, and now was settled wide-eyed before the mighty actor as though Martin were the Burning Bush. The boys having easily settled their pecking order, Tara was forcing the issue between the girls.

"I don't write, really," Anne replied.

"You should," Martin said, into his rye. He straightened. "I'm always saying you should write for television. Come on out to L.A. and do it."

"That'd be cool," William offered. "And I do listen to her."

"Good boy," said Martin.

"I don't own a TV," Anne said.

William persisted. "I totally listen to her. But she's a greenie. Grammar, yes. But the liberal stuff drives me crazy."

"Hey," Anne warned.

"Oh God, you're not one of those Young Republicans, are you?" Martin scoffed.

William's eyes were busy; he was furiously recalculating.

"What's your first choice, UVA or something?"

"SMU," grunted Tara. "TCU. Anything-C-U."

"Actually, Vassar," said William.

Now Tara beamed. "I went there! I loved it!"

"Hear, hear," said Martin, reaching for Tara. He fingered the three gold bracelets at her wrist. "Now, there's a recommendation for you, Will."

"But I can't apply there," William explained. "Parents won't let me."

Tara was angry. "Why the hell not?"

Martin stretched his face into mock horror. "No girls' school for my boy!" he bellowed, and laughed.

"Bingo," Anne said.

"Wow," said William.

"What an ass," spat Tara.

"It's not that shocking," Anne said, watching William's face.

"Not many Gippers at Vassar, kiddo," Martin said. The more he demeaned the boy, the more William adored him; he kept leaning across the table in Martin's direction and then catching himself, regrouping around his club soda with lime.

"That's okay," he said. "I'll probably be at Penn anyway."

"Why Penn?"

"I want to hear more about Anne's writing," Tara said.

"I don't think so," Anne replied.

"Is that how you met?" she pushed.

"No."

"Tell 'em, Annie," Martin urged. "How did we meet?"

He loved the story, seeing as it placed him on his pedestal from the very first moment—as indeed he had been, coming in as a guest on the morning talk show at the local public radio station, one of Anne's internships straight out of college. Anne thought she'd like to be among those confident, chalky voices she'd grown up with. But she hadn't got far enough to imagine a beat for herself, finding it surprisingly dull working on the day's headlines. Radio production was just at that time changing over from manual to digital, and most of the senior reporters used China-white pencils and tiny bits of masking tape to form their stories. Three minutes: the lede, a few voices, some ambient, a concluding note, and out. The work of spinning the reels and fitting together tiny snips of tape appealed to Anne a good deal. It was solitary and meticulous, done in tiny editing rooms. But she did not have the gumshoe instinct, and quailed at cold-calling. Nor did she yet have the larger sense of social justice that might have driven her to seek out stories of lesser civic interest.

Then, one dull Tuesday, came Martin. She was prepping the talk-show host for an interview with a hot young actor at Steppenwolf, who also wrote, and had a new play being workshopped uptown, etc., etc.—she gave all the guests their laurels—and the world kindled when he walked in. Her skin grew hot. Her shirt itched. She kept feeling pieces of hair fall from her barrette and into her eyes. She sat in the booth and watched the way Martin worked the microphone, cocking his head at the host but leaving his smile for the listeners. He put them all to shame. She followed him immediately. He had a dozen years on her; was big and lean, unapologetically ruffled and with an air of urgency: someone traveling far and fast. Martin quit the studio and asked her, sotto voce, to lunch. She gathered her notebooks and walked out. There had been, that night, a pair of women's shoes—ugly black flats, scuffed, of a sort she would never wear—cast askew on his living room floor. She was twenty-one and didn't ask. In fact, it pleased her to be the usurper. The shoes had disappeared soon enough. But remembering them now, she knew that Tara would know whose they were. Tara knew Martin then, knew his life, would have seen Anne come in and wondered, What on earth? It made Anne feel not much older than William, who was vibrating with surprise at his good fortune, to be sitting in Whiskey Blue with two accomplished actors late on a Friday night.

Anne told the story of their meeting, bare bones. "*The Tom McLean Show,*" she said. "I was an intern, he was the guest, I smiled, he asked me out. That was that."

"I remember that junket," said Tara. "You were just getting to be a big cheese."

Martin smirked at her. "Not half as big as you, my dear," he said. "You were brilliant up there tonight."

Tara was radiant. William was missing all of it. "You used to be on the radio?" he asked Anne.

"Only a few stories," Anne told him. "Mostly I was an assistant."

"Man," he said, shaking his head. "Why'd you quit that?"

"Yeah, why'd you quit that?" echoed Martin.

"Mmm?" Tara urged.

"Just not cut out to be a reporter," Anne said. Her voice was dead. It was increasingly uncomfortable to be answering questions in front of William. She sensed a prior conversation between Tara and Martin; there was something Tara was out to demonstrate.

"I've got to be heading home," Anne said, wrestling herself back into control. "William, it's late, I don't want to get into trouble on your account. Martin, I gotta walk Mitchell. Let's go."

"Aw," moaned Tara. It was half purr. "Stay for one."

"You think?" asked Martin.

"Come on. How often are you going to be back in Chi-Town now that you've made the great leap?"

"You're right," he said. He reached across to enclose Anne's hand. "Babe, I'll be right behind you."

There was no refusing this in front of William. "Cool, see you later," she said, standing. She beckoned a reluctant William out of his seat.

Tara gave a small wave. "Bye, kids."

Anne turned quickly so no one would see the sting.

In the taxi, William leaned his head against the glass and stared up. He held his rolled playbill—autographed by Tara, of course—as gently as a stray bird in his lap. "Man . . ." He sighed, and then he was quiet. Anne watched him walk up the marble steps and through the double set of doors, only a few blocks from her lonely apartment. He took home all the gold that night, she knew—piles of dreams, and a whole lotta hope. She was empty-handed. Maybe it was better that way. Maybe William Kantor needed it more than she.

MARTIN, WHO WAS still on California time, was finishing his morning exercises when Anne's telephone rang. He turned and scowled at the sound. Anne was pleased. She was busy, you see, with a rich and full life. She forced herself to wait two rings before answering.

From the floor Martin, mid-crunch, looked up, the batwing muscles along the tops of his shoulders rising tightly into his neck. "Who's that?"

She ignored him. Already she'd forgone her run with the dog in case Martin wanted to fool around. Morning always seemed a good opportunity for romance, though for some reason whenever they were in the same city they spent very little time in bed. Martin preferred to have sex on sofas and in cars, and in ways he'd seen in movies, like up against the fridge. It was sexy to be held—no mistaking how broad and strong he was—but logistics tended to preclude intimacy. This applied to bedtime in general, actually, if she thought about it. He did one hundred push-ups every night, and hopped out first thing in the morning to work his core. As a result, when he was actually in bed, he was always the tiniest bit rancid. Mitchell, much the better date, was waiting patiently by the door.

Anne picked up the phone. A small voice rapidly explained the rather convoluted reason for the call, which was, as best she could work out, to ask a few questions relating to a course Anne had once taken with Toni Morrison at Princeton. The reporter sounded young. He was calling from the East Coast, some paper whose name made sense to Anne but which she then immediately forgot. The *Rahway Review*. The *Hopewell Sentinel*.

"Who is it?" repeated Martin.

Anne cupped the phone in her palm. "Just someone who wants to talk about Toni Morrison."

He leaned back, letting his muscles tighten further, and gave her a deep nod of approval. She took the phone into the kitchen to get a Diet Coke, and because it would keep his curiosity aroused.

"How can I help you?" she asked the caller.

"You studied with Professor Morrison, is that right?"

So, yes, she'd been accepted into a class with Toni Morrison. A small writing seminar. It was the sort of point of pride that had a sell-by date, being more about promise than achievement, and lately it made her wince to remember. That spring had followed the awarding of the Nobel, and when Professor Morrison sailed across campus, students found themselves at their windows looking out before they knew what had drawn them there. All semester Anne had sat, mostly terrified, and studied the writer's dreadlocks—those gorgeous silver ropes—which had had a kind of Medusa effect. She'd never worked up the courage to ask her first question: how were you supposed to pronounce *Sethe*?

"I did," Anne answered the reporter. It sounded like a confession.

"Creative writing, is that right?" asked the reporter.

"Yes. Long fiction."

Martin had followed her into the kitchen and was sitting, in his boxer shorts, on one of two tall kitchen stools. He shook out a cigarette but made a show of waiting to light it until they were outside, a courtesy he extended when he felt Anne deserved respect.

"That's great," said the caller. "Amazing. Could you tell me a bit about what she was like? As a professor?"

As teachers went, Toni Morrison was not nice, but she'd been honest, and—hell—she was *Toni Morrison*. Sitting there with their sheaves of short fiction in her lap while the late-Friday light fell across Nassau Street. This was why you went to the top colleges, right? To get in front of the big guns. Such an excess of opportunity, it was almost alarming. Princeton hitting its high notes. Though every campus had its stars—you could swing a paperback and hit a great writer anywhere in higher education, really, and in some ways, the grander the grandee, the less learned. Nobody was fool enough to think they were writing the next *Beloved.* Anne and her classmates just wanted to hear Toni Morrison talk. As a teacher, she had resisted the oracular but had on occasion given out life advice, which they'd cherished so fiercely they repeated it only to each other.

One afternoon a junior, a lovely Indian woman, had come in stifling sobs. Morrison observed her for a long moment and then proclaimed, "When a man says he doesn't deserve you, he's right."

Martin had never said this, incidentally. Anne had been listening for it since the day they'd met.

To the reporter, Anne said, "She was great. She was Toni Morrison. What do you want to know?"

"Tell him she gave you an A," whispered Martin. She shook him off.

"Well, maybe a bit about what you worked on with her, and where you are with your work now?" said the reporter. "Something about how she helped you get your start?"

"Tell him!" Martin hissed.

She took her drink and turned away.

"Oh, it was just a sophomore story," Anne explained, hoping to sound as modest as she felt. "You know how that stuff is. I don't even remember it now." And she was pretty sure everyone had gotten an A. It was creative writing, for heaven's sake. Not that she'd tell that to Martin.

"You don't write anymore, then?"

"Not really, no."

"Oh," he said, deflated. She heard him shuffling through some pages. God, this is why I quit public radio, she thought smugly. The earnest rookie tones were making her cringe.

Martin had come round to face her and set his hands on her hips, pressing himself against her, in part to distract her from her focus on something other than him, and in part because he was radically excited by the sort of attention Anne was receiving now. She bobbed away from his nuzzling.

"So let's see . . ." the reporter said, buying time. "There were six of you in that class, is that correct?"

"I think so, yeah."

"And what can you tell me about your classmates? They're, let's see . . . Nina Gupta. She's a writer."

Postcolonial novelist. Long-listed for the Orange Prize. "Yep, she is," Anne said.

"Right." He shuffled again. Anne imagined a short, overweight hack, some would-be book critic for a dogpatch New Jersey paper. "Okay. And Seth Gantrim? Also a writer."

Anne recalled a monster book, the size and weight of a cinder block, called *Block*—thirteen hundred pages of experimental fiction she had no intention of facing. The publisher had designed the book to look like a cinder block, too, so when it had come out, to mostly puzzled reviews, the front table at the Barnes & Noble looked at first glance like they were doing some patch-up work to the wall behind. Among other things, Gantrim was interested in the ability of words to take up space.

"He is, yes," she answered. Martin had hooked one finger under her waistband and was running another across her belly.

"Right. And, let's see, Amelia Jenkins, she's teaching at Yale—"

"African American studies, I think, yes."

"Right, and Emily Bruton is a district attorney . . ."

"What's the question?" Anne asked, growing suddenly hot. Thank God Martin couldn't hear this guy. So everyone else had taken flight. So what? Did they have a man like Martin in their living rooms? An actor and real-live playwright, just on the cusp of landing big in L.A.? Someone with those amazing little hollows at the base of his hipbones, where the elastic from his shorts sat light as a touch? Anne gulped soda and pulled away, cradling the phone. Over her shoulder she gave Martin a big smile that she hoped looked conspiratorial.

"No, just, it's just that your class was, is, full of people who are pretty amazingly successful," said the caller. "And pretty young, I mean, not even thirty. So I was just wondering, you know, what Toni Morrison did or said that helped people, or whether it was just the power of her course, or just luck?"

Anne was quiet. This was unbelievable. Well, it was totally believable, given her attitude of late, but what made it unbelievable was that Martin was there, so she couldn't just hang up and cry.

"Have you talked to Professor Morrison?" she asked the reporter.

There was a pause.

"Well, no. She's not been available for comment as of yet."

"Have you talked to anyone else? From my class?"

"Ah. No."

Anne shook her head and frowned. "Sorry, who did you say you wrote for, again?"

He cleared his throat. "The *Metuchen H. S. Quarterly*."

"I don't think I know . . ." Anne stumbled.

"Right," replied the reporter. "Well, technically, it's the *Bulldog's Bark*. It's a high school paper. I'm in high school."

"Now?" Anne squeaked.

"No, right now I'm outside," answered the kid. "I have a second period free."

Martin, seeing her eyes grow big, chased round to face her and grinned. "Is it the *New York Times*?" he whispered. "The *Atlantic*?" His eyes were wild. "Print or glossy? Give me a clue."

"Sorry, do you need a moment?" continued the kid.

"I'm good," Anne said. "That was just my dog."

"Ah. Because, actually, I was going to ask your help with that. The others. Your number was the only one I could find. And hey, what did you say your job was now—tutoring, is that right?"

"I didn't say," she stalled. Then something occurred to her. "I can help you with the others," she offered, quickly shifting to her desk chair. It was easy enough to find everyone through the alumni network. "Tell me which numbers you want. Or do you prefer e-mail?"

"Oh, really?" said the kid. "So you all keep in touch? That's wonderful. Yeah, I suppose you would. Wow. Because a lot were hard to get, you know, from the people who are authors or whatever. So that'd be cool."

He rattled off names. Anne typed. Their profiles popped up, trailing accolades. Four women and one man. Anne smiled to see the name of the one person she'd befriended a bit in that chilly class, a screenwriter named Kellie Walker. Now she lied: "Sorry, there's nothing listed for Kellie Walker. She was always very introverted. She must want real privacy."

The kid let out a stream of profuse thanks.

Anne interrupted him. "How did you get my number?"

"Oh," he said, at his most sheepish. "My aunt? She lives in Short Hills? And she knows a woman on her street whose daughter worked with an independent college counselor who studied with Toni Morrison. So, yeah. So that was you, I guess."

"Guess so," said Anne. "Bye-bye."

Martin, exhausted by the exercise of patience, had opened a window to the cold morning and lit up. He exhaled toward the frosty air. "What was that all about?" he asked. "You didn't give him any good quotes."

"Just someone writing about Toni Morrison. Happy to help," she said.

"Writing for who?"

"I don't remember. New York local."

"The *Post*? *Village Voice*?"

"Something like that."

"And what's the deal with Kellie Walker? You don't mean *Kellie Walker*? The real one?"

"Are there fake ones?"

"She's brilliant. You didn't tell me you knew her. Do you know her?"

"I used to, sure."

"My God. You should call her. Let's have dinner next time you're out."

Next time?

Anne was struggling. Her apartment was filling with smoke, but she couldn't blame that for the ache in her chest. She decided to be bold.

"Martin," she said, sitting down across from him. "I'm actually kind of sad. This hurts. All these other people in that class, they're kicking ass now. I hadn't thought about it before now, but I just had to hear all about what they're up to, and it's all this cool stuff. And I'm . . ."

She didn't want to damn herself completely. She raised her shoulders in a shrug and was quiet. He could finish the sentence, of course, any way he wanted; they both saw his opportunity. They waited.

Martin exhaled again, forgetting the window and sending a cloud toward her face. "The thing is," he said, "it was her first full-length script, the one they nominated last year. I heard she just wrote it and sent it to an agent. No wonder, though. I've read it. It's like the plot points just float to the surface, totally inevitable. You can't see the ropes. A wizard."

Anne waved smoke from her eyes. "What are you talking about?"

"I was at a party with her not long ago," he continued. "She's a tiny little thing. I was going to go up and say something."

"Martin, please."

"Annie, what." It was not a question. He brought his eyes back down to her, as if lowering himself, by force, to the level of her feelings. He said, "Don't dwell on that stuff."

"Don't dwell?"

"No. Just get on with your own business."

"That's my point, exactly, though," she said, and now she did begin to cry. Fucking kid. Standing there on his cell phone in a high school parking lot. He'd unraveled her. And when Martin was in town. And when she had only a few hours to pull herself together before joining Gideon Blanchard, of all people, for lunch at a fancy place downtown.

"What's your point?" Martin prompted, softening some.

"That I don't know what job I want. I just don't know."

He stubbed his cigarette out in a saucer and sat back, looking at her. She watched him enjoy being watched. Don't give me the actor, she thought; give me the playwright. I need you to be smart and wise. Make something happen. I need help here.

He reached forward and took her glass from her hand, gently, and then drained it—the last, ice-cold gulps, perfectly citrusy. He set it down.

"I think," he answered, "by this point in your life, you don't need a job so much as you need a career."

She felt pitched into the deep. She was exhausted. How many times could a person fail to be kind before you concluded that he was cruel?

The morning was getting late. "I need to walk the dog," she said.

COMMON APPLICATION SHORT ANSWER

Anne this is supposed to be 150 words but I have 162 and can't figure out what to take out. Thanks, Hunter

Other than spending time with my friends, probably, tennis is the most important activity in my life. During the season and summer training I practice up to four hours a day and although my body gets tired, I never really get tired of playing the game. Tennis is the perfect sport because unlike in so many sports, where something happens and then it's over, like a race, with tennis you have so many chances to make it perfect. The ball is always coming back. (Unless you hit a winner). Also it's perfect because you can play with other people but you are still solely responsible for your own wins and losses. They like to say, "There's no "I" in "Team" but to them I reply, "There is an "I" in "Tennis". I like the responsibility of chalking up the W – L for my own day, and contributing to my team in that way, by giving it my very best on the court.

Was any space too small to represent the whole conflagration of the teenage soul? Hunter's work was so wonderfully, tragically consistent, it made Anne smile. He opened with his chronic ambivalence, designed to hide his commitment to things. The reporting of his hours of duty signaled the burden of keeping numeric tabs on his efforts and wasted valuable words in the process. He demonstrated the run-on ideas of a writer who doesn't have the discipline to plan what he'd like to say, and employed a terrible cliché that was even cheesier in the subversion. (You could crush a kid's spirit by revealing such tricks as trite; for a seventeen-year-old, they were novel to the point of revelation.) And there, buried at the center of the paragraph, a truly interesting idea that gestured to the writer's heart: *The ball is always coming back*. A line about possibility, responsibility, forgiveness, opportunity. Hunter loved to play tennis because it was the one place he was allowed to feel, for long minutes at a time (or up to four hours a day in season, if you prefer) that he might actually get things right.

Poor Hunter Pfaff. Why did this boy feel so trapped? Never mind; she'd take that one line and help him revise the paragraph to frame tennis as a space of dedication and promise. Anne set the page to the side.

SHORT ANSWER #1 (OF 6)

ALEXIS GRANT

One doesn't need to study Modigliani to know that the way the musician bends around a cello is an image of romance. Every day I have the good fortune to experience this myself, when I practice or perform on my cello. My love of music began with piano lessons when I was three; I can barely even play scales now, but I do remember loving the way the entire instrument would vibrate with the strings, and how powerful that made me feel when my fingers were still so little. Once I graduated to the cello, I adored the way the instrument not only resonates with the strings beneath my bow but also how the instru-

> ment becomes one with my arms and my knees, as though I'm the actual instrument. I have a terrible singing voice, but I like to imagine that this is what it feels like to be a songbird, or a humpback whale, calling out across entire oceans with my whole self. That I'm able to learn and express the compositions of some of the greatest musical masters with this remarkable instrument makes the pleasure expand beyond my own context, and makes me feel part of an orchestra of time.

So she ran a little bit long; but heavens, who would stop her? Anne might point out a few places to clip words; the poetry might be reined in a bit. Alexis might read it out loud to see where her voice flattened, noting a redundancy: words like "remarkable" or "instrument" a few too many times. A couple of clauses could vanish with no loss of meaning. Was "orchestra of time" exactly the right fantasy? It wasn't perfect, but Anne wouldn't change it: Alexis was in command of what she wanted to say and how she wanted to say it. Maybe, Anne thought fatuously, what I do isn't so much about editing as it is about aligning execution to intention. It's about waking kids up as writers.

Then she looked up, across the restaurant, and was returned to some humility. And don't forget, she chided herself, your kids are always just trying to get someplace else.

Gideon Blanchard was running late. A waiter had come over to tell her so. He'd offered her a glass of Prosecco, which she had declined, preferring instead to sip ice water with her folder of essays spread across the table. On her left, a wall of glass looked out over Michigan Avenue and the busy midday crowd one story below. Anne was pleased to be a part of it. She wasn't sure of Gideon Blanchard's expectations, but she was flattered. She'd been able to kiss Martin good-bye and head over here in a shift dress and heels. Large rain had begun to pelt the glass. Below her, commuters picked up their steps. Martin would be getting caught in it on his way to meet an old colleague. She wondered if it was a woman but couldn't summon enough energy to care.

Even now, in her late twenties, by which age her mother had been married for nearly a decade and had a child, Anne had not gathered in the lesser angels of her romantic desire. She was aware that she was generally attractive to men, but their interest had the disturbing habit of shading into her own, so that sometimes she wondered if she was attracted to a man because he was attracted to her. And the corollary she then feared: Was she actually just attracted to the version of herself that attracted the guy? In which case, why not just occupy that lovelier, more confident, happier self, and cut out the middleman?

All banal observations, she understood. Cupid and Psyche, Narcissus and himself, the Lacanian mirror, etc. But knowing that they were universal did not defang them. This was the bit about psychology and myth she did not get. As with fairy tales: even the smallest child understands that knowing the wolf is in the dark wood does not flush him from the trees. Nor does it mean you can go around. You can't. And age twenty-seven seemed calculated, for her, to be the moment of maximum awareness with minimal evolution: a time of excruciating self-examination, locked in the irons of the last of her adolescence.

She had the sense that her current confusion had ambition at its core. Anne was attracted to the power that some men possessed. So yes, she'd put on quite a nice getup for lunch with Gideon Blanchard. She didn't yet see that this was all a nifty way of avoiding feeling ambition herself, like distracting snarling dogs with a ball lobbed over a fence. So Martin could swagger while she swooned, and both were sufficiently occupied, neither really attending to the other.

Nor did it occur to her that men might suffer the same uncertainties. They seemed to know what they wanted, even if that was only more time to figure out what they wanted. Anne forced her feelings to counterpoint and let the guys play the tune. If her heart resonated, great. If not, she silenced it.

And she hoped that somehow, someday, everything would work out. It usually did, didn't it? Didn't it?

The anxious swell was threatening again. Like reaching for a sandbag, Anne turned to another essay.

COMMON APP SHORT ESSAY QUESTION BY SADIE M. BLANCHARD

Ding ding ding! Its my alarm going off. I roll over and hit the Off Button. It is only 5:30 AM. Every morning, my alarm goes off half an hour earlier than I need it to to make it to school by 7:45 with shower, breakfast, and everything else. Why? Because every morning, I get up alone and walk our family's dog. Tassel is little and doesn't need a ton of exercise, however, ever since she was a puppy, Tassel was my responsibility—and therefore I walk her every morning; no matter how dark or cold it is, or how tired I am from doing homework late the night before, I roll out of bed and put on my shoes. Walking the dog may not seem a challenging activity but it is something I do every single day, rain or shine. I love the way the city streets are quite so early; and how I can be alone with my thoughts even before the day begins. I love that first thing I have taken care of something other than myself. Other people may exercise or write in their journals or just read the paper but this is my quiet routine that I do not think it too much to call, a Discipline.

"You'll have to forgive me," boomed Gideon Blanchard, darkening the page. "The rain came on and there were just no cabs to be had. Have you had a drink? Let us fix that. My goodness, Sadie M. Blanchard. I think I know that name."

"Indeed," said Anne quickly, instinctively covering the page, as though to protect the girl.

"Don't get up, don't, don't," he said, patting down his suit. His lapels were wet. Rain was lashing now, and the dark outside made the restaurant glow. In the glass Anne saw him reflected, very tall and spindly, cast by several floods on a track overhead. He sat across from her and tucked in his tie. "Heavens, what a mess. What's my girl thinking?"

Anne was stumped. Blanchard cocked his head to one side and nodded down toward the page.

"Oh. Sadie!" she said, embarrassed. "Right. It's the short-answer question on the Common Application, about a significant activity in her life. She's writing about—well, about Tassel, actually."

"Oh. So is that the right answer?"

"Not really."

"Ah, dear." He sighed dramatically. "Well, do break it to her gently. She loves that dog."

"Of course." Anne wondered at how gently broken Sadie had been. The poor girl was always protesting how good she was. Every run-on sentence was a headlong argument for how she was really quite a good girl indeed.

"Anne, if I may . . ." he said uselessly. He rolled his eyeballs at the page again. "How's she doing?"

Probably it seemed a matter of convenience to him, to have a seventy-five-dollar plate of pasta while he touched base regarding his daughter's college applications. Every year this work grew stranger.

"She's doing well," Anne told him. "She's written her long essay about her volunteer work, of course, so we're sort of casting about for a subject for her shorter essay." Gideon Blanchard nodded carefully, reached into his jacket pocket, and pulled out his BlackBerry. He began scrolling. "She's chosen to write about walking the dog every morning, which maybe doesn't make the best use of that space on the application to showcase her strengths. So we're going to talk about how to adjust that."

She stopped talking. He was still reading his little screen.

The silence prompted him. "Okay, right . . ." he said, to no one. After a moment he looked up. "So sorry. Going to put this down. I think that's smart, what you say."

"I'm glad."

He was busy, of course he was. She understood. So why were they doing this? Why not just tell her what he wanted?

"You know, Anne," he began, "I made some calls before we hired you, and you really have a terrific reputation. I've actually heard parents say you're responsible for their kids' careers."

"That's very kind." He'd never asked for references. She had no idea whom he knew. Probably everyone.

"And when Margaret said she was talking to you, you know, I thought, It's probably a good idea for Sadie, who's had to endure so much as a result of her dyscalculia. She really does freeze up in the face of qualitative assessment by now. But I hadn't really thought it through, the notion of an essay writer. Coach. An essay coach. But I see, if we can be honest here—and I hope we can be honest, Anne—how there could be a place for that. Just how rigged this whole process seems to be. And how we're all just part of the system, which is, let's face it, much larger than any individual applicant. There are wheels turning that no one child can be held responsible for, right or wrong, admit or deny."

"Right," Anne said provisionally. "That's true. But—"

"So I have to ask. I mean, these parents positively glow when they talk about you. But you really don't write the essays for them, is that what you're telling me?"

She opened her mouth to answer. He signaled for the waiter.

"I don't . . ." she started, unsure. He was gesturing to her menu, indicating she should choose.

"We'll need to order," he told the waiter, an older man, who smiled widely at the two of them. Anne wondered what he imagined was happening there. "Bring everything at once, please, soon as you can, thank you," said Gideon Blanchard. He waved the waiter to stay put, and finished: "So how do you get them in?"

Anne didn't know whether she should order or reply. "Well, I don't do that either. I just make sure they have good essays."

It wasn't what Blanchard wanted to hear, so he ignored it. "What'll you have?" he asked Anne. He looked up to the waiter. "It's so hard to decide." He made a show of frowning over the menu. "I'll have the duck."

Anne really was having a hard time deciding. Pasta represented too much of a commitment. She wanted a salad, but feared fumbling the greens. She settled for soup.

"I'm paying, dear," he said.

"Really not terribly hungry," she replied.

He flicked at the air to send the waiter away. "So anyway," he continued, "that's it? Just fix up the essay, and they get the fat packet?"

"Well, no, of course not," she admitted. It wasn't clear if the word "dear" was meant to be affectionate or patronizing—maybe both—but it was like a stick to a beehive. Anne felt frantically unsettled. She heard herself elaborating: "There are grades and scores and recommendations and extracurriculars and everything else. But most of the time, it begins with the essay."

"Because that's the hardest thing."

"Because that's the only place where kids have a chance to reveal what matters to them. It is amazing how much changes when they figure out what they want. If they can make the jump from interest to discipline—that is, learn how the things that excite them manifest in the world, then they can see their way to the next step."

His face was blank.

"I'm not making sense, I know," she ventured.

"Try me again," he said.

Anne's mind skittered across her years of students, looking to form an explanation. Gideon Blanchard kept his eyes on her and raised his top lip in a wide sneer so he could pick at something lodged between his incisors. It was aggressive and disgusting, but also a little bit freeing.

"Okay," she began. "So, take a boy who, say, loves sharks." She paused, but he kept digging at his teeth. She went on: "He goes scuba diving in St. Barths and decides all he wants to do is live in shark cages. So over the summer he goes and gets his diving certification, and now he can be trusted to take his tank off and put it back on in the water. Standard stuff. He writes his college essay about great whites, and for good measure he'll mention that everything is endangered, and he'll lean on the scuba certification as proof of his dedication. And then he won't understand why he doesn't get in anywhere. Worse, he won't understand why he ends up ten years later in a job he hates and he's browsing tropical hotel Web sites every spare moment he's got."

Blanchard worked his tongue over his teeth and then flashed her a smile.

"But that kid," she continued, "if I get a chance . . . Let's say he'll let slip to me that he happens to have memorized all the Latinate names of the animals. Suddenly he knows genus and species for a zillion critters in St. Barths. This kid who can't conjugate *être* and *avoir*. There's ability there, because he *cares*. Because it's his and his alone and he *loves* it. If I can help him to understand that he can take that feeling he had underwater and apply it to his life—that there is a whole field of approach to such things, populated by people who treasure them—maybe then he realizes that he's fascinated by marine biology because it actually means devising smarter and finer ways to understand these creatures and what they do and what they need. Now, he could also be interested in maritime law or conservation ethics or underwater photography, I don't know, but you get my point. So this kid will go home and, usually without telling anyone, research marine biology departments, and discover several universities with killer programs that allow him to spend entire semesters in flippers. Suddenly college is there for *him,* not for anyone else—his parents, the annoying college counselor, even me. So that fall he steps it up in his AP bio class and the teacher takes a shine to him, because the teacher is flattered, and that teacher wants to write him his recommendation. And the boy's essay is focused and clear, and the school college counselor, who has sixty kids assigned to her and doesn't know a thing about him, realizes that he's a marine-biologist-in-training and that he's a great science student, which is a good handle, so she writes him a stronger school recommendation. And his list of schools is whittled to the ones where he really wants to go, and in his supplemental essays he's able to write intelligently about what each school offers and why it's a good fit for him.

"Now think of the admissions office: if they're assembling a class of people, not just grades, and they can hear this boy's voice and think, Hey, this kid tells a good story, I'd like to bump into him on the cobbled path out there on his way to the lab, then maybe he'll get in instead of the other kid whose transcript looks exactly the same, whose grades and scores are equivalent, but who wrote about something dull as dirt. Do you see? I mean, who knows? It's all nuance and chance. I can never tell. Maybe these kids would all get in, anyway."

Gideon Blanchard pursed his lips. "Maybe."

She didn't think so either.

Gideon Blanchard shoveled bread into his mouth and swept the crumbs to the floor.

"What can I say?" Anne continued. She felt a rush of sincerity and resentment, a dangerous mix. "I'm a hedge. A rich parent's hedge. I'm an SUV instead of a hatchback. Boarding school when the local private is great, private school when the local public is great. Any of it. A multivitamin. The mom who puts her daughter on the pill and says it's to help her cramps."

Now his eyes were very round. She watched him chew. He worked his jaw decisively.

Well, that must be it. She'd finally said enough to get cashiered. She'd called him rich, which he was, of course, but it wasn't right to say it. She'd announced her distrust in her own methods, pointed out the absurdity of his hiring her, and probably caused him to think his daughter was having lots of underaged sex on contraceptives. Well, fine. So something would happen. Maybe something interesting. Call the cub reporter. If she could just be released from this table, to fetch her coat and get back out into the rain.

Gideon Blanchard gathered up his large white napkin in his large white hands and tented it alongside his plate. He cleared his throat, pushed back his chair, and stood up halfway, leaning over the table toward her. She went to stand, too—she would at least be upright when he put her in her place—but he stilled her by reaching across to take both of her hands in his. He closed them up tightly and sought her eyes and, after taking a visible breath, said emphatically, "I think you do wonderful work."

He retook his chair and beamed at her. He had a great smile. He aimed it and let it shine and waited for her to soften.

The waiter, approaching with their food, let this moment pass. Anne pulled her shaking hands into her lap.

Blanchard took a knife to his duck. "Don't worry," he said, slicing around. "I place the highest premium on honesty. You call it like it is. I respect that, I really do."

Anne saw him considering her. She wondered if he thought she was pretty. As busy as she was, attempting to look sleek and polished, she had not guessed that the subtle proposals she was sensing had nothing to do with romance.

"I want to tell you a story," said Blanchard.

Anne started buttering a new slice of bread, to have something to do, the way people shovel in popcorn during horror movies.

"You began but did not complete a doctorate, is that right?" he asked.

"It is."

"Well, I did complete one." Anne knew—everyone knew—that he had done a Ph.D.; it was in his signature and on the door. "At the University of Chicago, like you. In economics, probably not like you."

"No, English," she said.

"Right. Well, I spent my twenties working on a dissertation about employment hierarchies and promotion practices in corporate settings, how to value them, how critical they are to helping workers succeed. Interesting, right?"

"Very."

"And my dissertation adviser, he'd been there for a thousand years, and he was working on his own thing, which turned out to be a study trying to link falling crime rates in this city with the passage of *Roe v. Wade.*"

Anne didn't touch this.

"In other words, he thought he could demonstrate that about eighteen years after *Roe v. Wade,* crime rates would begin to fall. That the bad kids weren't even being born."

"Wow."

"Wow is right. And you see, I had nothing to do with that work—nothing. I'm not all that interested in crime rates, except in as much as I don't get mugged. But once his study was published, everyone who had worked with him became a racist. Instantly. You'd have thought I wore a white hood."

"I'm sorry," Anne said. She was fascinated that nobody had ever cast his background against his wife's public image. Maybe they had in law, and didn't care, but she thought some talking heads might have a field day claiming Margaret Blanchard was married to a bigot.

Gideon flagged down the waiter for more wine. Specifically, "a nice big Barolo."

He continued, "So I had this degree, but I couldn't do anything with it. Anywhere in the field, people knew about that study."

"Of course." Anne remembered the academic hothouse, inside of which one obsessed over topics and tropes that basically could not even be explained on the sidewalk outside the seminar room.

"So do you know what I did? I went to law school. I had to do something *in the world*. I had to do something real. I couldn't stay and teach even if I wanted to."

"I see that."

"I imagine you can relate?"

"Sort of, yes," she said. Though God help me, she thought, if feeding off the college frenzy was to be the sum total of the "real" in her own life.

"And the kind of law I practice," explained Gideon Blanchard, "focuses on minorities—of color or background, you see, ethnic or social, who haven't been given the fair shake owed to them by this country. I do the opposite of what people said I did, what they thought I did. It's a point of pride. It would be anyway, but now it's even more so, you know, that I've come so far without any of that university stuff on my side. In fact, with it all working *against* me."

"That's really neat," Anne offered. He beamed.

"So I am thrilled to support your student Cristina. I believe that a college degree may open doors for her that would not otherwise be possible. And I want Sadie to feel confident and excited by the opportunities available to her at Duke. I loved it there, and she will, too. But the thing I just can't get my head around, the thing I get so angry about, is this assumption that these colleges are the arbiters of all things intelligent. Tell me this: Why should they be the ones to pick the next generation of American leaders? Why not, say, judges? Or entrepreneurs, small-business owners, real folks who have made it in the real world? Wouldn't that be more fair to someone like Cristina? Or, much as I hate to say it, Sadie?"

"I understand," said Anne, feeling herself rise in Sadie's defense, "though I think Sadie—"

"Don't get me wrong," he interrupted her. "Sadie might not be selected for Harvard, I get that. But she has skills and gifts that will serve her well in this world, believe me. And any self-respecting group of successful adults, actually successful adults, would see that. This whole application process? Now that, I just don't know. What the hell does it matter whether she writes about her dog? What does it matter what she says at all?"

His protest slipped into resentment, and his voice soured. Anne flinched. His idea for reforming college admissions was an odd, almost sweetly capitalist fantasy, and easily expressed over a balloon glass of Tuscan red. And there was some truth in what he said, of course. But also it was crazy. It did matter what these kids wrote; if not for the colleges, then for themselves. "A good essay," Anne argued, "a good college essay, it becomes a powerful thing for a student. It's personal mythology. It tells them where they've come from, and where they might be headed."

"Yeah?"

"Yeah."

He swallowed, nodded, twirled his nearly empty glass between his fingers. She wondered if he was feeling a bit loaded.

"I'm going to tell you something more," he continued. "Something I wouldn't say if Margaret were here."

"Okay."

"I know that Sadie is going to get into Duke. Of course I know that. I'm not sure Margaret does, but I do. This whole thing is an exercise in irrelevance. But it's good for Sadie to go through this, like everyone else. I see that, too. I think it's important that Sadie be put through her paces, to think that it might not come through. You know, to feel she's earned it."

"Then why . . ." Anne paused.

"Why hire you? Because I want them to be knocked out. I want them to *want* her. That's why."

"And you don't think she could do that on her own."

He set down his glass.

"Now, that's not a fair question," he said.

"Why not?"

"Anne," he said, "I love my daughter."

Anne was quiet.

"Good," he declared. "Now, you say Sadie's struck out with her essay about the dog. How do you know?"

Anne considered a gentle reply. He noticed her hesitation.

"Do you mind me asking? I hope you don't mind sharing your secrets."

"Not at all." No one had ever asked before. Parents just paid her and expected great things.

"All right," he said. "So how do you know when it's a good essay or a bad one?"

"Oh," she replied. "That's not the difficult part. You see, kids do this thing." Anne began to speak naturally as the ideas came to her, thinking in real time. She felt her shoulders relax and noticed how hard she'd been crossing her legs. And it was a relief to talk rather than face slurping her soup. "When they're asked to write in the first person," she explained, "and for something this important, kids switch into what I call English-teacher mode. Their voice on the page—you can hear it when they read out loud—gets higher, affected, like they're pretending to have an accent from an impressive country they've never been to. They choose a topic that bores them witless. Their sentences run on and on because they mistake length for persuasiveness. They dangle modifiers and bury antecedents. They capitalize like Germans. They use the word 'extremely' and start sentences with 'However, comma.' They drop in semicolons everywhere because they think it looks stylized. They're reflexive and jumpy, and they strangle every idea they have so they can hurry on to the next one. Nothing is cumulative. They forget where they started and they forget where they were going, and when they start to feel really disoriented, they'll use an em-dash. If they totally lose it, they add an exclamation point. Somewhere toward the end, it'll occur to them that they should mention college, so there will be a spasm of references to some school or preferred major or 'the future' or 'the rest of my life.' If they're feeling poetic, they'll end on the word 'beyond.'"

Gideon let his head fall back, showing her his Adam's apple, which for a moment revolted her—like a neck knuckle, jogging up and down—but when she realized he was laughing, hard enough to return to her red-cheeked and puffing, she felt proud, and forgave him. How much older was he? Twenty-five years? Twenty? Maybe men, by that age, just looked knobby like this, and with the visible pores on his nose. Would this happen to Martin? She didn't much care. In fact, she was surprised to find that she didn't want to think about Martin at all. She felt free and a little bit reckless, as though she too had polished off a few glasses of wine.

"That's great," he said, still sputtering. "Sounds exactly like what a teenager sounds like!"

"No, but that's the thing," she said, annoyed now at how he'd just insulted Sadie and somehow, it seemed, herself. "It doesn't. They don't. If you get a seventeen-year-old talking about something that really matters to him, just talking, telling the truth, it's the best. They're deadly serious and funny as hell and really original. They have great voices with better rhythm than you or I because they haven't read all the boring crap yet. They don't know how they're supposed to sound, so they sound fabulous. All that melodrama, it has a real keening to it, if you can tap into it. It's wonderful."

He sobered. "And how do you find that? The keening?"

"Well, you listen for the sound of their voice. Sometimes, it only comes up in actual conversation. They're so guarded, especially in the first drafts. But something will slip through—an image, an idea, a memory, something that they talk about in a simpler, softer, lower tone." Like I'm speaking now, she thought, but watching his big mouth chew, she figured there was no risk he'd notice. "It's when you feel their heart has shown up. That sounds silly, but it's true. That's the art of it, I guess. I have to help them to write about that thing, in that mode. And then it's easy. From there it's just Strunk and White."

He nodded knowingly. She knew he had no idea.

"And how do you do that?" he asked lamely. "Help them write about the special thing?"

She'd never thought of it in exactly this way, but the answer appeared to her instantly: "You make them forget they're being watched." In her mind she added, for the first time since they were born.

"Evaluated, you mean," he said.

"No, I mean watched. They've internalized all the judgment. They supply it themselves."

He made a high humming noise. "Sounds intimate. What you have to do."

"It can be done at Starbucks," she told him. "Or the kitchen table."

He raised an eyebrow. "Can you give me an example?"

"Sure. I had one student, a few years ago, whose mother was fighting breast cancer." The woman was not from Chicago, so this seemed safe to mention.

Gideon Blanchard gave a deep moan. Anne wondered if she shouldn't have specified "breast."

"Right. Terrible," she said. "But her college counselor had warned her, as usual, don't write about sick relatives. Like you don't write about community service or breaking the law. To which I would add dead pets, expensive vacations, the trials of caring for your horse, the teacher who screwed you over, cheating scandals, or your cousin who already goes there."

"You can't write about community service?"

She ignored this. "So this poor girl, she wrote a miserable essay about concern for the environment. Her college counselor thought it was great. But she wasn't a scientist and she didn't belong to her school's green club. She didn't even recycle. The essay was nonspecific, and therefore naive. She didn't know the first thing about environmental awareness, but then, that's not what she was writing about. It was a whole essay about the end of the world coming and how she couldn't do a thing to stop it but feel sad. Do you see?"

"No."

"She was writing about her feelings about her mom. But she didn't think she could say that. So her essay was terrible."

"Mmm. So what did you do?"

"I told her to just say what was true."

"Which was?"

"Her first sentence was, 'I know I'm not supposed to write my college essay about my mother having cancer, but if you want to know anything about me, you must know about this thing that I'm living with every single day.' "

He nodded slowly. "And?"

"And she got in."

"And her mom?"

Anne frowned at him. The girl's mother had died, halfway through her daughter's freshman year.

It was too dark. You're so depressing, Anne, she thought to herself. Quickly she added, "Or another student, my very first year. She wrote about mushrooms. She used to go out in the woods every fall, by her house, and hunt for mushrooms. She included all of these crazy mushroom details, things I'd never heard before. Some of them glow in the dark. Some of them bleed when you cut them, did you know that? It was fabulous."

"And?"

"She turned down Yale and went to Princeton."

"Wow." Gideon Blanchard finished his wine and set the glass down. He looked out at the rain. "I don't think there are mushrooms in the Gold Coast."

"That's not really my point."

"No, I know it's not," he said. "I know." She watched his thoughts shift away from Sadie; his mood brightened, and he turned back to her. "And what about you?"

"What?"

"What about you?" he repeated. The question had an unseemly pressure behind it, like fingers. "What's your passion? Is it this? Working on college applications? Is this the thing you've chosen for your life? Your one *wild* and *precious* life? That's from a poem by Mary Arnold."

"Oliver."

"What?"

"No, nothing." She shook her head.

"Because I've been thinking." He waited for her to meet his gaze. "You know that I'm a lawyer."

They both smiled, she captive, at his joke.

"I do."

"And I don't know if you've even thought about the law, but I think you should. Just the way you present, I . . . think it could be a splendid fit. Textual interpretation, attention to detail, questions of social justice. Have you considered it?"

"I was an English major," she told him, meaning, "Of course I've considered law school." It was the standard penance for wasting your late adolescence in novels.

"And?"

"Law school's expensive."

"That's why you make lots of money after you graduate."

"Hard to get into," she blurted.

"Not for you, I hope!" he said.

She smiled at the table. "Fair point."

"Because I see in you, if you don't mind me saying so, a young woman with a lot of intelligence and talent who is in need of a little direction."

Well, how dare you, she thought. But instead she said, "Thank you."

"Which is why I wanted to spend some time. To figure this out. I'm not sure if it means you should come try a paralegal post at the firm, or something else. But I thought maybe I might help you find that thing, that passion, that you're talking about with all these teenagers. I can open doors, Anne."

She was amused for a moment to think that he'd somehow understood this idiosyncratic detail about her—and that what had seemed a setup for an embarrassing seduction was actually a pitch for an internship. It was the way to Anne's heart, absolutely. How did he know this?

Still Anne saw the hook was barbed. She could not be seen to be uninterested in her students, when his own child was among them.

"You're very kind," she said, sounding completely insincere. "I really appreciate the offer to help. But I'm doing great. I like what I do."

The disappointment was plain on his face.

"Anne, let me try this a different way, because I know you've got a full plate today and certainly I do."

She nodded brightly.

He said, "Cristina, she's a very impressive girl."

"Cristina?"

"She's a damn impressive kid. I'm all set to make some calls and change her life. But I've got a daughter applying, too, and, you know, the first thing these people are going to ask me is, 'Gid,' they'll say, 'Gid, how is that Sadie?' "

"Of course."

"And I want to be able to say, 'She's terrific.' Even better, you know, I don't want to have to say it at all. Because her file will make that so clear. Am I making sense?"

"She's going to have a great application," Anne said. She still didn't see what he was driving at. But she was alarmed at how tempted she was to become whatever it was he was looking for: adviser, colleague, conspirator.

"Is she? That's good. Because if I'm going to be sending in two applications, as it were, one for this other girl and one for my own daughter, I don't want there to be—how shall I put it?—an incline. A differential. A matter of comparison."

Anne considered Cristina's transcript and scores next to Sadie's. "There's only so much I can change."

"That's exactly my point," he said, and leaned back. He smiled. "That's what I'm saying. And I think that, if you're able to make that change, then it will be a really good step for all of us."

My God, Anne thought. Write your daughter's essays and you'll give me a job. Is that it?

"You want me to write them," she said quietly.

"I didn't say that. Far from it."

"Sometimes I have taken a strong hand, I guess," she admitted. "But only in critical situations," she added, "only with a phrase here or there, you know, a conclusion at eleven fifty-nine on the day of a deadline . . ."

"So, good," said Gideon Blanchard, looking pleased. "Who doesn't like a strong hand? And we'll see to Cristina's needs, meanwhile, and Duke will have two excellent incoming freshmen to celebrate. It's such a pleasure to help, as of course you know."

"Of course," Anne said. She felt mugged. She touched her hands to her sides, pressed on her belly, as though something had gone missing from her pockets. Nothing, she told herself, I've promised him nothing.

"And we'll have to do this again," he said, signaling for the waiter. "In the New Year, when all of this is behind us. To talk about you. I've got ideas for you, Anne. I think you have really great things awaiting you."

"That's very kind," she said.

"And next time, you'll eat something."

"Ha."

He continued to issue a stream of vague ideas as they gathered up their coats. "Maybe you're interested in educational issues at large?" he offered, holding open her raincoat. She rolled sleeve to sleeve and stepped away quickly. "Maybe you'd like to consider a job at city hall, the department of education. Have you given that any mind?"

As Anne followed him out of the restaurant, fielding his wild offers of jobs and leads, she considered that the problem with old boys' networks wasn't who you needed to know, it was that you needed to know what to ask for. She was searching for yet another new demurral when she was stopped short by the sight of Martin leaning alongside the elevators, an unlit cigarette on point in his fingers.

He smirked at her. "Torrential," he said, referring to the rain. "Had to come inside."

"Gideon Blanchard," said Blanchard, extending a long arm. "Pleasure."

"Oh, of course," said Martin effortlessly. As though he recognized him. Though maybe he did, Anne thought. Who knew what these men knew about one another, even across fields, across cities? "Martin Waverly."

The elevator opened. Both men reached to hold the doors, one on either side. Anne passed through. "Thanks," she muttered.

She stood at the back and watched their shoulders—Martin was much broader—and how Mr. Blanchard squared and resquared himself a few times, as though unconsciously measuring. "Working with my daughter, lucky girl, whole process so wildly out of control . . ." he was saying, and Martin was replying in supplicant terms: "Indeed, absolutely, amazing, lucky girl."

"Well, lucky *you,*" finished Blanchard as they stepped into the lobby. He unsnapped the tail of his valet's umbrella and grinned at Martin, then at Anne. To her he said, "Give it some thought. I'm not finished with this." She understood he was referring to the problem of her career, and she felt the cryptic pronouns rile Martin, who drew closer. Blanchard lifted his chest and released his giant umbrella, a pinstriped peacock, and swept out onto the sidewalk.

Martin stopped her at the doors. "What the fuck was that?"

"I told you. He's a client. I'm working with his daughter."

"The little retarded girl." He popped open his umbrella and raised it over them both. They stepped out.

"Stop it," Anne said, into the wind. She ducked closer under Martin's arm. "She's very sweet. And perfectly bright."

"Yes. She just has—what was it? Dis-test-ia? Dis-homework-ia?"

"Discalculia."

"Ah, right. Dis-it's-just-fucking-school-ia. So math is hard. This is not news. They don't give a Nobel in, you know, language arts."

"You know, they sort of do," answered Anne, thinking of Toni Morrison.

"No," he said. "They don't."

"Actually, Martin, it's math that they don't . . . Well. Anyway, it's a real thing, the inability to keep numbers straight."

"Sure it is."

"It is!"

"I can't believe you buy into that. Does lunch at Spiaggia come with it? Some vino? Awfully nice grub. Do they have one star now or two?"

"I don't buy into anything," she said. "She's been to a learning specialist, she's been diagnosed, and that's all there is to it. My job isn't to assess her, it's to help her handle this along with everything else. Which doesn't matter anyway, because that guy you just met is chair of the board of trustees."

He stopped and turned to her. On the sidewalk pedestrians broke right and left around them. "And they need you why?"

"Well, they don't. But they want Sadie to have some support. To be honest with you, I think I was just asked to write her essays for her."

"You're kidding."

"No."

"Well then, do it! Save you a crap load of time. Go home, write them up, ask for your check, and be done with it. Sounds good to me."

"No, Martin. I can't do that, and I won't."

He shrugged wildly. "Why the hell not? Don't be so damn earnest, Anne. It's not attractive."

"Because it's not right," Anne said. She was too proud to add, *Because my work is real. And because it would break Sadie's heart.*

"Oh, but it's right for her to have you holding her hand all freaking fall? And it's right for her to get out of every math test since the fourth grade?"

"I can only deal with my part, Martin, Jesus. I want to help her write her essays on her own, and I want them to be decent."

"Which they wouldn't otherwise be."

"Well, no. Not really."

"Like I said. The little retarded girl."

Anne didn't bother to object a second time.

"So do all the dads take you to lunch?" Martin pressed.

"Not usually."

"He's not to be trusted."

"No shit."

"I'm not talking about essays, Anne."

Anne felt a thrill run across her shoulders. Not the reality, but the risk; the thought that she might be the uncertain one, for once, the one who might not be where she said she'd be.

"He's married," she explained. "To a very powerful woman. That's not a concern."

"Bullshit," said Martin, giving her an incredulous smile. "And have you seen that woman? She'll probably hit on you, too."

"Don't be ridiculous. They have children."

"Grow up, Annie," he huffed, sounding annoyed. Jealousy did not please him the way it sometimes intrigued her. He had no patience with sharing. "The man's a creep and you should not be accepting free spaghetti from him. Don't do it again."

He reached for her hand as he said this, clamped it tightly in his fist, and propelled them forward.

"I won't," she said.

To: Anne@mynextfouryears.com
From: Grant.Alexis@mssphs.edu

Dear Anne,

Here's my common application essay for Harvard (so far). I've written three versions of it, and I'm going to send them through to you later unless you tell me not to (Mom says you may not want to read all three?). This is the best one, I think, but it's all over the place and Dad isn't sure of the point of it. Anyway, let me know what you think. Questions:

* Is it okay if Mom is just "homemaker" on the common application part about parents' occupations? Or should she put down that she works too? She's always doing stuff but it's not really paid?
* Do I have to submit the supplemental essays at the exact same

time as the common app? If so, how do I do that? Do we use two computers? Or do I do one and then the other? Which one first?

* Is it okay if the credit card I use to pay the application fee is my dad's and not mine? I don't have one.
* I don't want to wait until Hallowe'en to send it in, but I'm worried if I send it too soon they'll think I didn't work hard enough on it. What do you think? Should I wait extra days just so they know I was really careful?
* Is it okay if I ask my teacher recommenders to address the envelopes themselves, or should I address them for them? Handwriting or typed?
* I have taken several AP tests. Is it okay just to put down all the 5s I got on the common app or do they need me to send them some sort of proof of this?
* Is it lame to title my essay?

Thanks! Hope to hear from you soon!

ALEXIS GRANT'S THUMB

One afternoon soon after I began tutoring Somali refugees at a local non-profit, I brought a map of the world so that we could all study together the country my students came from. After all, I've never been to Africa (though I very much want to go!) and I had to admit I had no idea where literally in the world these kids had been born and raised. I commented on the shape of their huge nation and how some of the boundaries are as straight as rulers while others are bumpy and jut out, and a counselor made a joke about "Churchill's thumb," which the kids smiled at, so I knew it wasn't the first time they'd heard it. Apparently it is said as a legend that when the English partitioned Africa after WWII they tried to take into account rivers, lakes, deserts, natural tribal patterns and other issues but some of the drawing was so arbitrary that one imagines the men leaning over the big map and just tracing around their fingers—leading to the protrusions, and the joke about Churchill's thumb. I don't see anything obviously hand-like on today's map of Africa, but it doesn't take the presence of dozens of Somali refugees in my town in Minnesota to tell us that the process of partition and the movement away from colonialization has hardly been a successful one.

Twice a week, when I bike home from my tutoring sessions, I think about these kids and what it would be like if the tables were turned. What if I were the one who had been transported to an entirely new place, where it was hot all the time when I was used to snow, where I didn't speak the language and had no job or school to go to, where my belly always hurt because I had to eat things I'd never seen before? Add to that the consideration that my family most likely had fled a war or worse, and it makes me wonder, riding down the streets that I know so well, what virtue there is in notions of nationality or, for that matter, statehood in general. It seems to me that boundaries are drawn by those in power, and rarely in the consideration of those not in power. Does it matter to someone in my town where the state line of Minnesota is? Well, no, not to me—I could bike over it and not notice that the sidewalk suddenly belonged to Wisconsin (or to Canada, for that matter), but I understand that governmental bodies require an understanding of their domain—the limits—so they know what is theirs to take and what is theirs to take care of. In school I've had the chance to study various forms of government and community-building, ranging from Native American tribes here to the trials of the US Civil War and the fight to avoid secession of the Southern states. On the one hand, when I think of the Native Americans and how the process of expulsion and confinement to reservations decimated that great people, I am full of sorrow to think that the requirements of a collective state are, paradoxically, the privatization of everything. If land belongs to everyone, to all our children and their children and so on, then is there really any need to declare, This is mine and This is yours? If we can barter successfully to acquire the things we need to survive, do we need a central government to support a currency and a marketplace? On the other hand, I read of the intention of the Southern states to build their own nation based on slave labor, and I realize that it has been critically important in history that the government of the Northern states refused to tolerate this move and were willing to send thousands to die to protect their vision of a better nation.

As in all political issues, I am learning, there is the dream and there is the reality. The dream of an independent Africa exists but the reality is in part the little kids I'm teaching to read on Tuesdays and Thursdays, who are freezing their tails off in Minnesota in search of a better life. These are big ideas, I realize, and I am idealistic to think about tackling them. But it is my highest hope for the next several years of my education to learn more about the requirements of the successful modern state and the challenges posed to the development of young states around the world. If there is a way for people to live mostly in peace by virtue of drawing and maintaining boundaries, may we learn to create boundaries where they naturally fall, rather than imposing our own images like shadows across the earth. I believe in the goal of our common humanity, and I hope one day to work to ensure the success of all nations by understanding more fully the ways people must draw lines in order to be more free.

To: Anne@mynextfouryears.com
From: WinnetkaOrion@yahoo.com

"You must be joking," I told my parents. "There is no way."

I think I laughed out loud when my mother told me I was

going to spend one month of my summer on a field trip investigating the "American West By Page and Range" with the English teachers from my school. It was just one of her latest ideas for my college application, I thought, and there was no way I was going to forfit my summer for that.

"I am not joking" mom told me "you are already signed up."

So in July there I was, at Ohare airport, waiting to board a flight to Bozeman. Which I thought sounded like a good dogs name but not a place I wanted to spend my summer. Little did I know what I would find there. Did you ever lay back and see so many stars overhead that they blurred together like snow? Well, I have. And it was amazing to think that I spent every night of my life until that day in Montana looking up and not knowing what was really there. Light from the nearby city of Chicago makes it impossible to see the stars, except for the Big Dipper and a few others, and mostly the sky is sort of pink. I had no idea what the sky was *supposed* to look like. You can't even see the constellations where I live.

Did you ever stand in a braided river? Or watch a moose try to get a piece of sawgrass off it's antler? Or a beaver go back and forth making it's damn? Or spot mountain lion tracks and wonder how far away it was? Well, I have. These are the things I did during the day, when at night we had the incredible stars, in Montana, in the Bitterroot Range. But the coolest thing about my school trip to Montana are the wild horses, or mustangs. They were completely wild. They had never had to take the bit (that metal part that horses have stuffed in their mouths all day) and when we went horseback riding along the trails and saw them in the fields way out, it's like the horse I was on was jealous, and I wanted to get down and take all the tack off of him and just let him free. I guess I think it's like seeing the stars in Montana. You don't know about how it's supposed to be until you get out of your own prison, and my prison is Winnetka, Illinois, and like the horse I wished I could run free.

I know it sounds spoiled to call Winnetka a prison but I realized this summer that so much of the time when I react with anger to what my parents tell me to do or sign me up for its because I am at a time in my life when I am starting to find so many things I want to study and do. I loved the mustangs because they represented for me a way of living that was about my own independence and my own interests. I had no idea that I would love the mountains so much, or as I said what the sky looks like at night when you aren't blinded by the city. And I guess growing up is a little bit like that. Your parents shine so brightly that you don't really know what's out there until you get away from it all by yourself. We need parents, like cities, to keep us safe and give us the things we need to survive. But we also need open fields and dark night skies so we can discover the things in our own hearts.

I've spent my time in high school working on things that I liked and that were important to my parents and teachers, like tennis, guitar, peer leader and homework. I feel very lucky to have been able to do all these things. But I was surprised to learn this summer that I feel passionate about things that are completely new to me, like caring for the wilderness or finding ways to be sure that wild horses are protected in our nation's west. It has made me eager to get back to school and history and science classes, and I've signed up for US Government so I can learn about the laws that govern our land. When my parents ask me about these changes, I sometimes find I don't want to share with them everything that I've discovered, not because it will prove they were right about the trip this summer but because it's important to keep our own interests to ourselves sometimes, when they are brand new. But when I think about college, it is with a new sense of excitement for all the things I will discover there. College, like Montana, will show me things I never knew were there, and give me the chance to find new directions for my passions. I believe that ____ will be the best place for me to explore my new interests.

To: Anne@mynextfouryears.com
From: Michelle_Delong@ExcelCiceroNorth.org

Anne
Please find attached Cristina's personal statement, which I've typed up for her as she has no computer and the school's lab has been closed since the TA is out this week. Can you send on to Blanchard, please?
Thx
Michelle

"No, Mami," I said. "It's the *supreme law of the land."*

"The high law?" asked my mother.

"Supreme law of the land," I repeated.

We had been working on this question, "What is the Constitution?", along with 100 others to prepare for the United States Citizenship Test. It was all we had talked about in my house for many weeks. My mother knows what the Constitution is, but we've been told that it is important that she give exactly the answer the testers want and not try to explain herself. It was late and Mom was tired. She had been working all day. My sisters offered to clean up dinner so I could keep quizzing Mom. She had only three days to prepare.

The preparation made me think about tests. This test, for example, was one that I would never have to take, being born in the United States. The answers were not things that any of my classmates would know. And truly, I wondered if my teachers could answer all of them, or that policeman by the front doors, or the principal, even. I was tempted to go up to them and ask: What are the stripes on the flag for? What about the stars? What is the First Amendment? But I know that these aren't the things that actually make citizens. It seems unfair to me that my mami should have to take this test while my sisters and I don't even have to learn these things, not even in school, to pass. It's enough just to be here.

But there are other tests, we all face them. For me, it's every test and quiz in school that my teachers prepare. If I want to go to college, I have to perform excellently on every single one of them. No exceptions. But the harder tests are out of school, I know, and they are harder to explain. There is the test of a very long day: can you get three little sisters up, dressed, and ready for school, feed them breakfast, and then do well on your own schoolwork? Can you also pick them up and make them dinner and make sure they are healthy and ready for bed before you start your homework? There is the test of doing this day after day, and coming home and finding out that it's still not enough, because maybe Mami has had to take a week off because her back is out again, and then there is not much money for that week. So this new test is: Can you figure out how to cook meals without any new ingredients from the store? We would do very well on the Citizenship test if one question was: You have beans, rice, water, salt, and cheese. Make three dishes for five people!

There are tests that are even more complicated, such as the test of how to be a top student at school, which means to speak a certain way and act a certain way, and then walk home and not have anyone give you trouble, which means to leave all that school behind and be just the kid that everyone knows. You have two vocabularies and two sets of voices. You say Yes in one word and Si or Yeah in the other. If you don't want trouble, you must pass this test every day.

> I think again about the supreme law of the land. We are lucky to live in a country with the Constitution, which guarantees freedom for all of us who are citizens. Of course it is important to test new citizens to ensure they understand and can uphold the Constitution. But when I see Mami with flashcards in her apron, I wish I could go with her to take the test, and stand up with her and have her perfectly say, not only, "The Constitution is the supreme law of the land," but also explain how many years she has worked to create our home, and raise her daughters to speak English even though she barely does, and how she takes only Sunday off, all because she wants her children to have this dream of a country. Because in my opinion, she has already passed the test, every single day. And I think that is an honor for even the Constitution.

So Cristina's familiarity with the United States government that first Saturday morning stemmed from her preparations with her mother for the citizenship test rather than her general acuity or, God forbid, a comprehensive U.S. history and politics curriculum. Perhaps she was even savvier than Anne had guessed, communicating to Mr. Blanchard and all his cronies that she was legal and that there was no tangle they should anticipate. It was just spicy enough to serve their need for the subordinate voice, defensive in her pride, but of course all within the lines, so they needn't be forced to address actual injustice. Or maybe she just wrote about the thing that had been shadowing her family's life for months or years, and got lucky in aiming it at the right sort of sop. Anne clipped Michelle's terse headnote, added a graceful note of thanks, and forwarded the essay on to Gideon Blanchard. It'd do nicely. She busied herself with other stray notes, all "urgent." Mrs. Pfaff had written to ask where on the Common App to indicate that Hunter was left-handed. Dr. Kantor was concerned that William's stated first choice of intended major—theater arts—would communicate a "soft" academic commitment. Then came two notes in succession that sickened her:

Annie,

I'm back here in lonesome La-La Land without you and I have an idea for a scene:

I'm just coming in from a shoot, and it's been a long day. You've been working yourself on your latest book, about Victorian novelists, and you have a screenplay on the side that your agent is hassling you about because producers are fighting over it. We're both exhausted and tired of pleasing others but it's a warm night, so we head out with Mitchell to hike Runyon and watch the sun set. The city is hazy but we're up in the clear, the lights on the hills are winking on, Mitch is getting lost in the shadows in the brush. We drop him home, shower, and make love. Then we head out to supper under the stars so you can tell me about the chapter you're working on and I can regale you with tales of my demanding co-stars. Maybe we're talking about making a baby, once our projects are wrapped? I see a bottle of wine on the table, a chocolate dessert. Two spoons. It's a late evening. Then we go home.

Wanted to see what you thought. Notes, please.

Love-

M

Dear Anne

Mr. Blanchard thanks you for your e-mail today and requests that you phone him at your earliest convenience. He may be reached on the numbers below.

Regards

Brenda Hollow, executive assistant to Gideon Blanchard

As with previous Blanchard communications, the body of the note was dwarfed by the lengthy legal disclaimers printed at the bottom, and for a moment Anne smiled to think that Martin's e-mails would better be printed with such warnings of improper use. You'd know how to handle them. The humor softened her, and then, dangerously, opened toward gratitude. She dialed Martin's cell. He'd taken the time—she should thank him. So it was early; but who minded a loving voice? The call was shunted immediately to voice mail, sharp as a rebuke. Anne stiffened. Suitably armed, she hung up and dialed Blanchard instead.

She was asked to hold. After much clicking, he came on the line. All business this time.

"I've received the essay," he opened. "Very nice, very moving." He paused.

Anne felt the shifting in her gut that accompanied the challenge of an older adult's strong will. Her confidence resettled itself, but it was precarious. She pictured Cristina—her long skirts rolled three times at the waist to stay up, her T-shirts, obviously donated, too tight or cut for men. She waited.

"But my first allegiance is, and must be, to my daughter," continued Blanchard. The partial non sequitur, and the tone, invoked a podium. Anne scrambled to figure out what was going on. He was taking a totally different line with her now, and having done so, he had distanced himself immensely—he was more a stranger to her than he'd been when she had known him only by reputation. And what could she say? *Hang on, what about lunch? I thought we hit it off?* She imagined him in the courtroom; he must sound like this. Then it occurred to her, suddenly, that Mrs. Blanchard was silently on the line.

"Of course it is," Anne replied, in the most grown-up voice she could manage.

"And I cannot proceed with fast-tracking the application of another student if it is to the detriment of my own daughter's planning. Or, God forbid, her future."

How did he arrive at that formula, the one at the expense of the other? Where was this coming from? But she just said, "No, you can't."

"So you'll understand why I may well have to stand down."

"I do," Anne said, because what else could she say? "Cristina will be very disappointed."

"There's nothing keeping her from applying by the regular routes, of course," he said, as if correcting Anne. She wondered for a moment if she had in fact been greedy to ask for help for Cristina. Then the logistical tangle reasserted itself in her mind. "Mr. Blanchard, the placement office at her high school isn't even set up to handle the application-fee waiver. There are holes in her transcript through no fault of her own, there's the financial-aid situation—"

Blanchard interrupted her. "Then you will have to reassure her that her qualifications are sound," he said. "And help her to understand that life hands all of us a few curveballs. It's how we handle them that reveals our character."

"I doubt that will be news to her," Anne said.

"I'm sure there are plenty of wonderful schools that will welcome her with open arms."

The wagons were circled. She could practically feel Mrs. Blanchard nodding on the line. It was clear she was not to mention anything about lunch at Spiaggia or the conversation she and Blanchard had there. Though how she knew this, she couldn't say.

"You, with your experience," he went on, "will be able to steer her toward the best outcomes."

She imagined him as a spider, spinning out ego, his silk growing thinner and thinner. For a moment she felt exhausted on his behalf: the solid public image, the sodden private self. She almost sympathized with him. Clearly Sadie was upset, and now she was refusing to apply to Duke, no matter who wrote her essays. And her mother must have lowered the boom. Fine, then. "Mr. Blanchard," she dared, "what if I can talk to Sadie? What if this is a simple misunderstanding, and we're able to help her to feel confident again about her next step?"

"Anne, could I ask you to wait just a moment? Something's come up." More clicks, and the firm's holding music. Then Mr. Blanchard's voice again: "Sorry about that. Well, we'd have to see, of course, but if Sadie is able to move forward, I'd be able to support the other girl's application, I suppose."

"She's really very upset," blurted Mrs. Blanchard, betraying herself.

"Margaret," he scolded.

"Sorry, Anne, but I'm here, too," she protested quickly, and then recovered her haughty tone. "I'm a mother. My daughter is miserable. I told Gid this would happen . . . That girl should never have come to our home."

"Margaret, easy," warned Blanchard.

"I understand," Anne said, addressing them both. "Let me come talk to her."

"Well, I'd think you'd come talk to her anyway," Mr. Blanchard said, angry to have been exposed. "You are contracted to work with her. We are paying you, after all, and I believe I have made my expectations clear." He paused for an extra second. Then he added, "And she didn't invite this upon herself."

"Yes, she doesn't deserve this," said Mrs. Blanchard. "That girl can go anywhere, can't she? Aren't they all looking for kids like that? Why does it have to be Duke?"

It didn't, of course. But if Anne and Michelle couldn't communicate somehow to an elite admissions office, at a school with the resources to fund her, that Cristina was the real deal, and then, somehow, give her mother the confidence to let her daughter travel thousands of miles to an unknown place of high stone gates for four years in directions unknown, especially after forcing her to fill out those FAFSA forms, which terrified anyone, and asking provocative questions about birth parents and bank accounts, not to mention the small amount of tuition almost any school would require, well . . . it was a long way down to a local school, community college, whatever was easiest and had night courses to accommodate work. Anne had been relying, in part, on Mr. Blanchard's pride, and here he and his wife diverged. They both loved feeling like saviors, but only he was the trustee, and only he was the alumnus. Anne realized Mrs. Blanchard's alma mater had never come up. Given her public persona, it most certainly would have, had she wished it to. So Cristina's matriculation at Duke would be his victory alone. And any cost to Sadie at all would be a price too high for her mother to bear.

"It doesn't have to be Duke," Anne conceded.

"No," said both Blanchards.

"Although," Anne corrected, "Duke would be lucky to have her. As they will be to have Sadie." She paused to be sure they heard this. Her support for Sadie was sincere. "Listen, what if I come by tomorrow? We can talk this out. Does that work for Sadie?"

"I'll make sure it does," Blanchard said.

Sadie had a spectacular pout. Her lovely bow mouth, inherited from her father, had been drawn to a fierce, petulant point. She hurled herself into a chair and crossed her arms. "I have nothing to say," she said.

"Okay," Anne replied, looking around Sadie's room, which she had never seen. It faced the front of the house, where the street trees were visible in yellow and green through heavily swagged curtains. The canopied bed was a king. The entire room appeared to be slipcovered. On the walls, posters of pop stars alternated with collages Sadie had made of her various destinations—Sri Lanka, Calcutta, Bali—which resembled travel brochures spattered with the scissored-out faces of family and ragged locals. A blank expanse was explained by a black-and-blue Duke banner in a heap on the floor. Meanwhile, Anne noticed Sadie studying her with smoldering eyes, and let her continue; she knew the girl was angry, and her parents would have stoked this, too. It was okay. Anne had to admit relief at the way Sadie's parents had aligned themselves behind their daughter. She hadn't thought they had such loyalty in them.

"I mean, what the hell am I supposed to make of it?" Sadie went on. A few breaths more and she was crying. Her face was immediately sodden. Anne saw that there had been days of this. "My parents tell me my entire life to do this, do that, to prepare myself for the future. And it's always Duke, Duke, Duke. So I bust my ass, I mean my butt, I do all this volunteering, which of course I really love, I don't mean to say I don't see that it's important, but I do it all the time, really every time, and sometimes I really just want to, like, go to the beach or just hang out. And I don't. And there's homework and sports and, just, everything. And then there's Dad's whole big law thing, and Mom's always doing her thing, and Charles is just a kid, so it's me. And the whole time, you know, I feel like I have this thing that's mine, and then I find out that all along I didn't have to do any of this, I could have just stayed home from school, I could have gone to the crappiest high school in town, it doesn't matter, and I could still go to Duke because my dad will make them take me and meanwhile this girl who has nothing that I can never have is, like, the apple of everyone's eyes."

"Oh, Sadie," Anne began, and the girl's crying sharpened. She looked about for a box of tissues, but Sadie used her fingers again and again to wipe away her tears—protecting eye makeup, Anne realized, even through the storm. She felt a moment of sympathy for her own mother—were all seventeen-year-old girls this dramatic?—and then remembered that she was not innocent in this crisis. "Sadie," she said gently, "I don't think you did all of those things so you could get into college, did you?"

Sadie stopped heaving for a moment to think. "No," she sniffed.

"I'm pretty sure you'd have been a good student and a wonderful volunteer no matter what."

"But no matter what, what?" asked Sadie. "I mean, if what? If I didn't want to go to college? If I was just going to, I don't know, *die* when I turned eighteen?"

"What I mean to say is that I don't think your qualities and successes emerge from your parents' expectations of you."

Sadie shook her head firmly. She was right, of course; Sadie's parents didn't actually have that many expectations for their daughter herself. Her job was to redeem their jobs, their titles, their ambitions, but they weren't much interested in her own. They didn't pay much attention to her at all, in fact. Anne's comment led to a dead end, and Sadie had known this all along; Anne was only seeing it now. It was the thing she'd missed in getting Mr. Blanchard involved in Cristina's search in the first place. To bring in a young woman whose future they could get behind, with pride, was to expose the ropes behind those two-story damask drops, and it had devastated Sadie.

Anne tried a different tack. "You know, I was really shocked when it turned out that Inez knew Cristina."

"You think?" asked Sadie ruefully. But she laid on the sarcasm lightly. This spot was cruelly tender, Anne knew.

"Inez adores you." Anne knew it to be true, so it seemed not wrong to say.

"Inez is paid to adore me," Sadie replied.

"Hey. That's not the Inez I know. She doesn't work like that."

The tears came anew. "And that's the other thing," Sadie sobbed. "That was the one other thing."

"What was?"

Sadie hunched forward over her lap, revealing that her chair was monogrammed: *SBM* hung over the weeping girl like a sign.

"You mean Inez?" asked Anne quietly.

Sadie nodded.

"She's really special to you."

Sadie unhooked pieces of wet hair from behind her ears so they fell forward, hiding her face. "Just, the one person, you know?" she whispered. "Always, every day, except Sunday, every day she was there."

It was then Anne realized that Sadie might have been bothered not at all by her father's adoption of Cristina's cause. That horse had left the barn a long time ago. It was this new affront that she couldn't stomach—that would stand in, of course, for the missing parents, as Inez had been standing in for them since Sadie was a baby.

"It's why I take Spanish instead of French," Sadie added, to drive home her point. "Everyone else takes French. That's honors track. It cost me an AP."

In some parts of the Midwest it was still the case in those days that French was considered the more sophisticated language and appropriate for more advanced students. This was not least because so many public school students already spoke Spanish, proving that it couldn't be either useful or challenging to acquire.

Time was passing and Sadie was only crying harder. Anne didn't know who, if anyone, was home; an unidentified housekeeper had answered the door, and no one could be heard through the halls. Anne had no idea where to go with Sadie, but she thought it time for a little bit of truth. Certainly Sadie was already most of the way there, and how much more damage could she do?

"Sadie, listen," Anne started. "It's true that your father is a very powerful alumnus of Duke. He's earned that position. He has worked hard for the university, he has supported it with donations, and he is a widely admired lawyer whom Duke is proud to name as an alum. You know all of that."

She sniffled. "Of course."

"It's also true that Duke is going to want to accept you. And that's not wrong. It's not wrong for universities to want to admit the families of people who support them. These places don't get by on tuition alone. They don't. And even if they did, they don't get full tuition from half of the kids who go there, or more. Most qualified kids come from families that can't dream of that price tag. So the school has to raise the dough. What do you think the football team is for? Creating student athletes?" At this Sadie smiled. "It's critical that top colleges build communities of support from alumni, and Duke does that very well. And if you're going to be a good student and a good person there, which of course you are, then why shouldn't they admit you?"

Sadie nodded and permitted her face to be seen. Her skin was hived from crying. Big welts raised her eyes and cheeks. She seemed ten years younger than her wrap cashmere sweater and tight jeans suggested, like a little girl playing dress-up.

"So I'm absolutely going to get in, then," she said.

Danger, thought Anne. But why not be honest? Sadie deserved it.

"Well, pretty much."

"What if I, like, did drugs or something?"

This seemed a sincere question, but by the way it was asked, Anne knew Sadie had never tried a mood-altering substance in her life, save wine at the altar rail.

"Okay, yes, if you got arrested for drugs, they might reconsider," Anne admitted, smiling. "Prison might be a tough one to overcome, even for you."

But Sadie didn't brighten. "So," she said. "So what?"

"So here's the thing. You have this opportunity open to you. It's fantastic. I spend my life working with kids who are terrified about getting into even one school as good as Duke. They're freaking out. You don't have to waste your energy feeling that way. You can focus on school, your volunteering, your friends, whatever you want, and know that you're going to be okay. And when you get to Duke, you can be grateful and make the absolute most of that opportunity you've been given. Take every class you want to take. Drop Spanish and start French. Hell, spend a year in Paris! Or maybe you'll find that all your volunteering has made you want to, I don't know, go into public interest law. Or become a social worker. Or a priest. I don't know. But you can get started on that road."

"Uh, not a priest."

"Okay. Or a doctor, or a teacher, or who knows what? But you'll have all of that available to you. So your job is not to sweat college; your job is to apply yourself to whatever it is that's going to make you feel the most useful. The most fulfilled. That's wonderful. And really important."

Sadie's eyes were clearing. She sat back against her initials and straightened her sweater, picking it out over her slim torso. "Yeah, that makes sense," she said.

"It does," Anne agreed. "I really think it does. So don't waste your time crying. Spend it deciding what you want to do. Get there. Hit the ground running."

"What about you?" Sadie asked. She had a new light in her face, and the welts were cooling. "Will you always do this? Work on college apps?"

"I don't know," Anne said, not wanting to give away her dissatisfaction. How could she ask Sadie to accept her own lot if she didn't? "Point is, you're about to head into a whole new world. So that's the thing to focus on. What's coming up. Let the whole Cristina thing go."

"And apply early to Duke."

"Yes, I'd think so."

"Well, no," Sadie said.

Anne was shocked at her resolve.

"I'm going to apply regular admission. And I'm going to apply to other good places, too. Like Middlebury and Georgetown and Yale. Just to see if I can get in."

For a moment Anne resented the girl forcing the world's hand; it would not hesitate to prove Sadie's point. She was a very privileged girl with a B-plus average and some dark marks where, as her mother put it, the teachers had "failed to enable" Sadie's success. Not to mention the issue with numbers. Her college counselor would know Duke was in the bag and slack off on every other school. What was the use?

"It's up to you," answered Anne. Her only hope was the appeal to virtue. "I'll help you with your applications to wherever you want. But you might think about whether you want to take away spots from other students if you know you're going to go to Duke."

"Maybe I don't know it," Sadie said. "Maybe Gid and Marge will just have to wait and see."

If it weren't for the disappointment Anne saw in the cards, she'd have embraced Sadie for this bit of sass. It would save her.

"Amen," said Anne, and both girls smiled.

It was on a jewel of a fall day that Mr. Grant found Anne on her cell phone, just turning onto the long, crepuscular private drive leading to the Pfaffs' suburban manse. She'd been feeling optimistic. Hunter's essay was coming together, and she could see how his application would lead to a fairly good story about himself. It wouldn't be enough for Amherst, unless the tennis coach came through, but it would be enough for a few schools on his list, and he wasn't wild about Amherst anyway. Anne believed his parents could be brought around. He'd do fine. She felt that Hunter's promise was her promise. She was young and healthy and the sun on her hair felt as real as a human touch. Her phone rang, and of course it would be Martin—late lunchtime in L.A., he'd be in between appointments, having a smoke—so she spun the wheel onto the Pfaffs' gravel drive, slowed to a crawl, and from the tunnel of trees on their estate answered her line. It took more than a moment to realize that the man's voice wasn't truly Martin's.

"Anne, oh, good, I got you!" it said. Definitely not Martin: his enthusiasm gave him away. "Can you speak? Are we disturbing you? We only need a quick second. Just one question. Or two."

Anne stopped the car halfway down the long drive, uncertain of cell reception within the estate itself—all those mature oaks—and put down the windows. The air was softer here. The oaks had coppered with the season, and the sugar maples fluoresced.

"Of course," she replied. She let go the image of Martin in a sunbeam in L.A. She couldn't see him, couldn't imagine him at all.

"You've read Alexis's essay, is that right?" asked Mr. Grant.

"'Churchill's Thumb'? I have, yes. It's terrific. I've sent her a reply by e-mail."

"Yes, good—thank you—but I wonder if you've not had time to make a few corrections?"

She spun through her memory to think what she might have missed. Anne pushed her students when they needed it, but she didn't fiddle. A voice was a voice, and Alexis's essay was great. "Mmm, no, that's not the case, actually. I thought it fine just as it is."

"Oh." Anne heard Mr. Grant whispering, and voices in the background. "Listen, we had just a few questions, then. Could I put you on speakerphone?" The line opened up. "You've got Alexis and her mom here, too," he added. "And Marlo's somewhere." There was a soft round of "hi's." "So we're looking, Anne, at page one, the first paragraph, here. Have you got the essay in front of you?"

"I don't. Just read me the sentence."

"Okay. 'I commented on the shape of their huge nation.' That's Alexis, talking about Africa and, you know, the map she brought in—"

"Yep, I remember."

"Right. So: ' . . . the shape of their huge nation and how some of the boundaries are as straight as rulers while others are bumpy and jut out, and a counselor made a joke about Churchill's Thumb, which the kids smiled at' "—here he paused—"so I knew it wasn't the first time they'd heard it.' "

The line buzzed with speakerphone static. Anne imagined the Grants sitting in their family room, waiting for her to crack some code, to deliver them to a perfection they did not think achievable on their own.

"What's the question?" she prompted.

"Well, you hear it, don't you?" asked Mr. Grant. "The preposition? 'Which the kids smiled *at*'? Clearly that should be, 'at which the kids smiled,' right?"

Oh, man. Anne switched off her car's ignition.

"We're not at the end of a sentence, Mr. Grant, so I think it's fine," she said.

"No, but it is a clause, and it does sound incorrect there, I think. We think."

Alexis chirped up from the background. "Yeah, when he reads it like that, I just, like, cringe! I can't believe I almost sent that in!"

"In fact," continued Mr. Grant, "there are places where she does just what you describe—the preposition actually ends the sentence! Like, here—bottom of the first page—'I understand that governmental bodies require an understanding of their domain . . . so they know what is theirs to take and what is theirs to take care of.' Did you hear that? Of! Right smack at the end! Like it's got bells on it!"

It shouldn't have, Anne realized, but this made her angry. It got her back up. She might be casual in her manner, but she did not miss a thing in a sentence. Nothing. This was the bit of her work about which she was most sure, quite simply because she loved words most of all. She checked her watch. Already late. But this was worth handling correctly.

"All right. Here's my take," she said.

"Yes?"

"In the first instance, it would be belabored to create the work-around 'at which the kids smiled' right in the middle of the sentence. It would halt the flow of the essay very early on and immediately after a critical piece of information, Churchill's Thumb, is first introduced. You risk your reader noticing the baroque wording and glossing over our title phrase, which of course will no longer be a title because we don't have space for title formatting on the Common Application."

"Okay, we see that," said Mr. Grant, though not a millisecond of family consulting time had elapsed. "But what if Harvard thinks she doesn't know the rule? What if they think she made the mistake because she didn't know better?"

"It's a matter of style and not correctness," Anne replied. "This is a not a misspelling or a misused word we're talking about. It's an issue of fluency. That's the level Alexis is now working at."

She let the prepositions dangle for effect. And wondered if anyone caught the split compound verb.

"Yes, but how can we be sure they know that? I mean, in that second instance, at the end of a sentence?"

"In the second example, well, that's a line of poetry, frankly, that I wouldn't dare touch. Alexis has repeated her full phrasing—'what is theirs to take and what is theirs to take care of,' which shows that this is a deliberate construction. Ending on the preposition in this case calls attention to her lovely reversal, which is at the heart of the essay's theme regarding the balance between boundaries as protective or as problematic. Alexis has taken the essay to a level above what college applications ask. She's actually entertaining her reader here. She's in full command. No good reader would wonder if she knows the basic rules of style." She did not add, *If Harvard has a heart, she's in.*

There was a short pause. "Okay," said Mr. Grant dubiously. "But I wonder if in some other essay she should, you know, include a workaround, just so they know she can do it."

"Alexis?" asked Anne.

"I dunno, seems like maybe a good idea," her voice called.

"Can we just keep musing on it?" called Mrs. Grant, from a vantage point even farther away.

"Yes, love," said Mr. Grant crisply, like an air-traffic controller. Anne pictured him leaning over the speakerphone, arms solid on the table, framing the error-filled essay just as Alexis had envisioned Churchill's men looming over their map. Civilizing her. In that moment she loved Alexis. In fact, she loved teenagers; she really did. They had so much heart. And it was so damn hard.

"Goody, are we done?" asked a most distant voice.

"Marlo, this is important for you, too," replied her father. "You are not far behind your sister."

"No, sweetie, not at all," added her mother.

"Tell that to my teachers," snapped Marlo.

"All right. Anne, we'll let you go, then," boomed Mr. Grant. "Thank you for thinking through this with us. We're so grateful to have you to bounce things off of."

"Dad!" squealed Alexis. "You just did it, too!"

"We're so glad to have you off of which to bounce things," piped Marlo, in a terrible British accent. "Righty-ho."

"Enough," said Mr. Grant. "Lordy, I don't know what's got into us!"

The chorus of "byes" was actually, if unintentionally, in tune.

Anne started back up the drive, feeling it criminal to disturb this harvest afternoon between the trees. She checked the clock. Ten minutes of misplaced prepositions. Did one charge for those minutes? Could one, in good faith, charge anything to Alexis's parents when really, the only thing anyone could do was get the hell out of the girl's way? The Pfaffs' drive curved to reveal the front lawns and the side rank of beeches, silvering in a bit of breeze. She parked at the stoop and scooted up, truly late now, and horrified to see a black Mercedes smack in front, which she knew meant Mr. Pfaff would, of course, be home. So finally they'd meet. The big front door was open, so she stood outside the screen and rapped softly at the frame.

There came a shout from inside. "A freaking *Muslim,* Mom? Are you serious?"

This was Hunter, somewhere on the ground floor. Anne checked her watch. It was Tuesday, wasn't it? It was. She was supposed to be here.

"It wasn't—I didn't—" sputtered Mrs. Pfaff. Anne recognized her whimpering from the phone. She considered backing out to her car, but even if they'd forgotten about her completely, the spray of gravel in the drive would give her away.

"Stupid, stupid, stupid, *stupid,*" came a man's baritone, deep and almost melodic in the variation of each repetition. He was a baron of disapproval. He seemed to be savoring it.

"For Christ's sake, Gerry, back off!" Mrs. Pfaff shouted back. "You've had precious little to do with this. Don't think you can start now."

"And what, a job at Jewel? Or what was it, Mom? Did you at least give me Whole Foods?" yelled Hunter. His voice hit adolescent skids at the top, edging his anger with shame. They were just past her view, down the hall, in the kitchen. Anne heard a sob, and a chair scraping across the floor. She shifted from foot to foot. Through the screen she studied the odd grandfather clock in the corner of the entry hall, which revealed itself to be, in fact, a very tall gun cabinet with bronze fretwork on the door. Just then the dog, sensing her, came trotting into view. It was a large, hairy, deliberate mix, a Rotterdoodle or something, and it looked almost alien. Behind it, Hunter peered around the doorway.

"She's here," he groaned.

As usual Anne scrolled feverishly through her memory to determine if she had done something to cause this uproar. The mustangs? They weren't so far out, and in any case she hadn't invented them. But Muslims—well, they were nowhere in the application, so far as she had seen, at least—and she could only be responsible for what she had seen, right?

"You must be Anne," said Mr. Pfaff, approaching her in the hall, led by his round gut, which was exactly halved by a needlepoint belt: mallard ducks, flapping round his equator. He hoisted his trousers and Anne snapped her eyes up to his.

"I can come back?" she started.

"Nonsense," he barked, and extended a plump hand. "Gerald Pfaff. We seem to be in the middle of a thing, here. Maybe you can help us make some sense of it. Please do come in."

WASPs were so good at feigning inclusion, especially to distract from real conflict. Not for the first time Anne realized that her fair ponytail was a considerable boon with some clients. The rangy dog followed his master, knocking Anne to the hand-glossed corridor wall.

The kitchen she had only seen through doorways: a vaulted space hung with gleaming copper pots. Except for an elaborate seasonal centerpiece, there was no evidence of food anywhere. Mrs. Pfaff sat at the end of the long refectory table, all in a heap, twisting a Kleenex in her manicured hands. Her blond hair was limp. She looked very thin and very clean, as though her features had been recently detailed. A laptop was half open before her. Hunter was kicked out atop a seat at the opposite end of the table, his feet and his head seeming miles from each other, in a flagrant display of uninterest that wasn't remotely convincing. He wagged a few fingers to greet Anne.

"What's up?" he said. "Change in plans. I'm a chick."

"Stop it, Christopher," snapped his father.

"Whatever, Dad."

"Sorry?" Anne said.

"Ask Mom. She'll explain everything."

Marion Pfaff shook her head. "I really don't think we need to go into—"

"Oh, heavens, Marion, just let's out with it," said her husband. "You can't be the first one."

"Oh, she can," said Hunter.

"And say what?" his mother wailed. Then she sniffed hard, and adjusted her small face toward Anne. "Hi, Anne."

"Have a seat," said Mr. Pfaff. He lowered himself over a ladder-back chair, which, as he leaned back, caused his flesh to bulge through the rungs at even intervals. He hitched up his trousers. His socks had ducks on them, too. "Coffee?"

"Nope, thanks, I'm good."

"So it seems," he began, "that Marion here took a turn at filling out this Internet form—"

"The Common App," supplied Hunter.

"—and made a few changes that we find suspect." He chuckled to himself. No one else was smiling.

"Like, I'm an Arab chick who works at a grocery store," said Hunter. "How's that for changes?"

Mrs. Pfaff had her head in her hands. She spoke from between her palms. "I was just playing around. This application is so . . . well, have you seen it?" She looked up at Anne, pleading. Anne nodded. She let her head fall again. "It is just so . . . *sterile*. And you hear, you know, about how hard it is for white kids to get in, and especially white boys, and especially white boys from the suburbs, and I just thought, you know, what would it look like if I made it, like, the exotic application they're looking for? You know, some extreme ethnic person with no money who does all the right stuff. The slam dunk. The home run."

She paused. Hunter's eyes were fixed out the French doors at the back lawns, glazed orange with the late light. The dog clicked over and stuck its nose in Anne's crotch. She shifted.

"Rommel!" yelled Mr. Pfaff. "Sorry, dear, he's a bird dog."

By which he meant the dog was a tracker, not a letch.

" 'S'okay," Anne said. "I like dogs."

The interlude gave Marion Pfaff new strength. She sat up to face them. For all her crying, her forehead was smooth and her face dry, not a furrow or streak in sight. "Look, I'm sorry, okay?" she said. "Hunter left his computer open here, with the application up. And I was reading it. So shoot me. It's not a secret, is it? And I saw all these great things he's done, but I just . . . it just . . . it seemed so . . . *thin*. And that made me, makes me, so angry. All these years, all your work—" Here her voice broke, and her face looked as though she was going to cry, but it remained still as glass. Anne was terribly confused. "I wanted to just shoot the moon for a moment, you know, as a 'fuck you' to them." Anne watched the expletive send a shiver over Marion's preserved skin. "To just see what it would look like to make you the *perfect* applicant. The one they all say they want. Just because I think you deserve that."

Still staring out the windows, Hunter explained: "Right. So she changed my bio info to make me a Muslim chick who works at the grocery store. I think I'm a bagger. Or am I a checker, Mom? Did you promote me?"

"Hunter, it was not *for real*!" she hissed at him. "Cut it out. Now."

"Mom, it's my application!"

"And Christopher happened upon his computer, here," explained Mr. Pfaff, finishing the story for Anne, "and saw these unfortunate changes."

"The phone rang," wailed Mrs. Pfaff.

"What if that had got submitted, Mom? Jesus!"

"I was going to change it right back!"

"That's not the point. What the hell are you doing on my application?" He was glaring at her now. "There's a reason I have a password. It's *my* application. Do you even get that?"

Mr. Pfaff was bouncing his round fists softly on the table, biding his time. Mrs. Pfaff glanced at him, and then at Anne, and then stood up from her chair, trying to gather force. She leaned across the long table. "Do you think," she asked her son, "that you alone are going to college? Do you think this is only about you? Your life? Your future?"

There was a silence. Mr. Pfaff's eyebrows were halfway up his head.

"Um, yeah, I do," said Hunter. "That's exactly what I think."

"Because you're wrong. You are my son. Our only child, Hunter. For the last eighteen years, I have done nothing but try to raise you and give you *everything*. Everything! And when they tell me that you don't have a prayer at Amherst . . . well, have you told your father that? Would you *like* to tell your father that? Because we have some skin in this game, too, you know. What you put down on that thing, there"—she gestured toward the laptop—"it comes from all of us. You work hard, and I am very proud of you, but do not for one second think that you came into this world with manners and a one-handed backhand."

Oh, but she'd just missed it! Been so close to a real, tender spot—the true measure of a mother's projection onto her only child, which Anne knew so well she couldn't decide if she sympathized more with Hunter or Mrs. Pfaff. It confused and upset her, that cataract of feelings. It made this big, gabled house seem almost Gothic as the fall afternoon gave way to dark. But Mrs. Pfaff had taken a perilous turn in her expression, away from what she had expected of her boy and toward what she now claimed of his life. There was no surer way to alienate him. Anne watched Hunter steel himself. He balled up his enormous hands and cracked each knuckle.

"That is a disgusting habit and you know it," his mother said.

"Marion, not now," said Mr. Pfaff.

"Well, I'm sorry you had to work so hard and all you got was this white kid," Hunter snarled. "I'll try harder to be an Arab. I will."

"Christopher, cut it out."

"Oh, Anne, is it true?" wailed Mrs. Pfaff. "Is it true that all of this stuff—the tennis, the photography, guitar, that it's just normal that every kid has it? I mean, what do we have to do?"

Anne tried to get a foot in the door. "What do *we* have to do?" she repeatedly gently.

"Tennis is the only thing that counts, anyway, Mom," growled Hunter. "I quit all that other stuff."

"I know!" she cried. "And you showed so much promise!"

"Boy's like a carp," said Mr. Pfaff, focusing on his grappled hands. "Gets only as big as the pond he's swimming in."

Anne felt her skin ice over. Hunter, accustomed, didn't flinch.

"So what, Gerry," said his wife, her voice rising now in desperation. "Should we just send him to New Trier? Throw him in with the big fish?"

"I'm just saying, maybe then he'd have learned to compete a little bit."

"Compete, Dad? What, like play number one on the tennis team? Like that? Or should I just go shoot some retarded stock duck with clipped wings? Is that a better way to spend my weekends?"

"That's more than enough, Christopher," said Mr. Pfaff, hauling himself upright. His belly mashed the table's edge and pushed it back an inch or so, sending candlesticks wobbling. Mrs. Pfaff shot her arms out to steady her tableau, which included wheat sheaves and a host of tiny pumpkins.

"Fine," the boy spat back. "It is enough." He spoke through his teeth. From his father came a low warning sound, almost a growl. Mrs. Pfaff frantically rearranged her gourds. "You're right," said her son. He narrowed his eyes and squared his jaw in that inimitable adolescent way, heaping scorn on everything before him. "It's more than enough for me, too. Have fun writing my applications, Mom. Best of luck with Amherst."

Hunter scrambled from his chair and lurched out of the room, his long, strong stride making all of the adults seem sickly somehow, and spent. Anne recrossed her legs in front of her and sighed, hoping to sound experienced, as though this happened all the time. Par for the course. Somewhere above their heads, Hunter took the stairs three at a time.

"Oh, Anne," said Mrs. Pfaff, "will you explain? I just—I just don't know. I've tried everything to get us to this point, I really have."

"What does that mean?" asked Anne. *"Tried everything?"*

Marion Pfaff pressed her fingers across the bridge of her tiny nose, closing her eyes as though trying to channel spirits. As she spoke, she kept them closed. Anne had the sense that Mr. Pfaff was figuring it all out for the first time. He was silent save for periodic grunts that sounded vaguely gastric, so Anne couldn't be sure he wasn't just dyspeptic; but his quiet amounted to an endorsement, that much was clear.

The thing was, Mrs. Pfaff explained, once, before Hunter was even in high school, she had received a haunting piece of advice: "Every kid has gotta have a hook." And this was particularly true, everyone knew, for white boys; even more so for privileged white boys. The wisdom had come from a Chicago matron whose two girls had come out at the Passavant Cotillion and whose sons had rowed at Yale, and all of them, Marion Pfaff noted, had returned home to Chicago to live. One Thanksgiving at The Racquet Club, she'd taken advantage of a corner table to study the eldest, Barnett, a right-angled, gold-hued creature with a boarding school ring, and determined that this was within her reach. Her own son was dynasty trust-funded and a forehead over six feet, with an excellent first serve. He was a prize fish in a big, strong net of alumni and family connections that would lead him through every gate he approached.

And yet, when it came to college in these modern, "multicultural" days—she said the word as though it had bitten her—he was doomed. White suburban boys were everywhere. Rich white suburban boys were everywhere. One read the newspapers, of course, so one wondered: was it worse for California-born Asian boys? Mrs. Pfaff figured that unless you were shooting for Stanford, no, it was not. At least we don't live in Greenwich! she said. Maybe the Midwest counted for something. And one night when Hunter was nine, she sat up late on the Common Application Web site and scrolled through the questions. If only she could fill it out for him, she realized, she might have a shot at making them see how wonderful he really was. But there were more drop-down menus than text boxes, and the whole thing was user-unfriendly: private equity wasn't even an option under *Occupation* for Gerry. She supposed *banking-finance* came closest. He'd shudder to hear himself called a banker. And what should she choose for herself? *Homemaker?* Were they kidding?

Year after year she monitored the evolution of the Common Application, but they never seemed to learn. And more and more colleges capitulated to the form. Then interviews became optional, and then they weren't even offered by admissions officers anymore, only by alumni, and who knew who you'd draw? Some kid, some nobody with a chip on his shoulder, when a former trustee lived just next door and had watched your child grow up, but could you choose *him*? Oh, no. Not without seeming to be grasping at straws, not without looking desperate. But the truth was that colleges weren't interested in the whole child, clearly. She counted exactly two places on the form—three, with an "optional" space for God knows what—where a student could even write a full sentence. In her mind she saw—had always seen—her son, honest and eager, in a wood-paneled office talking with men who would decide admissions; this was the meeting she'd been raising her child for. When had it happened that meeting the child, knowing the child, no longer mattered? Whatever became of the gentleman scholar? Nowhere in the application's crotchety boxes could she explain what made Hunter special. The form seemed designed to strip him of his dignity.

So she determined, all those years ago, that Christopher Hunter Pfaff would have a hook. As a nine-year-old, he seemed to choose tennis. She called up the head pro and worked out an arrangement. Before long he was attending Nick Bollettieri's camps, and with Mrs. Pfaff doing the paperwork, he was steadily earning a north suburban ranking for Illinois boys twelve and under. But Hunter had gotten only as good as he needed to be to play number one on his high school team; like a carp, his father said.

"It's true," Gerald declared now.

So Marian Pfaff had decided Hunter should travel. And indeed, he had surprised them one morning at breakfast with a question about South America, so that summer she had arranged for him go hiking in Chile and then crew on a Caribbean yacht. The trip came at some expense to his tennis, but that was acceptable because of the language skills he stood to gain. But halfway through the trek, he'd come down with terrible diarrhea, and spent the time holed up with a trip manager who'd flown in from Santiago to look after him. The fiasco darkened when his passport was misplaced—Hunter was sure it had slipped from his pocket as he paid for some bottled water—and it had required Gerry flying down there to sort it out and bring him home.

But the trip was a wonderful thing in that while Hunter was so ill, he'd lain in bed and taken photographs out the window of his room, and Mrs. Pfaff could have slapped herself for not thinking of his photography: he'd been taking pictures forever, as long as he could hold a camera in both little hands, and some of them were even pretty good. His high school had only a one-semester photography course, which he took as a freshman. But sophomore year there was a brilliant photographer in residence at the Art Institute of Chicago, Richard Mandalay, and while he hadn't taught in years, she'd been able, with a little wrangling from a friend in the development office, to talk him into giving Hunter a few lessons. Twice a month she'd driven her son downtown to the man's River North loft and waited in a coffee shop downstairs while Hunter studied his craft. Once, on the way home, she offered an idea she'd had: "It must be wonderful to work on your gift without having to worry about grades."

But Hunter had only shrugged. "I guess so," he said. In truth, he'd have preferred receiving a grade to the surly brows of the old man Mandalay, who didn't care for Hunter's pictures of the girls' field-hockey games, even the cool black-and-white one from the knees down that showed motion and captured the speed of the athletes. He and the photographer mostly sat in silence in the overheated loft and turned the pages of coffee-table books. Occasionally the old man would point to one and say, "That's what I mean by balance."

Mandalay's residency ended and he returned to Vermont or New Hampshire or wherever, and Hunter slid his camera under his bed and left it there. At which point his mother overheard him picking at a guitar, which he'd bought secondhand from a kid who took a year off before college and wanted to pack light. He had a certain feel for the strings. So guitar lessons were arranged, and Mrs. Pfaff found front-row tickets to see James Taylor at Ravinia, now that Hunter could appreciate his talent. And so on.

All of which was set out now in Hunter's Significant Activities list, and detailed in his résumé. "Why didn't you keep up with your photography?" Anne had asked him. "Your guitar?" This falling off in his commitments was a bad thing; one wanted to show increasing dedication to singular pursuits, even though that seemed precisely contrary to the natural inclinations of a confident, curious adolescent. "And your Spanish?"

Hunter's résumé reminded Anne of the chalked outline of a homicide victim: perfectly correct, but without anyone inside. Mrs. Pfaff had managed to kill every interest he revealed. Her Midas-by-proxy was among the most devastating examples of crap parenting Anne had ever seen. No wonder the mustangs.

Mrs. Pfaff's voice was as slender as a whisper now. "So that's what I mean," she said. "I tried everything. I give up." Her sorrow was genuine. Anne hated her, and she hated her husband, and she hated the colleges; and somewhere upstairs, Anne knew, Hunter was hating her—Anne—too, maybe just as fiercely, for witnessing this, and for acting as his parents' tool.

"Well, to hell with it," said Gerald Pfaff. He shook his head. "Who the hell cares about these places if to give our kid the world is to put him at a disadvantage? Sorry. In my book, you open every door you can. That's the right way. If they want to fault our son for being who he is and not black or brown or what have you, well, that's about as blatant racism as I can figure, but nothing I can say about it anyway."

"So that's it?" asked his wife. "We just let go?"

"Um, of Amherst, maybe," dared Anne. She sensed an opening here. It could all turn, it could all be so good. Hunter could study environmental science in Billings! Or Denver! Or Tacoma or Boulder! He could spend every summer working for the Park Service! He could take those guns from the front hall and set out west . . .

"Not a chance," said Mr. Pfaff. "Christopher will apply early to Amherst. Let them prove me wrong. If it's as good a place as they say it is, they'll let him in. He's a good kid. And I'm no slouch. We know folks."

"Fine," said Anne. "The application's due in two weeks. So maybe have Hunter call me when he's feeling up to meeting."

"Will do," said his father, like it was nothing at all. He ambled toward the French doors and peered out.

"What a mess," said his mother. She smoothed her hair over her temples and those oddly shiny cheeks, and turned to Anne. "Now probably isn't the best time to work on essays," she said. "Dinner and all. May we give you something for the road? A piece of fruit?"

"Don't worry, she'll bill us," muttered Mr. Pfaff. He was studying his grounds, his back to them, his bottom embarrassingly feminine in its bulges. Mrs. Pfaff switched on the kitchen lights against the evening, which had now fallen, and immediately Anne made out his face reflected in the glass. His eyes, unlike his wife's, were brimming with tears. He still thought himself unseen.

"Lord, it's dark early," he said.

"Okay, well, so, I get it now," Anne told Hunter, in opening.

"Get what?"

"That's a lot of stuff you have to deal with there."

"Oh. Yeah."

They had his latest draft before them on the table at Starbucks. She never wanted to set foot in the Pfaff house again, so she'd suggested an alternative for a few days later. Late afternoon. The Winnetka Starbucks was full of anxious mothers in cashmere coats, zooming in for enormous lattes prior to suppertime. Anne kept her voice down, and Hunter his hat low. But it was better than the gabled manse. The carp. Christ.

They were working line by line. " 'It was just one of her latest ideas for my college application, I thought,' " Anne read out loud, pointing with a pen nib. "About your mom. It's funny. But are we comfortable with what that might suggest about your mom's involvement in your activities?"

"It's the truth," said Hunter.

"Of course it is. But you don't owe them a confession, you're telling them a story. It's up to you."

He was mute.

"Is there a fear that someone reading this might think your mom has helped things a little too much, do you think?"

"Oh," he said, scraping his finger along the outside of his iced drink. It was a frigid, iron-gray day, and he wore only jeans and a T-shirt and his big, scribbled-black sneakers. "I see what you mean. Like I've been packaged."

"Yes."

"Well, but it's true—that's what I thought. She was signing me up because it's totally the sort of thing she falls for. And it's important, like, to say why I didn't want to go on that trip."

"Okay, then leave it. But can we find a way to pick up that thread later? So we don't let them wonder on their own?"

He took the page from her and bent his head.

"What if here," he said, pointing to a sentence toward the end, "I changed 'When my parents ask me about this stuff . . . I don't want to share it with them' to something about, like, being grateful for the idea but wanting to make it my own now? Or, like, how I already have made it my own?"

"Great," said Anne. "That's the right turn to make, I think."

"That's nicer than I feel."

"It's the right thing to do. Not because it's nice, but because we don't want the admissions people thinking you hate your parents."

"I don't hate them."

"I applaud that."

"But calling Winnetka a prison is maybe not that cool?"

"Could sound a bit spoiled, I think, maybe."

"Right," he said, and leaned back again. He stretched his length under the table, and with one hand idly twisted a rope bracelet on the other wrist. Anne knew, as though it were her own memory, that Hunter's girlfriend had given it to him.

"Hey, nice man-jewelry," she teased.

He smiled, but didn't look up. "It's kind of starting to smell."

"No worries. You can just rub a little Tide on it, on the inside there, before you shower."

"Really?"

"Yeah. Works a charm."

He spun the bracelet a few more times. "I'm not gonna get in, am I," he said.

"What?"

"Amherst. Not happening."

"Oh. Well, I'm not making the decisions. But I think it's probably not going to be that easy. No."

"You know what?" He raised his shaggy head on his long neck, a teenage lion. "I don't even want to. My cousin, she's the junior there? She's sweet and all, but she's, like, so uptight. I mean, have you ever been to Darien? Craaaazy. She's basically, like, applying to law school after she finishes her homework and everything. Like, no time to think. Or chill. Or just, whatever."

"Mmm. Those East Coasters," Anne said.

"They're all like that?" he asked. She was spooked to realize he was serious. Sometimes she forgot how young these kids were.

"Oh, it's just a stereotype. You know, of suburbs like Darien, or New Canaan. But your cousin sounds like a great student."

"Humph."

"So anyway, what do *you* want?" Anne asked.

"To go back out there," he said. "To Montana. Idaho. I don't know. Can you go to college there?"

"You can, in fact, yes."

"So, like, where?"

Anne flipped over his essay and started writing names. "These are schools I want you to go home and look up. Read about them, see what you think."

"Cool."

"And this one, in particular"—she starred Colorado College—"pay close attention. They have this thing, a block schedule, that lets you really focus on one area at a time. I think you might really love that. Then let's talk."

"So should I wait to work on the essay, then?"

Nice try, thought Anne. She shook her head, flipped back the page, and said, "No, listen." Then she read him his own words: " 'I've spent my time in high school working on things that I liked and that were important to my parents and teachers, like tennis, guitar, peer leader and homework. I feel very lucky to have been able to do all these things. But I was surprised to learn this summer that I feel passionate about things that are completely new to me, like caring for the wilderness or finding ways to be sure that wild horses are protected in our nation's west.' "

"Yeah . . ." he said warily. "It should be 'peer leadership,' shouldn't it?"

God, the corrections this boy had endured. "Or some other wording, yes, but that's not why I'm reading it. This is the heart of it, Hunter, right here. This is the story you're telling. You've spent your life doing things other people asked of you and guided you to. And that's not wrong—that's called being a kid. Okay, so your mom's a little intense. Your dad kind of scares me, but then again I don't hunt. Even your dog kind of scares me."

A laugh escaped his throat. He'd rather have belched, Anne knew, but he couldn't help but give her the smile.

"You have beautiful images in your essay, and great ideas. The braided rivers, the stars, the mustangs. About needing to be in the dark so you can see stars, about parents like cities. Keep all that. But go back to this passage I've read"—she drew a box around it—"and make sure that the whole thing is telling that story. Own it. Tell it straight up, as though you know what you're saying, because you do now. And tell us about those new passions. What are they, and how will you act on them?"

"Okay. That it?"

"Maybe lose the prison bit."

"Right."

"And go easy on your folks. Not because they deserve it, but because you don't want to sound like a dick."

"You shouldn't talk like that," he told her.

"You're right."

"I won't tell."

"And your language—be careful, now," she instructed. "It's time to pay attention to every word. Look up here—you list homework as something you've done, and then in the next sentence you say you feel lucky to have done it. Do you really?"

"No. Freaking hate it."

"All of it?"

"Most of it."

"Okay. So if those lines are in there, then it's just sloppy. It's not what you mean. Be as careful as you would be with a precal problem set. Line by line. Make sure it follows, it all adds up. That'll save us some time."

"What, it's—ten days now?"

"Exactly."

"Cool."

"So you'll get it done? I can look forward to revisions?"

"Totally."

"Good. Want another Frappuccino for the road?" she asked, standing.

Hunter shook his head. "These things are gross." He straightened, raised his arms as though for a free throw, and tossed his almost-full Venti several feet to the bin. It wobbled, end over straw end, through the café. People in line had to lean forward and back to clear the way. The cup fell in without a ding. The mothers among them shook their heads. One lowered her phone and scowled at Anne.

"Dude, Mom should've made me black," Hunter said.

"Gosh, I know. She totally doesn't know you at all."

"Craazy," Hunter said again. He sped to the door to hold it open for her. "Thanks for the tip on the thing," he said. "You know, Tide."

"Nicole will appreciate it," she told him, heading to her car.

"Awesome." He stalled for a moment on the sidewalk, clutching his essay draft, with Anne's list of alternatives inked on the back.

"Yes?" she asked.

He shook his head. Then he held the essay up toward her, as though he'd caught it after a long pursuit. The page snapped like a flag in the chilly wind.

"Cool," he called, and turned toward home.

"ANNE. MARGARET BLANCHARD. Have you got a moment?"

Anne held out her phone and studied the plastic. Seriously, her friends would have gotten such a kick out of this. They'd recently had an e-mail round about Blanchard's latest book, *Call Down Your Career*, now that so many of them had reached safe perches in law, medicine, and finance. Seemed they were convinced of Anne's potential as the lone one among them who could "still do anything," which, roughly translated, meant that she was the only one among them who had done nothing. Anne hadn't realized she had solicited their reassuring tones, which grated. She'd have loved to correct them the tiniest bit by mentioning Sadie; alas, she had a strict confidentiality rule about her students. She couldn't breathe a word.

The Margaret Blanchard in the books and magazines would've

loved to get her coaching hands on a girl like Anne. So much potential, so little power.

"I've really got a bone to pick with you," said the real Margaret Blanchard.

"I'm sorry?" Was it lunch? Who told her? Why would she care?

"Yes, well. Frankly, I can't believe I'm having to make this call."

Anne's fingers began to shake. She hated this, how quickly she could be cut to the quick, like a little girl. She sat on her floor next to Mitchell and placed a shivery hand on his warm side. "What's happened?" she asked.

"First our daughter says she's not going to apply to Duke at all. That whole mess with the Mexican girl, you know. Then you meet with her, and next we hear, she's applying but not until January, when all the other kids apply, and I'll tell you, that's not sending the right signal to the admissions committee. And those people are our *friends*. But the real issue at hand today is this: is it true that you told my daughter that the only way she could not get into college is if she becomes a drug addict?"

Ah. Finally, a bit of comic relief. A conversation out of context could be explained much more easily than the real issues, like the imagined contest between Sadie and Cristina, or the fact that for these parents, college had nothing to do with their daughter and everything to do with themselves.

Anne allowed a little chuckle. "No, that's not exactly what I said. Not at all."

"Really? *Not exactly?* Because that's what my daughter told me, and Sadie does not lie."

Now Anne was both frightened and annoyed. She stood up, woke up her computer, and softly Googled "Margaret Blanchard." Certainly Anne had seen her a million times, but in the moment she couldn't think. The screen offered a hundred thumbnails of a brunette who would have been beautiful save a vicious underbite, a jaw so deliberate she resembled an anglerfish in some deep-sea trench. "Honestly, Mrs.

Blanchard, those were not my words, and in any case they're completely out of context."

"So you're saying it's not true."

"I had a conversation with Sadie about college and her opportunities. She was, as you know, quite upset."

Margaret Blanchard cut her off. "You know, Anne?" A bit of song had crept into her voice. "What I teach my children is useful here. When we're confronted with a mistake we've made, we have to face that head-on. We have to honor our choices, even when they're the wrong ones. We don't resort to things like 'context.' "

Anne felt her own jaw grow as hard as she imagined Margaret Blanchard's bones must feel in her own skin. "I'm not resorting to anything. I am happy to detail for you the exchange I had with your daughter, if you'd like to hear it."

"Sadie told me that you said that the only way she wouldn't get into Duke is if she was a drug addict. That it's a sure thing. And, you know, my husband and I have spent her entire life trying to impress upon her that her achievements are her achievements alone, and now you have just gone and undermined everything we have worked to create for her. What will that admissions letter mean to her now? I mean, Merry Christmas, Sadie!"

"I think Sadie will be very pleased when that letter arrives."

" . . . Though of course she's refusing to apply early now, so we have to wait until April for that letter, not that it will delight her anymore. I'd think you have ruined Duke for her completely. And to bring up drugs, well, I just don't even know what to say to that. I'm not sure if drugs are routine in your world, but we do not find the use of illegal substances to be appropriate subject for conversation with a teenage girl."

"Look, Mrs. Blanchard, this is just a terrible misunderstanding. Sadie was casting about for a scenario in which Duke would not be in her future. Frankly, she can't imagine one. And that's a problem for her, believe it or not. It's lovely to want her to feel her achievements are her own. But getting into Duke is one achievement that will not be. I'm sorry, but it just doesn't work that way. So I chose to be honest with her, since she already knows the truth, and talk to her instead about being a good steward of her opportunities. Those are hers and hers alone."

"What do you know about my daughter's opportunities? What place is it of yours to talk to my daughter about stewardship? I beg your pardon."

"Would you have preferred I lie? Would you have preferred I tell her that she should be praying every night for a spot at Duke?" *Or would you prefer I tell her how her father's too ashamed of her to even let her write her own essays?*

"We don't think it's inappropriate to allow her to feel that she's earning her success. But perhaps you do."

"I don't!"

"In fact, perhaps it's hard for you to see these young kids succeeding. Perhaps a part of you wants to take that away from them."

"Mrs. Blanchard, that's just ridiculous."

"Don't be so quick to answer, Anne, you give yourself away."

"Excuse me?"

"I don't hear a considered response, I hear knee-jerk. And knee-jerk means I've hit a nerve."

Anne wanted to say, *It means you're a crazy bitch,* but knew she couldn't, and her brain refused to produce anything milder. She saw this woman's name on the covers of magazines in every checkout aisle in the city. She was everywhere, like some horrid self-help mushroom reaching its long, pious filaments blindly through everyone's thoughts. Anne felt helpless. She was silent.

"Ah. That's right," said Margaret Blanchard. "It takes a few moments to really hear what we don't want to hear, doesn't it?"

"Mrs. Blanchard," Anne said, "I'm sorry you're under the impression that I'm not trying to help your daughter, because I really am. I like Sadie very much. But I'm not going to be lectured by you."

Anne made some quick calculations. Sadie was close to her final essay drafts; she'd get into Duke and likely Duke alone, but that wasn't any the worse for Anne's influence. She could just end the whole engagement right now. She had more than earned her first payment, and it was more than fair to forgo any balance. The novelty of being fired kept her from crumbling. This sort of thing had never happened before. Usually, parents sent her champagne and houseplants.

Anne continued: "If you think, in fact, that I'm not able or willing to help Sadie, then we should stop working together immediately. I'll be happy to forward all the essay drafts and materials I have to you."

"Oh, Anne," said Mrs. Blanchard, her tone shifting again. There was a long pause. "Dear, I'm sorry I didn't see this before."

Anne waited while Margaret Blanchard took a long, audible breath.

"I should have done better than to come down on you," she continued. "I can be formidable, I know. And now you're trying to just run away. You're young, you're alone. Do you have a partner? A boyfriend? I don't think you're married."

Anne took the bait; in her confusion, it seemed like self-defense. "Boyfriend."

"Long time?"

"Um, five years."

"Ooh, yes. Excellent. Listen. You really should attend my seminar next weekend. It's oversubscribed, of course, but I could make an exception for you. 'Strife to Wife: Empowering Women to the Altar.' It's right here in Chicago. My assistant can get you signed up. You must be lonely. We should get you sorted."

"Oh, thanks, but my boyfriend's in L.A. He's an actor. He can't be here next weekend."

"Oh, it's not for him!" she said, aghast. "No partners allowed! This is a safe place for the girls to come together. We like to blame the men, of course, but we have to get our own homes in order first, now, don't we?"

"What?"

"Listen, Anne, there's nothing to be ashamed of. You must want to move forward with your life. Come next weekend, you'll see."

"Kind of a busy time of year for me, as I'm sure you can imagine," Anne said quickly. "But thanks so much."

"Shame, dear. A real shame. I had thought we might be able to connect here."

"I doubt it," Anne said, exhausted.

She practically heard the flame shoot up. Mrs. Blanchard's voice lost its dulcet tones and flattened, like sharpening steel. "In that case," she said, "we will be clear on a few things. First, my daughter will complete her applications with you, and I will read every one of her essays. Second, there will be no more talk of the Mexican girl's desire to attend Duke or anywhere else until Sadie has applied and we are settled."

So there it was. Anne pictured Cristina's file, meticulously compiled, the essays and forms and waivers and recommendations, all of it in a red folder Michelle carried to and from Cicero North every day. She didn't dare leave it in the office lest the school's own darkness swallow up the possibility. To think it came down to this woman, Margaret Blanchard, life coach to the stars, who had never even met Cristina—how strange this world could be, the way money tangled up lives so very far from its own concerns.

There was nothing to say.

"I hope you'll consider my offer to help you work on your antagonism," said Margaret Blanchard. "That's an opportunity lots of women would die for, you know."

If I were a stronger person, thought Anne, I'd go to her damn seminar and write funny e-mails to my friends at night. I'd use it to better understand poor Sadie, I'd give this woman what she wants so Cristina could get on with Duke and all of this would end. But she herself wasn't that nimble of heart. And she was all but gagging on the offer of life correction.

Then in a flash she thought, My God, is this how my students feel?

But Mrs. Blanchard was making excuses for hanging up, a busy life and a world that needed her desperately. Anne punched off the receiver and leaned back in her chair. Margaret Blanchard's head shots were still stacked on her computer screen. Even this, in the angry moment, seemed baffling: that some people were in such demand that they needed formal materials so the world could have more of them. Head shots. What were those? Little self-products, little iterations designed for a world so hungry that just a smile, just your own face atop your own self, wouldn't do? She remembered Sadie and her monogrammed chair. How much she must feel was riding on everything she did. The girl was always crossing her arms, Anne realized now, always standing as though she were cold. Or bare. Her mother would never know it, and in fact would probably always be disappointed by Sadie's grades and leadership posts, but the girl's greatest achievement was kindness. It was a feature Margaret Blanchard had no use for.

On the last Saturday in October Anne rose especially early, walked Mitchell in gusting rain, and led him back up the puddled fire escape before setting out for Cicero North to see if she could find a few minutes to talk with Michelle about the situation with Cristina. She wasn't looking forward to it. It was bad enough that she had to reveal that Cristina's future at Duke was now riding on the tender back of Miss Sadie Blanchard's aspirations. That Margaret Blanchard, advocate for underempowered women everywhere, was holding Cristina's application hostage. That now that they'd had a glimpse of what a fast-tracked, power-glossed application could look like for a girl with no strings to pull, it would be impossible to just shrug and say, "Let's send the damn thing in ourselves."

Worst of all was the fact that at no time did Anne's daily work seem as frivolous as it did when she confronted the fact of Michelle. Broke, single, out-of-shape Michelle, in her ill-fitting slacks, trying against hope to change lives in linoleum classrooms. Where did she go at night? Whatever else did she do? The police officer who rummaged through her handbag four times a day at the high school doors probably got closer to this woman's secrets than anyone else on the planet. Meanwhile Anne, whose life was similarly monastic—though she'd never have admitted it, since her full-color imagining of her future with Martin in Hollywood seemed to give her life a dimension it simply did not have—tinkered with kids' sentences. They delivered essay drafts that reminded her of piles of matches: thin, disordered stacks, pointing every which way but without the realization that they could be made to ignite. Year after year, draft after draft. At Cicero North, Anne waved to the Saturday security guard, who sat folded up in his hood in his rain-streaked van; she felt like an impostor crossing the twin beams of his headlights.

As a kind of talisman, she'd brought in her bag the two-page final essay Hunter had e-mailed the night before. It was clean, it was smart, and it was strong. He'd come through. His final section especially made her beam:

> Like so many young men in American history, I went West and found the way I want to live. I loved the mustangs because they represented the pursuit of my own independence and my own interests. Before Montana, I had no idea what the sky looks like at night when you aren't blinded by the city. And I guess growing up is a little bit like that. Your parents shine so brightly that you don't really know what's out there until you get away from it all by yourself. We need parents, like cities, to keep us safe and give us the things we need to survive. But we also need open fields and dark night skies so we can discover the things in our own hearts.
>
> I've spent my time in high school working on activities that I liked and that were important to my parents and teachers. I'm very lucky to have been given the chance to develop these skills and gain an

> education. But I was surprised to learn this summer what it feels like to come across your own passion, something that you find on your own, without anyone suggesting it, the way you come across a field of wild horses when you had no idea such a thing existed. Aside from my concrete interests in environmental preservation and in particular the ecosystems of the West, I will bring to college this new sense of excitement that stems from discovery and passion that comes from within. It has already inspired me to adjust my classes so I can take U.S. Government to better understand the politics of environmental conservation. In college I hope to study both politics and ecology so I can find the best way to address this new interest. I feel that I have a new compass that points me toward my truest goals, and like the mustangs, I want to run, run, run.

Did Hunter's words hold up in the damp corridors of Cicero North? Yes. Yes, they did. Anne could repeat some of the phrases in her head, and even here, where the tall, morguelike locker walls had been permanently padlocked to prevent storage of drugs and trash, even here, Hunter, for all his privilege, still seemed to be a real, live boy. Go, Pinocchio.

With that thought, it took a moment longer than it might have to figure out what was going on in Michelle's office, which was brightly lit against the rainy gloom and which held not just Michelle, but Michelle dressed in a black hat and cape, her cheeks streaked with green, and, sitting across from her, Cristina Castello in her usual too-long skirts and dogged sweaters with a woman beside her who was clearly her mother—the same lovely cheekbones, high and broad—and who was wearing the same drapes but in larger sizes. Cristina smiled brightly and sat up full in her chair to greet Anne. A small plastic headband on her head was adorned with twin eyeballs, like some alien lobster. On the table between them all was the red folder, thick as a steak now, neatly squared at the corners and ready to go.

"Oh, perfect!" said Cristina. The twin eyeballs bobbed a bit. "We were just about to give this to you!"

Halloween. Of course. Michelle was grinning, her green cheeks greasy and tight.

Mrs. Castello rose. She pressed her lips into a smile. Then she reached both arms, slowly, to take Anne's elbows in her hands and hold her still, as though she could radiate gratitude directly into Anne's bones. Anne wanted to be sick. There was the betrayal, of course, but part of the lurching in her belly was caused by the sense that this woman's firm arms were holding her more still than she had been held in years, like a finger on a spinning top. When was the last time Anne had really paid attention?

"Is it complete?" Anne asked Cristina, in part to avoid her mother's eyes.

"Yes! Mami's just signed all the last forms, so we're all ready."

Michelle scooted her little metal chair a bit to take the stage. "We thought you could deliver it to Mr. Blanchard," she explained. "Seems he told Cristina that was the best way to submit, under cover of a letter from him direct to the admissions director."

"I know it's only a few days, but can you get it to him? Is that okay?" asked Cristina. "It's all there now. Sorry it took so long!"

All three women looked up at Anne: good witch, good mother, good daughter. Anne was aware of a real danger that she might begin to cry.

"You know," she said, as matter-of-factly as she could, "as it turns out, it's not going to have to be there on such short notice after all. I just was talking to them, the Blanchards, and apparently because of the FAFSA forms and all, it's best to just submit under regular decision. That way they can assemble a proper aid package, no questions. So, by January first."

The lie just unfurled before her, bright as a spinnaker. It filled the room. No one seemed to mind. Still, Mrs. Castello gave Anne's elbows a little squeeze and then resettled herself in her chair, leaving Anne standing there, feeling as ungainly as Alice after a Drink Me bottle—she didn't belong there, couldn't ever fit herself in that room, but now she was well and truly trapped.

Michelle bought it. "Makes sense," she said. "A little disappointing, but not surprising. That's how it is for the financial-aid kids, in any case." She turned to Cristina. "Well, kiddo, you've got plenty of time to rest now. We'll just send it off to him so he'll have it in hand."

"I'll take it," Anne said, shuffling the folder into her bag. "Cristina, will you be applying anywhere else? Because you might want to photocopy some of these—"

"Why would she?" asked Michelle.

Cristina shook her head. "Not really. Should I?"

Mrs. Castello was frowning now. Cristina reached out and put a hand on her mom's knee.

"No reason," said Anne. "Just wondering if you needed anything in this file before I hand it over."

"We'll talk about that later," Michelle said. She tipped open her tote to reveal piles of chocolate. "Here, I brought candy. Did you remember, Anne?"

She had not.

"Okay, well, that's okay. Let's head in. It's time."

Cristina rose, lobster eyes bowing, and led her mom by the arm through the door and down the hall. Anne fell behind.

"Not even the U of I?" she asked Michelle.

"With board and books, they'll want, what, five K a year? Six? Seven? No. Can't be done. They don't have the resources to give her the full ride."

"Right."

"What's this, anyway? Why would she think about Champaign?"

"No, you're totally right. I'm just, you know, in that mode—I think everyone should have a backup. But that's just my job."

"Cristina is the sort of girl for whom there is no such thing as a backup. That's the point."

"I know."

They had slowed in the hall. Michelle turned to Anne and removed her peaked black hat.

"You know," she said, "I'm really proud of you. It can't be easy kowtowing to that man and his crazy family. I mean, I fight the system every day, but I don't have to sit in their living rooms. God knows how you charge enough to put up with it. I didn't think you could pull it off, after that whole afternoon at their apartment. But you did. You've done a really good thing here."

Anne looked sideways at the top of Michelle's head. She had pulled her hair into a tight bun, with rows of pins to keep in the strays, and she'd sprayed some sort of gray paint over the whole pile. As she walked, her long black witch's skirt swished.

"Lord, I need a broom," Michelle added. "I can't believe I forgot a broom."

"You're still pretty impressive," Anne told her. "Great costume."

"So what're you this year?"

"Oh, you know, just—a girl. Me."

"Hmm. Well, to that mother down there"—she gestured up ahead toward Cristina, who was leading her mom through the front doors—"you're an angel. I'd take it."

They stopped at Anne's classroom. Thirty-something souls sat slumped in their chairs, silent and bowed, like the very old. The fluorescent tube lights buzzed overhead. Anne stood in the doorway in her blue jeans, no costume to cheer them, no candy, nothing in her bag of tricks but a rain-soaked *New York Times,* some ACT books, and Cristina's college dreams in a big red file. Oh, and the folded-up essay of poor Hunter Pfaff, the Winnetka carp, bound for certain rejection in Amherst, Massachusetts. Michelle patted her arm.

"Thanks," Anne said.

Returning home, she welcomed the sleeting rain as a fitting sort of cloak for her conscience and a reasonable celestial response to her behavior. She parked miles away and staggered into the vestibule. A long envelope had been wedged into her mail slot, her name handwritten on the front. Special business. More BS about Mitchell? Some further clipping of her daily routines, some further intrusion from that bitch April? She pulled it open, hands almost shaking, and sat on the stairs to read two perfect, tiny, handwritten pages:

VASSAR PERSONAL STATEMENT

BY WILLIAM SAMUEL KANTOR

My father is a plastic surgeon. Lately this has made me think a lot about angels. Let me explain.

Dad spends his days performing procedures that are not needed but that people undergo because there is something about their body they want to change. Sometimes he'll talk at night about the girls who get their nose jobs as sixteenth birthday presents or ladies who'd like larger breasts (without names of course) but mostly, it's people who don't like the way they are getting older in the mirror. My own mother has had a face lift. I don't judge her. She is beautiful to me, no matter what. And my father's hard work has made it possible for me to live in a nice home with a view of Lake Michigan and go to good schools, for which I'm thankful.

But there has always been something that bothers me about people cutting themselves up to stop what is simply what happens over time. (Maybe this is easy to say when you're seventeen, as I am.) It wasn't until I read "Angels in America" by Tony Kushner that I understood what this was. I saw half of the show, "Millennium Approaches," at Northwestern University in a student production and when the angel crashed through the ceiling at first I was embarrassed for the director because it was such a mess. You could see the wires and the angel's wings looked like they were falling off. But I bought the play and went home and read about Tony Kushner and how he was inspired by the figure of the Angel of History imagined by Walter Benjamin, a German Jew who died in 1940. Benjamin's Angel was his way of understanding progress. The Angel has his wings held constantly open by a gale wind that blows from Heaven, which is Time, and which causes the Angel to have to keep flying, though he's facing backwards so all he sees is the wreck of things piling up in front of him. He sees wars, cities, and all the people who died. He wants to close his wings and make it stop, but he can't. The wind is just too strong.

When I read about this figure I researched Walter Benjamin, who killed himself rather than be sent to the Nazis. Many of my own family members perished in the Holocaust. I never met them, but my father has a book of pictures of some of them, like his two uncles who were young men who used to live in Poland. Though there are some who's names we won't ever know. When I read about the Angel I imagined my uncles' faces there in the pile of stuff that the Angel is looking at and that he is helpless to stop. It made me want to cry, though I never knew these men.

Kushner said that the Angel in his play should not be slickly done. He wanted it to be kind of a mess, to show the work involved in putting on live theater and also, I think, to show the messiness of people when it comes to Time and History. In Synagogue it's nice to think of G-d as having everything sorted out perfectly and we are all written in the Book of Life, but Kushner sees it very differently, and that's how it is for people, I think. Certainly it is for all the people who go to my father to have their skin cut open and parts of themselves taken off or rebuilt so they can pretend that that wind is not blowing. Certainly for me, since I sometimes wish that I could stop Time and change some things to make them perfect. I would bring my dad's uncles to New York City like my grandfather and they would have children and I'd know their children. (I am an only child, except for my half sisters, and cousins would be nice.) Also, since seeing the play "Angels in America," I would also change other things, like that I know that I am gay. I think it's like the Angel. It is a truth that is very messy. It kind of crashes through the ceiling. And I worry about all the things that will be wrecked by it.

I know that because my father spends his days making people more perfect it will not be something he will want to hear. He did not even want me to go see the play! Someday it will be obvious but for now, I am reading "Angels in America" again and thinking of Walter Benjamin and his Angel, and I'm glad to know that some people think that even Angels aren't always perfect, either. Maybe the one thing we can do with all that wind of Progress is make really wonderful theater performances so we can all be somewhere together at exactly the same time, because facing things together is what makes it easier to be a human being in the world.

Because this play, and theater in general, has opened my feelings and my thoughts, I intend to major in dramatic studies in college. I hope one day to work in New York City, maybe as a director. Maybe I will direct the first major revival of "Angels in America." I would dedicate the show to my uncles, who never got to grow saggy and old.

NOVEMBER

THOUGH IT WAS bitterly cold, Anne walked the few blocks east to William Kantor's Lake Shore Drive apartment tower. There was nowhere to park on the Drive, and in any case she wanted time to think through what she was going to say. She couldn't decide if she should feel proud or foolish that she'd overlooked the obvious. On the one hand, it was good not to be in possession of private insights into her students' sexual inclinations. On the other hand, how could she not have seen? Poor, ever-prepared, proud William. His devotion to Martin. His Cheney-esque political aggression. His button-downs. His shoes.

She considered her obligations in the light of his revelation. Should she celebrate him? She had no experience to fall back on here. Remembering her own high school love life, which was limited, except for one aborted groping episode with the wrestling-team captain when she was sixteen, to her first love, Benjamin—a complete romance that spanned one academic year, and died on the vine shortly after she'd arrived at Princeton and found it hard to keep him in mind among all those college men—she realized she had always preferred to keep her private life private. Her mother had taught her this, inadvertently, when in a flush of pleasure Anne had admitted that she was in love with this boy, Benji. Her mother had sighed, and not with nostalgia. "But why do you need a boyfriend?" she'd asked. "You should be thinking about your schoolwork, and getting to see the world."

Anne's mother was a member of the first generation of American women to attend four-year colleges en masse and the last generation to marry when just barely out of their teens, and that overlap had caused a good deal of pain. Her education hijacked by the wifely duties of the sixties, she'd found herself the wife of a navy cadet and then the mother of a little girl and then it would be years until she could begin what she called, to Anne, "my own life." Even after she'd gone back to graduate school to launch a career, Anne's mother suffered periodic crises, linked to some internal rotation Anne could not discern. When the dark moons struck, she'd storm and swear that she never should have been married in the first place, that all of it was a mistake, her entire life a failure, and then slam her bedroom door on the smoking scene. By evening, she'd be back in the kitchen, making supper, with her melodic chatter daring anyone to point out that just hours ago she'd laid waste to their lives. But Anne's father never would have dared, in any case. Marriage in that house was not a choice but a condition, a state of being, which did not vouch well for love.

Anne said nothing more of Benji, and when it came time to have sex with him, she drove herself alone to a Planned Parenthood clinic out by the airport to get on birth control and get *checked out,* which she somehow thought was important before the fact. She paid in cash, using her babysitting money, counting out tens at the reception window like someone posting bail. But Benji was young, too, and kind. They had a good deal of fun. They took nothing from each other. And then it was over.

What would she have wished her mother to say? And did this have any relevance, anyway, given that she wasn't gay, and wasn't facing the wrath of her conservative dad?

Well, in truth, she'd have wanted her mother to say: *Tell me about him.*

So when she sat down across from William at the little Eames table in his study, she said, "Your essay is wonderful. Are you in love?"

It was the one thing he hadn't been expecting. He shifted his skinny shoulders in his broadcloth shirt, as though something had gotten caught inside.

"In love?"

"Yes. Have you met someone?"

"Who would I be in love with? All the other gay guys in my class?"

Anne shrugged. "I have no idea. But you seem to have a world a little bit bigger than the senior class at Parker. And your essay was just radiant. I thought it was fabulous. So I wondered if you'd met someone special, and that had prompted it."

"Oh," said William. He frowned at her.

Anne waited, unsure. The picture window beside them was fogged a few feet up from the floor, where puddled trays of orchids cast humidity on the frozen glass. Outside, the lake had not yet begun to ice over at the breakfronts, though it wouldn't be long now. It occurred to Anne that William cared for the orchids. Of course he did.

"Not really," he finally answered her. "Maybe."

"Hmm," Anne said. "I don't remember falling in love as a 'maybe' kind of thing."

"That's because you're talking about Martin Waverly. So yeah, no kidding."

In fact, she'd been thinking of Benjamin.

"Are you going to marry him?" asked William.

Anne turned her gaze from the desolate lake. William was patient and sincere, as though he, too, were only gathering clues about how this whole love thing worked for everyone.

"Yes," she said.

Last Christmas, just before Martin had left for Los Angeles, they'd gone downtown to hear David Sedaris read—that old, great one about being an elf at Macy's—and as they walked back up Michigan Avenue, fairy lights a-twinkle, Martin had pulled her nearly off her feet into Bulgari and led the way to the diamond rings, where he stood before the gleaming case and said, "Tell me which." Then he'd stepped aside.

Way aside. So much so, you'd have thought they were strangers. Anne pointed shyly, and the saleswoman placed the winking jewels on a velvet cushion. Anne wasn't sure which finger to use to try them on. Even in this, instructing her to choose a diamond ring, Martin caused her so much uncertainty that she'd ended up sliding a cushion cut on her extended index finger and studying it aloft, like an insect that had landed there.

"Thank you," he'd told the saleslady, and led Anne back out onto the street, where a brass quartet was playing "The First Noel." It was dark. Anne remembered a curious thing, that on the corner Martin had reached deep into his pocket and rifled around for a moment, so long that Anne almost let herself believe he'd managed to buy the ring in that instant, and she'd allowed herself to look up at the lights and the Water Tower outlined against the pink city sky, laying down the memory, readying herself; but then he'd pulled out a fistful of small change and dropped it into the red charity bucket at the trombone player's feet.

"That's really great," said William now. "I'm really happy for you. He's a really talented guy."

"So what are we going to do?" Anne asked, having had enough of Martin. "About Vassar?"

"Well, what can I do?"

"I think you can do anything you want, really."

"You mean apply there."

"I don't mean anything specific. I just want to talk about it."

"Well, I could apply, and just not tell them. Of course I could. My college counselor doesn't care. And I've got a credit card. But why? It's not like Dad's going to let me go."

"How can he *not* let you go, exactly?"

"By not paying for it."

The boy had a point.

"Do you really think he'd do that?" she asked him.

"Yes."

Anne raised her open palms, as if to indicate the spacious condo, the long, split-screen gray of winter sky over winter lake. There was plenty. "Why?" she asked.

William stood up. "Tea?" he asked, and left the room.

In his absence, Anne looked around. William had one entire wing of the condo, his bedroom and en suite bath and this study that fronted the lake, what might have been a living room or parlor for a different family. Through a doorway she studied his bedroom. He slept on a platform on the floor. A stack of books held a goosenecked reading lamp, and there was no other furniture. She heard him set the kettle and was keenly aware that she had no idea what she was doing. There was no essay on the table. His applications—Penn, Cornell, Yale, Columbia, U Chicago—were mostly finished. Usually, when she was correcting awkward teenage sentences, Anne could let herself feel that she had a lot of mileage compared to her students. But William "when you're seventeen, which I am" Kantor was right alongside her. She remembered the way he'd looked at Martin at Whiskey Blue. Turns out it wasn't the theater he'd wanted (though that, too); it was sex, and recognition, and life. All the things Anne wanted, and should, by all accounts, be receiving from the great up-and-comer. But when it came time to cash in, she looked away. Went home and stayed there. William? He kept going out, kept seeing shows, kept reading, kept writing. Most of it here alone, she imagined, in this apartment full of hard edges. No desk had a drawer. The cabinets were without visible door pulls. Interiority was impossible in a home like this. It was like an architect's dream of self-realization. Anne thought of her parents' house in the suburban woods, full of overstuffed closets and keepsake boxes with ribbons sewn on top. She'd been imagining it lately because Thanksgiving was approaching, and Martin was spending the holiday with her family, which meant the possibility of a talk with her dad. He knew which ring she wanted, and it was time to join him in California. Her students would be finished soon. It would be spring. She knew her parents were expecting the proposal, and she was, too.

The Kantors' apartment heat came on, causing the floor vents to vibrate and setting the orchids shivering, as though the frost on the window were finally getting to them.

William returned with a pot of tea and two mugs. "Jasmine green."

"Perfect."

He sat down. "Well, you see," he said, having chosen his words, "if I go to Vassar, if I do theater, I'm gay. If I go to Penn, if I go to law school, I'm not gay. Get it?"

Anne nodded. "So he knows," she said stupidly.

"Well, who knows what he knows. But yeah, I think he knows. It's not like I'm a hockey recruit."

Anne thought to point out that a hockey star might be gay, and then thought better of it. "So tell me how I can help," she said finally.

"You can't."

Anne sipped her tea.

Then William said, "Do you think I can apply? Really?"

"I don't see why not. You're not committing to anything."

Which couldn't have been more false, of course, but in the moment, hands cupped around the mug he'd poured for her, Anne wanted only to console this boy. Vassar would require nothing from him but a reply, yes or no. But to apply in this way, or maybe, as William argued, to apply at all, was to commit to coming out. Of course it was.

"You could use that essay everywhere," she added. "It's much better."

"You just like it because it's not anti–polar bear."

"That's not fair."

"Not worth it," he declared. "I've got a fine essay. It's fine, no matter what you say, and I'm going to use it for Penn and everywhere else. If I apply to Vassar, well, then it's up to me. I'd have to just not say anything here—he tossed his head back to signify his home—tell the counselor to add it, just do it."

"I think you should," Anne said.

He lowered his full lips over his mug and looked at her. He slurped.

Then he asked, "Have you seen the show?"

"*Angels?* Yes. At the Walter Kerr."

"In New York," he finished.

She nodded. William let his features go soft, just thinking of it. Without him across from her, about the same age she'd been, she never would have remembered that night, the way she'd sat on the floor in the far balcony corner, peering down through ranks of dark shoulders at a stage erupting with story. She'd gone back to campus and managed to wheedle her way into a dramaturgy workshop with Oskar Eustis, the director who'd midwifed the show. She remembered how he'd shown up in the seminar room lugging an enormous blue binder glutted with Xeroxes of Brecht and Artaud. "One day, in college," she told William, "Tony Kushner and Oskar Eustis—he was—"

"I know," said William quickly.

"—they did a workshop on campus about dramaturgy. Theater in context. The role of history, literature, text on the performative space."

It had been deepest winter, the dead months. Kushner wore a turtleneck and had big, wiry hair that seemed like his very ideas, just casting around for lightning to strike. Anne remembered reading somewhere that lightning began at the ground up, and that if you had the right sort of lens you could capture these same, streaky little tendrils, poking the skies.

A wash of love came over her body. She set down her tea and wrapped her arms to her chest as though that binder were there to clutch for herself, and longed for school again. Suddenly it became clear that Martin was meant to be a conduit back to all of this. A way to follow them—the playwright and his director—out into the world. What had it been, a Tuesday workshop? One long, deep, lustrous day. But by nightfall the brilliant men had met the train back to Penn Station and Anne had gone back to her dorm, the world still off-limits to her. As it remained.

"That's amazing," William said. "What did they say? What did you read?"

"I can go back to my notes," she told him. "I've got the syllabus. It's huge. But that's not my point."

"I know, I know, just get to college," William droned, mocking her. "It'll all be better then."

"Well, it will," she told him. Her voice sounded hollow, but William didn't notice.

"All right," he replied. "I'll do it."

For a moment they looked out the window together. Then he elaborated. "I'll shoot for Vassar. Why not?"

Anne didn't want to claim the victory. Her heart thought a great thing had been decided here, but her belly told her otherwise. She was in a no-man's-land, not parent and not child, and she knew she ought to excuse herself as soon as possible.

"Poor orchids," she said, gesturing down. She thought William might appreciate her sympathy there. "Can't be easy to live in this freezing city."

"Naw," William told her. He shook his head briefly. "Not at all. They love the morning light. Couldn't be happier."

As ever, the approaching end of the year brought the parents around tight as a mob at nightfall, torches aloft. Marion Pfaff rang daily to follow the progress of Hunter's other applications, this being the only way she could soothe her nerves while they waited to hear from Amherst. In particular, she wondered if it might not be worth e-mailing Admissions to point out that he'd been born four weeks early, since this represented a handicap from day one. Mr. Grant had called from Minneapolis to alert Anne to the fact that Alexis would be traveling to Chicago with her debate team the week of Thanksgiving. This lousy holiday timing required her to fly out of nearby Midway Airport, on Chicago's south side, to make it to her grandmother's house in Kansas City, where the rest of the family would be waiting. Could Anne chaperone their daughter from debate to terminal on that Wednesday afternoon? And while she was at it, might she talk some sense into the girl, who was crying her eyes red late into the night with second thoughts about Harvard? Even Dr. Kantor had rung in between procedures, to clarify that Penn would not hold it against William that he'd not applied early decision. "It really is the best fit," he'd said. "But the boy's a stubborn one."

When Gideon Blanchard had a request for Anne, however, these days it was Brenda Hollow, his assistant, who placed the call.

"I've been asked to contact you regarding the firm's annual Christmas lunch," she opened tersely. Her voice made Anne think of nail clippers. "Are you familiar with the event?"

"I'm afraid I'm not," Anne said.

"It's an annual tradition here at Blanchard, McHenry. A very lovely, formal lunch during which the firm announces its philanthropic investments for the coming year, and honors one person or organization in particular."

"Sounds very nice."

"This year, I'm pleased to be able to tell you, the firm's focus is education, and to mark this focus the partners have chosen to honor Cristina Castello with a full scholarship to university."

"Um," Anne managed. Hearing Cristina's name in this woman's mouth was like discovering the girl had been kidnapped. "To which university?"

Brenda Hollow continued: "Cristina Castello will be honored as a representative of the firm's contributions to the pursuit of higher education in the coming year. Mr. Blanchard has requested that you help Cristina to prepare a short speech, ten to fifteen minutes, to deliver on that day."

"A speech?"

"Yes, a talk. Honorees usually share their experience leading up to this point. Not a dry eye in the house."

"Cristina—she's seventeen."

Brenda Hollow said nothing.

"I think that's a lot to ask of a kid in high school."

Still Brenda Hollow said nothing.

"Look," said Anne. She felt her frustration fraying her elocution, and she regretted giving Brenda the upper hand, but for God's sake, there was a *child* in the mix here. Two children, actually, if you counted Sadie. "Mr. Blanchard has been a little . . . *ambivalent* regarding his ability to help Cristina with college at all. So I think it's odd to ask her to speak, unless, of course, this is his way of informing us that he's going to support her application to Duke. Or maybe he intends to pay for her wherever she goes? If so, that's fabulous. I'll let her know. She can start those applications now. But we need to know which it is."

"Shall I say she's available, then?" asked Brenda.

"You're not hearing me. I need to know: what's in it for Cristina?"

"I don't understand," said Brenda.

Anne sighed heavily into the phone. It was meant as another flag for the woman on the other end, a semaphore from one subordinate to another, but it got her nowhere. "What, exactly, is Cristina supposed to say?" she asked finally.

Brenda began to explain, but Anne's mind wandered to the instruction she'd been given, that first, muggy day, to present herself at the service entrance of the Blanchards' five-story town home. She'd been fool enough to think it a matter of logistics. A broken doorbell, or a faulty stair.

" . . . many powerful professionals committed to charity," Brenda Hollow was saying. "About fifteen minutes, as I mentioned. She will be provided lunch, and is welcome to bring one guest. Mr. Blanchard suggested that you might accompany her. He also asked that I alert you that Sadie does not routinely attend."

"Which means it's a secret?" Anne asked, rudely.

"Dress is business formal," answered Brenda Hollow. "December eighteen, the Drake Ballroom, noon."

Anne pulled out a pen to scribble down details, which she tended to forget when her mind went white with anger.

She tuned in again to hear Brenda actually saying, "Thank you ever so much," before hanging up the phone.

The Blanchards were prescient in their apprehension of charity as a public game, elevated as it increasingly was from the sorry confines of clerical orders and therefore now useful as a sentiment-rich playing field for the wealthy seeking prominence among themselves. To brag about the achievements of one's own children was crass, but to brag about the achievements of children one had funded, well—that was magnificent. The annual lunch at Blanchard, McHenry, Winsett & Blair would become a landmark event, copied not only in Chicago but in New York, where the investment banks piled on, and in the glass atriums of the big studios in L.A. But Anne hadn't yet been to such a thing, so she was stuck imagining what it might look like. She saw Cristina in a Christmas dress—or should it be a suit? Where would she find Cristina a suit?—standing before a ballroom full of lawyers dressed to the nines, eating winter salads. She saw gold and silver baubles on the tables. Maybe candles. Hurricanes. She imagined the Blanchards tucking in their chairs the better to reach their wineglasses when the room fell silent and Cristina Castello began, in truth, to sing for her supper.

It was a high price for Cristina to pay. But whether it was a price too high, Anne realized, was not a decision she could make for the girl. There was a role for the skills of self-promotion in this world, after all, wasn't there? Feeling as cynical as she was just then, she thought the occasion simply the most blatant example of the elaborate marketing-and-PR exercise she completed with her kids every year: Make yourself believable. Make the big men feel moved. Make them proud of themselves for helping you on your way.

"I don't see why not," said Michelle cheerfully, when Anne found her later that week at Cicero North. This was a surprise.

"You don't?"

"No. Can't think why not. Cristina's articulate, she's confident, she'll present beautifully. Might lead to a job. Who knows?"

Of course Michelle didn't know that Cristina's application to Duke was being held hostage to Sadie Blanchard's tender feelings, which, as of the first week in November, were unyielding. Nor did she know that Anne had lied through her teeth about why the application hadn't been made early. Not to mention that Anne hadn't even been able to discover from the executive assistant—the *secretary,* for heaven's sake—whether there really was a scholarship in the offing, or just a fancy spin on the red carpet Duke would roll out if Gideon Blanchard could be convinced to make the call.

"Why, do you have doubts?" asked Michelle.

"Sadie Blanchard isn't invited to the lunch, apparently," Anne replied, sacrificing her last bit of dignity. "His own daughter." Anne was shaking her head, but not for the reason Michelle understood. Apparently her need for approval was so great that she was reduced to this, plying Michelle for confidence, goosing her already-successful lies. Inexplicably to her, Martin came into Anne's thoughts: he accompanied this feeling of desperation, as though his wide shoulders were the form it took as it moved from her heart to her mind. Never had an application season felt this dire.

Her comment worked like magic, of course. Michelle loved the idea that Cristina would have access where Sadie did not. "Sounds like a very sophisticated occasion," she said. "Cristina will have a lovely time! We'll start working on her remarks."

The image of Michelle and Cristina sitting together, dark heads lowered, in that sad little cinder-block office gave Anne a useful edge with Sadie, who was acting like a spoiled brat. She was flat-out refusing to meet now, saying she didn't have time in her schedule. So it was a race. Sadie needed to finish her Duke application. Let go of her fantasies of Yale and so on. Submit the damn thing. Then Cristina could apply, and her speech wouldn't be just a Christmas minstrel show. And Anne could be done with all of it. She was now quite conveniently angry at Sadie for putting her in the difficult spot to begin with. Maybe it was unfair, but it worked.

"Well, you have to eat," Anne told Sadie, when finally she caught her on her cell. "I'll find you at lunch."

To Sadie's mannered ears, this was a kind of social assault. She chose a restaurant near school and said she'd have forty-five minutes.

Anne understood that the shift in Sadie's attitude resulted from the very common phenomenon of girls siding with their parents when a conflict arose. It had happened before, and in general Anne considered it reasonable. But she sensed that Margaret Blanchard had been disparaging her in Sadie's earshot. Just the way Sadie looked her up and down as she approached the tiny window table, as if Anne were a nerdy new girl in school—just this told her she was right in her suspicion.

"Listen," Anne told Sadie, before she'd even removed her coat. It was chilly by the window, and Sadie was sitting there, arms folded, looking frozen and frosty both. "I know you're sick of this college stuff. Truth be told, I am, too. So let's just get this finished as quickly and easily as we can, okay?"

"Fine," said Sadie.

Anne looked around the packed restaurant, where customers mobbed the front counter beneath a huge chalkboard listing salads and soups. "How does this place work?"

"You have to go up."

"We only have forty-five minutes, is that right?"

"Yeah. So you'd better go now."

Anne looked at the girl's empty place. She had a blank notebook before her, and a blue pen, and nothing else. "You've eaten?"

"Not today. Not hungry."

"No dice," Anne said kindly. "Come with me."

"Really, I'm not hungry."

Anne was still standing. "Let's go, Sadie. Just see if there's something you can eat. It's a long day at school, and it's cold."

"No, thanks." Sadie bit off the ends of her words, leaving her teeth exposed.

"Jesus, Sadie. You're young and growing. Have some soup. A piece of bread. It's not a big deal."

Slowly, Sadie stood, and lightly tipped her chin up toward Anne, who was taller by several inches. "Who do you think you are, my mother?"

She was clever enough to ask the question straight, and not as mere challenge, as though Anne actually were delusional. It made anger rise up the back of Anne's shirt. The diners around them had set down their forks, so she kept her voice low. "Not in a million years," she replied, thinking of Margaret Blanchard. "But I am about a decade older than you are, and I'm asking you to just have one bite of something while we work."

"I don't think you're paid to monitor my diet," said Sadie. But still she shouldered her fancy leather tote to follow Anne to the counter.

"It's not at all clear what I'm being paid to do, I agree with you," Anne called back.

Sadie didn't respond. Anne replayed her words in her head and wondered what Sadie was making of them, and how much worse she'd just made things. Meanwhile, in front of her, something was familiar about a woman waiting: a long, shaggy, faux-shearling coat, needle-toed boots. Anne figured she needed to apologize, but she couldn't think what to say.

"Wow," Sadie finally said.

Anne turned to face her. There were tears brimming the girl's eyes, magnifying her kohl liner and making her look animated, like a tiny, bright-eyed Disney character, something small and skittish and likely to bolt. Anne gave up what remained of her hope of boosting the girl's confidence, giving her voice newfound strength, helping her to feel she could make her own choices. Why she'd ever thought she could bestow these things, she didn't know. Sadie lived with a level of privilege that made things different for her. Why did it matter that she sent in a subpar application, got in only to Duke, and matriculated there? The broad contours of her life were assured. Anne could tip them neither up nor down.

"Sadie, I'm sorry," she said. They shuffled forward with the line. Sadie was careful to keep her distance from Anne, who had to raise her voice to reach her. "I'm just frustrated, and that was inappropriate. This has gotten so complicated."

"It's because of that girl," Sadie replied. Her nose was beginning to run. She wrinkled it and sniffed. "Cristina."

Again Anne was aware of the woman ahead of her in line, who was shifting back and forth widely, as though to make out the chalkboard menu overhead, but some part of her attention was unclaimed. Anne lowered her voice.

"Is it? Really? I'm so sorry about that, if that's true. But she doesn't change anything about our deadline. January first. And your parents are frantic that you're not going to apply to Duke at all. They have dreamed of having you there since the day you were born."

"But what about everywhere else? If I apply to Duke, they're going to take me. Miss Hughes won't bother with my other applications. I know how it works."

"That may well be true."

"And if I go to Duke, it's like, 'Oh, here comes Sadie Blanchard.' Everyone already knows me, why I'm there. My dad is giving the new practice gym, did you know that?"

Anne did not know that.

"Like, for *basketball,*" Sadie continued. "It's just embarrassing. I mean, I'm proud of him, but it's a lot." She wiped at her cheeks again, and then something over Anne's shoulder caught her attention. "What is that woman's deal?" she asked.

Anne turned just in time to catch the faux fur ahead of them swiveling fast, but not fast enough to avoid revealing a tangle of highlighted curls and large, scrolled earrings hovering like a kind of mania. The face was thickly made up and sour.

"April," Anne said, not in greeting.

"She keeps staring at me!" Sadie said.

April Penze narrowed her eyes. She looked from one to the other, then settled on petite Sadie.

"I'm not staring at you, kid." Her voice was a tinny sneer.

Anne's body tensed up. Her appetite fled. "This is my neighbor," she told Sadie, as calmly as she could.

Sadie was still staring back, shaking her head slowly. Fearless, thought Anne. Then she said one word, "Weirdo," with enough poise in her voice to set April to strike. She seemed to rise from within, like a snake preparing. She huffed a tight little "Tah!"—sending a spray of saliva out over the glass deli case before them, and split the line, shoving her way through the crowd and out the door. The little bell on the hinge jingled behind her.

"What the hell?" Sadie asked.

But the moment was broken. She'd forgotten Duke, her parents, Anne's casting around for some calm place of authority.

"She's this crazy bitch who lives upstairs from me. She hates my dog. She makes my life hell."

Sadie laughed. "Oh my God. What a nightmare."

"Yeah. We're in a huge fight."

"I can tell."

"What do you think I should do?"

Sadie smiled and held up one finger while she gave her order to the counter girl, a green salad and some carrot soup. Anne followed.

"Move," Sadie told her.

"I wish I could."

They took their number and wound their way back to their tiny, drafty table. "No, seriously," Anne said. "What would you do if you were me?"

"Honestly?"

Anne nodded.

"I'd just totally ignore her. Path of least resistance. That's a chick looking for a fight. Did you see her, the way she, like, spat at us? The whole thing—she's just . . . *nasty*. Like, ghetto nasty. Like, you aren't going to be her friend, no matter what. I've seen that sometimes. I'd just totally ignore her. Rise above. Do what you gotta do and get on with it."

Anne was quiet.

"Look. She was totally staring at me because I'm rich," Sadie continued, spreading her fingers on the table to demonstrate. A Cartier tank watch, a little ruby ring on her right hand, some narrow enameled bangles on the other wrist. Even the manicure, clear, buffed to a shine. Anne hadn't noticed any of this. She figured she must be used to it by now. "She hates me for it."

"Well, plus you're with me, which makes you extra heinous," Anne said.

Sadie smiled. "Totally."

Anne leaned in. "You know better than anyone that some people are just going to resent you, no matter what. Right?"

"Yeah. That's my point."

"Mine, too. So don't let that get in your way. You know? The gymnasium. Who cares?"

Sadie studied her hands. As she did so, Anne observed her. Her hair was freshly blow-dried and fell straight, the chestnut tips in military rows on her cashmere shoulders. She sat with her hips squared and her ballet flats pressed to the floor. Her tiny body seemed perfectly proportioned, immaculate, and contained. How did an adolescent come to project such a total absence of need? Anne thought of Hunter, who was always underdressed, as though announcing: *I need a mother.* His huge, trip-on-things sneakers, better designed for the moon than the burbs. Even William Kantor, in his sartorial displays, revealed a desire to be seen. But Sadie was wrapped up tight. A done deal, wholly committed, fed from within. She drew circles in her carrot soup with a flattened spoon.

"Okay, you're right," she said.

Anne imagined those hands on the Miserable Children of the World Tour. Did she remove the watch? The ruby ring? She'd had years of enforced gratitude. Surely this created a child who knew to ask for nothing. And, of course, to confess to a problem was to risk her mother's life-coaching the very blood out of her own heart. The family was its own little cult of correctness. Sadie just wished to be invisible, for fear of being fixed.

It was why her writing was so insipid. It was why she wasn't a standout student. She shied from proving grounds, wherever they lay.

Anne picked up half her turkey club. "You know, I don't know that I have anything to offer you about this college thing."

Sadie looked up, puzzled.

"Except that I am good with grammar. Commas, etc. So whatever you want to do, it's fine with me. I'll just help you out with the words bit." Anne took a huge bite and chewed slowly, as if formally out of commission.

Sadie puffed air from her bottom lip to clear her bangs from her brow. After a moment she asked, "What was that woman's name, again?"

"April Penze. Pen-zay. Pence. I have no idea how it's pronounced."

"Hmm."

"Do you have your essay with you?" asked Anne.

"No. Sorry."

"It's okay."

"Maybe I should write about April," Sadie mused. "More interesting than what I've got."

"What would you say?"

"I don't know. Something about resenting strangers. Or kindness to strangers. Or, I don't know. I'm just sick of all of it. Wish I could do something new."

"You can," said Anne. "That's sort of my entire point, here. You can do this however you want to do this."

Sadie set her spoon down carefully against her bowl and laced together her little hands.

"What if," she began, smiling askance, deep in thought, "what if I did write about April? But April as a person and as a metaphor? You know how, like, at first I had that star metaphor but I took it out? Well, I think my essay needs something like that. And April is April, but it's also the month when the colleges send their letters. So, like, maybe I can play on that somehow? I can write about this woman who has all these ideas about me and is really mean even though she doesn't know me, which is kind of like the colleges who have to, you know, guess based on just some grades and things?"

Anne felt helpless and panicky, as though a bounding dog had just bolted into traffic.

"Um," she stalled.

"You think that's stupid," said Sadie. She let her hands come apart and placed them in her lap.

"No, it's not stupid. I just don't want my crazy neighbor to get any airtime in your essay. She'd put a copy of it on her fridge."

It was a punt, but it worked.

"Oh." Sadie nodded. "Got it."

"But certainly the month of April, and all that that portends for a high school senior—certainly that's a terrific subject, I think."

As she spoke, Anne imagined the directions Sadie might take. She saw that this subject could be made to solve everything. The kids who applied early admission heard from their schools in December; there was no long winter wait for them, no April week of stiff spring winds and shivering by their in-box. In writing about April, Sadie could address her choice not to apply early, thereby putting to rest any uncertainty about her focus on Duke, and maybe even placate her parents about her shifting intentions. She could explain it all.

Sadie wasn't intending any of this, of course. But what harm was there in showing her the chance? The idea had been hers, after all. And it was much, much better than writing the damn thing for her.

Sadie was still riffing on her inspiration. "So maybe I just write about, like, the process—the waiting, you know, for schools to tell you where you're in. I wonder, can I talk about Duke? Probably not, if I'm writing for all of them, right?"

"Well, you can personalize, if you wish—"

"No, no," said Sadie, waving her hands over her uneaten lunch. "I've got an idea now. I don't have to be specific. I'm interested in, like, the difference between planning and being told? How you just find out where you're going to be for four years, which, like, changes your life. You know?"

"I do know, yes," said Anne.

"Cool! This is cool! I'm excited now!" Sadie pushed aside her salad, uncapped her pen, and began to take furious notes. Her handwriting was tiny and straight and perfectly rounded, like a stitch. Anne found herself imagining lost generations of women bent over tiny, delicate crafts, complicated things no one else appreciated and that fell apart.

"Okay," said Sadie. "I've got it. I'll send it through to you soon."

For the first time in a while, the girl actually looked seventeen. Eager and clear, with a busy mind.

"Can't wait," Anne told her.

By this time of year, Anne's students were assembling piles of essays—at the core of each application the Personal Statement, a five-hundred-word massif around which were arrayed various shorter exercises, the usual paragraph about a "significant activity," and any other "supplemental" essays a university wished to request. Though the topics varied from school to school and even from year to year, with a list of eight or twelve schools the average student ended up answering the same questions in one form or another: Tell us about a teacher, coach, or mentor who impacted you in a significant way. Tell us about a work of art that challenged, surprised, or upset you, and why. Tell us where you'll be in ten years. Tell us what is special about our school/program/major. Tell us why you want us.

It really did grow quite dull.

The centrality of the Personal Statement was courtesy of the rise of the Common Application, and in Anne's opinion this did not represent progress. When she had applied to colleges, each school had had its own elegantly printed form that posed specific questions for the applicant to answer. The feeling was of writing a letter to a school, which in turn genuinely wished to hear the answers. Now her students were given the convenience of completing essentially one application, and then, with the nuisance of a few extra questions here and there—and these mostly confined to the most elite schools—sending it to anyone and everyone they wished. It was no longer about making contact with a great institution and entertaining one's dream of attending. There was no longer imagination in the drafting. You didn't envision walking the quadrangles on a snowy day or scanning a packed cafeteria for somewhere familiar to sit. Didn't loll over the phone-book-thick course catalog and wonder at seminars labeled "400.1." Instead, it was an exercise in self-branding. The schools were secondary. Marketing the student came first.

The intention was to introduce convenience, and as with all leaps of efficiency, the result was to depersonalize what had been a private process. Was it any wonder the professional college counselor cropped up now? Applying to college used to be like asking someone out. Long-considered, long-desired, heart-in-your-throat. Now it was like posting an ad.

Not to mention the monotony. Hunter Pfaff was industriously sending through supplement after supplement: "I believe Bates College is the perfect place for me because of its northern, rural setting, its emphasis on the liberal arts and academic exploration, and its opportunities for close contact with professors"—which, of course, distinguished poor Bates not at all from its dozens of small, rural, liberal-arts competitors in the American Northeast. The truth would have read something more like this: "I believe Bates College is the perfect place for me because my college counselor put it on my list as a yellow-light school, my parents are okay with it, and it doesn't make me write another long supplement except for this one." Anne and Hunter were complicit in crafting these friendly lies; everyone was.

William Kantor, meanwhile, was just moving commas around in drafts: "The most significant activity in my life, outside of school, is the time I spend performing *tzedakah*, whether it's by sitting with patients in the elder home, preparing meals for the house-bound, or donating from my allowance to our synagogue's ministries in Chicago and beyond"—intuiting, perhaps, that religious and ethnic minority interests, particularly when expressed in their native tongue, were unimpeachable. Sadie Blanchard had yet to send through her new essay, but she was dithering with a question regarding a character in literature with whom she'd like to have lunch ("I'm thinking Scout Finch or Ophelia? Does it matter that Ophelia's dead?"). Only Alexis Grant was seeking to set the world on fire. She overlooked no opportunity to address a desperately complex or traumatic topic: genocide, the failure of public education, the inability to take all the courses Yale had to offer in the four short years she'd be there. Anne read her essays with pleasure, suggested curlicue phrases to cut, and sent them back. From their pruned forms, three more essays would sprout, like old roses in spring.

So she was hardly surprised to find Alexis almost bobble-headed with excitement when she met her at the University of Chicago following her debate.

"Oh my God, so they argued," Alexis explained fitfully, "that you can *freeze* a person. Never mind the ethics of this, the legality is clear! It's absurd!"

For a moment Anne said nothing. She was suffering from a sort of emotional vertigo to find herself back on the Hyde Park campus, having parked along the Midway, where the long, low light was streaking east to the lake. She'd allowed it to blind her momentarily to the fact that she was about to come through the archway into the same quadrangle where she'd spent several years in graduate school, and which she'd finally walked out of a few years prior. Not that she regretted the decision to leave. But being grateful to be out of there didn't mean that going back didn't stir up her heart. She tried to fast-forward through the afternoon, picturing the long drive ahead, picking up Mitchell in Lincoln Park, and heading north to the suburbs for the holiday. And in the morning, Martin arriving, having booked the red-eye to save money.

The debate had been held at Cobb Lecture Hall. Now clusters of high school kids stood shivering in the frosty air all around the quad, where occasionally an unshaven philosophy or classics scholar would stumble down the stairs of an entry onto the walkway, study the groups of young minds, and look up at the fading sky before zipping up and hunching away. Alexis was radiant, standing there, bundled in a pink parka with her hair in a high ponytail. Behind her the long expanse of Gates-Blake Hall was like a quiet ship at mooring. The English department was there, and inside, Anne's old mailbox, with a new doctoral candidate's name assigned it.

"Sorry," Alexis was saying, giggling. "I should have explained! Okay, so it was, 'Resolved: Life begins at conception, so reproductive technology constitutes murder.' I was Negative. First speaker. And you can't talk about God, of course, though there was this one Catholic kid on the Affirmative who shouldn't have been there, I can't believe his coach didn't switch him, it's just stupid to be all passionate like that. You can't think. So it came down to policy which is already in place, all these practices and procedures, did you know about IVF, what they're really doing? Did you know that there are pregnancies that, if they are left to continue, will absolutely kill the mother, no matter what? And the baby?"

She was speaking faster than Anne could track. And doing so with a small wad of pink gum in her mouth, which Anne spotted periodically behind her teeth, and which made a kind of syncopated cracking sound as Alexis spoke, as though her tongue were wearing tap shoes. A faint strawberry cloud hung in the air between them. Alexis reached up, undid her ponytail, rebound it, and kept talking.

"So anyway we won, it was fine, but it was, like, I've never seen a team less prepared on pure policy. No takeouts, just this, like, they took *offense*. I think one girl cried. She was Chinese."

"Congratulations," Anne said. "You must be tired. And thirsty."

"Thanks. But I'm totally revved. Do we have time to walk around? When do we have to leave? You're so totally nice to do this!"

They had half an hour or so. The weather was clear, but they'd hit traffic heading west toward the airport. "How about some tea?" Anne offered.

They turned past the chapel toward a little café Anne remembered tucked up on the second floor, in a corner where two long corridors met. The holiday was descending, but maybe some straggler work-study kid was still closing up. "Why do they schedule debates the day before Thanksgiving?" she asked.

"Oh, 'cause it's the only time everyone's not in school! And it's not a religious holiday, so it's okay to cut into it a little."

"Ah. Of course."

"Oh my God," said Alexis, looking around. "I think I want to go here."

"To Chicago?"

"Yes! Look up." She was pointing along the cornices. "See those? Gargoyles, beside every other window! It's like a cathedral!"

Anne had loved the little guys when she was on campus, and this made her wish for a moment to put her arm around Alexis, as though she were her daughter.

"They fascinate me," Alexis continued. "They were an expression of Gothic fear. A way of manifesting all the nasty things the people couldn't control. They didn't have the science to understand famine, plague, you know, dying. So they envisioned these monsters. Expressions of their insecurity, but lovable, too. I like to wonder what we do now. Like, what gargoyles do we have?"

"I don't know," Anne said. "Weird little lapdogs?"

"You know what I think? I do this thing where, at night, I write down something I'm really worried about as though it has happened. Write it like a headline or something. Sometimes with a date and a place, like they do in the papers. And then I just look at it, and think, 'Okay, so that happened.' When of course it didn't. Then I just tear it up into, like, a zillion pieces. That's like my gargoyles. Only not as cute."

"Have you reported on not getting into Harvard?"

Alexis stopped. They were at the café's entryway. The other students had begun to clear out, and the last activity in the courtyard belonged to the frantically rummaging squirrels. Anne wondered if it was due to snow.

"No," she said. "Why? Should I?"

"I wouldn't think so. But I'm wondering why you're interested in coming here, all of the sudden."

"Oh." They climbed the stairs and came out onto a long, low hallway. Alexis lowered her voice, but they were alone. "Because in truth, maybe not getting in, it's not the worst thing. I mean, maybe I don't want to go to Harvard. Maybe it's not the best place for me! And if I get in, like, how can I *not* go? But then I won't be seeing all these other places. Like, really *seeing* them. You can't see them when Harvard's in your head. If you got in, I mean."

Anne was quiet.

"I guess I'm foreclosing on my options, is what I'm saying," Alexis finished. They came to the café, a paper-strewn set of laminated tables on uneven legs and a smattering of mismatched chairs. Behind the counter, a tired girl with magenta hair in a headband was shoveling sugar packets into a basket. "Oh my gosh, this is so cute and cozy!" said Alexis. "I can't believe you knew this was here!"

She seemed not to know, or to have forgotten, that Anne had been a student there, and Anne didn't want to remind her; it would have meant explaining why she'd left, and she couldn't yet talk about that decision and keep her confidence about her.

"Can I have a coffee?" Alexis asked.

Anne wasn't sure what the prohibition was—caffeine? Spending cash? She raised her brow.

"Oh, just because, you know, just asking," Alexis said.

Anne ordered two coffees. They sat.

Anne had never formally withdrawn, actually, from the university. She was technically still on leave. She could, theoretically, still march downstairs to the dean's office and reclaim her spot.

She poured milk in her coffee and watched Alexis do the same. Then followed with sugar. It occurred to her that Alexis had never had a cup of coffee before.

"Like it?" she asked.

Alexis removed her gum from her mouth and strapped it delicately to the side of her cup. She took a sip. "Delicious," she lied.

Anne waited.

"But what if, like, I could get into Yale? Or Princeton?"

"I think you probably can." Anne had never told a student this before. She studied Alexis's face, the pure enthusiasm sitting smooth across her cheeks, and waited for the shadow. Surely there must be something else the girl wished to talk about. What was it that drove her so hard? What specter stalked this cheerful achiever?

"Oh my God," moaned Alexis. "So what do I do? Like, in the debate, there are, like, a million ways to think about a thing. You know?"

"All too well."

"Like, for example, if you consider the resolution—that life begins at conception—then a person exists before the mother's body even knows it's there. There are invisible people—we can't see them, can't detect them, but we are obligated to protect them. Or so this is what you'd have to argue, to be in the affirmative. And here we have all these in vitro clinics—you know about those?"

"I do."

"So they create these people, literally *make* them, in the lab. Pipettes, plates, the whole thing. And then, if the mom and dad aren't ready or something, they *freeze* them. Think about that. About half the time, they survive and can be put back into the mom and become a baby. It's impossible. It's like Frankenstein. If you're in the affirmative, you have to believe all of this is wrong."

"Because you can't freeze a person."

"Exactly! I mean, I couldn't just take you and freeze you. At least, not without your consent. And they pointed out that the biology isn't the same for adults, but that's irrelevant to the ethics. A person's rights, as we understand them, are sacrosanct, at least in this country. It's not different with respect to age, not when it comes to having a fifty percent chance of surviving. And there's no law against enforced freezing, but we may imagine there should be, or ought to be. I mean, you couldn't freeze a baby that was, say, six months old. Or six weeks old. So why six days? Why is that okay? It's okay because it's not a person."

"Right . . ." Anne said carefully. For an instant she wondered if Alexis might be pregnant, but knew immediately that this was not so. Not even close.

"So my question is, how late is too late to freeze a person? Just 'cause you're not ready for them? 'Cause you have others to choose first? And it's not directly relevant for the purposes of the debate, but it totally wrong-footed the pro-lifers, who as I said shouldn't have had that side anyway, 'cause they were really upset. But here's the thing."

She stopped to sip at her coffee, which she didn't seem to care for much at all, then continued: "The thing is, I think of myself, now, as, like, having a thousand versions. There's the me who could go to Harvard—I mean, if I get in. And the me who could go to Yale. And the me who goes to, I don't know, Stanford. And the me who takes a year off and does something totally different. And the me who, like, decides college is an inappropriate use of my parents' money and that I should work instead. Or—" She broke off, frustrated, and rustled through the discarded flyers on a table beside them. Flipping over one pink sheet, she read, " 'Graduate fellow opportunity in London, England! International comparative education study, tenure one year!' " She slid the page across to Anne. "Or I could do that! Why not that? You see?"

"I do. I really do."

"All I have to do is just freeze all of the me's except one. But then, I can't ever go back. I don't remember ever feeling this way before. High school was just, like, what they called the years after eighth grade. But now it's like, I have to choose that one *me,* and that's the only one I can have for the rest of my life. And the rest will die. And I just can't face that."

Alexis blinked her clear blue eyes. She wore no makeup. Her cheeks were pink. A soft, pale mustache on her upper lip was almost shockingly candid, as though the girl had never looked in a mirror before. Anne raised her coffee and squinted a bit, to signify thought.

There were, at that time, some four thousand two- and four-year institutions of higher learning in the United States. Anne had often thought of the graduating hordes every spring, jostling to find their places, pouring into the cities and onto the trains, writing reading calling knocking. It made her crazy to think of it. But Alexis was not speaking of competition. This was something different.

"Your other students," she added now, "what do they do?"

In all of Anne's years working with kids, not one of them had asked a question about the others. They seemed not to want anyone else to exist.

Anne set down her cup. "Alexis, where you go to college is not the same as who you are."

"No, but it shapes me. It, like, shapes everything."

"Unless you consider that there's a trajectory to all of this passion. That you have a destiny, an intellectual and an emotional destiny, and that this force you feel is driving you toward that. Regardless of whether you turn left or right, you'll get there. You can't *not* get there."

"Oh!" Alexis exhaled, sending a little squall over the surface of her coffee. She set it down and put her palms to her cheeks. "Oh my gosh, that makes me cry."

"Why?"

She looked, quickly and shyly, at the magenta-haired counter girl, who was prone over a magazine. She turned back to Anne. Her eyes shone.

"Just that it's inside me."

"Yes. Where did you think it was?"

"I don't know. Out there. In everything out there." She pursed her lips. "Hang on." She bent below the table to dig through her book bag, resurfacing with a small wooden gavel with a fake metal plaque on one side. First speaker's award. She set it between them.

Alexis continued: "I guess it sounds silly now. Freezing the Yale me. Sorry. That's really embarrassing." She peeled her gum from the side of her Styrofoam cup and popped it back in her mouth.

"No, no," Anne told her. "It's true. Sometimes, growing up—it does feel like playing God. Like being in the lab and having to just, make things happen. Make a person. It's kind of amazing that no one's there over your shoulder, telling you how to do it."

Alexis rolled her gavel back and forth, over the pink flyer. "I guess that's why we love teachers," she said. "And parents."

Anne knew from the Grants' e-mails that Alexis had long ago passed her parents in aptitude and ambition. She wasn't riding their fantasies.

"Are yours helping you with this one?" Anne asked.

"Well, you heard them. Grammar and stuff. That's their way of helping."

"Mine, too," Anne admitted.

"So what do I do?" Alexis asked.

"Well, you come with me to Midway. And you get on an airplane and you fly to Kansas City and you have turkey with your grandma. And in May, or January or March or whenever, you write to some lucky college and tell them *yes*. And then you go."

Alexis nodded. She was chewing softly. She picked up her trophy and began to whack her half-spent sugar packet. "I'll never have this much choice again, though," she said sadly.

"Actually, it's going to happen over and over," Anne corrected her, sounding sad enough herself.

Her tone startled Alexis, who stopped her gavel and looked up.

"And that's bad?" she asked.

"I guess it just depends on how you feel about not knowing things," Anne answered.

"I *hate* not knowing things," Alexis declared.

"Maybe that's the thing we have to actually work on."

Anne was only half right: she needed also to let herself face the things she *did* know. Martin. Her work. But Alexis, for her part, was content. She seemed to have received what she needed to weather the trip to Kansas City and the weeks until Harvard would send her good news. She pointed to the silly gavel, now rocking slightly on the crappy table as they stood to gather their things.

"You should keep that," she said, handing it to Anne.

It rested on the dashboard all the way home to her parents' house in the suburbs, north and west of the city, not far from the Wisconsin border, those deep woods. *First Speaker, First Speaker,* it flashed, as the orange lights of the highway swept over the dash. It seemed a message to keep her mouth shut. Or else a message to figure out what it was that she should be saying, should have said a long time ago. And to herself, not to anyone else. *Enough talking,* said the little gavel. *Enough, now.*

"And what about that student in Colorado, do you remember that?" Anne's mother was saying. "What was it, Aspen? And the parents told you what about her ski schedule?"

"That she needed her R-and-R, that it was an important part of her development, so I was only to expect to hear from her after her morning runs."

"That's right. I remember."

"Ridiculous," Martin declared. He swiveled his glass, whiskey, two cubes. Anne's mother and grandmother had pulled their chairs closer to him, as to a hearth. Her father paced. Folded newspapers. Recapped pens and stowed them in a cup on the countertop.

"Well, she *was* burned out," Anne said, feeling guilty she'd ever discussed the student in the first place. It had been years ago: Tilly Benson, a Chapin girl. They'd worked remotely except for the annual Christmas trip, where Anne was put up in a back room at the chalet, in an enormous bed made of logs. Not a skier herself, she spent mornings tramping through snow along the golf course, looking up into the mountains and wondering what it was like to be so little and so exposed on the slopes. Tilly emerged after lunch, flushed and slightly smelly, and sat in her long underwear to work with Anne until supper. She'd ended up at Sewanee. A failure, as she'd been aiming for UVA.

Anne wondered if this was what her mother was remembering—the failure. Anne had been very upset. But that was overly cynical. The machinations of her wealthy clients always made for good sport at the Thanksgiving table.

"And the kid in Paris? The boy?" Her mother held out a platter heaped with food, enough for three times the five of them.

"He was a doll," Anne answered, shaking her head at seconds. "He went to Harvard."

"You still had to fly there to help him get in," said her father.

"Nothing wrong with a trip to Paris," said her mother. "Or Aspen. Or New York City. Or any of these places, frankly. And they pay you awfully well."

But she sounded angry, not proud. Anne realized, with a bit of shock, what her mother was doing: she was trying to impress Martin. As though this was what was keeping the ring off Anne's finger.

"Or what about that one in Florida?"

"The sport fisher," Anne answered. "A nice boy. Wasn't his fault."

"It's not anyone's fault, to hear you talk about it," said her mother.

"Well, it's not," Anne replied.

"I know!" Martin laughed, leaning toward her mother. "I agree with you. No way I'd excuse these kids their behavior! Spoiled brats. I tell Annie all the time she should aim higher."

"I'll say," said her father.

"Like what, screenplays?" Anne asked Martin.

He ignored her. "All that talent, going to waste on teenagers. Let them find their own way to college. God knows we all did."

"That's the truth," said Anne's father.

"I took the train by myself to Mills," added Anne's grandmother, looking at no one in particular. Divorced for fifty years, she was most comfortable in scenes of abandonment. "No one went with me at all."

"Anyway," said Anne's mother, "I always think it's wonderful that these kids have Anne. It's just amazing that such a thing exists nowadays. And of course the parents adore her."

"Of course they do," said her father.

"Then, once I had your mother," continued her grandmother, gesturing toward Anne, "I used to say to myself, 'So this is what I went to college for?' "

Anne's mother rolled her eyes skyward. She could be seen breathing in deeply. With Martin at the table, Anne thought for the first time of how very little she knew of her grandmother as a young woman. Only the story she'd absorbed of the train to Mills and the flyboy she'd met there, at a Saturday-night dance at the Sir Francis Drake in San Francisco. A tall man from Sacramento. Eventually he'd up and left, circumstances unknown, leaving his infant girl and her mother. All of this was visible in Anne's grandmother's curled claw hand, with its engagement ring still securely in place, sharp as a little pick.

"Well, Annie's going to be moving on to other things soon, I'm sure," said Martin, and there was a collective pause. Anne felt a rush of excitement in her belly.

"La-la land," offered her mother.

Anne held her breath.

"Or wherever her heart takes her, God knows," said Martin expansively.

At this, her mother flashed Anne a look of such hot frustration that Anne felt it on her skin, like peering into an oven. Fed up enough herself, she refused to indulge her mother with any sorrow or frustration of her own. She shrugged in return.

Martin stood. "That was the most delicious meal," he said, giving her mother his best stage smile. Cross as she was, her cheeks peached up a bit in response. Martin could always, always pull that off; he always would. "As ever. Annie, want to take Mitchell?" This was code for needing a cigarette.

"Oh!" said Anne's grandmother sharply, not willing to let pass an affront. She looked around the table, still laden with platters, and at her own, half-full plate, as though a storm were blowing through. She knew something was offtrack, but she was wrong about what it was.

"I'll clear," said Anne's mother, folding her napkin. Anne's father had already stepped out.

"But we're not done here!" Anne heard her grandmother say.

Martin held out her coat and she twisted into it. Outside they sat on the stoop. Mitchell sniffed at the scrub trees in the yard, barely visible at the edge of the lawn. When Anne's parents had bought this ranch house, when Anne was three, it had stood alone, a good twenty minutes from the nearest shop. But that was—what?—almost twenty-five years ago. The prairie was gone. Now the cornfields, all mowed, bristled with new bay windows and ragged yearling trees. The effect was to make her parents' home seem even more remote. Anne wished Martin weren't there, so she could cry. It was easier, missing him when he was away. Far more painful to do so when he was right beside her.

Something of the yard put her in mind of Hunter Pfaff's big suburban home, the grounds, that dark night he was called a carp. Anne thought of something new to say to Martin.

"I'm my parents' only child, you know," she told him.

He turned to her, inhaled, and exhaled off toward the sky. "Yeah. And?"

"Just, you should know that."

"I do."

That hadn't been the plan, to raise Anne alone. By the time she was five, her parents' desire for a second child was so loud and took up so much space that it was as though there had been a baby in the house for years. As a small girl, Anne concluded that she was not a child, since if she had been, the problem would not have been so grave. They were three little adults, smart and capable and largely self-contained. It was only that they could not have a baby.

Long ago Anne had worked out that the second child was intended to be the genius, her father's Bobby Fischer, but they'd had to settle for her; and now, it seemed, they were already looking to the next generation.

"That's why they're so annoying," she said now. "There's just a lot riding on me. Sorry about that."

"Why don't we go back down to your apartment?" Martin suggested. "Just us. And Mitch. We can have a drink, take a walk. Your grandmother drives me crazy. Plus they're gonna make us sleep in separate rooms again."

" 'Cause we're not engaged."

"Annie, I'm *forty*."

Their point exactly. But anyway.

"Sure, I'll tell them," she said. "Watch Mitch?"

Inside, her mother was elbow-deep in the sink. "Fine, I guess," her mother said. "If that's what you want."

"It's just easier in the city," Anne replied.

"Whatever works best for you two."

"Thanks, Mom."

Her mother pressed her lips together. Small creases had gathered above and below them, Anne saw, not unlike her grandmother's face, and she wondered when this started—how long it would be before it happened to her, too. Sometimes lipstick crept up her mother's upper lip, like tiny red veins. Anne was sure she was the only person who noticed. It made her at once furious and sad.

"Okay, well, we're off, then," she said.

"Your father's gone off somewhere."

"Tell him I'll see him maybe next weekend?"

"Of course."

Anne felt bolted to the kitchen floor. She pictured Martin outside, on the stoop, and Mitchell wandering idly. In the living room, her grandmother, sitting alone, sighed loudly. Her mother held up a dripping plate and studied her daughter, who dropped her eyes to the floor. So many hoops she'd made it through. High school, college, graduate school (some of it, at least). Working. Her first apartment. This handsome, near-celebrity boyfriend.

There are things parents wish for a child, and things parents want for the child, the difference being that wishes are received with a feeling of hope and goodwill, while wants are rightly heard by children in the imperative. Anne couldn't recall her parents speaking of her getting married or having a family. But still she felt a missed command. It was as though they'd been blowing a dog whistle all her life that she couldn't quite hear. She tried every trick she knew, learned every lesson, and still it wasn't quite right. So was this it? Marry Martin? Get a ring, get on with it?

But her mother spoke first. "What is it that you want, Anne?" she asked.

She meant, *want from me*.

"Nothing, I'm good," Anne replied. "Fabulous meal. Thanks again."

Her mother returned her attention to the dishes. It was the good china and could not be run through the machine. On the counter, wineglasses were drying upside down. The heavy silver would be rinsed and put away for another year. Something should have happened, but it hadn't. Anne felt responsible.

"Just drive safely," her mother said.

THAT NIGHT MARTIN was as attentive as he'd been in those first months, when he'd used to kiss her so hard it hurt her back.

"You've gotten skinny," he told her, lowering over her belly. "It's sexy."

"I was always skinny," she said.

"I know, but now you're hungry skinny. Very L.A."

Come to think of it, she had lost her appetite. And she'd been running more. Skipping breakfast because of the damn *New York Times,* which wasn't there to read over her cereal.

"You don't mind the boobs?" she asked him, conscious that everything had slackened some.

"Not if it means these hips," he said, cupping her bones.

Afterward he'd kissed her good night, and then leaned away to tuck his phone under his side of the bed, as he always did. There, under Anne's eyelet bed skirt, the phone pulsed like a cricket. She could feel Martin's muscles working not to respond. "Could be Lawrence," he said. His agent.

"At this hour?"

"Time difference."

"On Thanksgiving?"

"He may just have met with somebody. Lots of people out today."

"He can leave a message."

"He hates that."

Anne had left her parents home alone on Thanksgiving to be here with Martin. Lawrence could damn well wait. "Well, tough. I hate it that we have to always be available to him."

"Thanks for supporting my work," Martin answered bitterly. "Do you have any idea how tough it is out there?"

"Do you have any idea how tough it is here?" she answered.

"What's tough about Chicago? College essays? Hell, it's a seasonal industry, Anne. I don't have a long time. I'm trying to make it for both of us."

"I don't have forever either," she answered. She wasn't sure where this came from.

"What's that supposed to mean? Am I not successful enough for you yet?"

"I'm not talking about your success, Martin. Jesus."

"Then what?"

Anne sat up and pulled on her nightshirt. Her body felt skimpy and cold. "It's just—you're away. That's hard, is all."

"Look. I'm here now," he said. "Can we not fight when I'm here? Can we not just fucking fight when I'm actually here?"

"Of course," Anne said softly.

"Good."

They lay there. Eventually Martin leaned over. By the rise and fall of light, Anne knew he had checked messages and switched off his phone. He resettled himself beside her, seeming somehow accompanied. She waited for the news.

He said nothing. His breathing slowed.

Finally, she sat up. "Martin, what happened?"

"Hmm?"

"With Lawrence. Was that him?"

"Jesus, Lynn!" Martin snapped back. "I'm trying to get some sleep."

Lynn?

It was so bitter and so true, she played it over a few times to be sure.

It was not the name she would have expected: so simple and uninteresting. What did a Lynn look like? She knew only one, her third-grade teacher. Wide cheeks, pinned hair.

"Oh," Anne said aloud.

"What?" asked Martin, pretending to be half asleep, but even he couldn't sustain the lie. "I don't know why I just said that," he added easily. "That was ridiculous."

"Who's Lynn?"

"There is no Lynn. That's what I'm saying. It's ridiculous."

"No Lynn?"

"No. I don't even know a Lynn. Anne, come on—it's me. It's Martin. Listen to me. I don't even have anyone by the name in my life." He switched on the light and rubbed his eyes. "I was half asleep. I was already dreaming. I just snapped. I'm sorry. Can we just go to sleep, please?"

The light illuminated Anne's room: the floral wallpaper her mum had insisted on; the set of doors across the shallow, overfull closet; the curtains intended to soften the grimy, wire-hatched window that faced the fire escape. What was remarkable about being called Lynn was not even that it evoked another woman, who Anne had always half believed was there anyway. It was the way he had said it, in practiced exasperation: he fought with this *Lynn,* too. They were in deep enough to argue, plain as day. Anne wasn't special even in that way.

"You just called me by somebody else's name."

"It's nobody else's name."

Upstairs, April Penze dropped a book or a shoe, causing a thump just over their heads. Her proximity in this raw moment was more than Anne could take. She lay back down. On the floor in the hall, Mitchell turned and sighed, licked his long teeth.

Martin pulled her close. "Sweetheart," he said. "I'm an actor. I run lines for a living. Every day, I'm a different person. Every day, I have to remember names and then forget them. And sometimes they just stick, like some number you memorized, a license plate or something, sitting in traffic. Like some song you can't get out of your head. I'm sorry. I know that was crazy. But, love, there's nothing there. There really isn't. Even you, with your big imagination, can't turn that into something it isn't."

As hot as her emotions could be, as anxious and riled as she felt moving between students and her parents and the looming emptiness of the rest of her life, there were also moments of nonfeeling. Almost of nonbeing. Had circumstances been a bit different, Anne might have recognized in her own blankness the nullifying sentences of her students. She might have recognized how false a note was sounded by the "I" in her own mind, the same "I" she saw over and over in those churned-out essays the kids knew their parents would tear up and rewrite. Anne lay there and studied the ceiling as Martin repaired her. "I'm here, and I love you," he said smoothly. "I love you. Now let's sleep here in this bed together and be happy to have each other, okay? Please?"

"Turn it off," she asked. Martin leaned for the lamp.

The sodium alley lights came through the window. The fire escape was frozen tonight. The wood had sung beneath her heels when she walked Mitchell up for the last time. It would be Christmas soon. Then her birthday—she would be twenty-eight.

"My God, I'm going to be twenty-eight," she said into the darkness.

"Hmm," murmured Martin, hugging her in. His lips were on her ear. "Perhaps I should marry you, then."

Anne said nothing.

"You think?" he asked.

"Think what?"

"In fact," Martin continued, nestling even closer, "in fact, well, why not. Why don't you sit up?"

He scooted out of bed and into the hall, where his suitcase was spilled across her floor. She heard him rummage and return. He hopped back up beside her. "How about something like this?"

Her eyes still adjusting to the alley light, she studied his hand. There was a sparkle, a lone glint. He held up his fingers. She felt for the ring. "Oh God," she said. "Really? Now?"

"I think it's probably time," he answered. "I think you're right. Let's just do it."

She was holding up the ring, examining it. She knew by its weight that it was not the one she'd tried on, but no matter that. And she knew better than to turn on the light and expose them both, but not better than to say yes. After all this time, how could she say no?

"Should I put it on?" she asked him.

"If you want."

He watched her press it over her knuckle. She'd imagined a key in a lock, when the little diamond slid into place. But no such feeling attended. Instead it felt like something she should remove before bed, like a watch or a barrette. She fingered it with her right hand. It was as awkward and hard as a lost tooth.

"My God, Martin," she said, buying time.

"Are you happy?" he asked her.

"Yes."

"All right, then."

"Should we call our parents?" she asked.

"At this hour?"

"No, you're right."

"Love you," he said. He lay back. She tucked up under his arm. He adjusted a hand over her waist. She felt herself breathing into his palm, which was large and warm, wonderfully so. And all too soon limp with sleep.

In the morning she found him at her desk, waiting. His suitcase was beside him on the floor. It was closed.

She wandered into the center of her tiny living room and stood there. He studied her body, the short nightshirt, her undies, her storky legs with their dry skin and peeling pedicure. His eyes were pitched up in the center and full of sadness.

"Oh, Annie." He sighed hugely. "There *is* a Lynn."

"I know," she heard herself say. Then she couldn't hear anything else, because a kind of rushing filled her ears, the cottony panic of a doomed flight.

He'd hugged her, suitcase in one hand, and he'd bent to hug Mitchell. He'd taken up her hand with the ring and kissed it, and promised her something about sorting it all out, about not coming back until he'd done so. About doing right by her forever. About not wasting any more of her time.

Sitting there, folded up into her shirt, alone on the cold love seat, Anne looked at the morning and thought that all she had was time. It was actually, now, the only thing she had, and it was all around, oceans of it. But it felt thinner than water, even thinner than that—it was vinegar. It was lifeless and clear and there was nothing at all she could do except sit there, crinkle up, and weep.

DECEMBER

As it turned out, heartbreak was a fabulous state from which to understand the mind of a teenager.

All the puerile melodrama that previously had made Anne crazy now seemed quite appropriate in a world in which nothing good came true. "April is the meanest month," wrote Sadie Blanchard, opening her new essay draft, ". . . because it's when colleges make a decision that will decide the rest of your life, even though they've usually never even met you."

Seemed about right. But: "Why 'meanest'?"

"Oh, because T. S. Eliot said 'cruelest,'" answered Sadie.

"Yes, and—"

"So I had to change it. Otherwise that's plagiarism."

Oh, honey, you should talk to your father, thought Anne. "Still is," she said. "You don't want to just cite the original?"

Sadie gave her a withering look. "The Common App doesn't have room for footnotes."

Fair enough. See? Teenagers were right. Life was just obstacle after obstacle.

Sadie's voice came to Anne through the haze that had lowered the morning Martin left. That haze had a specific gravity and a low, static sound, and it seemed to fill her belly, crowding out appetite. It even had something close to a smell, metallic and cold, like the street-side doorknob on these December mornings. He had not been in touch since the latch had closed behind him. She replayed that last clacking note over and over. Six years, and this. Her entire twenties, and this.

Oh, and *Lynn*. Lynn was Everywoman now: blond or brunette, tall and slim, short and curvy. Because Anne knew nothing, she imagined everything, as though to see which phantom hurt the most. That one would surely be correct. Intuition had sorrow's nose.

"Okay, next sentence," Sadie said. Finally proud, she was actually, at her own instigation, reading her essay aloud. She sat curled on her bedroom sofa with Tassel sleek in her lap, both of them posed as though for a seventeenth-century Dutch portrait. Winter light softened their lines and made Sadie's skin glow. It was a Saturday. No one else was home.

"I am the person who has been taught since being small that it is necessary to disregard the opinions of other people and to consider my own conscience and moral compass. Except for my parents and teachers, I have always worked hard to ignore the feelings of other people because they do not know the real me, and their opinions can only make me be someone I'm not."

Anne was surprised to hear that Sadie, for all her graces, was uncomfortable with the phrasing of her own words; she read as though she'd never encountered an essay before, let alone this one. She paused before commas and ran out of breath before her sentences ended. She even seemed surprised by some of the words she came to. Anne wondered if her parents had ever read to her when she was little. Come to think of it, had anyone read to her? When would she have heard the written word aloud?

Something came into clearer focus about the way the Blanchards had raised their girl, about the gifts they had attempted to give her, while overlooking the most ordinary things: taking her to visit refugee camps, for example, though they were never home for supper. As though they had taught her hang gliding while neglecting that boring bit about walking. In the Blanchard home, other people's tragedies were useful, but one's own, everyday feelings were inconvenient at best. Sadie's heart was in hiding. As was Hunter's, though he had been railroaded by a more typical pressure to achieve. As was William's, though for an even more ordinary reason still, which was that he desired the wrong sex. Alexis, by contrast, suffered a surfeit of want, but it supported her talent and drove her success; her bewildered parents, long outpaced by her gifts, could only watch. They policed her prepositions with all the utility of a farmer swatting at a rising flock of birds. And Cristina? No one had had the time to interfere on her behalf. The adults worked all day and night, or they left. On balance, it seemed to Anne that a kind of benevolent neglect might be the best form of parenting available. Provided, of course, that every now and then you sat down and listened to your child talk.

Sadie continued: "This is a lesson my parents reinforced by choosing to have major careers even though that meant not a lot of time with my brother and me. When you come home from school and do your homework alone every day before putting yourself to bed, you learn to be self-sufficient and not to rely on others for things."

Inez had been erased. Anne considered this. Inconvenient? Or was this punishment for her attachment to Cristina? When in fact it was neither; Sadie was anticipating her parents reading her words, and she was protecting them from the quite accurate image of their only daughter spending her every day with the housekeeper. Anne would later reflect that she might have caught this instinct for filial propriety and directed Sadie's revisions accordingly. But it was late in the game, and Sadie had finally taken charge.

"But I see April in a different way," she continued. "April, like spring, is an opportunity for new growth. Every year high school seniors have the chance to take the opportunities given to them and make the most of it. College is a privilege. This is a lesson I have learned through years of volunteer service performed in communities around the world."

"There it is," said Anne. "I like it. Right there."

"It's really true, don't you think?"

"I do. I love that you're thinking of college as a privilege. And it'll give you a great platform for discussing your volunteer work."

"Well, just think of it!" Sadie said, visibly excited. She cast her eyes quickly about her room. "Like, for example, take the dining hall. There are, like, a dozen places you can go to for every meal. Pizza or Chinese or sushi or whatever. And in college, it's free! You don't even pay! The whole thing is just amazing."

"A rich offering, I agree."

"Okay, so let me finish," Sadie said. She picked up her page. Anne was relieved. They could work with this essay. It posed the problem of privilege and handled it, openly. It recognized educational opportunities as legitimate gifts, which would charm Duke. And it might well disarm readers at other schools, too.

Anne listened quietly. The house was silent. A few cabs went by on Delaware outside. Sadie hadn't remarked on the date, December 14, one day before the traditional response date for early-admissions applications. This year, the fifteenth fell on a Sunday, and no one knew if the colleges would give their answers on Saturday or wait until Monday. Some of them were using online notification systems, while others still sent proper envelopes, large or small. Anne had heard from a few remote students the day before—all good news, kids headed to Johns Hopkins and Northwestern and Tufts—but today she was on high alert. She was eager to leave Sadie to her rewrites and get home to her phone, just in case. In case of Harvard and Amherst. Also Martin.

Sadie could have been speaking for both of them when she read her concluding lines: "I hope that I will always believe that every new beginning, no matter whether it's what I hoped for or not, is an opportunity to grow."

THE CALLS CAME just after dark.

"Ohmygod ohmygod ohmygod!" said Alexis.

There was laughter behind her, the whole Minnesota family.

"Well, congratulations," Anne said.

"I can't thank you enough!" Thank-yous echoed around.

"I didn't do a thing." Anne replied, truthfully. "You are a fantastic student and they are lucky to have you."

"Well, yes, but now I'm really excited to go there, too. So, thank you."

So it was always Harvard, then.

"What about Yale? Stanford?"

"What?" Alexis laughed. Getting into Harvard had that effect on a kid. "Oh, right! Well, we'll see!"

"Going to be a marvelous Christmas," Mr. Grant called out.

"We wish we could have you over!" called Mrs. Grant.

"She's the first to get in from her school in nine years," he said.

"The principal just called!" added Alexis.

"You'll make them proud," Anne said. "Already have. I can't wait to see what you choose to do once you get there. And afterward."

Anne pictured their home: lit Christmas tree, thick carpet, maybe a cat. Snow piled against plate-glass doors. Sky as bleak as the Chicago night and even a few degrees colder. Something braising in the kitchen.

"Are you drinking champagne?" she asked.

"Sparkling juice!"

"Right."

"They have blood orange at the Cub Foods now!" added Mrs. Grant. "It's delicious!"

Absurdly, Anne found herself tearing up, which often happened when the colleges said yes. When the college in question was Harvard, and the season was right, on an evening like this it seemed the apotheosis of a young person, and it made Anne feel her work might be worthwhile after all.

"Wish I were there," she told them, and meant it.

The feeling gave her the briefest repose from the crisis of Martin's betrayal and the grim everything of her life that remained. "Briefest" because the next call came almost immediately, and the tone was of morbid urgency.

"Anne." It was Mrs. Pfaff.

"Yes?"

"I thought I'd best call."

It seemed Hunter had been not just deferred from Amherst—which was to be expected—but, somewhat alarmingly, flat-out *rejected*. There was no chance, the fine school reported, that he would be competitive for admission with the pool of general applicants. They wished him luck in his search. They wished not to waste his time while they considered their options through the spring.

Rather like Martin, Anne reflected.

"We're not sure what to do now," said Mrs. Pfaff.

This had only happened once before in Anne's career. That Amherst had said no was not a surprise. That the school had said *not ever* was a dark sign for the rest of Hunter's applications. "Shall I come by?" she asked.

"No, you'd better not," replied Mrs. Pfaff. "Gerald is home."

In light of the pull they'd accessed, Mr. Pfaff would be royally offended that the school had not offered the WASPish courtesy of a deferral. Such deferrals were almost a kind of etiquette, like saying, "We're so busy this month" when what you mean is, "I'd rather die than give you a Saturday night." White boys from certain families might not make the cut come spring, but they weren't to be pitched into the deepest dark space of the early rejection. This sort of candor was usually reserved for big state schools, which, as everyone knew, used complicated algorithms to make their somehow less critical decisions. Wow, Anne thought. Little Amherst was showing some muscle.

Still, she knew that what would sting the most was the fact that Hunter's cousin was already a Lord Jeff. A family that set its pride on one heir at such a school could not simultaneously forgive the rejection of another. Blood is thicker than water and all, but for blue bloods, one's strongest fidelity is to the notion of the meritocracy, so Hunter would have to be tarred, however silently. It meant shame, false or true condolences, and a real rift that would be detectable at family gatherings for years. Perhaps even this year. Anne tried to remember where they'd said they were going for Christmas. Was it east?

"So you'll have to step it up with the remaining applications," continued Mrs. Pfaff. "We have to get them in. We leave for Jackson Hole on Tuesday."

"They're complete," Anne told her. "We need only to go over them one last time. You might read them now; Hunter's okay with that, he said. I'd like your thoughts. Especially now."

If they were going to blame her, she needed them to see that what remained to be submitted was as strong as could be. And it was.

"Fine," said Marion Pfaff.

Anne waited. Then she said, again, "I am so sorry." Though, of course, she'd never encouraged this application; though everyone in a position to know had, in fact, discouraged it. Hunter had been set up to fail and he had.

Mrs. Pfaff did not reply. Anne let sit her apology awhile longer and then asked, "How is Hunter?"

"Oh, he's fine. A little shook up, but I don't think he was wedded to the idea. Not sure what he's interested in, frankly, except that Nicole. They're together now. Christmas shopping."

It made Anne smile to hear that Mrs. Pfaff had bought the oldest trick in the suburban teen's book: "We're going to the mall."

"Well, good," Anne said.

Another moment passed, during which Anne cast about for a way to end the call, and then Marion Pfaff could be heard crying gently into the phone. It seemed rude to interrupt her. As silently as she could, Anne tapped out a text message on her cell:

> TO HELL WITH THEM. NO BRAIDED RIVERS IN AMHERST, MASS.

Mrs. Pfaff's crying grew louder. So she wished Anne to hear.

"Please don't be so sad," Anne told her. "There are wonderful schools out there. He's going to be fine. He's going to do great."

"I'm not sure I can handle this," Marion wept. Her voice was guttering. "I'm really not. I have never. I mean, never."

To which Anne thought, rather uncharitably, Never? This is the worst that has happened to you? And you're sobbing?

But she did not yet have her own child, so she could not imagine how it felt to have some stranger tell your little boy no. Even if it had been a long shot. And it wasn't, in the end, the prospect of the gloating sister or the awkward graduation parties next year that had Mrs. Pfaff so rattled. It was that a door had, for the first time, been closed forever on her child. He was growing up. And the world was hard.

"I'm so, so sorry this is so difficult," Anne said again. "But Hunter is really terrific. He's a great kid, and he's going to have a wonderful life. He really is. Amherst is tiny and uptight and they wouldn't have helped him flourish there in any case. Let's just take a few days and then regroup and figure out how to go from here."

"Yes," sniffed Mrs. Pfaff. "Yes, you're right. Thank you."

Her voice was a kind of wet whisper. Anne wondered where in the house Mr. Pfaff was grieving.

It was decided that Anne would come around the following week. School would be out. She'd take Hunter for hot chocolate, they'd get this sorted. Mrs. Pfaff gathered herself up and thanked Anne heartily. Anne used her best to-hell-with-it tone, professional and generous and even a bit chummy. She did not want Mrs. Pfaff to know that she was rocked deeply. Because, in truth, she hadn't helped Alexis get into Harvard, and she hadn't prevented Hunter's being rejected from Amherst. She was helpless to reframe eighteen years of parenting and generations longer of expectations. She was just a custodian of fate, as she pictured herself now, an orderly, shuffling alongside these kids. Perhaps offering a bon mot. Sending them through the next set of doors, and turning back each spring to where the new year's kids were waiting.

Anne's cell phone chirped.

ITS COOL THANKS WILL BE BETTER IN MOUNTANS ANYWAY

read Hunter's reply.

DECEMBER 18 WAS a mess of a winter day. All night rain had fallen, and by dawn, cold air had moved in from Canada and crystallized the city, including the sky. Hard little bullets of freezing rain sleeted under cuffs and down collars and made everyone walk sideways nearly into everyone else. Anne pushed her way up Michigan Avenue toward the Drake, which in this weather seemed to be perched at the corner of the city and the northern edge of the planet, the lake stretching beyond it to Canada and this polar wind. Had she thought, when accepting this invitation, that she'd be passing the same Bulgari store in the same festive season, even the same brass quartet on the same corner, as though she'd been given the opportunity to correct a bad dream? Not consciously, no. But it was in her stride now, in both her speed and her determination to make something go right. Cristina, at least, would pull this off.

She found the reluctant star and her mother in the lobby, perched awkwardly on chairs set astride an enormous sideboard that supported an equally enormous arrangement of lilies. The air around them was wet with scent. The chairs were too far apart for conversation, so Cristina and her mother sat silently, wearing the same uncertain expression, and both seemed deeply relieved to see Anne come in from the street.

"I hope it's okay that Mami came," said Cristina. Her mother nodded fiercely.

As though there should be a question, Anne thought, with her best smile steering them back toward the ballroom. The halls were crowded with professional types and their wives, clumped toward the middle of the runner carpet and channeled by younger people who had the look of busy but entirely natural hangers-on, like cleaning fish, darting here and there to tend to someone's gills. Anne spotted the mayor about ten suits up. Nobody took notice of the Latina girl and her mother until they arrived at the set of long tables stacked with printed name tags, each bearing a red ribbon and a sprig of greenery. Anne found hers and Cristina's. There was no tag for her mother, of course, who had not been included.

"Oh." The young woman behind the table frowned. "Hmm. Well, let me see what I can do." She turned and left them to consult with a pack of women holding clipboards.

"I'm sorry, who did you say you were?" she asked Mrs. Castello, returning. After a moment's silence, she gave up and turned her questioning face to Anne.

"That's Cristina Castello and her mother," Anne told the woman, who was actually, now that she looked at her, a girl, probably her own age or a bit younger. How did you get into a job like this? What *was* her job, anyway?

"I'm sorry," said Cristina, and Anne worried that the table silliness would cost her the confidence she'd need at the podium. "I didn't realize . . ."

Anne said clearly, "Cristina is being honored today. She's speaking."

Several heads turned. The young woman's eyes opened wide. "Ohhhh," she said. "Of course! You're in the program! I'm sorry, I didn't recognize—I didn't understand the name, here, under *C*—it's not—anyway . . ." Her voice trailed off. She wagged her fingers in the direction of the ballroom.

But none of the snafus of their arrival—not the unfestooned tag with *Sra. Castello* scrawled in Sharpie, pinned ceremoniously to her sweater, not the chair hastily added and the place settings shuffled to accommodate her, not even the blank greetings every adult gave, assuming even "Hello" and "Merry Christmas" would be foreign to her—managed to rile Cristina, who, after a vague introduction from

Gideon Blanchard's partner Donald Winsett, stood and talked for twelve minutes, during which time nobody so much as lifted a fork.

Hers wasn't, in truth, a terrible story. There were no coyotes smuggling children across the sand under a desert night, no abusive men or drunken minders, no brothers lost or in jail, though of her seven aunts and uncles, both uncles were dead—one the victim of political murder in Guatemala, and the other of the drug-related depression that followed this first loss—and two aunties were still grinding out their lives back in Central America. The phrase "gunned down" drew the predictable gasp from the crowd. But more often the audience nodded, as though being reminded rather than informed of this girl's home on the northwest side, where she lived with her mom and aunt and two other women (Inez among them, of course) and their children, four kids to a room plus a crib in the hall, eleven total if everyone was home, which almost never happened. In fact, it was rather an ordinary American story, only that nobody listening to it was the slightest bit ordinary, socioeconomically speaking. They were flattered to find that it lined up with their imaginings of the lives of others, and even more flattered by the reach and focus of Cristina's language, which was articulate and graceful, and which made them feel not the tiniest bit unequal to her, above or below.

"The opportunity to continue my education," Cristina said, "is one that I will meet with pleasure, gratitude, and enormous energy. I am hungry to learn."

The mayor was the first to stand, rapping his hands together like bear paws and grinning around him as though she were his.

Cristina returned to the table, patted and pressed as she made her way through the crowd. Donald Winsett reclaimed the stage and impelled his guests to give and give generously. The envelopes at the center of each table filled with checks. Anne watched Cristina and her mother watching this, eyeing the envelope by their very own centerpiece, and noticed that neither woman ate a single bite of food, and perhaps not for nerves; maybe this was their lone refusal of this torrent of abundance, which must have made them as suspicious as would a gang of men in a dark alley. Anne felt an odd affinity with the neo-Marxists at the U of C when she wondered at the degree of complication at play here: the law firm, the ballroom, the girl who has to stand and deliver, all to wrangle the checks in the envelopes on the table not a foot from the child herself. Why not, she thought, just have a guest slip off a Cartier cuff and press it directly into Cristina's hand? But still it was all quite lovely, and Christmasy, especially when the chocolate desserts came round and a black boys' choir began to sing up on the makeshift stage.

Then Margaret and Gideon Blanchard were upon them. Everyone stood.

"Well, how moving!" Gideon bellowed, reaching his long arms for Cristina and folding her in like a pin-striped spider. "And Anne." He nodded carefully. "How proud you must be."

"In fact, this is Cristina's mother," Anne said, gesturing.

He took a big, mock step back, and stared. Then he turned to Mrs. Blanchard and said, "Honey, this is her mom! How wonderful. Gideon Blanchard. Margaret Blanchard. And you are? Señora Castello, *of course*! Our pleasure. My goodness. And how proud *you* must be!"

Margaret Blanchard managed not to look at Anne at all, as though she weren't standing there, flanking Cristina's other side. Well, so be it. Sadie wasn't there to sense her envy, so what did it matter?

"Your daughter is very special," she said. Unprompted, she repeated herself in Spanish.

Mrs. Castello said, "Thank you." But her eyes were turned to another couple who had approached them, a short pair, one round and the other slight. For a moment Anne did not recognize Gerald and Marion Pfaff. She did not expect to see them here, and indeed she had not seen them since the afternoon of the Muslim-applicant incident, since they had both taken pains to be out when Anne had gone to look in on Hunter and the remainder of his applications. It took what was for her an uncomfortably long minute to recall their names. But no matter; no one else seemed to expect her to know them either.

There was first a raucous round of greetings: "Gid!" "Marion!"

"Gerry!" "Margaret!" Heads lowered and rose again, kisses and thumps were exchanged. Jewelry clinked. Programs were shuffled and folded away. Then their four heads came up as though from underwater, and Gideon Blanchard feigned embarrassment.

"Here, let me introduce you," he said. "Marion, Gerry, this is Cristina Castello, our student of honor. And this is her mother."

The Pfaffs cooed and lowed.

"And this is Anne, the young woman who works with Cristina at her public high school on the northwest side. She's a volunteer college counselor there."

Mrs. Pfaff smiled as though to demonstrate what was meant by the term "smile," assembling her face into an approximation of pleasure. Her traced lips allowed no teeth to peek through, but Anne detected the smallest crinkle at the bottom corners of her eyes, which gave, graciously, a tiny hound-dog angle beneath a brow smooth as cream. The expression was balanced perfectly between recognition and the sense that Mrs. Pfaff had only just been caught deep in thought about something else. "Marion Pfaff," she said, and extended her hand.

Anne felt her cheeks tighten in a blush. She had been ignored, on city sidewalks and at school performances, but never summarily denied. She had to work to take in enough breath to manage, "Hello."

Gideon Blanchard, the most comfortable liar of the bunch, caught nothing. "Cristina was wonderful, Anne," he said. "Thank you."

"Don't thank me, please."

"Anne works with the kids up there every Saturday," he continued. "Isn't that right? So she spotted Cristina's gifts, and now here we are."

"How wonderful."

"Mmm," added Gerald Pfaff.

"It really is a labor of love," observed Margaret Blanchard, the first words she had spoken to or of Anne. It was her television voice, confidence atop a rolling purr, and it confirmed that she wasn't about to give up the game either. "Anne, you must tell us more about it sometime."

"Must be very rewarding," replied Marion Pfaff. "Now tell me, did she apply early anywhere? She must be admitted already."

Only now did Anne notice that Cristina and her mother had faded back to the table, where they were sitting alone.

"No, regular admission," Anne replied, noting that Margaret Blanchard's camera-ready grin was flashing again and again, almost involuntarily, like a lighthouse. She added, "It's a decision related to the financial-aid process."

"Which is of course a moot point now," said Gerald Pfaff, rolling forward onto his toes in the direction of Gideon Blanchard. Together they were like a comedy duo, one small and round, one tall and jutting. It was clear that Margaret Blanchard was claiming victory in this display. She took a step closer to her husband so that she was more nearly above Gerald Pfaff. Mr. Pfaff did not possess the self-observation required to notice such one-upmanship. He'd been short and round all his life and it bothered him not at all. But Mrs. Pfaff was irritated, and working to keep conversation light.

"And such lovely hair, too," she said.

There was an embarrassing silence. Cristina did indeed have lustrous long hair, but it was unique only because nearly everyone else in the room was blond. Or bald.

Speaking of which. "Where has she applied?" asked Mr. Pfaff, giving Anne his best neutral gaze. "Let me guess: Harvard, Princeton, Yale, Williams, Amherst?"

Anne studied him. She remembered their fantasy Muslim girl, the—how had his wife put it?—"extreme ethnic." Well, here she was. He had determined that Cristina was the enemy. And there was Mrs. Pfaff, too, for whom Anne felt rather sorry. Her ankles seemed too thin to hold up her slender frame, wrapped as it was in a quilted black suit, couture, expertly tailored to her wrists, which were turned to a sleek bag. The look was designed to be both elegant and warm, but on her bones it gave the impression of being purely decorative and somehow wrong, as though she were a throw pillow in search of a chair. Marion Pfaff wore her breeding in a uniquely Midwestern way, a phenomenon

Anne had not understood until she'd gone east and returned: the Pfaff bank accounts may well have been big, and indeed Marion's cousins by marriage in Greenwich lent her additional claim to that old world, but there was always something a touch *off* about her choices. And the tiniest bit defensive. Harbor Springs was not Fisher's Island, after all, any more than Lake Shore Drive was Park Avenue. The suit, the brooch, the clutch—it was just a little bit too much. Her sister in New York would have known to forgo the jewelry or wear a higher heel. Still, Marion Pfaff's Second City berth had seemed utterly secure until the arrival of such as Margaret Blanchard, a wholly new kind of arriviste: not just new money, but celebrity money. And some of it was *her* money. Much of it, in fact. Earned by her, in her lifetime.

And, of course, there could be not a soul in that ballroom who did not know that Gideon Blanchard chaired the board at Duke, which meant that when it came to college admissions, the only truly relevant test scores for Sadie were her Apgars (eight and nine). Marion, with nothing to show for her labors but an early rejection from Amherst and ten outstanding applications, stood trembling. She clutched closer her lizard clutch.

"She has applied to several places," answered Anne, when in fact the truth was Cristina had applied only to the U of I, and the Duke application was waiting, stamped and sealed, for the high sign. Anything else was out of the question in terms of financial support. "She's looking into a bunch of schools."

"Probably the very same schools as young Hunter, eh?" said Mr. Blanchard, addressing the Pfaffs. "Such a bright kid. So much potential."

"Some of them, I think," said Gerald Pfaff.

"Don't I remember that he has cousins at Amherst? Isn't that so?" This was Margaret Blanchard. "I think we met them last Christmas, didn't we?"

"One, yes," said Mrs. Pfaff.

"So Hunter must have applied," concluded Mrs. Blanchard. "How wonderful."

"No. "

"No? Oh."

Mrs. Pfaff recovered. "No, no. So small! No, he's looking to play tennis, so we're working with coaches, you know. It requires waiting to see how things shake out, the team ladders, it's a process on all fronts that way."

"Of course," said Gideon Blanchard. "I will never forget that kid's forehand. Comes at you like the Concorde, I swear."

"That's nice, thank you."

"And what about Sadie?" asked Mr. Pfaff.

"Well, she's quite fond of Duke, so we're pleased," answered Margaret Blanchard. It was another sign of the difference between her and Marion Pfaff: she felt no shame, saw no need to trim her sails.

All four parents smiled, but only one of them was genuine. Gideon Blanchard hadn't a doubt in the world. So for the benefit of them all, he said, "Well, Anne, this must be so boring for you! You can't have much to do with this side of things, seeing as you serve the population you do at Cicero North."

By now Anne was game. "Not at all. It's a challenging time for every student, no matter her background," she replied.

All four adults nodded gravely.

"Well said," pronounced Gideon Blanchard.

Marion Pfaff nodded lightly to Anne. "Well, nice to meet you."

"Yes, very," said Margaret Blanchard. "Gid, we must—"

"Yes, Gerry we should—"

They moved off.

Anne was left at the empty table. Cristina and her mother had gone. On their plates remained chocolate mousse terrines, drizzled with raspberry glaze and dotted with berries. Their name tags lay neatly alongside their untouched spoons.

BUT IN THE foyer of the Pfaff residence, late in the evening of December 23, Anne was greeted not only by name but with an embrace. Mrs.

Pfaff reached round her twig arms and pressed awkwardly, as though measuring Anne for a dress. Her eyes beneath her plucked brows were hollow. You'd have thought the family had received a diagnosis rather than a denial. Anne stood by the gun case, uncertain.

"Rommel's been boarded," said Mrs. Pfaff, barely above a whisper. "You can come in."

The dog wasn't the one Anne was worried about.

"Gerry has—well, he's done some work," explained Mrs. Pfaff. "On the essays. He's very upset. I thought you should just come see where things stand. I know how hard you and Hunter have been working." She dropped her head and led Anne through the dark halls to a third-floor study where Hunter and his father were waiting.

Following up the stairs, Anne inhaled the carpets and paint and wondered at how casually Mrs. Pfaff overlooked the fact that just a few days ago she'd pretended not to know Anne at all. Maybe crisis trumped manners. Or maybe it was just understood that Anne should be ignored, like a therapist, say, or one's gynecologist at the grocery store. Maybe it wasn't that Anne was unimportant, but that she was very far on the inside indeed.

Noting that Mrs. Pfaff was wearing house slippers, Anne concluded the latter.

The study was low-shouldered at its gabled eaves and lit by a single floor lamp, under which Gerald Pfaff had parked himself in a wide leather chair. Scattered across the carpet were essay drafts and printed copies of the Common Application—the disorganization made Anne start to sweat—and across from Mr. Pfaff, seated with his knees folded up and his back to the wall, was Hunter. Gerald held pen and paper in his burgeoning lap.

"I'll be downstairs," said Mrs. Pfaff, like a nurse. "If you need anything." She descended silently.

Mr. Pfaff said, "Anne."

Hunter flapped one hand in greeting.

"What's up?" she asked, as lightly as she could.

"We've made some changes," replied Mr. Pfaff. "To the application, here. Some things more fitting for our current situation. Wanted you to sort out the last bits now."

Hunter said nothing.

Mr. Pfaff held out the page in his hand. He wasn't about to hoist himself from the chair, so Anne crossed the room, stepping around essays as best she could, to take it from him. She cleared a spot, knelt, and began to read. Only a few words in, Mr. Pfaff spoke again.

"So is that your day job, then?"

"I'm sorry?"

"Working with the poor kids. That's your day job, and this is just on the side?"

She might have said "just the opposite," except that both college-counseling roles were sort of on the side, and since she'd left her doctoral program, there really wasn't anything to speak of in the middle. But Hunter seemed fragile as blown glass, and couldn't be made to feel anymore that he was an also-ran.

"I volunteer at Cicero North," she said simply, "every Saturday. For years."

Mr. Pfaff said only, "Humph."

It was an uncertain verdict, but she had been warned: he doubted her motivation now. Her sincerity. She felt him watching her read the page in her hands. It was Hunter's personal statement, the primary essay, which had been polished to a sincere gleam. Now the last two-thirds were crossed out, with swift arrows tracing down and all around, like a winter weather map, to a new paragraph scribbled in Mr. Pfaff's hand:

> Like so many young men in American history, I went West and found the way I want to live. I loved the mustangs because they represented the pursuit of my own independence and my own interests. But I realized that they are not useful icons for a young

> man, because they are not responsible to anyone or anything. The idea of running free is fun to think about but no way to live.
>
> I've spent my time in high school working on activities that I liked. I'm very lucky to have been given the chance to develop these skills and gain an education. Colleges, like all communities, benefit from the participation of all different sorts of individuals. Not everyone can be exceptional, and in fact the foundation of any community is the group of average, hard-working people. Mediocrity has just as much place as anything else, and in fact it is important for a community to boast diversity of achievement. My grades and test scores may not be in the 99th percentile, but this offers value to the institution. Instead I will bring to college my many interests and well-rounded experience.

Thereafter a long, sinuous line traced back up the page to the original, though the concluding sentence about the mustangs had been vigorously inked out.

Anne took a deep breath and let her eyes travel up. Mr. Pfaff's words swam in her brain like little piranhas, toothed and quick. *Offers value to the institution,* writes the private equity chief. *Useful icons for a young man,* writes the one just fifty. And cruelest of all, yes, there it was—the word "mediocrity." A word Hunter would never use, perhaps didn't even know, applied to himself in his father's hand. Anne blinked several times. The study was overheated and the lamp's shadows made it hard to see. Her body seemed to be failing to get things right. She was hot, tearful, panicky.

"So this is the new version we've got, then," said Mr. Pfaff. "We're just wanting your spell-check before we send it in. Marion thought you should come by rather than do it on the phone."

What Anne was feeling, of course, was rage. But she was not familiar with that emotion, which she habitually twisted like hanger wire into prodding self-doubt, and she was certainly no good at using it. So she stalled.

"Okay. It's really late—could we take a day or two? I always think it's best to do that after a major revision."

"Nope," he replied. "We leave for Jackson in the morning, and I want this done."

"Right," she said. "It's just that if—if the mustangs are useless as a symbol, then they don't really belong in the essay, is all. Logically speaking. So we should take those out, which really leaves us with not much to ground the setting in the first place. It doesn't need to be about Montana, or anywhere else."

Mr. Pfaff narrowed his eyes at her. The lamp highlighted the deep pouches of his face and neck and shone off his protruding belly, where his shirt was stretched tight.

"Good point," he said.

From deep in his throat Hunter let out a smack of sarcasm. He was out of words.

Hoping to establish camaraderie, Anne looked at him, but he kept his gaze level at the far wall.

Anne might have hated them both, the rich boy with his long legs coiled, his bags packed for the ski slopes. His father, who was an ass. But what was Gerald Pfaff searching for that hadn't been handed to him, and to his father before him? Hadn't the sons of privilege always been expected to inherit their fathers' kingdoms? And hadn't the sons always chafed at the narrow chute opening before them as adulthood dawned? Anne wondered if college madness in contemporary America wasn't, after all, the problem, but rather a poor solution to the problem: it was intended to give a young person the opportunity to pursue any professional life he could imagine for himself. These boys weren't facing recession or depression or war. College was four years to spend looking for something that was just right. It was a great idea, and a fine time to live it. But such an opportunity presupposed imagination, and fathers had always been the gatekeepers of their sons' dreams. You could turn that opportunity into just another chance to fail, if you were entitled enough and careless enough and far enough from your own boyhood self. Anne felt, in that stuffy, crow's-nest room, that she was in the presence of a crisis much older than college admissions.

Mr. Pfaff was making further decisions. "So I'll just cut that part, too, then," he said. "All the horse stuff." He held out a square paw for the page in her hand.

"Then we'll have not much left at all."

"How many words it have to be?"

"I'm not really thinking of word count."

"How many?"

"Five hundred limit."

"We're well under that. Is there a minimum?"

"Not technically, no, but it should be—something—"

"We've got plenty." Mr. Pfaff licked his lips, propped the page on one thigh, and drew lines through additional text.

"We really had that in pretty fine shape, I think," Anne said. She let him hear her sigh, let him see her check her watch. Ten more schools. Ten more schools that needed this application, and it was—what—ten at night now, and the family was leaving in the morning. And the essay had been months in the making, and Hunter, exhausted, seemed hung from his shoulders like a whipped dog. She thought of the elaborate display of Christmas lights across the boxwood hedge all along the front of the house—thousands of white fairy lights, and larger bulbs in the dogwood trees lining the lot. Of course they'd paid to have this done, not mounted ladders themselves, but why? The lights would shine all night long in front of an empty house while the family skied and didn't talk to each other out in Wyoming. You couldn't see any of it from the road. No one would even know. What role frivolity in the face of revisions like this?

"The essay was a strong one," she added, feeling braver.

He raised his eyebrows at her. "Well, obviously not."

"The essay did not keep him out."

"Sure as hell didn't get him in."

"Neither will this one. Trust me."

"Should I?"

"Up to you. But the word 'mediocrity'? Really, do you think that's the best way to approach this?"

Half Mr. Pfaff's face raised in a disbelieving smile. Had he used the word "chutzpah," he'd have been thinking it now. But his background supplied him with different terms, more like "floozy" and "gall." He turned to his son. "What think you, Christopher?"

Hunter raised his eyes, met his father's, and then looked away. They had broken him at last.

"Right," said his father. Gerald Pfaff turned back to Anne, triumphant. "So just give this the once-over, for the small stuff, and then you and Christopher here can type it up and be done with it." In a series of pulls and shoves, he raised himself from the chair and moved to the door. Before descending the stairs, he said one last thing: "And you'll see we're no longer applying to those mountain schools, the U Boulder whatever. We ski on vacation. He'll go east."

They listened to him lumber down a few stairs, waiting for something more.

"'Night, Dad," called Hunter. There was no reply.

DID "MEDIOCRITY" STAY? The word settled over Anne like a sort of moral, a key to her days that was as predictive as it was gloomy. She wore it while sitting in the chair by the fire at her parents' house Christmas Eve, beside her mother with a crossword puzzle and her father with his laptop. She hauled it back down to the city first thing the twenty-sixth, glad the holiday was behind her, watching her sparkleless fingers on the steering wheel as she drove the salted highways home. She'd left Martin's ring with her parents. She didn't yet have the heart to mail it back, but she didn't want it in her apartment either. Fondling the bright diamond over the kitchen sink, her mother had sighed and said, "Do you mind if I wear it out every now and then?"

For a week Anne lay about in her apartment, flipping through books that had once ignited her—all women, she noted glumly—Isak Dinesen and Adrienne Rich and Shirley Hazzard. She did not know, in the end, which essay Hunter submitted late the night of the twenty-third. When she'd left his house at midnight, she'd convinced him only that there were two choices, his essay or his father's, and that she could not choose for him. So she tidied up his father's scribble on the page, explained why she thought the admissions committees still might cotton more to mustangs than to mediocrity, and wished him safe travels. Hunter himself had been mute. She'd left him there, bent over his laptop on the floor, his wide shoulders crowding the useless keys, and concluded that the Common Application was a terrible bottleneck for all the energy and ambition of a young man, no matter how restless and spoiled he might be.

She'd asked him to drop her a line when the applications were submitted. That note was still forthcoming, but she wasn't surprised; Hunter was burned out. You couldn't blame him for not finding time for her administrative oversight.

She read there were tremendous snowstorms in Wyoming. Anne hoped at least the skiing was good. It was the sort of thing she discovered, idly clicking about online, which is what she was doing on New Year's Eve, just as the afternoon set in. Outside, the sidewalks were starting to crackle with high heels and the occasional illicit firework. Anne was in blue jeans and socks. She'd been invited to a party hosted by former grad school classmates, a couple who'd met as M.A. students and who were slogging through the Ph.D. together, mano a mano for the same funding dollars in their shared passion, nineteenth-century visual theory. She could already taste the boxed wine and watery hummus, could already see the low lights of Hyde Park out their porthole of a back window. Not sure what she would say when people asked what she was up to now, she'd sent her regrets. But casting about for phantom signs of Martin in the L.A. news was too solitary, even for her, so she leashed up Mitchell and set out to find some pizza.

Twice her phone rang, and twice she ignored it. It could have been Martin. But she had grown tired of hoping, and exhaustion had brought her closer to reason than careful thought ever had. Her kids were all taken care of. Her parents could wish her a Happy New Year in the morning. Her mother would only be rooting around to discover Anne's plans, anyway, and could be counted on to say something like, "You should be going to a big party."

But the third time it rang, in quick succession, she picked up.

"Anne, oh my God, thank God."

She recognized a breathless Marion Pfaff, on a crackly line from the mountains.

"Oh my God," she wailed. "They're not in. Hunter's applications are not in. Oh my God, they're due today, aren't they? Tonight?"

"Tomorrow . . ." interrupted Anne, feeling immediately ashamed but determined not to sound it. "Why on earth—"

"Oh my God," continued Mrs. Pfaff. "I just asked him, thinking, you know, of course they were done—I've been staying out of it all since, you know, Gerry stepped in—and today on the lift I just asked, because we were sitting there and I thought, 'How nice that all of that is behind him, he must be so relieved,' and he said, 'No, Mom, I haven't done it yet.' And I near about fell off that thing but I couldn't do anything and thank *God* Gerry was in the one behind us. I mean, he knows now but I think he might have pushed the kid right out of that seat."

"*None* of them are in?" asked Anne. "But they're all finished. They've been finished—all he has to do is hit submit. It's really nothing."

"The thing is, Anne, I don't even ski anymore, I really don't, I hate it. I get cold. But something told me, 'Today, Marion, you should go up.' And I wondered, was it that Hunter was going to get hurt? Was today the day he breaks a bone? But then when I asked him and he answered, I thought, that's it. Mothers always know, Anne. We always know."

"Okay. It's all saved on his Common Application. All he has to do is log in, and choose each school's application, and—"

"I mean, he wouldn't have gone to college next year! At all! Anywhere! Can you apply late? You can't, can you?"

"No, you can't. Is he there?"

"No no, they're still up on the mountain. But here's the problem, Anne, here's why I'm calling you. I came down to call you. I'm just standing here in the lodge now! Still in my boots and everything! The problem is, the finished essay—you know, the one he and Gerry pulled together—apparently that's on a piece of paper, not in the computer, is that right? And Hunter's got his laptop out here but not that. So he can't submit."

Anne was quiet. There seemed no solution. Not to the problem of the applications, but to the problem of stupidity. Gerry Pfaff wanted his essay, and Hunter had neglected to type it in. Of course he had. Clever boy. But what could she do now? Maybe the kid would finally get his way. His dad's essay was in Chicago! What was he to do? No way they could make it back in time.

"So what I need you to do," said Mrs. Pfaff, "is go to our home and dictate it."

"Uh—" Anne began, casting for an excuse. She didn't have one.

"I'll tell you how to get in, don't worry about that. Hunter said it should be upstairs, do you remember where? So listen. I told him I'd have you call his cell once you've got it in front of you. Then you can just read and he can type it in. Okay?"

"Now?"

Mrs. Pfaff sounded shocked. "Yes! Now! When else?"

Anne felt pitted against Hunter. On this side, a crowded and cowed only child, almost eighteen. And on this side, his insane parents, with their trusty sidekick, Anne. Off she goes now, to throw the last punch! The knockout blow! To dictate his father's essay into his ear so he can type it into his application as though his fingers doing so, rather than hers, or his father's, made it true.

"Anne?" pleaded Mrs. Pfaff. "We can't do this any other way. I'm sure you understand."

"Okay," Anne said. At least she could talk to Hunter, tell him again that he could submit whatever he wanted. Maybe he could take the bull by the horns here and just tell his father no. "Okay, fine. I'll call when I have it."

Anne hit the freeway. There was no one heading north out of the city, but the inbound lanes were choked. For a short while the gray expanse of asphalt was brightened by the feeling that she alone was escaping, with Mitchell, curious and patient, in the seat beside her. She exited at Willow Road and headed east toward the lake, deeper and deeper into the suburban shadows. There was the feeling of socking in. She saw no one. The sidewalks ran out, and tall hedges walled the road.

It was all as Mrs. Pfaff had said. The gate rolled open obediently when Anne punched in the code. The privacy of the driveway was broken only by the flight of a crow startled by a spray of gravel beneath Anne's tires. She counted four paving stones to the right of the front steps and located the gray rock that was not a rock. She slid out the key. The door wasn't even bolted. The way the knob turned, she figured a credit card or bobby pin would've done the trick.

She was grateful to Mitchell for following closely up the stairs, the first sweeping flight and then the second, smaller set, to the little study under the eaves. The vacant house was creepy. She thought of the gun cabinet in the hall. She imagined terrible things, in quick, fleeting glimpses, like flipping through a book of options for her own demise: surprised burglar, disgruntled ex-gardener, straight-up ax murderer. Enough light made it through the two dormer windows that she could spot the two pages of cruelly rewritten essay, Hunter's formatted paragraphs covered over in his father's hand like the work of some uptight, private-equity graffiti artist. Anne grabbed it and fled back down the stairs to the kitchen, which was still lit through the wall of French doors. She flipped out her phone and dialed Hunter.

Gerald Pfaff answered. "I hope this means you're there," he said, instead of Hello.

"In the kitchen, in fact," she said.

"Well, thank heavens. Good. Christopher's just in the hot tub. I'll have him ring you when he gets out."

"Sure." Though she didn't wish to spend one moment more in that house. She snapped her fingers to summon Mitchell, who was snuffling round Rommel's enormous bed.

"Lucky thing you were free," added Mr. Pfaff, the closest he could come to gratitude. "So typical of the kid to forget the most important bit." He eased his voice lower, as though in confession. "I keep thinking he'll outgrow it, but I fear it's just part of his makeup. Going to make for a tough life, I tell you."

"Oh, I think he'll do just fine," she said. She agreed, of course, that it might well be a tough life. Just for completely different reasons.

He heard her insincerity. "Ah, well," he said, resigned, as though there were nothing to be done about the boy. Amherst really must have been a cruel blow. Now the man was suffering a complete failure of imagination. He couldn't think there might be any other future for his son, or any value in traits other than servitude and solicitation. "Bye, now."

Anne heard him sign off and looked around his kitchen. The empty expanses of marble were as blank as an operating theater, washed in the flat light of the late afternoon. One framed photograph of Hunter as a little boy stood alone on the countertop. Over it the nest of bright copper pots hung low, like the autumnal foliage of a dying domesticity. It would have taken five children to make this a home, Anne thought, feeling the house sprawl around her. Or six or seven. She wished Hunter had had a sibling. Someone to help him face his father and laugh with him about his mother's frantic ministrations. In the picture he looked impossibly young, freckle-cheeked. He held up a toy boat to the photographer. The camera had caught him looking proud of something he loved.

She studied the two crumpled pages on the table. The light had faded further, but she was half afraid to get up and find switches. It was almost dark when from behind her came a loud click, followed by a reddish glow. She gasped and turned around. Mitchell trotted a few paces ahead of her into the hall, facing the vast living room. There they discovered the family Christmas tree looming, all lit up on its vacation timer. Anne approached through two sofa bays. The tree stood in a dry bowl, bronzing to its tips and covered with giant colored bulbs. Presumably so potential intruders would think the Pfaffs weren't out of town. The lights shone off the empty furniture, the lacquered wood picking up rich reflections of color, rainbows on the armoire.

Suddenly Anne was even more spooked, and she hurried with Mitchell back into the kitchen to find the overheads. The room came ablaze. She went to the fridge and opened it. There was a comforting clink. Many condiments in little glass jars, and a row of bottled beer. She took one. There was an opener right where she expected it in the utility drawer to the right of the sink. She selected a crystal goblet from the glass-fronted cabinet, which had its own internal lights. No Whirly Popper here, to be sure. Or Fun Size Snickers. Just easily forgotten bottles of Chimay ringing like jingle bells in the Sub-Zero's door. A stack of mail in a corner yielded nothing to read, so Anne pulled out some cookbooks and sat back down to wait. Mitchell settled in Rommel's memory-foam bed and let out a deep sigh.

She had almost finished a second beer—it was New Year's Eve, after all—when Hunter finally called. Her phone made her jump. The drinks, and the recipes, had caused her to forget that the house was probably bristling with escaped felons. Now she was shivery again, and she wanted to get the hell home.

"So hit me," he said.

Still sensing all the imagined violence around her, with a little bravado from the beer, Anne felt ready to fight. She'd never lived in a house like this, thank God, and she never would. But she needed to make something happen. It was not like her little apartment was going to work forever. Her little life.

She stared at his essay and said, "Hunter, I can't find it."

"What?"

"It's not here. I've looked." Her words were slow and clear, demonstrative, a tipping of the hand.

After a moment he said, "Oh."

"Must've got lost in transit. Maybe at the airport. Didn't you work on it there?"

"Oh, yeah, that's right," he said. "I did."

"I guess you'll just have to apply with what you've got."

"Yeah."

In the background she heard his father beginning to grow concerned.

"Dad, it's not there," said Hunter.

"Tell him I've looked everywhere. Tell him I'm so sorry."

She heard Mr. Pfaff yelling. "Tell her to rewrite it, then! Here, give me the phone."

He crowded the line. "That's impossible! We've just got to have that!"

Anne sipped her beer. His beer. The glass was almost empty, but the crystal was so wonderfully heavy it was as though it were full. She set it down gently as an egg and reminded Mr. Pfaff, "Or he could just submit his applications now with the essay we had polished. It's quite strong."

"The one about compasses and ponies?" She could hear the spit cracking between his teeth.

"Well, I don't know what to say, then. I'm so sorry. I have to get back to the city, I'm afraid."

"This is your *job,*" he said.

"I've done my job, Mr. Pfaff. And Hunter has done his."

"The hell he has. Those applications are not complete."

"I think they are. I have to get back to the city now, Mr. Pfaff. Could I talk to Hunter again?"

"I think you've had quite enough to do with my son," he answered her, and hung up. In retaliation, she switched off her phone.

She stayed long enough to wash and dry the crystal and replace it on the shelf. The ruined essay pages she folded into a tight square and tucked in her jeans. Empty bottles clinking in one fist, she flipped off the lights and found her way to the door by the jangling glow of the gasping Christmas tree.

Parking was a complete bitch. Had she thought about it, she might have said no altogether to Mrs. Pfaff's ridiculous request.

Still it was sort of fun to have passed the time up there, and now another terrible New Year's Eve was in full swing, which meant it was almost over. It was a freezing half mile home from the parallel spot she finally found. Perfect, though: Mitchell would be sorted for the night. She had popcorn to whirl and she was already two beers in. She thought she'd tape Gideon Pfaff's essay to the front of her refrigerator, just for fun.

In the same spirit of defiance she took the main stairs with Mitchell and his manky paws. It was a shame April was nowhere to be found.

But as she climbed, the thrill of her mini-revolution faded and she realized that she was taking a risk on behalf of Hunter, which wasn't fair. It was one thing to challenge his father's imperiousness, but another if doing so put college in the balance. There was a decent chance the kid wouldn't pull it together and get his applications in. He might be flummoxed by her lie and just pleased enough by her collusion to sink himself. She'd best get inside and call him.

She reached the landing only to find William Kantor sitting there, by her door.

"Sorry, I tried to call," he said. He held up a bottle of wine with a ribbon tied at its neck. "This is for you."

"You brought me wine?"

He stood. "I can't buy wine. Someone just left it here. Can I come in?"

"Um, sure?" She was not at all sure. She did not invite students to her apartment. Too small, too intimate, too inappropriate. "What time is it?" she asked, just to make the point.

"Nine-something."

He was very close behind her, like a small child. She unbolted her door and flipped on a light. William surveyed her space. She regretted the open bathroom door and the clutter of lotions on her counter. Books piled on her coffee table and on the floor. A tuft of dog hair scooted along the baseboard. She closed the door to stop the draft.

"Nice place," he said. "Cozy."

"That's one word."

"A great block, though."

"Yeah, that's why. My parents thought it would be safe."

"My parents would think the same way."

"Do they know you're here?" She took off her coat and gestured to the love seat, hoping he'd sit—he'd be more manageable if he weren't standing there, surveying.

"They know I'm out. Who's the wine from? Mr. Waverly?"

It hadn't occurred to her, and for a moment she thrilled to the possibility. She read the tag: *Happy New Year! from the Baldwins, 1B*. Complete with a picture. Very kind.

"No," she said, and left it at that. She suspected that whatever had driven William to her apartment, she still needed to be Martin Waverly's other half to earn the boy's revelation. And their breakup was none of his business, besides. "When's your curfew?"

"Not really an issue."

"You don't have one? Special night?"

"Right." He peered into the kitchen, a dark galley between the front room and the back door, which led to the fire escape and the yellowed alley beyond. She half thought he expected someone else to be there.

"William, what's up? Did something happen? Some admissions thing?"

"Just out walking," he lied, wandering now to her bookcase. He passed his thumb along the spines. She'd have rather he fingered the dresses in her closet—those, she wore and put away. The books were unfinished business. The ones she'd read even more than the ones from her orals lists, still shrink-wrapped from the press. The ones she'd adored, most of all.

She was distracted by how thin William was—his pants belted so tightly at the waist they puckered all along his back and hung from there with no interference clear to his shoes, which, Anne was surprised to note, were sneakers. Very hip, suede sneakers, but still sneakers.

"That why you put on your sneaks?" she asked.

He turned to her, and then down to his feet. He shook his head no. But when he returned his eyes to her, they were wider than before and seemed uncertain at the far corners, as though his words were gathering there rather than in his throat, and just as it occurred to her that he might cry, she said gently, "William, what's going on?"

He opened his mouth. The phone rang, sharply, her landline. William looked away. "No, go ahead," he told her, raising a loose hand to her desk.

"Oh, thank heavens," she said out loud, relieved that the Pfaffs would be calling so she could at least sort out Hunter's little gamble. The person on the other end of the line heard this rather than hello, and was confused. Also ticked off.

"I'm sorry, hello? Is this Anne? I need to speak with Anne. It's Margaret Blanchard."

Anne was surprised to realize that she was not terribly surprised.

"Speaking."

She waved a deliberate hand at William to suggest he sit, making a point of gritting her teeth and baring them: it might be a while.

"Gosh, am I sorry to have to make this call twice," said Margaret Blanchard, sounding not at all sorry. In fact, she sounded very much the way Mitchell looked when he spotted a cat: muscled and keen, his most primal self. "Anne," she said again, drawing out the consonant. "Anne." She paused once more before continuing: "I've just read Sadie's essay, the one I assume you're all ready to send in tomorrow, or tonight, who knows, and I have some very deep concerns about some of the things that are said in it. Very. Deep."

"Okay," said Anne carefully. "And you've only just seen it? Just now?"

"Sorry, dear," she answered coldly. "I have a rather full docket, as you may imagine, if you can imagine that, and I haven't had a chance until now. But here I am, now, on New Year's Eve, and I've had to send Gideon on to our party alone while I address this."

"I'm sorry," said Anne, about the party. "What's the problem?"

"First of all, I have to say that I hardly think it's Sadie's best work. Gid and I have seen her pieces from creative writing class, and she is much more talented than this. I really think you've not helped her to reach her potential at all."

Because she always asked to read several examples of a student's work, Anne had seen those very same pieces, and so she knew that Sadie's final essay for Duke was by far the most coherent, sophisticated, thoughtful bit of prose she had produced. And of course she had tuned her ear to the sound of Sadie's voice at its most fluent, so she could best recognize the ideas that came from her heart and help her to develop those. She knew what made Sadie most proud, and what had made other people make her think she should be proud. But the question of achievement wasn't Margaret Blanchard's point, and in any case they both knew it to be irrelevant in the case of Duke admissions, so Anne waited.

"More than that, though—which is of course the point of hiring you at all—is this other thing, which is that the essay has this crazy bit about both parents working, when there's no place for that in a college application. It makes Sadie sound spoiled. Most mothers do work, you know. I don't know if yours ever did but most do, and it's just not like Sadie to go on about it. It makes her sound truly very naive and that's not the case at all."

"Sadie thought it relevant that she spent a good deal of time alone as a child. This helped to form her character, her independence. That's not a bad thing to say, I don't think."

"Well, but it's simply not true. I mean, she goes on like . . . like she's Cinderella or something, you know, and that's just embarrassingly off.

The whole thing is just—I don't know how it got so wrong, but this is not our daughter's work. So it will be redone."

There was a moment when Anne might have responded in kind. She might have told Margaret Blanchard that, in fact, her husband had not wanted the essay to be his daughter's work at all; that he had already concluded that her work would be insufficient for his reputational needs. And he'd taken Anne to a really nice lunch to make this request, and then high-stepped his way back into some silly formality as though he'd never tried to offer her a job or career counseling or whatever it was he'd dangled before her. But William Kantor by now had settled on the floor beside Mitchell and was rubbing the dog's ruff. Anne wanted to return to him. Some feeling of guilt was nudging her, and it seemed the longer he stayed in her apartment, the more on the hook she'd be. "Could you read the sentences that trouble you?" she asked Margaret Blanchard. "Perhaps we can address those directly."

"Oh, I don't have it," said Mrs. Blanchard wearily, not to be bothered. "It's, you know, the stuff about both of her parents working long hours and being left to brush her teeth alone, all of which is nonsense that must have been put there by someone else, I'm not sure who."

"Those sentences are pretty much intact from her first draft," said Anne, in self-defense.

"Well, that's hard to believe."

"Believe it."

There was a pause.

"In any case," continued Mrs. Blanchard, "it makes her sound terribly privileged to suggest that all kids don't have two working parents. I mean, to even *have* two parents is lucky. That's just not a healthy view of the world. And it goes without saying, I should mention, that Gideon is appalled." She paused again, this time so Anne could do the math on the impact of Gideon's emotional state. She got it, loud and clear: one Cristina Castello, still in limbo. The stakes thus presented, Margaret Blanchard wrapped up: "Look, I'm sending her over now, I've given her money for cabs both ways, please see to it that she's safely back when it's been fixed. She's skipping the party, too, I might add. This really must end now. Really."

Not until Margaret Blanchard had hung up did Anne realize the power she now had over this woman, who had called, quite simply, to protest the truth in her daughter's college essay. And not a terribly unkind truth either. The woman was a workaholic, so was her husband, and their two children had been raised by a loving Guatemalan immigrant who saw her own babies only in the nights and on Sundays because that was what it took. And so what? Would this so surprise the Duke admissions office, and especially old what's-his-name from Choate? But the 489-word looking glass was not what Ms. Blanchard had intended to *call down,* and she hadn't thought to think that everyone else could see plain as day, too. So now she was sending Sadie over to have it fixed. On the night before it was due. As though they might rewrite her parenting choices, have her home rocking her baby girl. Reading to her, Anne thought cruelly.

"So, I have another student coming over," she told William.

His eyebrows went up. The usual, slightly insouciant slack had returned to his eyes. "Boy or girl?"

"Girl."

"Pity. Latin or Parker?"

"Latin."

"Of course. Do I know her?"

"Don't know. Probably."

"Name?"

"Sadie Blanchard."

"Hmm!" he said, sitting up taller. "I don't know her. Everyone knows *of* her, of course, but I've never met her. Supposed to be nice. Has that mother, is that who . . . ?"

Anne nodded.

"Oh gosh. You must get a lot of that."

"I do. Though yours has been very mellow on that score."

"Yes, it's not really her thing. More Dad's."

Anne looked around quickly and didn't wish to have Sadie show up to find another student, a boy, however homosexual he might be, sprawled on her floor nearing ten at night on New Year's Eve. She ran about switching on lights and poured some glasses of water to set on her table, as though they'd been working there. She fetched a pen and took some paper out of her printer. "I'm going to have to do some work with Sadie," she explained, "so we should sort out whatever it is you've got going on. Deadline tomorrow."

"It's okay," he replied. "I should get going."

Anne shrugged. "Whatever you want. I'm happy to talk, just maybe not right now? I don't want to be rude—"

The buzzer sounded.

"That'll be Sadie," she said. She gathered up William's coat. Then something occurred to her. "How did you get in?" she asked him. "Was the door propped open?"

"Some weird woman was coming in. I followed her. I think she went upstairs."

"Big hair, lots of perfume?"

"Yeah."

"Ugh, that's April. She does live upstairs." Over the intercom, Sadie sounded exasperated.

"She wasn't very nice," continued William. "Looked at me like I might be a mugger or something."

Anne opened her door and lowered her voice. "I know, she's terrible. She steals my newspaper every morning, can you believe it? Like she even reads. My *New York Times*."

Sadie was wrestling with the vestibule door. William fixed his eyes on Anne. "No, she doesn't," he said. "I do."

"Wait, what? Why?"

William shrugged, then smiled. "It's not cool, I know. I'm sorry. I walk by here mornings, on the way to school. I grab coffee then a taxi out on Clark. Used to see you with him"— he gestured to Mitchell— "and one day you turned in here, and I kind of followed you, but most mornings you weren't around, and the paper was there . . . But I didn't know it was yours! My dad swears it's propaganda, you know. The worst of the worst. Israel, liberals, they get it all wrong. So I just wondered. And then I just, I don't know, I liked the way it unfolded into your hands like these *slabs* of life—you have the news, the sports, the arts, they slide out of each other like everything is just there for you to have, like you might as well be in New York City that morning. I'm sorry. It's really not right, I know. I think if I'd known it was yours—anyway. I'm glad I told you." Sadie crested the landing. "Hi," he said.

Anne turned. Sadie was there, glossy lips and glossy hair, belted coat, flats so encrusted with crystals she looked like she'd been wading in geodes. "So much for going out," she said dispiritedly. "Can we just do this quickly? Who's he?"

Anne was thinking furiously. One dollar. "One dollar," she said out loud to William. "Everywhere, even at Starbucks, I think. Sadie, this is William Kantor, another student of mine. William, Sadie. He was just on his way out."

"I know, but it's not the same as nabbing it, sorry," he answered her, shaking Sadie's hand. They did this, these seventeen-year-olds, meeting like miniature versions of their parents. "Nice to meet you," he said.

"Where're you applying?" Sadie asked him.

"Well, that's just the problem, actually," he answered her.

Sadie studied him. "Ohhhh," she said. "You should stay!"

She dropped her overcoat and stepped into the room in a black dress, looking little and clipped, like a paper doll. William drew back into the apartment behind her. For a moment Anne was embarrassed to be caught so obviously without plans, but there was excitement enough here that neither teenager seemed to notice.

"So what're you deciding between?" Sadie asking him, scanning the room.

"Long story," he told her. "How about you?"

"Duke, Middlebury, Yale, Richmond, Georgetown, Tufts, UVA,

and Hamilton. But that's all settled. It's just that my parents just read my essay and they hate it."

"It's a little more complicated than that," Anne told her.

"No, it's not. I said some really stupid things."

Again, thought Anne. Like a goddamn compass needle, Sadie twirled back to her mother's side whenever an argument arose. Margaret Blanchard told her how to feel about what she'd written, and she agreed.

"Well, I disagree," Anne said, with as much reserve as she could. "But what matters is that you feel confident about your essay, so we'll work on it."

William dropped down opposite Sadie in Anne's chair and kicked his feet onto the blanket chest that served as a table. Sadie had crossed one skinny leg over the other and then hooked her fancy shoe around again behind her calf, as though to ensure she took up as little space in the room as possible. She flexed her hands and folded them in her lap. She was tiny and commanding. Her wealth calmed him: he knew these girls. And her problem, naturally, interested him. "So what's wrong with your essay?" he asked.

She sighed. "I don't have a good handle on my priorities," she answered, sounding notes of recitation on "handle" and "priorities." "What's wrong with yours?"

He smiled at the floor. "Hard to say, really. Or not, I guess. I wrote about being gay, and my dad saw it, and he kicked me out. So that's sort of it."

Sadie gasped. "Holy shit."

"Oh God," Anne said quietly. "William. What happened?"

He looked up to where she was standing, by the boarded-up mantel of a fireplace that had been filled in for decades. There was no room for her to sit, with these two on either side. "My college counselor told Mum how great she thought the essay was, didn't know that about my family blah blah, and Mum asked for a copy and I guess he just saw it tonight."

"And he kicked you out?" asked Sadie. "What does that even mean?" She was bolt upright now, two dazzling feet on the floor, her lower jaw thrust forward in an unconscious imitation of her mother's most unfortunate feature.

"He told me I was betraying my ancestors. He told me that nothing in his upbringing prepared him for a son like me. Then he told me to get out."

"Just, like, leave?"

"Yep."

"And go where?"

"I don't think he really cares."

Silently cursing his school counselor, Anne asked, "William, did she not understand . . . ?"

But he thought she'd meant his mother. "Mum's not like that. I mean, she doesn't care so much about . . . But with Dad, there was nothing she could do."

"What *did* she do?" asked Sadie. She was hanging on his words, this real-life crisis of her own kind, in her own city.

"Told me to drop the whole Vassar thing," he explained, looking up at Anne, to whom this would make sense. "Just pretend it didn't happen. She gave me some cash. Maybe for a hotel."

"God, my mom did that tonight, too," said Sadie.

"Oy, you, too? Why?"

"No no, I mean, just for taxis. You just reminded me. Anyway, sorry." She shook her head. "I thought Vassar was all girls."

He snickered. "Right now I wish it was."

"Wow," she said, sitting back. "I thought *I* was frustrated."

"William, I am so sorry," interjected Anne.

He was too kind to blame her, but he did give himself the luxury of ignoring her apology. He got up and walked to Anne's kitchen.

"Got anything to drink?" he called back, over his shoulder. There was a miserable lilt in his voice. Anne let him have the moment to blink away his tears.

"Not much," she said. "You could look—"

Then William stuck his hand around the kitchen door, Old Nassau dangling. "What the hell is this?"

"It's a fish," Anne replied. Sadie swiveled. "Please put him back."

He held it up to the lights. "Are you going to eat it?"

"No."

"Then why is it in your freezer?"

Sadie crossed the room to where William was standing, the bag up over his head. She rubbed frost off the outside and peered in. "Wow. Cool. And kind of gross."

"It's a long story," said Anne. "Please put it back."

She heard William rummaging.

"When my dad has cocktail parties," Sadie informed them, "he has the caterers put little sprigs of herbs in the ice."

"Can I have a Diet Coke?" called William.

"Of course."

"Do you have any ice without things in it?"

Anne didn't answer this. "Can I ask you guys something? If you were me, and one of your students had all of his applications complete but was just not able to get them in, what would you do?"

"What do you mean 'not able'?" asked William.

"Not willing."

Sadie asked, "You mean they're all finished, spell-checked, whatever, but he won't submit?"

"Right."

"Let him," she said.

"Easy," added William.

"Even though it means he won't have anywhere to go to college next year? Even though it means his parents might sue me?"

She didn't really believe this second part, but it was a remote possibility. Perhaps Gideon Blanchard would take the case.

Sadie replied, "Yeah. Totally. You can't submit for him. Isn't that illegal or something, anyway?"

"I mean, if it weren't, my dad would have applied to Penn, like, last year," said William.

"Oh my God, my parents at birth," added Sadie.

"But what if we're taking the long view on his behalf?" Anne pressed. "Should I really let a momentary act of defiance cost him the beginning of college?"

She wasn't sure if these two were the best or the worst people to ask.

"You're a tutor, not a truancy officer," announced William, emerging from the kitchen with two glasses. He extended one to Sadie. "So, anyway," he asked her, "what's your thing?"

"Thanks," said Sadie. She stirred her drink with a finger and decided to take the confessional line. It was rapidly proving that sort of night. "So, my dad's a trustee at Duke. So I'm totally supposed to go there. Which is fine. But he's, like, obsessed with my essay, and my mom's kind of even worse, because it matters to them that all their friends are going to see it. Like, everyone's been waiting for me to apply, and now here I am, so what am I going to say, you know? And I wrote some stuff that I thought made sense at the time but really I was just tired and kind of annoyed with them over this silly thing, so now it's the night before it's due and I have to rewrite it and I'm just fried. Plus it's New Year's Eve and that sucks."

"What kind of stuff did you write?"

Sadie produced a wad of paper. "Well, here."

William reached across, unfolded the page against his knee, and began to read: " 'When T.S. Eliot wrote, "April is the cruelest month," we can be sure he was not thinking of college admissions.' " He paused to smile. " 'But for today's eighteen-year-old, it's hard to read that line of his poem and think about anything else.' That's funny. What's wrong with that?"

"No, not that part. It's a ways down—stuff about my parents."

He scanned the page. "Oh, here," he said. " 'This is a lesson my parents reinforced by choosing to have major careers even though that means not a lot of time with my brother and me. When you come home from school, do your homework alone, and put yourself to bed every night, you learn to be self-sufficient from a young age.' "

Sadie cringed. "Yeah, that's it."

"So what's wrong with that?"

"It makes me sound spoiled."

"I don't think so. It's just a statement."

"Yes, but there's the—you know, the idea that it was one way when it should have been the other way. Like, that they should have been home with me every night. And that's silly."

"Why?"

" 'Cause it's, like, bragging, but in a reverse way. You know? Like I'm making up a problem when in reality I didn't have any problems at all."

William took his feet off the bench and leaned forward. He was frustrated. "Couldn't it be just part of what makes you *you*?"

"It's not like being gay," she told him, not unkindly.

"What *is* like being gay?"

"I don't know," she said. "Being black? You know, something that totally sets you out, and that you have to deal with in society."

"Never thought of that," said William.

"Well, I don't have any of that stuff," mused Sadie. "I'm white, we have money, my parents are together, I had a full-time nanny, everything."

"Christian, too, I bet."

"Presbyterian."

"Of course."

How these kids navigated the high-tension wires of class and code that ran between them, the ones they were supposed to pretend weren't even there! *Latin or Parker?* William had asked. There were two schools in their town. There were twenty colleges to which they might apply. But there were even fewer lives they might imagine for themselves. Twenty-five years ago, one generation, a girl like Sadie Blanchard probably wouldn't have gone to college at all, education not figuring in her birthright. And a boy like William Kantor probably wouldn't have come out—certainly not in high school, and possibly not ever. College rocked the boat. It forced the issue. And how? By inviting teenagers to write about themselves? Five hundred words, give or take, where their insecurities and their learned sense of propriety ran smack up against their hormones and their hopes—a dangerous exercise, indeed.

Maybe, Anne concluded, college was best thought of as four years in which adolescents might learn to use the pronoun "I" and mean it.

"So what are you going to do?" Sadie asked William.

"I don't know," he answered. "I'll figure something out."

"So you don't know where you're going?"

"Well, I want one thing, my dad wants another, who knows where I'll get in. Maybe I'll pull my application to Vassar. Too much trouble. Maybe I'll just wait and see."

"Oh. I meant tonight. Where are you going tonight. But 'wait and see'? What do you mean?"

"What choice do I have?"

"Well," she said, "I'm sure they only want what's best for you. I'm sure your dad is just worried that you won't be happy, being gay. Or maybe, I don't know, maybe they're worried about gossip? About it, you know, being messy?"

"My dad left his first wife when my mom was still his secretary, so no, I don't think messy bothers him all that much."

Sadie nodded gravely. Anne watched them both: their composure, their careful compassion for each other. She pressed her back into her mantel, empty except for her grandmother's silver candlesticks, which she polished twice a year, though she'd never got around to buying tapers. Her mother had said she might as well take them back if they weren't going to be used. For the hundredth time that year, Anne felt the fool. She had nothing to offer these epiphyte children, these trained climbers, who were expected to need no grounding at all.

"Anyway, I still don't see the big deal with your essay," said William. "I was here when your mom called. She was, like, yelling. Why does she care? You're not supposed to have any problems because you've been given a lot?"

"My parents aren't like that," Sadie said. She lowered her voice to soften what came next. "I mean, sorry, but they didn't throw me out for being gay."

"Try them."

"No, no. They'd be cool. I have a gay uncle."

"Mmm." William smirked, folded her essay back into its tiny scrunch, and tossed it back. "So anyway, if Dad's a trustee, it probably doesn't matter what you write in your essay anyway. Couldn't you, like, write, 'I want to go to Duke' in blue crayon and be done with it?"

This hurt Sadie, as he had intended. She shifted on Anne's little love seat and wrapped her arms around her sides. William may have been homeless, but Sadie was trapped. She simply couldn't imagine anything other than what had been handed to her. "Last summer I wrote an essay about my community service and volunteer work and I really liked that," she said, by her tone returning them to a more formal place. "I think I'm going to just send that in." She looked up at Anne. "The star essay."

"Star?" asked William.

"Yeah, a geometric star," she said, showing off a bit. "I used the five points as a metaphor, to explain my ideas."

"Sounds terrific," said William. It occurred to Anne that he was beginning to understand—Duke was as high, higher even than Sadie could reach; to encourage her to think for herself would cost her four years at a top university. Why not open the door when she had the key?

William said, generously, "But you must be excited about Duke, though, anyway, right? How great to be able to go there!"

"Not really," Sadie admitted. "I don't really want to go."

"Then why are you applying?"

"Because it's the best place for me."

She wasn't wrong. Not that there wouldn't have been a better fit for her college years—but that the Sadie who could have pursued that school was not the Sadie sitting there before them. She'd never gotten out of the gate, that one.

"So hang on," William said. "You're over here because your parents are making you rewrite an essay you liked to apply to a college you don't even want to go to?"

"That's not really fair." Sadie was looking out Anne's window, but it was backed in city grime and at night there was nothing to see.

"I agree."

"No, I mean, to them. You're not being fair to my parents. They are—well, let me tell you. My father is a lawyer. Big-time. He spends every day fighting in the courts for people who are wronged by bigger people. People who are hurt by doctors or hospitals or big companies. It's his passion, to help people find truth and justice. My mom, she's like this guru for women all over the world. She's on the TV and radio and all over the place. She helps women who are stuck in their lives. My parents have helped so many people. And I'm only seventeen. They know what's best for me."

William was nodding. Finally he said, "So what you feel is wrong. About Duke, at least."

"Well, yeah."

"Wow. I'm so sorry."

"Why?" she asked. "I'm so lucky!"

Anne watched him give up. He studied Sadie, his mouth slightly open, his manicured hands quiet in his lap.

"So anyway, I'm off," she said, and got up. She retrieved her coat from Anne's table and buttoned herself in. "I'll just submit the star essay, okay?" She turned to William. "And I'm really sorry about what you're having to deal with; that really sucks. Maybe you can, like, come stay at my place if you have nowhere else to go. I could ask my mom."

William stood behind her. "No, thanks," he said.

"You sure? We have a guest floor. And you could just be yourself, no need to pretend not to be gay. Anyway, if you change your mind—"

"I didn't pretend," said William. "That's the problem."

"Whatever," Sadie said. "I offered." She unbolted Anne's door. William's questioning had unsettled her, and she was finished thinking now. Flustered, Anne reached to open the door for her, feeling she'd failed again. Mitchell scrambled to his feet. William sprang up as though he'd had another thought, but she cut him off before he could speak.

"My parents are really great," Sadie declared and stepped out into the hall. Then, buckling tight her coat round her tiny waist, she looked up to see what Anne and William had already seen—William had grabbed Anne's arm on the door, and both for a moment stopped breathing—a commotion against the far wall: a tall man wrapped like a spider around a small, wriggling woman with big hair and big heels, Gideon Blanchard in his three-piece suit bundling April Penze's coat in one hand and her purple-skirted ass cheek in the other, grabbing and rummaging, his big hands all over her hair and perfume and her little moans all over the rotten landing.

"Oh my God," said Sadie, and then again she yelled, "Oh my God!"

Looking over the frosted curls, Gideon spotted his daughter and shoved April forcibly to one side to reach for her, but she was already dropping down, taking the steps three at a time in her little jeweled flats. "Sweetheart, sweetheart," he hollered, tearing down after her. April scrambled up and they heard her door slam, then the front door wheezed and Gideon was bellowing on the sidewalk, "Goddammit. Fuck. Darling, wait!"

Mitchell let out one late, excited bark. For a moment William and Anne stood there. She replayed what she'd seen, trying to think. In surprise and shame, they almost smiled. Then William turned to Anne with frightened eyes when they heard the door slam open again, and heavy feet climbing back up—together they were stepping back, crazily but instinctively not wanting to face Blanchard's rage, his lying, caught-out pace pounding the carpet as though he might salvage something by coming back for them.

"Shit," whispered William.

The pounding turned the corner. It was not Gideon Blanchard. It was Martin Waverly, looking puzzled and keen, extending a bouquet of daisies in airport cellophane.

"Annie?" he asked.

JANUARY

ANNE COULD TELL by the sound of the city against the glass that the snow was beginning to stick. The wind shifted to the north and east, drawing a muffle over the streets and the *grind-swish* of spinning tires. In the direction of the lake the sky was pink. It was not yet 7 A.M.

Inside, carnage: Martin slumbering across her bed, windmilled from corner to corner; in the front room, William, tucked beneath her mother's cashmere throw, his color-block socks extending on her love seat's arm; and on the floor, Mitchell, upside down, one big brown eye on her as she moved from her desk to the window and back again. Pacing like an inmate, penned in by sleeping boy-men.

She'd been able to convince Martin not to put William out in the dark, saying it wasn't safe, but that was more to postpone being alone with him than it was to protect a perfectly competent city kid. Martin had permitted himself to be entertained by the story they'd told, of the exposure of Gideon Blanchard, William's expulsion from his Lake Shore Drive bedroom, and even the newly solved thieving concern. But he would not tolerate William's presence much longer. He'd kick him out, and then she would have to face this thing. All night she'd lain there, sleepless, frostier than Old Nassau. Finally she got up and tiptoed to her desk, feeling the weight of the jilted everywhere. She tapped out a text to Sadie.

DON'T WANT TO CALL AND WAKE YOU. I HOPE YOU ARE DOING OKAY. CALL IF YOU WANT. ANNE

When there was no reply, Anne felt helpless. She studied the back of William's head. Quite a haircut, a million different lengths still immaculately indexed at his temples. She wished he'd wake up. Should she wake him up?

I've been hiding behind these kids for years, she thought, and now I am literally, actually taking cover behind the presence of a student. In my apartment. On New Year's Day.

For the first time in a long time, Anne knew what to do. She had been delivered, as if by the stroke of midnight, into cold certainty. In fact it was the stroke of Gideon Blanchard that had delivered her: the sight of his hand working April Penze's tush, like some cartoon of desire. What she'd seen wasn't lust; it was avarice. It was entitled. She recognized it because it reminded her of Martin. Then he had bounded up the stairs a few moments later and confirmed her impression.

She sat in the dawn, heavy with the ache that accompanies serious fear of change. She felt her body in space so acutely she could sense time pulsing past, like a fish suddenly made aware of the current. Anne figured she'd probably be single forever. She sighed to think of all the weddings as a plus-one. She'd have to freeze her eggs. When did one do that? she wondered. Thirty-five? What did it cost? But it didn't matter: she was already six weeks into this heartbreak, and the clump of daisies in a glass on her desk was not going to turn her back. Life was saying—it was unmistakable—*Go now.*

There was just one thing she needed to know. One reason she didn't just boot William, leash up the dog, and evacuate. After the revelation about Lynn, after so much dead time, what was it that drove Martin to fly unannounced across the country to reclaim her hand? What was he *thinking,* as he buckled in and felt the wheels leave the ground? "Lynn's no more," Martin had said. "She understands." As though Lynn were the one who deserved reasons. What blind bull heart beat in these men and made them think they could have anything they wanted?

Because she needed a little bit of that.

The boys snored. Anne's phone hopped.

CHECK UR EMAIL

She popped open her laptop and set it aglow. Sadie's e-mail read, in its entirety:

MY FINAL ESSAY THAT I SUBMITTED, xoxo.

And an attachment. Anne swallowed a whoop of triumph. Sadie had actually gone home and pulled something together and sent it in. It was remarkable; it made Anne love her fiercely. So there was hope for Cristina; and renewed hope for Sadie, too. Anne clicked to open the essay, and just then Martin emerged from her bedroom, in his underwear.

"Up and at 'em, Sebastian Flyte." With his toes he poked at William's side. "Let's move!"

William startled.

Anne closed her computer and glared. "Martin, quiet," she hissed.

He raised his voice. "Now."

"Okay, okay," grumbled William. He began to gather himself and sat up. He raised his arms overhead in a long, childlike stretch, yawning out loud. Martin sent out a fist to the boy's solar plexus, just enough to make him *huff* and roll up again into his arms.

"What the fuck?" said Anne. "Martin?"

"Just messing around," he told her. "Guy to guy. Let's go, kiddo."

"I'm going."

"Hang on, I'll walk you home," Anne said.

"No, you won't," said Martin.

"I'm fine," William told her. He hurried into his shoes and jacket.

"Mitch needs to go out anyway," Anne told Martin. "I will walk him home."

William stood by the door, scarf tight around his neck. "No. I'm good." He looked at Martin. "You're an asshole." Then he waved to Anne and left.

"Bye," said Anne, despondent.

"Good luck," Martin called after him. "Hands off the goddamn paper."

They heard the downstairs doors slam.

Martin sank back on her sofa, patting the seat beside him. "Finally."

"You've got to be kidding me," Anne said.

"Oh, honey." Martin's voice was calm, his demeanor mild. He smiled up at her. He was earnest and composed and quietly inviting. Martin Waverly, in his groove. As though Lynn and their broken engagement and the surprise flight from L.A. and the night with a teenager on her sofa were all just temporary blips on the radar screen, and it was clear sailing now. For so long, Anne had mistaken this apathy for perspective. How young she'd been, to give him that! What she saw now was simple and essential, like an element, like salt: Martin Waverly wasn't sophisticated. He was selfish.

"You are an asshole," Anne said. "He's right."

"Jesus, Anne," Martin said. "Let's not let the kid come between us."

"The kid? The kid come between us?"

"Annie." He stood up and approached her, set his hands on her hips. It had always been her favorite move and he knew it. Now she felt pinned, like a bug.

"Off," she said, and began to dress. She raked a brush through her hair, scrolled it into a loose knot, pulled on a sweater and thick tights. As she moved she realized that all she needed to do was walk out and this would end.

"Annie," Martin repeated. He bent to scratch Mitchell's neck, trying to lure her to his side. "Just tell me, what is it you need me to say? What do you need to hear? 'Cause I'm here. I know you're mad. I know I fucked up. But I went back to L.A., I dealt with it, it's over. I want you. I want you to move with me. I want to marry you. It's a new year. Let's go. What is it you need me to say?"

She stomped into her boots and paused. Outside, car tires whirred and whined in the snow. "I want you to tell me this," she said. "When—"

"I didn't love her."

She waved him off. "No, not that. Listen. I want you to explain this: when you're a stage actor, and you decide you're going to just get into TV and film, so you up and leave Chicago to head out to L.A., and you land there and go pick up your bag at luggage claim and head out to the curb and there's the city and there you are, starting again, and everything's new—when you do that, what is it you're feeling? What is it you're thinking?"

He frowned at her. Confusion made him angry. He may have been an intellectual, but he had never been curious.

"I don't know," he replied. "I guess I think, here's this thing I really want to do, and I'd be as good or better at it than all the people doing it already, so I just start knocking on doors."

"But you don't have TV training, you don't have movie experience, you don't have a degree . . ."

He loved being reminded of these things. His head bounced up and down in agreement. Then he said, "Smoke and mirrors, baby. Give them what they want. Who cares if it's true or not?"

He gave her his flippest grin, a tall salesman in his underwear.

"I see," Anne said. "And this person Lynn?"

He sobered up his face and nodded.

"What were you thinking then?"

"You know, sweetheart," he told her, wincing a bit, "monogamy is just not my strong suit. Never has been. But I promise you, with you, it's different. It will be different. Already is. I've never—"

Anne leashed up Mitchell and pulled on her gloves.

"Right," she interrupted. "That's helpful. Listen. I'm going to walk the dog. We'll head to the lake and back. That means you have about half an hour to pack up. When I get back, you'll be gone."

"What are you talking about?"

"I want you out."

"What?"

"Half an hour."

On his features, confusion turned to chaos. His jaw dropped and drew down his eyes and cheeks. He was almost crying, or trying to cry, or something—Anne wasn't sure—no feeling she could name passed over his face save an almost juvenile, helpless frustration. For an instant her heart lurched, and she felt a blast of panic—What am I doing?—and then, calmly, she remembered. Five years of bobbing and leaning and pining. The sucker punch to a sad teenage boy. Someone called Lynn. *Strong suit?* "Bye-bye," she told him.

She opened her door and led Mitchell to the hall.

And to turn the knife, she added, "You ought to say good-bye to Mitch, too. He liked you. You'll never see him again."

Now Martin really did weep. "Of course," he said. "Of course." He came to her side and dropped to his knees, pulling the dog awkwardly to his chest. Mitchell, pulled off balance, tapped on his feet to steady himself and snuffled Anne's glove, alarmed.

She looked down at Martin, who was shedding years in front of her, like some trick of visual editing, looking now like the Marty Waversky he'd been as a boy, a gawky, too-tall Jewish kid with wiry hair he could never really tame and a mother who insisted he take both Communion and center stage. He might have been one of Anne's students—that lost. Worse. He clung to the dog and cried. She thought of all of his trials and successes and arrogant fuckups and realized that he moved through the world like some untutored, lesser god, just hurling his thunderbolts all over the place.

"Of course you're going to leave me," he was saying, directly into the dog's coat. "Of course you are. Of course you are. You were never serious about me. You never really loved me."

Even Anne would not have been reduced to this.

She stared at him. "Oh, I loved you."

"No, you didn't," he said, and she wondered if he might be right. And marveled that it didn't matter. She'd work out later what love had meant, in this time and with this man. For now, who cared what they called it?

"The ring?" he asked then. He looked up at her. "Do you even have it?"

"It's at my mom's."

"Fitting," he spat. "She was always the one who wanted it anyway."

"You can bill me," she said, and pulled shut the door.

For a long time, Anne walked. The snow gathered along Mitchell's back and feathered his face until he looked like a wolf. She balled her icy fingers into her gloves. She was pretty sure Martin would take her orders and go—plenty of places for him to hole up in the city, if flights were hard to come by—but she didn't want to take any chances, so she stayed out, ignoring her cell phone's ringing deep in her pocket. Also it was unclear what to do next. Where to start over, to begin again.

The only bright spot was the opportunity to read Sadie's final essay, which would now be on the servers of the Duke University Admissions Office. She had half a mind to walk to Sadie's house and ring the bell. It wasn't far. What on earth would be going on in that home today? She'd almost have paid to witness it, though only the most heartless spectator could enjoy what would no doubt be shattering for Sadie and her brother.

Regardless, it was out of her hands now. Duke was in. Which meant that Sadie was in.

Anne scrunched along the unplowed sidewalks to her local Starbucks, but it was dark; so, too, the one just a few blocks down. The only lights anywhere belonged to the Donut Hole. It was a shit hole, really, but the orange neon from the illuminated sign fell on the frozen sidewalk like a red carpet rolled out just for her, and Anne walked in. Over the door a cold little bell rattled. A young man emerged from a back room behind the counter.

Anne closed the door on Mitchell's leash, to hold him, since the usual tie-up spots were buried or just too cruel to use.

"Oh, you can bring him in," said the coffee-shop guy. "It's cool. Owner's not around."

Anne settled Mitchell on the entry mat, stomped snow off her boots, and pulled her frozen hands from her gloves.

"Grill's down," added the man, "and no pastries came in today. Sorry."

He was young, not much younger than she was, with freckles, and eyes a little bit too close together. He seemed to be concentrating on her, but in fact it was just that tight focus over the bridge of his nose. Though of course he was paying attention, waiting to see what she wanted. Anne didn't really know. Two people in a coffee shop on a frigid day. The world felt new. For the first time all morning, she thought she might cry.

He gestured to a glass case fogged with grime. Anne could barely make out the shrink-wrapped muffins inside. He said, "We've got these here, but they're kinda old."

"Just hot chocolate. If you can."

He grabbed milk and a pitcher and began to steam. "Dog had to go?" he called out, over one shoulder. He tipped his head toward the window to indicate the storm.

"Yeah, but that was a long time ago. I'm just walking. Need to walk something off, actually."

"I know how that goes," he said. "I'm Doug."

"Anne."

Doug started dumping chocolate into a giant cup. He wasn't her type, this Doug, not at all, but watching him making her hot chocolate, his nice hands on the spoon and the steaming metal pitcher, she thought that there were other men in the world beside Martin, and that it might be nice to kiss one of them. Not now, maybe not for some time, but one day.

"Sorry you have to work New Year's," she said.

"Don't be," answered Doug. "Lousy tips, but it's cool. Space to think. You working today?"

"I really hope not."

"What do you do?"

"It's a long story."

He looked up.

"I work with high school seniors on their college applications," she explained. It sounded like a confession. It *was* a confession. "You know, I help them with essays and stuff, all the deadlines, the forms."

What was it she wanted? To be admonished, or absolved?

She went on. "So right now is kind of tough, because most applications were due at midnight. Or are due today. And people get kind of crazy."

A valediction. She wanted a valediction.

"College," Doug said. He shook his head. "I never went in much for all of that."

"No?"

"No. I did a year at City College, Harry Truman. I don't know. Maybe I'll go back someday. Not my thing now."

"Cool," said Anne.

He topped up her drink and set it down with a lid. "Here you go," he said, and smiled. His freckles shifted sweetly up over his cheeks. He thunked a solid, Saran-clad muffin on the counter. "Here's for Fido." Then he added, "Not that I have anything against more school, you know. Hope I didn't insult you just now."

"Not at all."

"Just that the degree isn't all that relevant to me right now. I want to be a photographer. I *am* a photographer. I like to shoot people. Portraits and shots of people out on the streets, in the city, on the El, you know. I've got a few gigs, so that's cool. So maybe, you know, later."

"Plenty of time," Anne told him.

"Yeah, maybe I'll call you," he joked. He rang her up, a buck ninety-nine, and she handed him a five-dollar bill.

"Scholarship money," she said, and smiled back.

"Yeah, right?" he said. "Like, who can afford college anyway?"

"I have no idea," she lied. "Probably people who don't really need it."

He nodded emphatically. "Oh, man, that's how everything works. But that's how you know what really matters. I say, if you gotta be rich to get it, it isn't that important to begin with."

"Nice theory. I like it."

"It's free with the cocoa," said Doug. "Stay warm out there."

THE OBSESSIVE PHONE calls she'd been ignoring all morning did not turn out to be from Martin. Nor were they from the Pfaffs, who would be dealing with Hunter's application however they were going to deal with it; she was quite sure Mr. Pfaff wouldn't stoop to asking for her counsel any longer. Anne felt only fatigue when she thought of these people, and she returned to her apartment wanting to throw open the windows and scrub everything down, change her number and e-mail address, bury her cell phone in a deep bank of snow. Martin was gone. No note, no dishevelment save her rumpled sheets and the wadded-up blanket that had sheltered William. She kicked off her boots, stripped to her T-shirt, and collapsed onto the sofa with her phone.

It was Margaret Blanchard's voice on the line.

"Please do call, it's imperative that you do so," she said. And, "Please do call, it's important." And, "Anne, I'd like you to call me, please."

But when Anne called, there was no trace of emergency. Just Mrs. Blanchard inviting her to join the family for their traditional New Year's cocktails at the Four Seasons Hotel. "We do an early supper for the kids," she explained, ridiculously, "and Gid and I raise a glass to the New Year."

Anne laughed out loud. Damage control, of course. Gideon Blanchard had come home and revealed all, and his wife had experienced not betrayal but shame. Or, hell, maybe Margaret Blanchard already knew her husband was diddling his paralegal and was grateful not to have to tend to him herself, but they had reputations to uphold. Big reputations. Rapid-response-press-team reputations. Anne had seen this before, when, say, she witnessed a fight between a student's parents; inevitably they'd summon her the next day for coffee or a kind word, to restore the fantasy. But that was just to keep things copacetic at the club. In this, the Blanchards would have to out-WASP even the best-soaped suburbanites she'd known. Starting with the Four Seasons.

"Uh, what shall I wear?" Anne asked, laughter in her voice, intending to provoke Mrs. Blanchard. She failed.

"Casual is fine."

Which, of course, it wasn't. When Anne arrived, having found a taxi to skate over the paved roads, she was underdressed in her long skirt and Christmas sweater. Around her, in the cocktail lounge of the hotel, minks clung like oil slicks to the backs of chairs. The women who had shed them had almost nothing else on, just strappy tops and miniskirts above shoes that could not possibly have navigated the salted sidewalks. Anne felt like a mountaineer coming in from the cold, her parka closed against the wind that emerged in gusts through the revolving doors, where the doormen whistled like trains.

But she felt dolled to the nines by virtue of a secret, which was Sadie Blanchard's final essay, neatly folded in her bag. It was a knockout. It made her feel invincible.

She looked for Sadie, but at table she found only Mr. and Mrs. Blanchard, impeccable, and Charles, his glossy head bent low over a handheld video console. His thumbs hammered on the plastic.

"Sadie will join us shortly," said Gideon Blanchard, rising alone. He tucked in his tie and reached across to greet her. "Happy New Year."

Anne kept her arms crossed and sat. Blanchard made his eyes small at her, and she thought she detected a warning. An involuntary smile made her mouth wobbly. Holy crap.

To steel herself Anne summoned the image of April Penze in flagrante. As silly as it was foul. This helped.

Mrs. Blanchard pushed a bowl of nuts across the table. "They have the most delicious spice glaze here," she said. "And can we order you a drink? Something warm to start? Let's get Manuel."

Gideon Blanchard raised a French cuff into the air.

"Where is she?" asked Anne. "Sadie."

"She's visiting with a friend," answered Margaret. "After all her hard work, we figured she could have a little social time. Also it affords us the chance to talk before." She looked at Gideon and then at Charles, who had not yet looked up.

"Charles," she said.

He raised sullen eyes at Anne. "Hi."

"Thank you," said his mother.

He returned to his game.

Manuel arrived. Anne ordered hot tea and he was gone.

"That's all?" asked Margaret.

Anne gave a tight nod and briefly scanned the room. She imagined the company they were in: couples hiding away together, or revelers taking the day off to explore the snowy city. How could she have explained her presence there, the complicated, ludicrous, and finally trivial set of expectations that had brought her to this glass table in a blizzard? A high school senior and her parents and the young woman they had hired, all party to a process that claimed to elevate young people and offer them the world, but which instead taught them to commodify their gifts, bury their struggles, deny curiosity, and murder whimsy. Never mind the adultery, Anne thought, if you could dismiss such a thing; why did parents like Gideon Blanchard let their children grow up in a world in which college admissions could poison them so? Sadie already had all the privileges any applicant ever sought by virtue of a top degree. The contacts, the carriage, the cash. Why make it all so difficult?

Why not, Anne wondered, just for one moment tell the truth?

Gideon Blanchard spoke. "Anne, we wanted to invite you to thank you for all of your work this fall. We can only imagine—we know it must be a terribly busy couple of months for you. Sadie told us she submitted her application this morning, so we're very happy and grateful."

"Of course," Anne said.

"And that girl," prompted Margaret Blanchard, her voice cross.

Anne straightened. *Here it comes.*

Gideon Blanchard said, "Oh, yes." His wide horse grin, half flare. "Cristina Castello."

"What?" said Anne.

His eyes were wide with feigned inquiry. "Cristina?" he repeated. "Your other student?"

"Oh, yes," Anne scrambled. "Yes. Of course."

"Yes. You will be happy to hear that her information is all in the hands of the director of admissions himself. I saw to it that he'd give her a special read, and the trustees are keen to ensure that she's in a position to take advantage of any opportunity the university may offer her."

Anne felt what should have been delight for Cristina crashing head-on with disgust for Gideon Blanchard and sheer bafflement at his ability to dissemble. The girl was a pawn to him, that's all; he moved her about as he needed to, forcing Anne's hand. Anne held her breath and felt her thoughts wheeling. Wasn't this right about when some people tossed a drink in a man's face? Threw a shoe? Pulled a gun?

Anne's forced smile made her cheeks twitch, like a threatened hare. "That's lovely, thank you," she said. She held her tea to her face and listened, and hoped something would come to her.

Margaret Blanchard said, "We're so glad that's sorted. Now. All Sadie will tell us about Duke is that the application is in. No idea what she wrote. I assume she used the essay she developed with her English teacher, the points-of-the-star piece. It was so clever and true."

Anne did not correct this.

Gideon Blanchard said, "Are you happy with it? Her essay?"

"Oh, yes," said Anne.

"Good. We just wanted to be sure. Because it turns out that Sadie came home from your office very, very upset last night."

"My apartment. Yes. I can imagine she did."

"She won't say why," added Margaret. With a shudder Anne realized she wasn't bluffing. Margaret Blanchard had no idea.

"No," added Gideon. "So we were a little concerned. Wanted to have the chance to clear that up before she arrived." He raised his voice slightly. "So," he asked Anne, "did something happen last night?"

Charles lifted his golden head and tuned in.

"Hey, kiddo," his father said quietly.

Anne sputtered. The boy paralyzed her, as Gideon Blanchard had known he would. She would not be the one to break a child's heart.

"What?" she said.

She was so stunned she had to start from the beginning to relocate herself in that chair in that room. She looked back at Gideon Blanchard, into his yellowed eyes with their pink rims. She thought of King Lear's vile jelly. She wanted this man to howl in pain on the great barren heath of his existence.

"So we just wanted to be sure," Margaret Blanchard was saying, "that there was no conflict between you two."

"Not at all," Anne managed.

"So what, then?" challenged Mr. Blanchard.

As if on cue, Charles said, "Sadie was crying!"

Anne took the only option she saw, substituting the already miserable son offstage for the boy in front of her, who was still young enough to sport hair that had been painted down with a wet comb and who in his alarm had let his video-game player drop into his lap unnoticed. "I had another student there last night," she told them, "a very nice boy. He had been kicked out of his home after a terrible fight with his father. I was talking with him, and Sadie grew upset just hearing about it."

Gideon Blanchard smiled.

"Oh, she does that, our Sadie," said Margaret, nodding deeply. Anne watched relief move through her. "She does. She gets so caught up in other people's problems. I think it's the mark of confidence that she can so easily find her empathy."

Anne felt she might be sick. She was the little girl again, opposite a grown opponent who was carefully, methodically, trapping her in a corner. She struggled to remember how she'd ever gotten free. How did she win? Did she ever win? Did she always go to bed with, as her father put it, "more to learn"?

Just then Sadie appeared. Anne noticed her because of the heads that were turning—this girl who had appeared on the lobby carpet and was threading her way past the banquettes, a lovely young woman in a blue dress. She held her overcoat draped over one arm. Her hair was dusted with bright drops where the snow had landed. Something hidden propelled her, some certainty Anne hadn't seen before, and Anne wasn't the only one to notice. Sadie wasn't tall or draped in jewels or angular as a model, but she moved through the room like a bird on a thermal, and everyone turned to look.

A waiter hurried to set her chair.

"Sorry I'm late," she said. "What'd I miss?"

"Nothing," said Anne.

"Good day, sweetie?" asked her mother. "You look so much better."

"Feeling good," she said. "Got my application in."

"We're so proud of you," said Margaret Blanchard.

"We were just talking about last night," said her father. "And what upset you so terribly. And Anne has explained to us about the other student, who was going through some trauma with his family, and how that may have upset you, too."

"Did she?" asked Sadie.

Her mother was staring at her. Sadie really did look radiant.

"I wasn't sure how much it was appropriate to share," explained Anne.

"Mmm."

Anne watched Sadie's hands, the corners of her mouth, for any signal that she should have told the truth. Sadie sat, composed.

Her mother reached out a hand to her daughter's cheek and brushed at something with her thumb. Sadie shook her off.

"Quit," she said.

"There was something there, is all," said her mom. "A lash."

Sadie shook out her hair so that it resettled over the collar of her dress. The portrait neckline showed off her collarbones and a small gold chain across her throat.

"That's such a pretty dress," said Anne. "Where'd it come from?"

Sadie opened her mouth to answer, but her mother beat her to it.

"You know," said Mrs. Blanchard, still gazing at her daughter, "when I met Gideon, I was wearing a blue dress. He fell in love with me because of my blue dress."

Anne turned to her, astonished. Gideon Blanchard shifted in his chair.

"Yes, he did," Margaret continued. She had forgotten them all; she was enchanted. "It was long, with a fluted waist." She leaned forward against the edge of the table to reach up to her daughter's hair, which she pushed aside. "A collar that dipped like this"—gesturing now toward her own fallen bosom—"and I had this bracelet with little sapphire flowers all around it, tiny, to match."

Half smiling, Sadie suffered this display.

"I looked so pretty," finished Mrs. Blanchard.

There was a terrible quiet at the table. Around them the room grew louder. Champagne flutes chimed on the tabletops. Anne had a moment to think. Witnessing Margaret Blanchard's embarrassing recollection, her slip back up the river from daughter to mother, something came clear. Something hard and bright and terribly freeing. It was so simple, it took only time to understand it—only time, but time alone: how very much this woman envied her daughter.

It was envy.

My God, it was envy. Anne thought certain parents hijacked their kids' applications and tortured their essays because they wanted to give their children the world, which of course they did. But there was something more. Something ugly in their vigilance that tasted of ownership. Money made it worse but did not explain it away; rich parents were not necessarily bad parents. Nor was it a class concern. This madness was not, in the end, about the preservation of means or the perpetuation of a self-assuming elite. No.

It was about the hoarding of time. The one resource parents could not renew, try though they might. This generation would not go gentle. Gideon and Margaret Blanchard, Gerald and Marion Pfaff, all of those baby boomers aging now in the soft fields of Darien, Palm Beach, Summit, Mill Valley, Lake Forest, in the high floors and single townhomes of cities from New York to Boston to Seattle: they had made their choices. They were not seventeen. They were deep in their ruts and shuttling at top speed through middle age. It must have terrified them. They couldn't release their grip, though their children heading to college meant that their time up front was just about done.

But these kids? Well, they had it all to play for. Everything lay ahead for them.

Anne looked at Sadie and was able to imagine her whole life, just waiting. The cities, the people, the parties, the work, the home, the love. Surely love.

How very much some parents wanted to take it all back.

"Well, you can't," Anne said, and only when the table turned to her in puzzlement did she notice that she had spoken.

"Can't what?" asked Sadie.

"You can't take back what's happened."

Gideon Blanchard stiffened. "What is it you're saying?"

Anne bit her lip. They were all looking at her. She saw the dominion in the faces of the adults—Gideon's indignation and his wife's blind hauteur—and was stunned by how little they understood. Did they notice Sadie biding her time, her knowing patience? Or detect the alarm in the eyes of their confused little boy? It was easy to think, You fools. To love a child, you launch the child, and then you get the hell out of the way. But it was not so easy for her to admit what followed: that it's the child's job to let go of everything else. Poverty tours and cruel chessboards and whatever hell Anne would visit on her own children, because someday she would—all parents did—it was a kid's job to jettison all that, and put on her best dress, and say what it was that she wanted.

"It's up to Sadie now," Anne said at last. "You're done. And, in fact, I have her essay with me. I just happened to print it out."

Sadie widened her eyes, first in surprise and then in anticipation. Anne felt a shiver of pleasure. Sadie said, "Perfect."

Anne tugged the page from her pocket and smoothed it flat on the tabletop. She spun it on the glass and slid it across. Beside her, Sadie took a deep breath. Mrs. Blanchard reached her claret nails to the page.

"It's terrific," Anne said. "You should be very proud of her."

She stood, gathered her coat, and set a hand on Sadie's shoulder. "Bye," she said. "Congratulations. Call if you need to." Gideon Blanchard's hands were flat on the table as though he was about to rise, but he stayed put. To him Anne said, "You can just mail a check for the remainder of my fee."

Then she waved to Charles and walked briskly through the sumptuous hall of the Four Seasons, out into the brightly lit dark.

PERSONAL STATEMENT FOR DUKE UNIVERSITY (FINAL)

By Sadie Marie Blanchard

I have always expected that I would go to college. To be honest, I always knew that I would go to Duke. Growing up, I had a Blue Devils banner on the wall over my bed. It was the only blue thing in my room—everything else was pink or yellow. Duke basketball games were the only television permitted in my house. I've gone to visit with my parents more times than I can count.

So lately, this past fall, people have started asking me: Are you excited about college? You must be getting so excited about Duke! And the answer, honestly, is No. But this is not because I'm not excited about college, or even about going to college at Duke. It's because when you grow up with expectations like that, you don't really imagine things on your own. Or, in other words, if you've always looked up at a blue banner on your wall, you haven't had a blank space in which to daydream. It was always already there for you.

If there is one word I think of when I think about the college application process, it is *expectations.* College is the final expectation teachers have of their students, starting from when they are very small. The colleges, meanwhile, have expectations of the applicants, in terms of grades and scores and so on, and then once they let students on campus, they have expectations of those students based on their applications. We like to think about childhood being a time all about imagination. About make-believe and pretending. College is the end of all of that. And unfortunately, the expectations surrounding college mean that the make-believe of childhood ends much sooner than I think it should.

In the last few months, I have learned alot about expectations. I have learned that expectations get in the way of imagination. I have learned that expectations make it difficult to see the truth. I have learned that while expectations can help us to succeed, they can also let us down. So I've done a little imagining about expectations vs. imagination. I like to think of them as characters, as people almost. Expectation, for example, speaks with a really deep, booming voice. Imagination is quiet and whispery. Expectation is typed in black. Imagination is handwritten, on the corner of your page, in purple. If you set up Expectation and Imagination in a debate, Expectation would win every time. Imagination would just stand there in a pretty dress with a crazy scarf and smile. Expectation goes for timed field hockey runs. Imagination jumps in Lake Michigan on a hot day. Expectation is a 2400 on the SAT. Imagination is zooming out of the building after they start the clock and hiding somewhere with your favorite book instead. Expectation is your dad, who you always knew is honest and faithful to your mom. Imagination is wondering what the hell he was doing making out with the slutty paralegal who lives upstairs from your college counselor. Expectation is going to Duke. Imagination is pretending I've never heard of the place and letting it be new so I can spend four years there that are all my own. Expectation is that I'll get in, because of my Dad's connections. Imagination is that the admissions office will think I might really be a good fit there. Expectation is the essay my parents worked on with me, that I wrote with my college counselor and that my English teacher and my school counselor both edited. Imagination is what I've used to write this.

I think Expectation comes with fear. Imagination comes with hope. So I'll just say it: I expect to attend Duke, and I imagine I will have a wonderful four years there.

Expectations are what have got me this far. But I sense that the braver, more difficult choice is to use Imagination, and that, I hope, is what will get me the rest of the way.

EPILOGUE

Sadie Blanchard majored in art history at Duke and pledged Delta Delta Delta. She spent her junior year in Florence, where she had her heart broken by a junior professor from Calabria who had taken her to Sicily for a spring break full of first things but was nowhere to be found by May. Her senior year was spent writing unanswered letters to him and securing a Manhattan-based internship with Sotheby's, where she now works in Old Masters. She lives in a classic six in the East Seventies. Since her parents' divorce, Tassel has come to live with her there. (Charles was sent to Eaglebrook.) Sadie's boyfriend, Preston, is an analyst with Bank of America. What little free time they have is taken up volunteering for junior boards and on Team In Training runs. She enjoys their summer weekends in a shared rental in Quogue, but some nights she still dreams about blood oranges and the tiny bright lizards of Taormina.

Alexis Grant graduated summa cum laude, Phi Beta Kappa from Harvard. She turned down the Marshall to accept the Rhodes Scholarship, which she used to study the ethics of international development at Balliol College, Oxford, while simultaneously pursuing an MSc at the London School of Economics. One autumn, connecting through Heathrow on his way to Prague, Michael Schleinstock staged a prolonged layover to spend two days wandering London by her side.

Standing before the Rosetta Stone, their rain-soaked jackets in his arms, he professed his love. She took his hand and said, "I love you, too!" Nothing happened next. He was still confused when she waved him good-bye on the Piccadilly line the next day. Her Geneva-based job with UNDP will follow an extended field placement in Kurdistan. Her first published paper, on tent libraries, indigenous language, and the integrity of refugees, appeared in *Foreign Affairs*.

C. Hunter Pfaff took a year off after high school. His parents engaged a private consulting firm based in Boston that specializes in planning such hiatuses. Consequently, he spent the autumn doing trail maintenance with the U.S. Fish and Wildlife Service in the Clearwater National Forest; for the winter he traveled to Bogotá to brush up on his Spanish and intern with a private equity firm that manages structured debt transactions in emerging markets; and in the spring he rented a condo in Miami, where he spent mornings teaching tennis to Cuban refugee children and afternoons focusing on his own game with a private coach. He submitted his college applications from Colombia. After all that travel, he was happy to settle at Bates, playing varsity singles on the tennis team and hiking the Maine trails on Sundays, but his parents disagreed that it was the right fit, and he came to see the light in time to apply to Cornell to complete his degree. Also at their urging, he switched majors from environmental science to economics, and graduated in five years. He is now an M&A analyst with UBS in London. He lives in a small flat in Battersea. From his bathroom window, when it is not fogged from the shower or the radiator, he can see the Thames rolling by. Its banks are concrete.

Cristina Castello graduated from Duke with honors in history. She was able to return to Chicago exactly twice during her four years in Durham. The law firm of Blanchard, McHenry, Winsett & Blair paid her tuition, room, and board, freeing her, upon graduation, to accept a Teach for America position in South Central Los Angeles. She lives in a rented bungalow in Silverlake. It shares an alley with a McDonald's, but she has her own little porch and a jacaranda tree. Her younger sister, a high school freshman, attends the Cicero North Excel program every Saturday.

William Kantor graduated from Penn with a major in politics and a minor in theater. He moved immediately to New York City, where he is a production intern for a small avant-garde company with a roving stage. He found a fabulous Reform shul that meets out of a Presbyterian church in the far West Village and that holds services on Monday nights to accommodate members who work in the theater. He and his boyfriend, Alan, go almost every week.

April Penze left her job at Blanchard, McHenry, Winsett & Blair to become a desk assistant at the local NBC News affiliate. She has been shopping her test reel as a weathergirl for about a year. The editor, a married man, assures her she's got what it takes.

Doug the Coffee Shop Guy is a portrait photographer whose loft studio is adored by local celebrities for the way the El rattles by its three huge windows and for its gentle morning light. He never completed his degree.

Anne applied for the graduate fellowship to study international comparative education in England, which turned into a long-term position. She took a small flat in St. John's Wood. Despite calls from parents at the American School, she has no time to work on college applications.

Several major philanthropic organizations, not to mention the current American administration, have shown interest in her team's proposals regarding vocational training and higher-ed reform in Western Europe. Mitchell is delighted to be off leash in London's lush parks. Occasionally Martin shows up with his new girlfriend, a pop singer, in the back pages of weekly celebrity magazines. The singer's name is always listed first. (It is not Lynn.) Anne hasn't bothered to remark on this to her fiancé, Greg. Every now and then, she finds herself doing the math to determine in what years their future children might graduate from college. It makes her heart drop and soar at the same time.

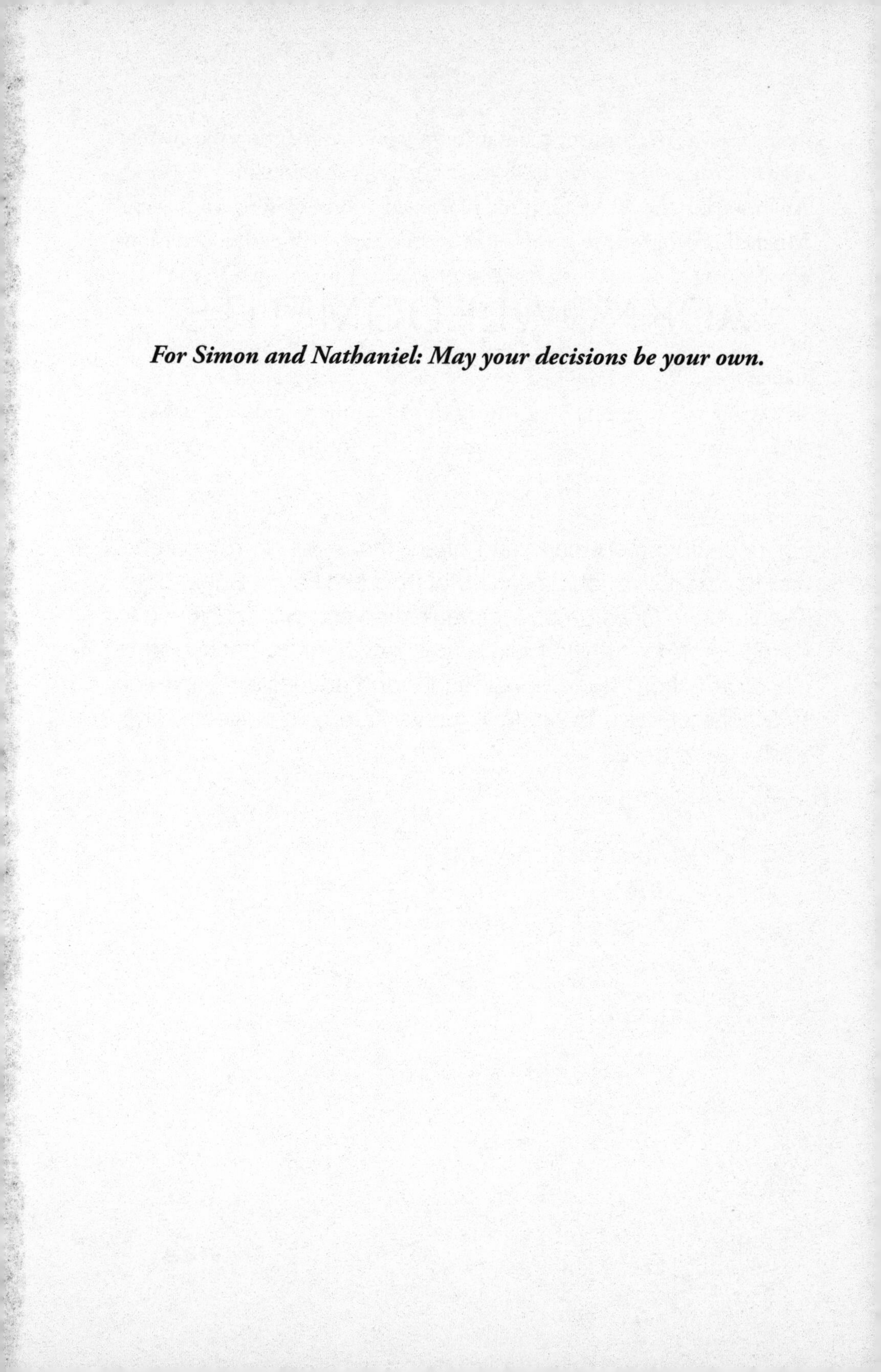

For Simon and Nathaniel: May your decisions be your own.

ACKNOWLEDGMENTS

For encouragement early and often, thank you to my parents and to the late Marion Strickland of the Lake Forest Book Store. Thank you to Chris Lynch for imagination and wit. Thank you to Carrie Feron for transforming a manuscript into a book, and to Christina Clifford, exceptional reader and advocate. Thank you to Stephen Grosz; to Maggie, forever free on the Heath; and, each day, to my E.